C.

Fai

Clive Stapl[...] [...] giants of the twentieth century and arguably [...] tial writer of his day. He was a Fellow and Tutor in English literature at Oxford University until 1954 when he was unanimously elected to the Chair of Medieval and Renaissance English at Cambridge University, a position he held until his retirement. He wrote more than 30 books, allowing him to reach a vast audience, and his works continue to attract thousands of new readers every year. His most distinguished and popular accomplishments include *The Chronicles of Narnia, The Cosmic Trilogy, The Four Loves, The Screwtape Letters* and *Mere Christianity.*

Also available:

C. S. LEWIS

ESSAY COLLECTION

Faith, Christianity and the Church

EDITED BY LESLEY WALMSLEY

HarperCollins*Publishers*

HarperCollins*Publishers*
77–85 Fulham Palace Road
Hammersmith, London w6 8jb
www.**fire**and**water**.com

Paperback edition 2002
1 3 5 7 9 10 8 6 4 2

First published in Great Britain by
by HarperCollins*Publishers* 2000

Text © C.S. Lewis Pte Ltd 2000
Compilation © Lesley Walmsley 2000

Lesley Walmsley asserts the moral right to
be identified as the editor of this work.

A catalogue record for this book is
available from the British Library.

ISBN 0 00 713653 6

Printed and bound in Great Britain by
Clays Ltd. St Ives plc

CONTENTS

INTRODUCTION

Clive Staples Lewis was born in Belfast in 1898 and became a renowned scholar of medieval English, in which he lectured, first at Oxford and then at Cambridge. He also wrote widely on that subject, but as an author is now best known for his religious writings, including such books as *Mere Christianity*, *The Screwtape Letters* and *The Chronicles of Narnia*.

He was also a prolific writer of essays on many subjects to do with faith and life, and although they have been published in various collections over the years, this present volume is the first time that they have all been brought together. To make for ease of reading I have tried to put them into logical sections, but in some cases an essay could happily fall into at least two, such was Lewis's breadth of approach, and within each section the essays are generally listed chronologically. There is a short introductory history for each one, including details of the latest collection in which it has been published, and at the front of the book there is a list of titles, with publication dates, of all the books mentioned as sources.

For all this background information, as for so much else to do with the works of C.S. Lewis, I am greatly indebted to Walter Hooper, whose *C.S. Lewis: A Companion and Guide* gives full details of all Lewis's writings, including of course his essays. I have also largely kept the helpful footnotes which he added for those reading the essays many years after they were written. One small addition should be a note about *The Guardian*, which was a religious magazine rather than the national newspaper now known by that name.

Lewis was writing over a long period, from the 1920s to shortly before his death in 1963, and the world has changed a great deal since then. For many people there is no firm religious background to life, and new mass communications have brought influences from all kinds of ideologies into our very homes, all presented with lavish and impressive marketing techniques, some of which we don't even realize may be changing the way we think. When Lewis made the broadcasts which were to form *Mere Christianity* Britain was at war, and his words came as a firm foundation to people who were looking for a faith to steady their lives. In reading them again I was struck by how directly they still speak to us at the turn of the century, despite having been written in that very different world of some fifty years ago.

Lesley Walmsley

BOOKS MENTIONED
IN THIS VOLUME

Lewis's adult religious books were first published by Geoffrey Bles, but in 1953 Bles was bought by William Collins, and his books then appeared under the imprints of William Collins Sons & Co (hardbacks) or Fontana (paperbacks), until in 1977 the religious paperbacks launched their own imprint of Fount. Collins later joined with the American publisher Harper & Row, and is now HarperCollins*Publishers*. Unless otherwise stated, the books listed below were all published by Bles/William Collins/HarperCollins/Fount. The dates shown represent the first and latest editions.

Complete publication details of all Lewis's writings, up to 1996, can be found in *C.S. Lewis – A Companion and Guide* by Walter Hooper, published by HarperCollins*Publishers*, London and San Francisco.

The Abolition of Man or, Reflections on Education with Special Reference to the Teaching of English in the Upper Forms of School, Bles 1946, Fount 1978
    US: Macmillan 1947, Macmillan Paperback 1965
Christian Reflections, Bles 1967, Fount 1981, 1998
    US: Eerdmans 1967
Christian Reunion, Fount 1990
Compelling Reason, Fount 1996, 1998 (formerly *Undeceptions* and *First and Second Things* – see below)
The Dark Tower and Other Stories, Collins 1977, Fount 1983, 1998
    US: Harcourt Brace Jovanovich, Harvest/HBJ paperback 1977
Fern-seed and Elephants and Other Essays, Fontana 1975, Fount 1977, 1998
First and Second Things: Essays on Theology and Ethics, Fontana 1971, Fount 1985
God in the Dock – Essays on Theology and Ethics, (US) Eerdmans hardback 1970
    UK: *Undeceptions* – (see below)
God in the Dock – Essays on Theology, Fontana 1979, Fount 1979, 1998 (This edition is much shorter than the American one)
Of Other Worlds – Essays and Stories, Bles 1966

US: Harcourt, Brace & World 1967, Harvest Book paperback 1975

Of This and Other Worlds, Collins 1982, Fount 2000 (The contents are not exactly the same as those of *Of Other Worlds*)

Present Concerns, Fount 1986, 1991

US: Harcourt, Brace, Jovanovich, Harvest/HBJ paperback 1987

Rehabilitations and Other Essays, Oxford University Press 1939

Selected Literary Essays, Cambridge University Press 1969

The Screwtape Letters and Screwtape Proposes a Toast, Bles 1961

US: Macmillan 1962; revised Macmillan Paperback 1982

Screwtape Proposes a Toast and Other Pieces, Fontana 1965, Fount 1977, 1998

Surprised by Joy – The Shape of My Early Life, Bles 1955, Fontana 1959, Fount 1977

They Asked for a Paper – Papers and Addresses, Bles 1962

Timeless at Heart – Essays on Theology, Fount 1987, 1991

Transposition and Other Addresses, Bles, 1949

US: *The Weight of Glory and Other Addresses*, Macmillan 1949 (see also *The Weight of Glory* below)

Undeceptions – Essays on Theology and Ethics UK edition of (US) *God in the Dock* (1970), Bles 1971

The Weight of Glory and Other Addresses (revised and expanded edition)

US: Macmillan Paperbacks 1980

The World's Last Night and Other Essays (US) Harcourt, Brace & World 1960

[PART I]

THE SEARCH FOR GOD

[1]
THE GRAND MIRACLE

This was preached in St Jude on the Hill Church, London, and later published in The Guardian *(27 April 1945). It was reproduced in* Undeceptions *(1971) and* God in the Dock *(1998).*

One is very often asked at present whether we could not have a Christianity stripped, or, as people who ask it say, 'freed' from its miraculous elements, a Christianity with the miraculous elements suppressed. Now, it seems to me that precisely the one religion in the world, or, at least, the only one I know, with which you could not do that is Christianity. In a religion like Buddhism, if you took away the miracles attributed to Gautama Buddha in some very late sources, there would be no loss; in fact, the religion would get on very much better without them because in that case the miracles largely contradict the teaching. Or even in the case of a religion like Mohammedanism, nothing essential would be altered if you took away the miracles. You could have a great prophet preaching his dogmas without bringing in any miracles; they are only in the nature of a digression, or illuminated capitals. But you cannot possibly do that with Christianity, because the Christian story is precisely the story of one grand miracle, the Christian assertion being that what is beyond all space and time, what is uncreated, eternal, came into nature, into human nature, descended into His own universe, and rose again, bringing nature up with Him. It is precisely one great miracle. If you take that away there is nothing specifically Christian left. There may be many admirable human things which Christianity shares with all other systems in the world, but there would be nothing specifically Christian. Conversely, once you have accepted that, then you will see that all other well-established Christian miracles – because, of course, there are ill-established Christian miracles; there are Christian legends just as much as there are heathen legends, or modern journalistic legends – you will see that all the well-established Christian miracles are part of it, that they all either prepare for, or exhibit, or result from the Incarnation. Just as every natural event exhibits the total character of the natural universe at a particular point and space of time; so every miracle exhibits the character of the Incarnation.

Now, if one asks whether that central grand miracle in Christianity is itself probable or improbable, of course, quite clearly you cannot be applying Hume's[1] kind of probability. You cannot mean a probability based on statistics according to which the more often a thing has happened, the more likely it is to happen again (the more often you get indigestion from eating a certain food, the more probable it is, if you eat it again, that you will again have indigestion). Certainly the Incarnation cannot be probable in that sense. It is of its very nature to have happened only once. But then it is of the very nature of the history of this world to have happened only once; and if the Incarnation happened at all, it is the central chapter of that history. It is improbable in the same way in which the whole of nature is improbable, because it is only there once, and will happen only once. So one must apply to it a quite different kind of standard.

I think we are rather in this position. Supposing you had before you a manuscript of some great work, either a symphony or a novel. There then comes to you a person, saying, 'Here is a new bit of the manuscript that I found; it is the central passage of that symphony, or the central chapter of that novel. The text is incomplete without it. I have got the missing passage which is really the centre of the whole work.' The only thing you could do would be to put this new piece of the manuscript in that central position, and then see how it reacted on the whole of the rest of the work. If it constantly brought out new meanings for the whole of the rest of the work, if it made you notice things in the rest of the work which you had not noticed before, then I think you would decide that it was authentic. On the other hand, if it failed to do that, then, however attractive it was in itself, you would reject it.

Now, what is the missing chapter in this case, the chapter which Christians are offering? The story of the Incarnation is the story of a descent and resurrection. When I say 'resurrection' here, I am not referring simply to the first few hours, or the first few weeks of the Resurrection. I am talking of this whole, huge pattern of descent, down, down, and then up again. What we ordinarily call the Resurrection being just, so to speak, the point at which it turns. Think what that descent is. The coming down, not only into humanity, but into those nine months which precede human birth, in which they tell us we all recapitulate

[1] David Hume (1711–76), Scottish philosopher and historian. See especially the 'Essay upon Miracles' in his *Philosophical Essays Concerning Human Understanding* (1748).

strange pre-human, sub-human forms of life, and going lower still into being a corpse, a thing which, if this ascending movement had not begun, would presently have passed out of the organic altogether, and have gone back into the inorganic, as all corpses do. One has a picture of someone going right down and dredging the sea-bottom. One has a picture of a strong man trying to lift a very big, complicated burden. He stoops down and gets himself right under it so that he himself disappears; and then he straightens his back and moves off with the whole thing swaying on his shoulders. Or else one has the picture of a diver, stripping off garment after garment, making himself naked, then flashing for a moment in the air, and then down through the green, and warm, and sunlit water into the pitch black, cold, freezing water, down into the mud and slime, then up again, his lungs almost bursting, back again to the green and warm and sunlit water, and then at last out into the sunshine, holding in his hand the dripping thing he went down to get. This thing is human nature; but, associated with it, all nature, the new universe. That indeed is a point I cannot go into tonight, because it would take a whole sermon – this connection between human nature and nature in general. It sounds startling, but I believe it can be fully justified.

Now, as soon as you have thought of this, this pattern of the huge dive down to the bottom, into the depths of the universe and coming up again into the light, everyone will see at once how that is imitated and echoed by the principles of the natural world; the descent of the seed into the soil, and its rising again in the plants. There are also all sorts of things in our own spiritual life where a thing has to be killed, and broken, in order that it may then become bright, and strong, and splendid. The analogy is obvious. In that sense the doctrine fits in very well, so well in fact that immediately there comes the suspicion. Is it not fitting in a great deal too well? In other words, does not the Christian story show this pattern of descent and re-ascent because that is part of all the nature religions of the world? We have read about it in *The Golden Bough*.[2] We all know about Adonis, and the stories of the rest of those rather tedious people; is not this one more instance of the same thing, 'the dying God'? Well, yes it is. That is what makes the question subtle. What the anthropological critic of Christianity is always saying is perfectly true. Christ *is* a figure of that sort. And here comes a very curious thing. When I first, after childhood, read the Gospels, I was full of that stuff about the dying God, *The Golden Bough*, and so on. It was to me then a very poetic, and mysterious, and quickening idea; and when I turned to the Gospels never will I forget my

---

[2] By Sir James George Frazer (1890).

disappointment and repulsion at finding hardly anything about it at all. The metaphor of the seed dropping into the ground in this connection occurs (I think) twice in the New Testament (John 12:24; 1 Corinthians 15:36), and for the rest hardly any notice is taken; it seemed to me extraordinary. You had a dying God, Who was always representative of the corn: you see Him holding the corn, that is, bread, in His hand, and saying, 'This is My Body' (Matthew 26:26; Mark 14:22; Luke 22:19; 1 Corinthians 11:24), and from my point of view, as I then was, He did not seem to realise what He was saying. Surely there, if anywhere, this connection between the Christian story and the corn must have come out; the whole context is crying out for it. But everything goes on as if the principal actor and still more those about Him, were totally ignorant of what they were doing. It is as if you got very good evidence concerning the sea-serpent, but the men who brought this good evidence seemed never to have heard of sea-serpents. Or to put it in another way, why was it that the only case of the 'dying God' which might conceivably have been historical occurred among a people (and the only people in the whole Mediterranean world) who had not got any trace of this nature religion, and indeed seem to know nothing about it? Why is it among *them* the thing suddenly appears to happen?

The principal actor, humanly speaking, hardly seems to know of the repercussions His words (and sufferings) would have in any pagan mind. Well, that is almost explicable, except on one hypothesis. How if the corn king is not mentioned in that Book, because He is here of whom the corn king was an image? How if the representation is absent because here at last, the thing represented is present? If the shadows are absent because the thing of which they were shadows is here? The corn itself is in its far-off way an imitation of the supernatural reality; the thing dying, and coming to life again, descending, and re-ascending beyond all nature. The principle is there in nature because it was first there in God Himself. Thus one is getting in behind the nature religions, and behind nature to Someone Who is not explained by, but explains, not indeed, the nature religions directly, but that whole characteristic behaviour of nature on which nature religions were based. Well, that is one way in which it surprised me. It seemed to fit in in a very peculiar way, showing me something about nature more fully than I had seen it before, while itself remaining quite outside and above the nature religions.

Then another thing. We, with our modern democratic and arithmetical presuppositions would so have liked and expected all men to start equal in their search for God. One has the picture of great centripetal roads coming from all directions, with well-disposed people, all meaning the same thing, and getting closer and closer together. How shockingly opposite to that is the Christian story! One people picked out of the whole earth; that people purged and proved again and again. Some are lost in the desert before they reach Palestine; some stay in Babylon; some becoming indifferent. The whole thing narrows and narrows, until at last it comes down to a little point, small as the point of a spear – a Jewish girl at her prayers. That is what the whole of human nature has narrowed down to before the Incarnation takes place. Very unlike what we expected, but, of course, not in the least unlike what seems, in general, as shown by nature, to be God's way of working. The universe is quite a shockingly selective, undemocratic place out of apparently infinite space, a relatively tiny proportion occupied by matter of any kind. Of the stars perhaps only one has planets: of the planets only one is at all likely to sustain organic life. Of the animals only one species is rational. Selection as seen in nature, and the appalling waste which it involves, appears a horrible and an unjust thing by human standards. But the selectiveness in the Christian story is not quite like that. The people who are selected are, in a sense, unfairly selected for a supreme honour; but it is also a supreme burden. The People of Israel come to realise that it is their woes which are saving the world. Even in human society, though, one sees how this inequality furnishes an opportunity for every kind of tyranny and servility. Yet, on the other hand, one also sees that it furnishes an opportunity for some of the very best things we can think of – humility, and kindness, and the immense pleasures of admiration. (I cannot conceive how one would get through the boredom of a world in which you never met anyone more clever, or more beautiful, or stronger than yourself. The very crowds who go after the football celebrities and film stars know better than to desire that kind of equality!) What the story of the Incarnation seems to be doing is to flash a new light on a principle in nature, and to show for the first time that this principle of inequality in nature is neither good nor bad. It is a common theme running through both the goodness and badness of the natural world, and I begin to see how it can survive as a supreme beauty in a redeemed universe.

And with that I have unconsciously passed over to the third point. I have said that the selectiveness was not unfair in the way in which we first suspect, because those selected for the great honour are also selected for the great suffering, and their suffering heals others. In the Incarnation we get, of course, this idea of vicariousness of one person profiting by the earnings of another person. In its highest form that is the very centre of Christianity. And we also find this same vicariousness to be a characteristic, or, as the musician would put it, a *leit-motif* of nature. It is a law of the natural universe that no being can exist on its own resources. Everyone, everything, is hopelessly indebted to everyone and everything else. In the universe, as we now see it, this is the source of many of the greatest horrors: all the horrors of carnivorousness, and the worse horrors of the parasites, those horrible animals that live under the skin of other animals, and so on. And yet, suddenly seeing it in the light of the Christian story, one realises that vicariousness is not in itself bad; that all these animals and insects and horrors are merely that principle of vicariousness twisted in one way. For when you think it out, nearly everything good in nature also comes from vicariousness. After all, the child, both before and after birth, lives on its mother, just as the parasite lives on its host, the one being a horror, the other being the source of almost every natural goodness in the world. It all depends upon what you do with this principle. So that I find in that third way also, that what is implied by the Incarnation just fits in exactly with what I have seen in nature, and (this is the important point) each time it gives it a new twist. If I accept this supposed missing chapter, the Incarnation, I find it begins to illuminate the whole of the rest of the manuscript. It lights up nature's pattern of death and rebirth; and, secondly, her selectiveness; and, thirdly, her vicariousness.

Now I notice a very odd point. All other religions in the world, as far as I know them, are either nature religions, or anti-nature religions. The nature religions are those of the old, simple pagan sort that you know about. You actually got drunk in the temple of Bacchus. You actually committed fornication in the temple of Aphrodite. The more modern form of nature religion would be the religion started, in a sense, by Bergson[3] (but he repented, and died Christian), and carried on in a more popular form by Mr Bernard Shaw. The anti-nature religions are those like Hinduism and Stoicism, where men say, 'I will starve my flesh. I care not whether I live or die.' All natural things are to be set aside: the aim is Nirvana, apathy, negative spirituality. The nature religions simply affirm my natural desires. The anti-natural religions simply contradict them. The nature religions simply give a new sanction to what I already always thought about the universe in my moments of rude health and cheerful brutality. The anti-nature religions merely repeat what I always thought about it in my moods of lassitude, or delicacy, or compassion.

But here is something quite different. Here is something telling me – well, what? Telling me that I must never, like the Stoics, say that death does not matter. Nothing is less Christian than that. Death which made

[3] Henri Bergson (1859–1941). His 'nature religion' is particularly evident in his *Matière et Mémoire* (1896) and *L'Evolution Créatrice* (1907).

Life Himself shed tears at the grave of Lazarus (John 11:35), and shed tears of blood in Gethsemane (Luke 22:44). This is an appalling horror; a stinking indignity. (You remember Thomas Browne's splendid remark: 'I am not so much afraid of death, as ashamed of it.') [4] And yet, somehow or other, infinitely good. Christianity does not simply affirm or simply deny the horror of death: it tells me something quite new about it. Again it does not, like Nietzsche, simply confirm my desire to be stronger, or cleverer than other people. On the other hand, it does not allow me to say, 'Oh, Lord, won't there be a day when everyone will be as good as everyone else?' In the same way, about vicariousness. It will not, in any way, allow me to be an exploiter, to act as a parasite on other people; yet it will not allow me any dream of living on my own. It will teach me to accept with glad humility the enormous sacrifice that others make for me, as well as to make sacrifices for others.

That is why I think this Grand Miracle is the missing chapter in this novel, the chapter on which the whole plot turns; that is why I believe that God really has dived down into the bottom of creation, and has come up bringing the whole redeemed nature on His shoulders. The miracles that have already happened are, of course, as Scripture so often says, the first fruits of that cosmic summer which is presently coming on (Romans 8:23; 11:16; 16:5; 1 Corinthians 15:20; James 1:18; Revelation 14:4). Christ has risen, and so we shall rise. St Peter for a few seconds walked on the water (Matthew 14:29); and the day will come when there will be a re-made universe, infinitely obedient to the will of glorified and obedient men, when we can do all things, when we shall be those gods that we are described as being in Scripture. To be sure, it feels wintry enough still: but often in the very early spring it feels like that. Two thousand years are only a day or two by this scale. A man really ought to say, 'The Resurrection happened two thousand years ago' in the same spirit in which he says, 'I saw a crocus yesterday.' Because we know what is coming behind the crocus. The spring comes slowly down this way; but the great thing is that the corner has been turned. There is, of course, this difference, that in the natural spring the crocus cannot choose whether it will respond or not. We can. We have the power either of withstanding the spring, and sinking back into the cosmic winter, or of going on into those 'high mid-summer pomps' in which our Leader, the Son of Man, already dwells, and to which He is calling us. It remains with us to follow or not, to die in this winter, or to go on into that spring and that summer.

---

[4] 'I am not so much afraid of death, as ashamed thereof.' *Religio Medici*, First Part, Section 40.

[2]

IS THEOLOGY POETRY?

A paper read to the Oxford Socratic Club in reply to one by Professor H.H. Price. Both papers were subsequently published in The Socratic Digest, *No. 3 (1945) and No. 5 (1952). Lewis's paper was reproduced in* They Asked for a Paper *(1962) and* Screwtape Proposes a Toast *(1998).*

The question I have been asked to discuss tonight – 'Is Theology Poetry?' – is not of my own choosing. I find myself, in fact, in the position of a candidate at an examination; and I must obey the advice of my tutors by first making sure that I know what the question means.

By Theology we mean, I suppose, the systematic series of statements about God and about man's relation to Him which the believers of a religion make. And in a paper set me by this Club I may perhaps assume that Theology means principally Christian Theology. I am the bolder to make this assumption because something of what I think about other religions will appear in what I have to say. It must also be remembered that only a minority of the religions of the world have a theology. There was no systematic series of statements which the Greeks agreed in believing about Zeus.

The other term, Poetry, is much harder to define, but I believe I can assume the question which my examiners had in mind without a definition. There are certain things which I feel sure they were not asking me. They were not asking me whether Theology is written in verse. They were not asking me whether most theologians are masters of a 'simple, sensuous and passionate' style. I believe they meant: 'Is Theology *merely* poetry?' This might be expanded: 'Does Theology offer us, at best, only that kind of truth which, according to some critics, poetry offers us?' And the first difficulty of answering the question in that form is that we have no general agreement as to what 'poetical truth' means, or whether there is really any such thing. It will be best, therefore, to use for this paper a very vague and modest notion of poetry, simply as writing which arouses and in part satisfies the imagination. And I shall take it that the question I am to answer is this: Does Christian Theology owe its attraction to its power of arousing and satisfying our imagination? Are those who believe it mistaking aesthetic enjoyment for intellectual assent, or assenting because they enjoy?

Faced with this question, I naturally turn to inspect the believer whom I know best – myself. And the first fact I discover, or seem to discover, is that for me at any rate, if Theology is Poetry, it is not very good poetry.

Considered as poetry, the doctrine of the Trinity seems to me to fall between two stools. It has neither the monolithic grandeur of strictly Unitarian conceptions, nor the richness of Polytheism. The omnipotence of God is not, to my taste, a poetical advantage. Odin, fighting against enemies who are not his own creatures and who will in fact defeat him in the end, has a heroic appeal which the God of the Christians cannot have. There is also a certain bareness about the Christian picture of the universe. A future state, and orders of superhuman creatures, are held to exist, but only the slightest hints of their nature are offered. Finally, and worst of all, the whole cosmic story though full of tragic elements yet fails of being a tragedy. Christianity offers the attractions neither of optimism nor of pessimism. It represents the life of the universe as being very like the mortal life of men on this planet – 'of a mingled yarn, good and ill together'. The majestic simplifications of Pantheism and the tangled wood of Pagan animism both seem to me, in their different ways, more attractive. Christianity just misses the tidiness of the one and the delicious variety of the other. For I take it there are two things the imagination loves to do. It loves to embrace its object completely, to take it in at a single glance and see it as something harmonious, symmetrical and self-explanatory. That is the classical imagination: the Parthenon was built for it. It also loves to lose itself in a labyrinth, to surrender to the inextricable. That is the romantic imagination: the *Orlando Furioso* was written for it. But Christian Theology does not cater very well for either.

If Christianity is only a mythology, then I find the mythology I believe in is not the one I like best. I like Greek mythology much better: Irish better still: Norse best of all.

Having thus inspected myself, I next inquire how far my case is peculiar. It does not seem, certainly, to be unique. It is not at all plain that men's imaginations have always delighted most in those pictures of the supernatural which they believed. From the twelfth to the seventeenth century Europe seems to have taken an unfailing delight in classical mythology. If the numbers and the gusto of pictures and poems were to be the criterion of belief, we should judge that those ages were pagan; which we know to be untrue.

It looks as if the confusion between imaginative enjoyment and intellectual assent, of which Christians are accused, is not nearly so common or so easy as some people suppose. Even children, I believe, rarely suffer from it. It pleases their imagination to pretend that they are bears or horses; but I do not remember that one was ever under the least delusion. May it not even be that there is something in belief which is hostile to perfect imaginative enjoyment? The sensitive, cultured atheist seems at times to enjoy the aesthetic trappings of Christianity in a way which the believer can only envy. The modern poets certainly enjoy the Greek gods in a way of which I find no trace in Greek literature. What mythological scenes in ancient literature can compare for a moment with Keats's *Hyperion*? In a certain sense we spoil a mythology for imaginative purposes by believing in it. Fairies are popular in England because we don't think they exist; they are no fun at all in Arran or Connemara.

But I must beware of going too far. I have suggested that belief spoils a system for the imagination 'in a certain sense'. But not in all senses. If I came to believe in fairies I should almost certainly lose the particular kind of pleasure which I now get from them when reading the *Midsummer Night's Dream*. But later on, when the believed fairies had settled down as inhabitants of my real universe and had been fully connected with other parts of my thought, a new pleasure might arise. The contemplation of what we take to be real is always, I think, in tolerably sensitive minds, attended with a certain sort of aesthetic satisfaction – a sort which depends precisely on its supposed reality. There is a dignity and poignancy in the bare fact that a thing exists. Thus, as Balfour pointed out in *Theism and Humanism* (a book too little read) there are many historical facts which we should not applaud for any obvious humour or pathos if we supposed them to be inventions; but once we believe them to be real we have, in addition to our intellectual satisfaction, a certain aesthetic delight in the idea of them. The story of the Trojan War and the story of the Napoleonic Wars both have an aesthetic effect on us. And the effects are different. And this difference does not depend solely on those differences which would make them different as stories if we believed neither. The *kind* of pleasure the Napoleonic Wars give has a certain difference simply because we believe in them. A believed idea *feels* different from an idea that is not believed. And that peculiar flavour of the believed is never, in my experience, without a special sort of imaginative enjoyment. It is therefore quite true that the Christians do enjoy their world picture, aesthetically, once they have accepted it as true. Every man, I believe, enjoys the world picture which he accepts: for the gravity and finality of the actual is itself an aesthetic stimulus. In this sense, Christianity, Life-Force-Worship, Marxism, Freudianism all become 'poetries' to their own believers. But this does not mean that their adherents have chosen them for that reason. On the contrary, this kind of poetry is the result, not the cause, of belief. Theology is, in this sense, poetry to me because I believe it: I do not believe it because it is poetry.

The charge that Theology is mere poetry, if it means that Christians believe it because they find it, antecedently to belief, the most poetically attractive of all world pictures, thus seems to me unplausible in the extreme. There may be evidence for such a charge which I do not know of: but such evidence as I do know is against it.

I am not of course maintaining that Theology, even before you believe it, is totally bare of aesthetic value. But I do not find it superior in this respect to most of its rivals. Consider for a few moments the enormous aesthetic claim of its chief contemporary rival – what we may loosely call the Scientific Outlook,[1] the picture of Mr Wells and the rest. Supposing this to be a myth, is it not one of the finest myths which human imagination has yet produced? The play is preceded by the most austere of all preludes: the infinite void, and matter restlessly moving to bring forth it knows not what. Then, by the millionth millionth chance – what tragic irony – the conditions at one point of space and time bubble up into that tiny fermentation which is the beginning of life. Everything seems to be against the infant hero of our drama – just as everything seems against the youngest son or ill-used stepdaughter at the opening of a fairy tale. But life somehow wins through. With infinite suffering, against all but insuperable obstacles, it spreads, it breeds, it complicates itself: from the amoeba up to the plant, up to the reptile, up to the mammal. We glance briefly at the age of monsters. Dragons prowl the earth, devour one another and die. Then comes the theme of the younger son and the ugly duckling once more. As the weak, tiny spark of life began amidst the huge hostilities of the inanimate, so now again, amidst the beasts that are far larger and stronger than he, there comes forth a little naked, shivering, cowering creature, shuffling, not yet erect, promising nothing: the product of another millionth millionth chance. Yet somehow he thrives. He becomes the Cave Man with his club and his flints, muttering and

[1] I am not suggesting that practising scientists believe it as a whole. The delightful name 'Wellsianity' (which another member invented during the discussion) would have been much better than 'the Scientific Outlook'. — C.S.L.

growling over his enemies' bones, dragging his screaming mate by her hair (I never could quite make out why), tearing his children to pieces in fierce jealousy till one of them is old enough to tear him, cowering before the horrible gods whom he has created in his own image. But these are only growing pains. Wait till the next act. There he is becoming true Man. He learns to master Nature. Science comes and dissipates the superstitions of his infancy. More and more he becomes the controller of his own fate. Passing hastily over the present (for it is a mere nothing by the timescale we are using), you follow him on into the future. See him in the last act, though not the last scene, of this great mystery. A race of demigods now rule the planet – and perhaps more than the planet – for eugenics have made certain that only demigods will be born, and psychoanalysis that none of them shall lose or smirch his divinity, and communism that all which divinity requires shall be ready to their hand. Man has ascended his throne. Henceforward he has nothing to do but to practise virtue, to grow in wisdom, to be happy. And now, mark the final stroke of genius. If the myth stopped at that point, it might be a little bathetic. It would lack the highest grandeur of which human imagination is capable. The last scene reverses all. We have the Twilight of the Gods. All this time, silently, unceasingly, out of all reach of human power, Nature, the old enemy, has been steadily gnawing away. The sun will cool – all suns will cool – the whole universe will run down. Life (every form of life) will be banished, without hope of return, from every inch of infinite space. All ends in nothingness, and 'universal darkness covers all'. The pattern of the myth thus becomes one of the noblest we can conceive. It is the pattern of many Elizabethan tragedies, where the protagonist's career can be represented by a slowly ascending and then rapidly falling curve, with its highest point in Act IV. You see him climbing up and up, then blazing in his bright meridian, then finally overwhelmed in ruin.

Such a world-drama appeals to every part of us. The early struggles of the hero (a theme delightfully doubled, played first by life, and then by man) appeals to our generosity. His future exaltation gives scope to a reasonable optimism; for the tragic close is so very distant that you need not often think of it – we work with millions of years. And the tragic close itself just gives that irony, that grandeur, which calls forth our defiance, and without which all the rest might cloy. There is a beauty in this myth which well deserves better poetic handling than it has yet received: I hope some great genius will yet crystallise it before the incessant stream of philosophic change carries it all away. I am speaking, of course, of the beauty it has whether you believe it or not. There I can speak from experience: for I, who believe less than half of what it tells me about the past, and less than nothing of what it tells me about the future, am deeply moved when I contemplate it. The only other story – unless, indeed, it is an embodiment of the same story – which similarly moves me is the *Nibelung's Ring* (*Enden sah ich die Welt!*).

We cannot, therefore, turn down Theology, simply because it does not avoid being poetical. All world views yield poetry to those who believe them by the mere fact of being believed. And nearly all have certain poetical merits whether you believe them or not. This is what we should expect. Man is a poetical animal and touches nothing which he does not adorn.

There are, however, two other lines of thought which might lead us to call Theology a mere poetry, and these I must now consider. In the first place, it certainly contains elements similar to those which we find in many early, and even savage, religions. And those elements in the early religions may now seem to us to be poetical. The question here is rather complicated. We now regard the death and return of Balder as a poetical idea, a myth. We are invited to infer thence that the death and resurrection of Christ is a poetical idea, a myth. But we are not really starting with the *datum* 'Both are poetical' and thence arguing 'Therefore both are false'. Part of the poetical aroma which hangs about Balder is, I believe, due to the fact that we have already come to disbelieve in him. So that disbelief, not poetical experience, is the real starting point of the argument. But this is perhaps an over-subtlety, certainly a subtlety, and I will leave it on one side.

What light is really thrown on the truth or falsehood of Christian Theology by the occurrence of similar ideas in Pagan religion? I think the answer was very well given a fortnight ago by Mr Brown. Supposing, for purposes of argument, that Christianity is true, then it could avoid all coincidence with other religions only on the supposition that all other religions are one hundred per cent erroneous. To which, you remember, Professor Price replied by agreeing with Mr Brown and saying: 'Yes. From these resemblances you may conclude not "so much the worse for the Christians" but "so much the better for the Pagans".' The truth is that the resemblances tell nothing either for or against the truth of Christian Theology. If you start from the assumption that the Theology is false, the resemblances are quite consistent with that assumption. One would expect creatures of the same sort, faced with the same universe, to make the same false guess more than once. But if you start with the assumption that the Theology is true, the resemblances fit in equally well. Theology, while saying that a special illumination has been vouchsafed to Christians and (earlier) to Jews, also says that there is some divine illumination vouchsafed to all men. The Divine light, we are told, 'lighteneth every man'. We should, therefore, expect to find in the imagination of great Pagan teachers and myth-makers some glimpse of that theme which we believe to be the very plot of the whole cosmic story – the theme of incarnation, death and rebirth. And the differences between the Pagan Christs (Balder, Osiris, etc.) and the Christ Himself is much what we should expect to find. The Pagan stories are all about someone dying and rising, either every year, or else nobody knows where and nobody knows when. The Christian story is about a historical personage, whose execution can be dated pretty accurately, under a named Roman magistrate, and with whom the society that He founded is in a continuous relation down to the present day. It is not the difference between falsehood and truth. It is the difference between a real event on the one hand and dim dreams or premonitions of that same event on the other. It is like watching something come gradually into focus: first it hangs in the clouds of myth and ritual, vast and vague, then it condenses, grows hard and in a sense small, as a historical event in first-century Palestine. This gradual focussing goes on even inside the Christian tradition itself. The earliest stratum of the Old Testament contains many truths in a form which I take to be legendary, or even mythical – hanging in the clouds: but gradually the truth condenses, becomes more and more historical. From things like Noah's Ark or the sun standing still upon Ajalon, you come down to the court memoirs of King David. Finally you reach the New Testament and history reigns supreme, and the Truth is incarnate. And 'incarnate' is here more than a metaphor. It is not an accidental resemblance that what, from the point of view of being, is stated in the form 'God became Man', should involve, from the point of view of human knowledge, the statement 'Myth became Fact'. The essential meaning of all things came down from the 'heaven' of myth to the 'earth' of history. In so doing, it partly emptied itself of its glory, as Christ emptied Himself of His glory to be Man. That is the real explanation of the fact that Theology, far from defeating its rivals by a superior poetry is, in a superficial but quite real sense, less poetical than they. That is why the New Testament is, in the same sense, less poetical than the Old. Have you not often felt in Church, if the first lesson is some great passage, that the second lesson is somehow small by comparison – almost, if one might say so, humdrum? So it is and so it must be. This is the humiliation of myth into fact, of God into Man: what is everywhere and always, imageless and ineffable, only to be glimpsed in dream and symbol and the acted poetry of ritual, becomes small, solid – no bigger than a man who can lie asleep in a rowing boat on the Lake of Galilee. You may say that this, after all, is a still deeper poetry.

I will not contradict you. The humiliation leads to a greater glory. But the humiliation of God and the shrinking or condensation of the myth as it becomes fact, are also quite real.

I have just mentioned symbol: and that brings me to the last head under which I will consider the charge of 'mere poetry'. Theology certainly shares with poetry the use of metaphorical or symbolical language. The first Person of the Trinity is not the Father of the Second in a physical sense. The Second Person did not come 'down' to earth in the same sense as a parachutist: nor re-ascend into the sky like a balloon: nor did He literally sit at the right hand of the Father. Why, then, does Christianity talk as if all these things did happen? The agnostic thinks that it does so because those who founded it were quite naïvely ignorant and believed all these statements literally; and we later Christians have gone on using the same language through timidity and conservatism. We are often invited, in Professor Price's words, to throw away the shell and retain the kernel.

There are two questions involved here.

1. What did the early Christians believe? Did they believe that God really has a material palace in the sky and that He received His Son in a decorated state chair placed a little to the right of His own – or did they not? The answer is that the alternative we are offering them was probably never present to their minds at all. As soon as it was present, we know quite well which side of the fence they came down. As soon as the issue of Anthropomorphism was explicitly before the Church in, I think, the second century, Anthropomorphism was condemned. The Church knew the answer (that God has no body and therefore couldn't sit in a chair) as soon as it knew the question. But till the question was raised, of course, people believed neither the one answer nor the other. There is no more tiresome error in the history of thought than to try to sort our ancestors on to this or that side of a distinction which was not in their minds at all. You are asking a question to which no answer exists. It is very probable that most (almost certainly not all) of the first generation of Christians never thought of their faith without anthropomorphic imagery: and that they were not explicitly conscious, as a modern would be, that it *was* mere imagery. But this does not in the least mean that the essence of their belief was concerned with details about a celestial throne room. That was not what they valued, or what they were prepared to die for. Any one of them who went to Alexandria and got a philosophical education would have recognised the imagery at once for what it was, and would not have felt that his belief had been altered in any way that mattered. My mental picture of an Oxford college, before I saw one, was very different from the

reality in physical details. But this did not mean that when I came to Oxford I found my general conception of what a college means to have been a delusion. The physical pictures had inevitably accompanied my thinking, but they had never been what I was chiefly interested in, and much of my thinking had been correct in spite of them. What you think is one thing: what you imagine while you are thinking is another.

The earliest Christians were not so much like a man who mistakes the shell for the kernel as like a man carrying a nut which he hasn't yet cracked. The moment it is cracked, he knows which part to throw away. Till then he holds on to the nut: not because he is a fool but because he isn't.

2. We are invited to restate our belief in a form free from metaphor and symbol. The reason why we don't is that we can't. We can, if you like, say 'God entered history' instead of saying 'God came down to earth'. But, of course, 'entered' is just as metaphorical as 'came down'. You have only substituted horizontal or undefined movement for vertical movement. We can make our language duller; we cannot make it less metaphorical. We can make the pictures more prosaic; we cannot be less pictorial. Nor are we Christians alone in this disability. Here is a sentence from a celebrated non-Christian writer, Dr I.A. Richards.[2] 'Only that part of the course of a mental event which takes effect through incoming (sensory) impulses or through effects of past sensory impulses can be said to be thereby known. The reservation no doubt involves complications.' Dr Richards does not mean that the part of the course 'takes' effect in the literal sense of the word *takes*, nor that it does so *through* a sensory impulse as you could take a parcel *through* a doorway. In the second sentence 'The reservation involves complications', he does not mean that an act of defending, or a seat booked in a train, or an American park, really sets about rolling or folding or curling up a set of coilings or rollings up. In other words, all language about things other than physical objects is necessarily metaphorical.

For all these reasons, then, I think (though we knew even before Freud that the heart is deceitful) that those who accept Theology are not necessarily being guided by taste rather than reason. The picture so often painted of Christians huddling together on an ever narrower strip of beach while the incoming tide of 'Science' mounts higher and higher, corresponds to nothing in my own experience. That grand myth which I asked you to admire a few minutes ago is not for me a hostile novelty breaking in on my traditional beliefs. On the contrary, that cosmology is

---

[2] *Principles of Literary Criticism*, chapter II.

what I started from. Deepening distrust and final abandonment of it long preceded my conversion to Christianity. Long before I believed Theology to be true I had already decided that the popular scientific picture at any rate was false. One absolutely central inconsistency ruins it; it is the one we touched on a fortnight ago. The whole picture professes to depend on inferences from observed facts. Unless inference is valid, the whole picture disappears. Unless we can be sure that reality in the remotest nebula or the remotest part obeys the thought-laws of the human scientist here and now in his laboratory – in other words, unless Reason is an absolute – all is in ruins. Yet those who ask me to believe this world picture also ask me to believe that Reason is simply the unforeseen and unintended by-product of mindless matter at one stage of its endless and aimless becoming. Here is flat contradiction. They ask me at the same moment to accept a conclusion and to discredit the only testimony on which that conclusion can be based. The difficulty is to me a fatal one; and the fact that when you put it to many scientists, far from having an answer, they seem not even to understand what the difficulty is, assures me that I have not found a mare's nest but detected a radical disease in their whole mode of thought from the very beginning. The man who has once understood the situation is compelled henceforth to regard the scientific cosmology as being, in principle, a myth; though no doubt a great many true particulars have been worked into it.[3]

After that it is hardly worth noticing minor difficulties. Yet these are many and serious. The Bergsonian critique of orthodox Darwinism is not easy to answer. More disquieting still is Professor D.M.S. Watson's defence. 'Evolution itself,' he wrote,[4] 'is accepted by zoologists not because it has been observed to occur or … can be proved by logically coherent evidence to be true, but because the only alternative, special creation, is clearly incredible.' Has it come to that? Does the whole vast structure of modern naturalism depend not on positive evidence but simply on an *a priori* metaphysical prejudice? Was it devised not to get in facts but to keep out God? Even, however, if Evolution in the strict biological sense has some better grounds than Professor Watson suggests – and I can't help thinking it must – we should distinguish Evolution in this strict sense from what may be called the universal evolutionism of modern thought. By universal evolutionism I mean the belief that the

---

[3] It is not irrelevant, in considering the mythical character of this cosmology to notice that the two great imaginative expressions of it are *earlier* than the evidence: Keats's *Hyperion* and the *Nibelung's Ring* are pre-Darwinian works.

[4] Quoted in 'Science and the BBC', *Nineteenth Century*, April, 1943.

very formula of universal process is from imperfect to perfect, from small beginnings to great endings, from the rudimentary to the elaborate: the belief which makes people find it natural to think that morality springs from savage taboos, adult sentiment from infantile sexual maladjustments, thought from instinct, mind from matter, organic from inorganic, cosmos from chaos. This is perhaps the deepest habit of mind in the contemporary world. It seems to me immensely unplausible, because it makes the general course of nature so very unlike those parts of nature we can observe. You remember the old puzzle as to whether the owl came from the egg or the egg from the owl. The modern acquiescence or universal evolutionism is a kind of optical illusion, produced by attending exclusively to the owl's emergence from the egg. We are taught from childhood to notice how the perfect oak grows from the acorn and to forget that the acorn itself was dropped by a perfect oak. We are reminded constantly that the adult human being was an embryo, never that the life of the embryo came from two adult human beings. We love to notice that the express engine of today is the descendant of the 'Rocket'; we do not equally remember that the 'Rocket' springs not from some even more rudimentary engine, but from something much more perfect and complicated than itself – namely, a man of genius. The obviousness or naturalness which most people seem to find in the idea of emergent evolution thus seems to be a pure hallucination.

On these grounds and others like them one is driven to think that whatever else may be true, the popular scientific cosmology at any rate is certainly not. I left that ship not at the call of poetry but because I thought it could not keep afloat. Something like philosophical idealism or Theism must, at the very worst, be less untrue than that. And idealism turned out, when you took it seriously, to be disguised Theism. And once you accepted Theism you could not ignore the claims of Christ. And when you examined them it appeared to me that you could adopt no middle position. Either he was a lunatic or God. And He was not a lunatic.

I was taught at school, when I had done a sum, to 'prove my answer'. The proof or verification of my Christian answer to the cosmic sum is this. When I accept Theology I may find difficulties, at this point or that, in harmonising it with some particular truths which are imbedded in the mythical cosmology derived from science. But I can get in, or allow for, science as a whole. Granted that Reason is prior to matter and that the light of that primal Reason illuminates finite minds, I can understand how men should come, by observation and inference, to know a lot about the universe they live in. If, on the other hand, I swallow the scientific cosmology as a whole, then not only can I not fit in Christianity, but I cannot even fit in science. If minds are wholly dependent on brains, and brains on biochemistry, and biochemistry (in the long run) on the meaningless flux of the atoms, I cannot understand how the thought of those minds should have any more significance than the sound of the wind in the trees. And this is to me the final test. This is how I distinguish dreaming and waking. When I am awake I can, in some degree, account for and study my dream. The dragon that pursued me last night can be fitted into my waking world. I know that there are such things as dreams: I know that I had eaten an indigestible dinner: I know that a man of my reading might be expected to dream of dragons. But while in the nightmare I could not have fitted in my waking experience. The waking world is judged more real because it can thus contain the dreaming world: the dreaming world is judged less real because it cannot contain the waking one. For the same reason I am certain that in passing from the scientific point of view to the theological, I have passed from dream to waking. Christian theology can fit in science, art, morality, and the sub-Christian religions. The scientific point of view cannot fit in any of these things, not even science itself. I believe in Christianity as I believe that the Sun has risen not only because I see it but because by it I see everything else.

[3]

THE FUNERAL OF A GREAT MYTH

This essay was first published in Christian Reflections *(1998), and develops one of the myths in 'Is Theology Poetry?' (see p. 10).*

There are some mistakes which humanity has made and repented so often that there is now really no excuse for making them again. One of these is the injustice which every age does to its predecessor; for example, the ignorant contempt which the Humanists (even good Humanists like Sir Thomas More) felt for medieval philosophy or Romantics (even good Romantics like Keats) felt for eighteenth-century poetry. Each time all this 'reaction' and resentment has to be punished and unsaid; it is a wasteful performance. It is tempting to try whether we, at least, cannot avoid it. Why should we not give our predecessors a fair and filial dismissal?

Such, at all events, is the attempt I am going to make in this paper. I come to bury the great Myth of the nineteenth and early twentieth century; but also to praise it. I am going to pronounce a funeral oration.

By this great Myth I mean that picture of reality which resulted during the period under consideration, not logically but imaginatively, from some of the more striking and (so to speak) marketable theories of the real scientists. I have heard this Myth called 'Wellsianity'. The name is a good one in so far as it does justice to the share which a great imaginative writer bore in building it up. But it is not satisfactory. It suggests, as we shall see, an error about the date at which the Myth became dominant; and it also suggests that the Myth affected only the 'middle-brow' mind. In fact it is as much behind Bridge's *Testament of Beauty* as it is behind the work of Wells. It dominates minds as different as those of Professor Alexander and Walt Disney. It is implicit in nearly every modern article on politics, sociology, and ethics.

I call it a Myth because it is, as I have said, the imaginative and not the logical result of what is vaguely called 'modern science'. Strictly speaking, there is, I confess, no such thing as 'modern science'. There are only

22

particular sciences, all in a stage of rapid change, and sometimes inconsistent with one another. What the Myth uses is a selection from the scientific theories – a selection made at first, and modified afterwards, in obedience to imaginative and emotional needs. It is the work of the folk imagination, moved by its natural appetite for an impressive unity. It therefore treats its *data* with great freedom – selecting, slurring, expurgating, and adding at will.

The central idea of the Myth is what its believers would call 'Evolution' or 'Development' or 'Emergence', just as the central idea in the myth of Adonis is Death and Re-birth. I do not mean that the doctrine of Evolution as held by practising biologists is a Myth. It may be shown, by later biologists, to be a less satisfactory hypothesis than was hoped fifty years ago. But that does not amount to being a Myth. It is a genuine scientific hypothesis. But we must sharply distinguish between Evolution as a biological theorem and popular Evolutionism or Developmentalism which is certainly a Myth. Before proceeding to describe it and (which is my chief business) to pronounce its eulogy, I had better make clear its mythical character.

We have, first of all, the evidence of chronology. If popular Evolutionism were (as it imagines itself to be) not a Myth but the intellectually legitimate result of the scientific theorem on the public mind, it would arise *after* that theorem had become widely known. We should have the theorem known first of all to a few, then adopted by all the scientists, then spreading to all men of general education, then beginning to affect poetry and the arts, and so finally percolating to the mass of the people. In fact, however, we find something quite different. The clearest and finest poetical expressions of the Myth come before the *Origin of Species* was published (1859) and long before it had established itself as scientific orthodoxy. There had, to be sure, been hints and germs of the theory in scientific circles before 1859. But if the mythopoeic poets were at all infected by those germs they must have been very up-to-date indeed, very predisposed to catch the infection. Almost before the scientists spoke, certainly before they spoke clearly, imagination was ripe for it.

The finest expression of the Myth in English does not come from Bridges, nor from Shaw, nor from Wells, nor from Olaf Stapledon. It is this:

> *As Heaven and Earth are fairer, fairer far*
> *Than Chaos and blank Darkness, though once chiefs;*
> *And as we show beyond that Heaven and Earth*
> *In form and shape compact and beautiful,*

In will, in action free, companionship,
And thousand other signs of purer life;
So on our heels a fresh perfection treads,
A power more strong in beauty, born of us,
And fated to excel us, as we pass
In glory that old Darkness. (II, 206–15)

Thus Oceanus, in Keats's *Hyperion*, nearly forty years before the *Origin of Species*. And on the continent we have the *Nibelung's Ring*. Coming, as I do, to bury but also to praise the receding age, I will by no means join in the modern depreciation of Wagner. He may, for all I know, have been a bad man. He may (though I shall never believe it) have been a bad musician. But as a mythopoeic poet he is incomparable. The tragedy of the Evolutionary Myth has never been more nobly expressed than in his *Wotan*: its heady raptures never more irresistibly than in *Siegfried*. That he himself knew quite well what he was writing about can be seen from his letter to August Rockel in 1854. 'The progress of the whole drama shows the necessity of recognizing and submitting to the change, the diversity, the multiplicity, the eternal novelty, of the Real. Wotan rises to the tragic height of willing his own downfall. This is all we have to learn from the history of Man – to will the necessary and ourselves to bring it to pass.'

If Shaw's *Back to Methuselah* were really, as he supposed, the work of a prophet or a pioneer ushering in the reign of a new Myth, its predominantly comic tone and its generally low emotional temperature would be inexplicable. It is admirable fun: but not thus are new epochs brought to birth. The ease with which he plays with the Myth shows that the Myth is fully digested and already senile. Shaw is the Lucian or the Snorri of this mythology: to find its Aeschylus or its Elder Edda you must go back to Keats and Wagner.

That, then, is the first proof that popular Evolution is a Myth. In making it Imagination runs ahead of scientific evidence. 'The prophetic soul of the big world' was already pregnant with the Myth: if science had not met the imaginative need, science would not have been so popular. But probably every age gets, within certain limits, the science it desires.

In the second place we have internal evidence. Popular Evolutionism or Developmentalism differs *in content* from the Evolution of the real biologists. To the biologist Evolution is a hypothesis. It covers more of the facts than any other hypothesis at present on the market and is therefore to be accepted unless, or until, some new supposal can be shown to cover still more facts with even fewer assumptions. At least, that is what I think most biologists would say. Professor D.M.S. Watson, it is true, would not go so far. According to him Evolution 'is accepted by zoologists not because it has been observed to occur or … can be proved by logically coherent evidence to be true, but because the only alternative, special creation, is clearly incredible.'[1] This would mean that the sole ground for believing it is not empirical but metaphysical – the dogma of an amateur metaphysician who finds 'special creation' incredible. But I do not think it has really come to that. Most biologists have a more robust belief in Evolution than Professor Watson. But it is certainly a hypothesis. In the Myth, however, there is nothing hypothetical about it: it is basic fact: or, to speak more strictly, such distinctions do not exist on the mythical level at all. There are more important differences to follow.

In the science, Evolution is a theory about *changes*: in the Myth it is a fact about *improvements*. Thus a real scientist like Professor J.B.S. Haldane is at pains to point out that popular ideas of Evolution lay a wholly unjustified emphasis on those changes which have rendered creatures (by human standards) 'better' or more interesting. He adds: 'We are therefore inclined to regard progress as the rule in evolution. Actually it is the exception, and for every case of it there are ten of degeneration.'[2] But the Myth simply expurgates the ten cases of degeneration. In the popular mind the word 'Evolution' conjures up a picture of things moving 'onwards and upwards', and of nothing else whatsoever. And it might have been predicted that it would do so. Already, before science had spoken, the mythical imagination knew the kind of 'Evolution' it wanted. It wanted the Keatsian and Wagnerian kind: the gods superseding the Titans, and the young, joyous, careless, amorous Siegfried superseding the care-worn, anxious, treaty-entangled Wotan. If science offers any instances to satisfy that demand, they will be eagerly accepted. If it offers any instances that frustrate it, they will simply be ignored.

Again, for the scientist Evolution is a purely biological theorem. It takes over organic life on this planet as a going concern and tries to explain certain changes within that field. It makes no cosmic statements, no metaphysical statements, no eschatological statements. Granted that we now have minds we can trust, granted that organic life came to exist, it tries to explain, say, how a species that once had wings came to lose them. It explains this by the negative effect of environment operating on small

---

[1] Watson, quoted in 'Science and the BBC', *Nineteenth Century*, April, 1943.
[2] 'Darwinism Today', *Possible Worlds*, p. 28.

variations. It does not in itself explain the origin of organic life, nor of the variations, nor does it discuss the origin and validity of reason. It may well tell you how the brain, through which reason now operates, arose, but that is a different matter. Still less does it even attempt to tell you how the universe as a whole arose, or what it is, or whither it is tending. But the Myth knows none of these reticences. Having turned what was a theory of change into a theory of improvement, it then makes this a *cosmic* theory. Not merely terrestrial organisms but *everything* is moving 'upwards and onwards'. Reason has 'evolved' out of instinct, virtue out of complexes, poetry out of erotic howls and grunts, civilisation out of savagery, the organic out of inorganic, the solar system out of some side-real soup or traffic block. And conversely, reason, virtue, art and civiliza-tion as we now know them are only the crude or embryonic beginnings of far better things – perhaps Deity itself – in the remote future. For in the Myth, 'Evolution' (as the Myth understands it) is the formula of *all* exis-tence. To exist means to be moving from the status of 'almost zero' to the status of 'almost infinity'. To those brought up on the Myth nothing seems more normal, more natural, more plausible, than that chaos should turn into order, death into life, ignorance into knowledge. And with this we reach the full-blown Myth. It is one of the most moving and satisfying world dramas which have ever been imagined.

The drama proper is preceded (do not forget the Rhinegold here) by the most austere of all preludes; the infinite void and matter endlessly, aimlessly moving to bring forth it knows not what. Then by some millionth, millionth chance – what tragic irony! – the conditions at one point of space and time bubble up into that tiny fermentation which we call organic life. At first everything seems to be against the infant hero of our drama; just as everything always was against the seventh son or ill-used step-daughter in a fairy tale. But life somehow wins through. With incalculable sufferings (the Sorrows of the Volsungs were nothing to it), against all but insuperable obstacles, it spreads, it breeds, it complicates itself; from the amoeba up to the reptile, up to the mammal. Life (here comes our first climax) 'wantons as in her prime'. This is the age of monsters: dragons prowl the earth, devour one another, and die. Then the old irresistible theme of the Younger Son or the Ugly Duckling is repeated. As the weak, tiny spark of life herself began amidst the beasts that are far larger and stronger than he, there comes forth a little, naked, shivering, cowering biped, shuffling, not yet fully erect, promising nothing: the product of another millionth, millionth chance. His name in this Myth is Man: elsewhere he has been the young Beowulf whom men at first thought a dastard, or the stripling David armed only with a sling against mail-clad Goliath, or Jack the Giant-Killer himself, or even Hop-o'-my-Thumb. He thrives. He begins killing his giants. He becomes the Cave Man with his flints and his club, muttering and growling over his enemies' bones, almost a brute yet somehow able to invent art, pottery, language, weapons, cookery and nearly everything else (his name in another story is Robinson Crusoe), dragging his screaming mate by her hair (I do not exactly know why), tearing his children to pieces in fierce jealousy until they are old enough to tear him, and cowering before the terrible gods whom he has invented in his own image.

But these were only growing pains. In the next act he has become true Man. He learns to master Nature. Science arises and dissipates the superstitions of his infancy. More and more he becomes the controller of his own fate. Passing hastily over the historical period (in it the upward and onward movement gets in places a little indistinct, but it is a mere nothing by the time-scale we are using) we follow our hero on into the future. See him in the last act, though not the last scene, of this great mystery. A race of demi-gods now rule the planet (in some versions, the galaxy). Eugenics have made certain that only demi-gods will now be born: psycho-analysis that none of them shall lose or smirch his divinity: economics that they shall have to hand all that demi-gods require. Man has ascended his throne. Man has become God. All is a blaze of glory. And now, mark well the final stroke of mythopoeic genius. It is only the more debased versions of the Myth that end here. For to end here is a little bathetic, even a little vulgar. If we stopped at this point the story would lack the highest grandeur. Therefore, in the best versions, the last scene reverses all. Arthur died: Siegfried died: Roland died at Roncesvaux. Dusk steals darkly over the gods. All this time we have forgotten Mordred, Hagen, Ganelon. All this time Nature, the old enemy who only seemed to be defeated, has been gnawing away, silently, unceasingly, out of the reach of human power. The Sun will cool – all suns will cool – the whole universe will run down. Life (every form of life) will be banished without hope of return from every cubic inch of infinite space. All ends in nothingness. 'Universal darkness covers all.' True to the shape of Elizabethan tragedy, the hero has swiftly fallen from the glory to which he slowly climbed: we are dismissed in 'calm of mind, all passion spent'.[3] It is indeed much better than an Elizabethan tragedy, for it has a more complete finality. It brings us to the end not of a story, but of all possible stories: *enden sah ich die welt*.

---

[3] John Milton, *Samson Agonistes* (1671), line 1758.

I grew up believing in this Myth and I have felt – I still feel – its almost perfect grandeur. Let no one say we are an unimaginative age: neither the Greeks nor the Norsemen ever invented a better story. Even to the present day, in certain moods, I could almost find it in my heart to wish that it was not mythical, but true. And yet, how could it be?

What makes it impossible that it should be true is not so much the lack of evidence for this or that scene in the drama as the fatal self-contradiction which runs right through it. The Myth cannot even get going without accepting a good deal from the real sciences. And the real sciences cannot be accepted for a moment unless rational inferences are valid: for every science claims to be a series of inferences from observed facts. It is only by such inferences that you can reach your nebulae and protoplasm and dinosaurs and sub-men and cave-men at all. Unless you start by believing that reality in the remotest space and the remotest time rigidly obeys the laws of logic, you can have no ground for believing in any astronomy, any biology, any palaeontology, any archaeology. To reach the positions held by the real scientists – which are then taken over by the Myth – you must, in fact, treat reason as an absolute. But at the same time the Myth asks me to believe that reason is simply the unforeseen and unintended by-product of a mindless process at one stage of its endless and aimless becoming. The content of the Myth thus knocks from under me the only ground on which I could possibly believe the Myth to be true. If my own mind is a product of the irrational – if what seem my clearest reasonings are only the way in which a creature conditioned as I am is bound to feel – how shall I trust my mind when it tells me about Evolution? They say in effect: 'I will prove that what you call a proof is only the result of mental habits which result from heredity which results from bio-chemistry which results from physics.' But this is the same as saying: 'I will prove that proofs are irrational'; more succinctly, 'I will prove that there are no proofs'. The fact that some people of scientific education cannot by any effort be taught to see the difficulty, confirms one's suspicion that we here touch a radical disease in their whole style of thought. But the man who does see it, is compelled to reject as mythical the cosmology in which most of us were brought up. That it has embedded in it many true particulars I do not doubt: but in its entirety, it simply will not do. Whatever the real universe may turn out to be like, it can't be like that.

I have been speaking hitherto of this Myth as of a thing to be buried because I believe that its dominance is already over; in the sense that what seem to me to be the most vigorous movements of contemporary thought point away from it. Physics (a discipline less easily mythological) is replacing biology as the science *par excellence* in the mind of the plain man. The whole philosophy of Becoming has been vigorously challenged by the American 'Humanists'. The revival of theology has attained proportions that have to be reckoned with. The Romantic poetry and music in which popular Evolutionism found its natural counterpart are going out of fashion. But of course a Myth does not die in a day. We may expect that this Myth, when driven from cultured circles, will long retain its hold on the masses, and even when abandoned by them will continue for centuries to haunt our language. Those who wish to attack it must beware of despising it. There are deep reasons for its popularity.

The basic idea of the Myth – that small or chaotic or feeble things perpetually turn themselves into large, strong, ordered things – may, at first sight, seem a very odd one. We have never actually seen a pile of rubble turning itself into a house. But this odd idea commends itself to the imagination by the help of what seem to be two instances of it within everyone's knowledge. Everyone has seen individual organisms doing it. Acorns become oaks, grubs become insects, eggs become birds, every man was once an embryo. And secondly – which weighs very much in the popular mind during a machine age – everyone has seen Evolution really happening in the history of machines. We all remember when locomotives were smaller and less efficient than they are now. These two apparent instances are quite enough to convince the imagination that Evolution in a cosmic sense is the most natural thing in the world. It is true that reason cannot here agree with imagination. These apparent instances are not really instances of Evolution at all. The oak comes indeed from the acorn, but then the acorn was dropped by an earlier oak. Every man began with the union of an ovum and a spermatozoon, but the ovum and the spermatozoon came from two fully developed human beings. The modern express engine came from the *Rocket*: but the *Rocket* came, not from something under and more elementary than itself but from something much more developed and highly organized – the mind of a man, and a man of genius. Modern art may have 'developed' from savage art. But then the very first picture of all did not 'evolve' itself: it came from something overwhelmingly greater than itself, from the mind of that man who by seeing for the first time that marks on a flat surface could be made to look like animals and men, proved himself to excel in sheer blinding genius any of the artists who have succeeded him. It may be true that if we trace back any existing civilization to its beginnings we shall find those beginnings crude and savage: but then when you look closer you usually find that these beginnings themselves come from a wreck of some earlier civilization. In other words, the apparent instances of, or analogies to, Evolution which impress the folk imagination, operate by fixing our attention on one half of the process. What we actually see all round us is a double process – the perfect 'dropping' an imperfect seed which in its turn develops to perfection. By concentrating exclusively on the record of upward movement in this cycle we seem to see 'evolution'. I am not in the least denying that organisms on this planet may have 'evolved'. But if we are to be guided by the analogy of Nature as we now know her, it would be reasonable to suppose that this evolutionary process was the second half of a long pattern – that the crude beginnings of life on this planet have themselves been 'dropped' there by a full and perfect life. The analogy may be mistaken. Perhaps Nature was once different. Perhaps the universe as a whole is quite different from those parts of it which fall under our observation. But if that is so, if there was once a dead universe which somehow made itself alive, if there was absolutely original savagery which raised itself by its own shoulder strap into civilization, then we ought to recognize that things of this sort happen no longer, that the world we are being asked to believe in is radically unlike the world we experience. In other words, all the immediate *plausibility* of the Myth has vanished. But it has vanished only because we have been thinking it will remain plausible to the imagination, and it is imagination which makes the Myth: it takes over from rational thought only what it finds convenient.

Another source of strength in the Myth is what the psychologists would call its 'ambivalence'. It gratifies equally two opposite tendencies of the mind, the tendency to denigration and the tendency to flattery. In the Myth everything is becoming everything else: in fact everything *is* everything else at an earlier or later stage of development – the later stages being always the better. This means that if you are feeling like Mencken you can 'debunk' all the respectable things by pointing out that they are 'merely' elaborations of the disreputable things. Love is 'merely' an elaboration of lust, virtue merely an elaboration of instinct, and so forth. On the one hand it also means that if you are feeling what the people call 'idealistic' you can regard all the nasty things (in yourself or your party or your nation) as being 'merely' the undeveloped forms of all the nice things: vice is only undeveloped virtue, egotism only undeveloped altruism, a little more education will set everything right.

The Myth also soothes the old wounds of our childhood. Without going as far as Freud we may yet well admit that every man has an old grudge against his father and his first teacher. The process of being brought up, however well it is done, cannot fail to offend. How pleasing, therefore, to abandon the old idea of 'descent' from our concocters in favour of the new idea of 'evolution' or 'emergence': to feel that we have risen from them as a flower from the earth, that we transcend them as Keats's gods transcended the Titans. One then gets a kind of cosmic excuse for regarding one's father as a muddling old Mima and his claims upon our gratitude or respect as an insufferable *Stammenlied*. 'Out of the way, old fool: it is we who know to forge Nothung!'

The Myth also pleases those who want to sell things to us. In the old days, a man had a family carriage built for him when he got married and expected it to last all his life. Such a frame of mind would hardly suit modern manufacturers. But popular Evolutionism suits them exactly. Nothing *ought* to last. They want you to have a new car, a new radio set, a new everything every year. The new model must always be superseding the old. Madam would like the *latest* fashion. For this is evolution, this is development, this the way the universe itself is going: and 'sales-resistance' is the sin against the Holy Ghost, the *élan vital*.

Finally, modern politics would be impossible without the Myth. It arose in the Revolutionary period. But for the political ideals of that period it would never have been accepted. That explains why the Myth concentrates on Haldane's one case of biological 'progress' and ignores his ten cases of 'degeneration'. If the cases of degeneration were kept in mind it would be impossible not to see that any given change in society is at least as likely to destroy the liberties and amenities we already have as to add new ones: that the danger of slipping back is at least as great as the chance of getting on: that a prudent society must spend at least as much energy on conserving what it has as on improvement. A clear knowledge of these truisms would be fatal both to the political Left and to the political Right of modern times. The Myth obscures that knowledge. Great parties have a vested interest in maintaining the Myth. We must therefore expect that it will survive in the popular press (including the ostensibly *comic* press) long after it has been expelled from educated circles. In Russia, where it has been built into the state religion, it may survive for centuries: for

> It has great allies,
> Its friends are propaganda, party cries,
> And bilge, and Man's incorrigible mind.

But that is not the note on which I would wish to end. The Myth has all these discreditable allies: but we should be far astray if we thought it had no others. As I have tried to show it has better allies too. It appeals to the same innocent and permanent needs in us which welcome Jack the

Giant-Killer. It gives us almost everything the imagination craves – irony, heroism, vastness, unity in multiplicity, and a tragic close. It appeals to every part of me except my reason. That is why those of us who feel that the Myth is already dead for us must not make the mistake of trying to 'debunk' it in the wrong way. We must not fancy that we are securing the modern world from something grim and dry, something that starves the soul. The contrary is the truth. It is our painful duty to wake the world from an enchantment. The real universe is probably in many respects less poetical, certainly less tidy and unified, than they had supposed. Man's role in it is less heroic. The danger that really hangs over him is perhaps entirely lacking in true tragic dignity. It is only in the last resort, and after all lesser poetries have been renounced and imagination sternly subjected to intellect, that we shall be able to offer them any compensation for what we intend to take away from them. That is why in the meantime we must treat the Myth with respect. It was all (on a certain level) nonsense: but a man would be a dull dog if he could not feel the thrill and charm of it. For my own part, though I believe it no longer, I shall always enjoy it as I enjoy other myths. I shall keep my Cave-Man where I keep Balder and Helen and the Argonauts: and there often revisit him.

[4]
GOD IN THE DOCK

Walter Hooper's title for 'Difficulties in Presenting the Christian Faith to Modern Unbelievers', published in Lumen Vitae, *Volume III (September 1948) (English text with French translation). It was reprinted in* Undeceptions *(1971) and* God in the Dock *(1998).*

I have been asked to write about the difficulties which a man must face in trying to present the Christian Faith to modern unbelievers. That is too wide a subject for my capacity or even for the scope of an article. The difficulties vary as the audience varies. The audience may be of this or that nation, may be children or adults, learned or ignorant. My own experience is of English audiences only, and almost exclusively of adults. It has, in fact, been mostly of men (and women) serving in the RAF. This has meant that while very few of them have been learned in the academic sense of that word, a large number of them have had a smattering of elementary practical science, have been mechanics, electricians or wireless operators; for the rank and file of the RAF belong to what may almost be called 'the Intelligentsia of the Proletariat'. I have also talked to students at the Universities. These strict limitations in my experience must be kept in mind by the readers. How rash it would be to generalise from such an experience I myself discovered on the single occasion when I spoke to soldiers. It became at once clear to me that the level of intelligence in our army is very much lower than in the RAF and that quite a different approach was required.

The first thing I learned from addressing the RAF was that I had been mistaken in thinking materialism to be our only considerable adversary. Among the English 'Intelligentsia of the Proletariat', materialism is only one among many non-Christian creeds – Theosophy, spiritualism, British Israelitism, etc. England has, of course, always been the home of 'cranks'; I see no sign that they are diminishing. Consistent Marxism I very seldom met. Whether this is because it is very rare, or because men speaking in the presence of their officers concealed it, or because Marxists did not attend the meetings at which I spoke, I have no means of knowing. Even where Christianity was professed, it was often much tainted with Pantheistic elements. Strict and well-informed Christian statements, when they occurred at all, usually came from Roman Catholics or from members of extreme Protestant sects (e.g. Baptists). My student audiences shared, in a less degree, the theological vagueness I found in the RAF, but among them strict and well-informed statements came from Anglo-Catholics and Roman Catholics; seldom, if ever, from Dissenters. The various non-Christian religions mentioned above hardly appeared.

The next thing I learned from the RAF was that the English Proletariat is sceptical about History to a degree which academically educated persons can hardly imagine. This, indeed, seems to me to be far the widest cleavage between the learned and the unlearned. The educated man habitually, almost without noticing it, sees the present as something that grows out of a long perspective of centuries. In the minds of my RAF hearers this perspective simply did not exist. It seemed to me that they did not really believe that we have any reliable knowledge of historic man. But this was often curiously combined with a conviction that we knew a great deal about Pre-Historic Man: doubtless because Pre-Historic Man is labelled 'Science' (which is reliable) whereas Napoleon or Julius Caesar is labelled as 'History' (which is not). Thus a pseudo-scientific picture of the 'Caveman' and a picture of 'the Present' filled almost the whole of their imaginations; between these, there lay only a shadowy and unimportant region in which the phantasmal shapes of Roman soldiers, stage-coaches, pirates, knights in armour, highwaymen, etc., moved in a mist. I had supposed that if my hearers disbelieved the Gospels, they would do so because the Gospels recorded miracles. But my impression is that they disbelieved them simply because they dealt with events that happened a long time ago: that they would be almost as incredulous of the Battle of Actium as of the Resurrection – and for the same reason. Sometimes this scepticism was defended by the argument that all books before the invention of printing must have been copied and re-copied till the text was changed beyond recognition. And here came another surprise. When their historical scepticism took that rational form, it was sometimes easily allayed by the mere statement that there existed a 'science called textual criticism' which gave us a reasonable assurance that some ancient texts were accurate. This ready acceptance of the authority of specialists is significant, not only for its ingenuousness but also because it underlines a fact of which my experiences have on the whole convinced me; i.e., that very little of the opposition we meet is inspired by malice or suspicion. It is based on genuine doubt, and often on doubt that is reasonable in the state of the doubter's knowledge.

My third discovery is of a difficulty which I suspect to be more acute in England than elsewhere. I mean the difficulty occasioned by language. In all societies, no doubt, the speech of the vulgar differs from that of the learned. The English language with its double vocabulary (Latin and native), English manners (with their boundless indulgence to slang, even in polite circles) and English culture which allows nothing like the French Academy, make the gap unusually wide. There are almost two languages in this country. The man who wishes to speak to the uneducated in English must learn their language. It is not enough that he should abstain from using what he regards as 'hard words'. He must discover empirically what words exist in the language of his audience and what they mean in that language: e.g., that *potential* means not 'possible' but 'power', that *creature* means not 'creature', but 'animal', that *primitive* means 'rude' or 'clumsy', that rude means (often) 'scabrous', 'obscene', that the *Immaculate Conception* (except in the mouths of Roman Catholics) means the 'Virgin Birth'. A *being* means 'a personal being'. A man who said to me, 'I believe in the Holy Ghost, but I don't think it is a being,' meant: 'I believe there is such a Being, but that it is not personal.' On the other hand, *personal* sometimes means 'corporeal'. When an uneducated Englishman says that he believes 'in God, but not in a personal God', he may mean simply and solely that he is not an Anthropomorphist in the strict and original sense of that word. *Abstract* seems to have two meanings: (a) 'immaterial', (b) 'vague', obscure and unpractical. Thus Arithmetic is not, in their language, an 'abstract' science. *Practical* means often 'economic' or 'utilitarian'. *Morality* nearly always means 'chastity': thus in their language the sentence 'I do not say that this woman is immoral but I do say that she is a thief,' would not be nonsense, but would mean: 'She is chaste but dishonest.' *Christian* has an eulogistic rather than a descriptive sense: e.g., 'Christian standards' means simply 'high moral standards'. The proposition 'So and so is not a Christian' would only be taken to be a criticism of his behaviour, never to be merely a statement of his beliefs. It is also important to notice that what would seem to the learned to be the harder of two words may in fact, to the uneducated, be the easier. Thus it was recently proposed to emend a prayer used in the Church of England that magistrates 'may truly and indifferently administer justice' to 'may truly and impartially administer justice'. A country priest told me that his sexton understood and could accurately explain the meaning of 'indifferently' but had no idea of what 'impartially' meant.

The popular English language, then, simply has to be learned by him who would preach to the English: just as a missionary learns Bantu before preaching to the Bantus. This is the more necessary because once the lecture or discussion has begun, digressions on the meaning of words tend to bore uneducated audiences and even to awaken distrust. There is no subject in which they are less interested than Philology. Our problem is often simply one of translation. Every examination for ordinands ought to include a passage from some standard theological work for translation into the vernacular. The work is laborious but it is immediately rewarded. By trying to translate our doctrines into vulgar speech we discover how much we understand them ourselves. Our failure to translate may sometimes be due to our ignorance of the vernacular; much more often it exposes the fact that we do not exactly know what we mean.

Apart from this linguistic difficulty, the greatest barrier I have met is the almost total absence from the minds of my audience of any sense of sin. This has struck me more forcibly when I spoke to the RAF than when I spoke to students: whether (as I believe) the Proletariat is more self-righteous than other classes, or whether educated people are cleverer at concealing their pride, this creates for us a new situation. The early Christian preachers could assume in their hearers whether Jews, *Metuentes* or Pagans, a sense of guilt. (That this was common among Pagans is shown by the fact that Epicureanism and the Mystery Religions both claimed, though in different ways, to assuage it.) Thus the Christian message was in those days unmistakably the *Evangelium*, the Good News. It promised healing to those who knew they were sick. We have to convince our hearers of the unwelcome diagnosis before we can expect them to welcome the news of the remedy.

The ancient man approached God (or even the gods) as the accused person approaches his judge. For the modern man the roles are reversed. He is the judge: God is in the dock. He is quite a kindly judge: if God should have a reasonable defence for being the god who permits war, poverty and disease, he is ready to listen to it. The trial may even end in God's acquittal. But the important thing is that man is on the Bench and God in the Dock.

It is generally useless to try to combat this attitude, as older preachers did, by dwelling on sins like drunkenness and unchastity. The modern Proletariat is not drunken. As for fornication, contraceptives have made a profound difference. As long as this sin might socially ruin a girl by making her the mother of a bastard, most men recognized the sin against charity which it involved, and their consciences were often troubled by it. Now that it need have no such consequences, it is not, I think, generally felt to be a sin at all. My own experience suggests that if we can awake the conscience of our hearers at all, we must do so in quite different directions. We must talk of conceit, spite, jealousy, cowardice, meanness, etc. But I am very far from believing that I have found the solution of this problem.

Finally, I must add that my own work has suffered very much from the incurable intellectualism of my approach. The simple, emotional appeal ('Come to Jesus') is still often successful. But those who, like myself, lack the gift for making it, had better not attempt it.

[5]

WHAT ARE WE TO MAKE
OF JESUS CHRIST?

Reprinted from Asking Them Questions, *Third Series, edited by Ronald Selby Wright (OUP, 1950), reproduced in* Undeceptions *(1971) and* God in the Dock *(1998).*

'What are we to make of Jesus Christ?' This is a question which has, in a sense, a frantically comic side. For the real question is not what are we to make of Christ, but what is He to make of us? The picture of a fly sitting deciding what it is going to make of an elephant has comic elements about it. But perhaps the questioner meant what are we to make of Him in the sense of 'How are we to solve the historical problem set us by the recorded sayings and acts of this Man?' This problem is to reconcile two things. On the one hand you have got the almost generally admitted depth and sanity of His moral teaching, which is not very seriously questioned, even by those who are opposed to Christianity. In fact, I find when I am arguing with very anti-God people that they rather make a point of saying, 'I am entirely in favour of the moral teaching of Christianity' – and there seems to be a general agreement that in the teaching of this Man and of His immediate followers, moral truth is exhibited at its purest and best. It is not sloppy idealism, it is full of wisdom and shrewdness. The whole thing is realistic, fresh to the highest degree, the product of a sane mind. That is one phenomenon.

The other phenomenon is the quite appalling nature of this Man's theological remarks. You all know what I mean, and I want rather to stress the point that the appalling claim which this Man seems to be making is not merely made at one moment of His career. There is, of course, the one moment which led to His execution. The moment at which the High Priest said to Him, 'Who are you?' 'I am the Anointed, the Son of the uncreated God, and you shall see Me appearing at the end of all history as the judge of the universe.' But that claim, in fact, does not rest on this one dramatic moment. When you look into His conversation you will find this sort of claim running throughout the whole thing. For instance, He went about saying to people, 'I forgive your sins.' Now it is quite natural for a man to forgive something you do to *him*. Thus if somebody cheats *me* out of five pounds it is quite possible and reasonable for me to say, 'Well, I forgive him, we will say no more about it.' What on earth would you say if somebody had done *you* out of five pounds and *I* said, 'That is all right, I forgive him'? Then there is a curious thing which seems to slip out almost by accident. On one occasion this Man is sitting looking down on Jerusalem from the hill above it and suddenly in comes an extra-ordinary remark – 'I keep on sending you prophets and wise men.' Nobody comments on it. And yet, quite suddenly, almost incidentally, He is claiming to be the power that all through the centuries is sending wise men and leaders into the world. Here is another curious remark: in almost every religion there are unpleasant observances like fasting. This Man suddenly remarks one day, 'No one need fast while I am here.' Who is this Man who remarks that His mere presence suspends all normal rules? Who is the person who can suddenly tell the School they can have a half-holiday? Sometimes the statements put forward the assumption that He, the Speaker, is completely without sin or fault. This is always the atti-tude. 'You, to whom I am talking, are all sinners,' and He never remotely suggests that this same reproach can be brought against Him. He says again, 'I am the begotten of the One God; before Abraham was, I am,' and remember what the words 'I am' were in Hebrew. They were the name of God, which must not be spoken by any human being, the name which it was death to utter.

Well, that is the other side. On the one side clear, definite moral teaching. On the other, claims which, if not true, are those of a megalo-maniac, compared with whom Hitler was the most sane and humble of men. There is no half-way house and there is no parallel in other reli-gions. If you had gone to Buddha and asked him: 'Are you the son of Bramah?' he would have said, 'My son, you are still in the vale of illusion.' If you had gone to Socrates and asked, 'Are you Zeus?' he would have laughed at you. If you had gone to Mohammed and asked, 'Are you Allah?' he would first have rent his clothes and then cut your head off. If you had asked Confucius, 'Are you Heaven?', I think he would have prob-ably replied, 'Remarks which are not in accordance with nature are in bad taste.' The idea of a great moral teacher saying what Christ said is out of the question. In my opinion, the only person who can say that sort of thing is either God or a complete lunatic suffering from that form of delusion which undermines the whole mind of man. If you think you are a poached egg, when you are looking for a piece of toast to suit you, you may be sane, but if you think you are God, there is no chance for you. We may note in passing that He was never regarded as a mere moral teacher. He did not produce that effect on any of the people who actually met him. He produced mainly three effects – Hatred – Terror – Adoration. There was no trace of people expressing mild approval.

What are we to do about reconciling the two contradictory phenomena? One attempt consists in saying that the Man did not really say these things, but that His followers exaggerated the story, and so the legend grew up that He had said them. This is difficult because His followers were all Jews; that is, they belonged to that Nation which of all others was most convinced that there was only one God – that there could not possibly be another. It is very odd that this horrible invention about a religious leader should grow up among the one people in the whole earth least likely to make such a mistake. On the contrary we get the impression that none of His immediate followers or even of the New Testament writers embraced the doctrine at all easily.

Another point is that on that view you would have to regard the accounts of the Man as being *legends*. Now, as a literary historian, I am perfectly convinced that whatever else the Gospels are they are not legends. I have read a great deal of legend and I am quite clear that they are not the same sort of thing. They are not artistic enough to be legends. From an imaginative point of view they are clumsy, they don't work up to things properly. Most of the life of Jesus is totally unknown to us, as is the life of anyone else who lived at that time, and no people building up a legend would allow that to be so. Apart from bits of the Platonic dialogues, there are no conversations that I know of in ancient literature like the Fourth Gospel. There is nothing, even in modern literature, until about a hundred years ago when the realistic novel came into existence. In the story of the woman taken in adultery we are told Christ bent down and scribbled in the dust with His finger. Nothing comes of this. No one has ever based any doctrine on it. And the art of *inventing* little irrelevant details to make an imaginary scene more convincing is a purely modern art. Surely the only explanation of this passage is that the thing really happened? The author put it in simply because he had *seen* it.

Then we come to the strangest story of all, the story of the Resurrection. It is very necessary to get the story clear. I heard a man say, 'The importance of the Resurrection is that it gives evidence of survival, evidence that the human personality survives death.' On that view what happened to Christ would be what had always happened to all men, the difference being that in Christ's case we were privileged to see it happening. This is certainly not what the earliest Christian writers thought. Something perfectly new in the history of the universe had happened. Christ had defeated death. The door which had always been locked had for the very first time been forced open. This is something quite distinct from mere ghost-survival. I don't mean that they disbelieved in ghost-survival. On the contrary, they believed in it so firmly that, on more than one occasion, Christ had had to assure them that He was *not* a ghost. The point is that while believing in survival they yet regarded the Resurrection as something totally different and new. The Resurrection narratives are not a picture of survival after death; they record how a totally new mode of being has arisen in the universe. Something new has appeared in the universe: as new as the first coming of organic life. This Man, after death, does not get divided into 'ghost' and 'corpse'. A new mode of being has arisen. That is the story. What are we going to make of it?

The question is, I suppose, whether any hypothesis covers the facts so well as the Christian hypothesis. That hypothesis is that God has come down into the created universe, down to manhood – and come up again, pulling it up with Him. The alternative hypothesis is not legend, nor exaggeration, nor the apparitions of a ghost. It is either lunacy or lies. Unless one can take the second alternative (and I can't) one turns to the Christian theory.

'What are we to make of Christ?' There is no question of what we can make of Him, it is entirely a question of what He intends to make of us. You must accept or reject the story.

The things He says are very different from what any other teacher has said. Others say, 'This is the truth about the universe. This is the way you ought to go,' but He says, '*I* am the Truth, and the Way, and the Life.' He says, 'No man can reach absolute reality, except through Me. Try to retain your own life and you will be inevitably ruined. Give yourself away and you will be saved.' He says, 'If you are ashamed of Me, if, when you hear this call, you turn the other way, I also will look the other way when I come again as God without disguise. If anything whatever is keeping you from God and from Me, whatever it is, throw it away. If it is your eye, pull it out. If it is your hand, cut it off. If you put yourself first you will be last. Come to Me everyone who is carrying a heavy load, I will set that right. Your sins, all of them, are wiped out, I can do that. I am Re-birth, I am Life. Eat Me, drink Me, I am your Food. And finally, do not be afraid, I have overcome the whole Universe.' That is the issue.

[6]
THE WORLD'S LAST NIGHT

First published in Religion in Life, *Volume XXI (Winter 1951–2) under the title 'Christian Hope – Its Meaning for Today', it was later published under its new title in* The World's Last Night and Other Essays *(US, 1960). It was also availab. Fern-seed and Elephants (1998).*

There are many reasons why the modern Christian and even the modern theologian may hesitate to give to the doctrine of Christ's second coming that emphasis which was usually laid on it by our ancestors. Yet it seems to me impossible to retain in any recognisable form our belief in the divinity of Christ and the truth of the Christian revelation while abandoning, or even persistently neglecting, the promised, and threatened, return. 'He shall come again to judge the quick and the dead,' says the Apostles' Creed. 'This same Jesus,' said the angels in Acts, 'shall so come in like manner as ye have seen him go into heaven.' 'Hereafter,' said our Lord himself (by those words inviting crucifixion), 'shall ye see the Son of Man … coming in the clouds of heaven.' If this is not an integral part of the faith once given to the saints, I do not know what is. In the following pages I shall endeavour to deal with some of the thoughts that may deter modern men from a firm belief in, or a due attention to, the return or second coming of the Saviour. I have no claim to speak as an expert in any of the studies involved, and merely put forward the reflections which have arisen in my own mind and have seemed to me (perhaps wrongly) to be helpful. They are all submitted to the correction of wiser heads.

The grounds for modern embarrassment about this doctrine fall into two groups, which may be called the theoretical and the practical. I will deal with the theoretical first.

Many are shy of this doctrine because they are reacting (in my opinion very properly reacting) against a school of thought which is associated with the great name of Dr Albert Schweitzer. According to that school,

Christ's teaching about his own return and the end of the world – what theologians call his 'apocalyptic' – was the very essence of his message. All his other doctrines radiated from it; his moral teaching everywhere presupposed a speedy end of the world. If pressed to an extreme, this view, as I think Chesterton said, amounts to seeing in Christ little more than an earlier William Miller, who created a local 'scare'. I am not saying that Dr Schweitzer pressed it to that conclusion: but it has seemed to some that his thought invites us in that direction. Hence, from fear of that extreme, arises a tendency to soft-pedal what Schweitzer's school has overemphasized.

For my own part I hate and distrust reactions not only in religion but in everything. Luther surely spoke very good sense when he compared humanity to a drunkard who, after falling off his horse on the right, falls off it next time on the left. I am convinced that those who find in Christ's apocalyptic the whole of his message are mistaken. But a thing does not vanish – it is not even discredited – because someone has spoken of it with exaggeration. It remains exactly where it was. The only difference is that if it has recently been exaggerated, we must now take special care not to overlook it; for that is the side on which the drunk man is now most likely to fall off.

The very name 'apocalyptic' assigns our Lord's predictions of the second coming to a class. There are other specimens of it: the *Apocalypse of Baruch*, the *Book of Enoch*, or the *Ascension of Isaiah*. Christians are far from regarding such texts as Holy Scripture, and to most modern tastes the genre appears tedious and unedifying. Hence there arises a feeling that our Lord's predictions, being 'much the same sort of thing', are discredited. The charge against them might be put either in a harsher or a gentler form. The harsher form would run, in the mouth of an atheist, something like this: 'You see that, after all, your vaunted Jesus was really the same sort of crank or charlatan as all the other writers of apocalyptic.' The gentler form, used more probably by a modernist, would be like this: 'Every great man is partly of his own age and partly for all time. What matters in his work is always that which transcends his age, not that which he shared with a thousand forgotten contemporaries. We value Shakespeare for the glory of his language and his knowledge of the human heart, which were his own; not for his belief in witches or the divine right of kings, or his failure to take a daily bath. So with Jesus. His belief in a speedy and catastrophic end to history belongs to him not as a great teacher but as a first century Palestinian peasant. It was one of his inevitable limitations, best forgotten. We must concentrate on what distinguished him from other first-century Palestinian peasants, on his moral and social teaching.'

As an argument against the reality of the second coming this seems to me to beg the question at issue. When we propose to ignore in a great man's teaching those doctrines which it has in common with the thought of his age, we seem to be assuming that the thought of his age was erroneous. When we select for serious consideration those doctrines which 'transcend' the thought of his own age and are 'for all time', we are assuming that the thought of *our* age is correct: for of course by thoughts which transcend the great man's age we really mean thoughts that agree with ours. Thus I value Shakespeare's picture of the transformation in old Lear more than I value his views about the divine right of kings, because I agree with Shakespeare that a man can be purified by suffering like Lear, but do not believe that kings (or any other rulers) have divine right in the sense required. When the great man's views do not seem to us erroneous we do not value them the less for having been shared with his contemporaries. Shakespeare's disdain for treachery and Christ's blessing on the poor were not alien to the outlook of their respective periods; but no one wishes to discredit them on that account. No one would reject Christ's apocalyptic on the ground that apocalyptic was common in first-century Palestine unless he had already decided that the thought of first-century Palestine was in that respect mistaken. But to have so decided is surely to have begged the question; for the question is whether the expectation of a catastrophic and divinely ordered end of the present universe is true or false.

If we have an open mind on that point, the whole problem is altered. If such an end is really going to occur, and if (as is the case) the Jews had been trained by their religion to expect it, then it is very natural that they should produce apocalyptic literature. On that view, our Lord's production of something like the other apocalyptic documents would not necessarily result from his supposed bondage to the errors of his period, but would be the divine exploitation of a sound element in contemporary Judaism; nay, the time and place in which it pleased him to be incarnate would, presumably, have been chosen because, there and then, that element existed, and had, by his eternal providence, been developed for that very purpose. For if we once accept the doctrine of the Incarnation, we must surely be very cautious in suggesting that any circumstance in the culture of first-century Palestine was a hampering or distorting influence upon his teaching. Do we suppose that the scene of God's earthly life was selected at random? – that some other scene would have served better?

But there is worse to come. 'Say what you like,' we shall be told, 'the apocalyptic beliefs of the first Christians have been proved to be false. It is clear from the New Testament that they all expected the second coming in their own lifetime. And, worse still, they had a reason, and one which you will find very embarrassing. Their Master had told them so. He shared, and indeed created, their delusion. He said in so many words, "this generation shall not pass till all these things be done." And he was wrong. He clearly knew no more about the end of the world than anyone else.'

It is certainly the most embarrassing verse in the Bible. Yet how teasing, also, that within fourteen words of it should come the statement 'But of that day and that hour knoweth no man, no, not the angels which are in heaven, neither the Son, but the Father.' The one exhibition of error and the one confession of ignorance grow side by side. That they stood thus in the mouth of Jesus himself, and were not merely placed thus by the reporter, we surely need not doubt. Unless the reporter were perfectly honest he would never have recorded the confession of ignorance at all; he could have had no motive for doing so except a desire to tell the whole truth. And unless later copyists were equally honest they would never have preserved the (apparently) mistaken prediction about 'this genera-tion' after the passage of time had shown the (apparent) mistake. This passage (Mark 13:30–32) and the cry 'Why hast thou forsaken me?' (Mark 15:34) together make up the strongest proof that the New Testament is historically reliable. The evangelists have the first great characteristic of honest witnesses: they mention facts which are, at first sight, damaging to their main contention.

The facts, then, are these: that Jesus professed himself (in some sense) ignorant, and within a moment showed that he really was so. To believe in the Incarnation, to believe that he is God, makes it hard to understand how he could be ignorant; but also makes it certain that, if he said he could be ignorant, then ignorant he could really be. For a God who can be ignorant is less baffling than a God who falsely professes ignorance. The answer of theologians is that the God-Man was omniscient as God, and ignorant as Man. This, no doubt, is true, though it cannot be imag-ined. Nor indeed can the unconsciousness of Christ in sleep be imagined, nor the twilight of reason in his infancy; still less his merely organic life in his mother's womb. But the physical sciences, no less than theology, propose for our belief much that cannot be imagined.

A generation which has accepted the curvature of space need not boggle at the impossibility of imagining the consciousness of incarnate God. In that consciousness the temporal and the timeless were united. I think we can acquiesce in mystery at that point, provided we do not aggravate it by our tendency to picture the timeless life of God as, simply, another sort of time. We are committing that blunder whenever we ask how Christ could be *at the same moment* ignorant and omniscient, or how he could be the God who neither slumbers nor sleeps *while* he slept. The italicised words conceal an attempt to establish a temporal relation between his timeless life as God and the days, months, and years of his life as Man. And of course there is no such relation. The Incarnation is not an episode in the life of God: the Lamb is slain – and therefore presumably born, grown to maturity, and risen – from all eternity. The taking up into God's nature of humanity, with all its ignorance and limitations, is not itself a temporal event, though the humanity which is so taken up was, like our own, a thing living and dying in time. And if limitation, and therefore ignorance, was thus taken up, we ought to expect that the ignorance should at some time be actually displayed. It would be difficult, and, to me, repellent, to suppose that Jesus never asked a genuine question, that is, a question to which he did not know the answer. That would make of his humanity something so unlike ours as scarcely to deserve the name. I find it easier to believe that when he said 'Who touched me?' (Luke 8:45) he really wanted to know.

The difficulties which I have so far discussed are, to a certain extent, debating points. They tend rather to strengthen a disbelief already based on other grounds than to create disbelief by their own force. We are now coming to something much more important and often less fully conscious. The doctrine of the second coming is deeply uncongenial to the whole evolutionary or developmental character of modern thought. We have been taught to think of the world as something that grows slowly towards perfection, something that 'progresses' or 'evolves'. Christian apocalyptic offers us no such hope. It does not even foretell (which would be more tolerable to our habits of thought) a gradual decay. It foretells a sudden, violent end imposed from without: an extinguisher popped on to the candle, a brick flung at the gramophone, a curtain rung down on the play – 'Halt!'

To this deep-seated objection I can only reply that, in my opinion, the modern conception of Progress or Evolution (as popularly imagined) is simply a myth, supported by no evidence whatever.

I say 'evolution, as popularly imagined'. I am not in the least concerned to refute Darwinism as a theorem in biology. There may be flaws in that theorem, but I have here nothing to do with them. There may be signs that biologists are already contemplating a withdrawal from the whole Darwinian position, but I claim to be no judge of such signs. It can even be argued that what Darwin really accounted for was not the origin, but the elimination, of species, but I will not pursue that argument. For purposes of this article I am assuming that Darwinian biology is correct. What I want to point out is the illegitimate transition from the Darwinian theorem in biology to the modern myth of evolutionism or developmentalism or progress in general.

The first thing to notice is that the myth arose earlier than the theorem, in advance of all evidence. Two great works of art embody the idea of a universe in which, by some inherent necessity, the 'higher' always supersedes the 'lower'. One is Keats's *Hyperion* and the other is Wagner's *Nibelung's Ring*. And they are both earlier than the *Origin of Species*. You could not have a clearer expression of the developmental or progressive idea than Oceanus's words

> ... 'tis the eternal law
> That first in beauty should be first in might.

And you could not have a more ardent submission to it than those words in which Wagner describes his tetralogy.

> The progress of the whole poem, therefore [he writes to Röckel in 1854], shows the necessity of recognizing and submitting to, the change, the diversity, the multiplicity, and the eternal novelty, of the Real. Wotan rises to the tragic heights of willing his own downfall. This is all that we have to learn from the history of Man – to will the Necessary, and ourselves to bring it to pass. The creative work which this highest and self-renouncing will finally accomplishes is the fearless and everloving man, Siegfried.[1]

The idea that the myth (so potent in all modern thought) is a result of Darwin's biology would thus seem to be unhistorical. On the contrary, the attraction of Darwinism was that it gave to a pre-existing myth the scientific reassurances it required. If no evidence for evolution had been forthcoming, it would have been necessary to invent it. The real sources

---

[1] '*Der Fortgang des ganzen Gedichtes zeigt demnach die Notwendigkeit, den Wechsel, die Mannigfaltigkeit, die Vielheit, die ewige Neuheit des Wirklichkeit und des Lebens anzuerkennen und ihr zu weichen. Wotan schwingt sich bis zu der tragischen Höhe, seinen Untergang zu wollen. Dies ist alles, was wir aus der Geschichte der Manscheit zu lernen haben: das Notwendige zu wollen und selbst zu vollbringen. Das Schöpfungswerk dieses höchsten, selbst vernichtenden Willens ist der endlich gewonnene furchtlose, stets liebende Mensch; Siegfried.*'

Fuller research into the origins of this potent myth would lead us to the German idealists and thence (as I have heard suggested) through Boehme back to Alchemy. Is the whole dialectical view of history possibly a gigantic projection of the old dream that we can make gold?

of the myth are partly political. It projects on to the cosmic screen feelings engendered by the Revolutionary period.

In the second place, we must notice that Darwinism gives no support to the belief that natural selection, working upon chance variations, has a general tendency to produce improvement. The illusion that it has comes from confining our attention to a few species which have (by some possibly arbitrary standard of our own) changed for the better. Thus the horse has improved in the sense that *protohippos* would be less useful to us than his modern descendant. The anthropoid has improved in the sense that he now is ourselves. But a great many of the changes produced by evolution are not improvements by any conceivable standard. In battle men save their lives sometimes by advancing and sometimes by retreating. So, in the battle for survival, species save themselves sometimes by increasing, sometimes by jettisoning, their powers. There is no general law of progress in biological history.

And thirdly, even if there were, it would not follow – it is, indeed, manifestly not the case – that there is any law of progress in ethical, cultural, and social history. No one looking at world history without some preconception in favour of progress could find in it a steady up gradient. There is often progress within a given field over a limited period. A school of pottery or painting, a moral effort in a particular direction, a practical art like sanitation or shipbuilding, may continuously improve over a number of years. If this process could spread to all departments of life and continue indefinitely, there would be 'Progress' of the sort our fathers believed in. But it never seems to do so. Either it is interrupted (by barbarian irruption or the even less resistible infiltration of modern industrialism) or else, more mysteriously, it decays. The idea which here shuts out the second coming from our minds, the idea of the world slowly ripening to perfection, is a myth, not a generalization from experience. And it is a myth which distracts us from our real duties and our real interest. It is our attempt to guess the plot of a drama in which we are the characters. But how can the characters in a play guess the plot? We are not the playwright, we are not the producer, we are not even the audience. We are on the stage. To play well the scenes in which we are 'on' concerns us much more than to guess about the scenes that follow it.

In *King Lear* (III, vii) there is a man who is such a minor character that Shakespeare has not given him even a name: he is merely 'First Servant'. All the characters around him – Regan, Cornwall, and Edmund – have fine long-term plans. They think they know how the story is going to end, and they are quite wrong. The servant has no such delusions. He has no notion how the play is going to go. But he understands the present scene.

He sees an abomination (the blinding of old Gloucester) taking place. He will not stand it. His sword is out and pointed at his master's breast in a moment: then Regan stabs him dead from behind. That is his whole part: eight lines all told. But if it were real life and not a play, that is the part it would be best to have acted.

The doctrine of the second coming teaches us that we do not and cannot know when the world drama will end. The curtain may be rung down at any moment: say, before you have finished reading this paragraph. This seems to some people intolerably frustrating. So many things would be interrupted. Perhaps you were going to get married next month, perhaps you were going to get a raise next week: you may be on the verge of a great scientific discovery; you may be maturing great social and political reforms. Surely no good and wise God would be so very unreasonable as to cut all this short? Not *now*, of all moments!

But we think thus because we keep on assuming that we know the play. We do not know the play. We do not even know whether we are in Act I or Act V. We do not know who are the major and who the minor characters. The Author knows. The audience, if there is an audience (if angels and archangels and all the company of heaven fill the pit and the stalls), may have an inkling. But we, never seeing the play from outside, never meeting any characters except the tiny minority who are 'on' in the same scenes as ourselves, wholly ignorant of the future and very imperfectly informed about the past, cannot tell at what moment the end ought to come. That it will come when it ought, we may be sure; but we waste our time in guessing when that will be. That it has a meaning we may be sure, but we cannot see it. When it is over, we may be told. We are led to expect that the Author will have something to say to each of us on the part that each of us has played. The playing it well is what matters infinitely.

The doctrine of the second coming, then, is not to be rejected because it conflicts with our favourite modern mythology. It is, for that very reason, to be the more valued and made more frequently the subject of meditation. It is the medicine our condition especially needs.

And with that, I turn to the practical. There is a real difficulty in giving this doctrine the place which it ought to have in our Christian life without, at the same time, running a certain risk. The fear of that risk probably deters many teachers who accept the doctrine from saying very much about it.

We must admit at once that this doctrine has, in the past, led Christians into very great follies. Apparently many people find it difficult to believe in this great event without trying to guess its date, or even without accepting as a certainty the date that any quack or hysteric offers them. To write a history of all these exploded predictions would need a book, and a sad, sordid, tragi-comical book it would be. One such prediction was circulating when St Paul wrote his second letter to the Thessalonians. Someone had told them that 'the Day' was 'at hand'. This was apparently having the result which such predictions usually have: people were idling and playing the busybody. One of the most famous predictions was that of poor William Miller in 1843. Miller (whom I take to have been an honest fanatic) dated the second coming to the year, the day, and the very minute. A timely comet fostered the delusion. Thousands waited for the Lord at midnight on 21 March, and went home to a late breakfast on the 22nd followed by the jeers of a drunkard.

Clearly, no one wishes to say anything that will reawaken such mass hysteria. We must never speak to simple, excitable people about 'the Day' without emphasizing again and again the utter impossibility of prediction. We must try to show them that that impossibility is an essential part of the doctrine. If you do not believe our Lord's words, why do you believe in his return at all? And if you do believe them must you not put away from you, utterly and for ever, any hope of dating that return? His teaching on the subject quite clearly consisted of three propositions: (1) That he will certainly return. (2) That we cannot possibly find out when. (3) And that therefore we must always be ready for him.

Note the *therefore*. Precisely because we cannot predict the moment, we must be ready at all moments. Our Lord repeated this practical conclusion again and again; as if the promise of the return had been made for the sake of this conclusion alone. Watch, watch, is the burden of his advice. I shall come like a thief. You will not, I most solemnly assure you, you will not, see me approaching. If the householder had known at what time the burglar would arrive, he would have been ready for him. If the servant had known when his absent employer would come home, he would not have been found drunk in the kitchen. But they didn't. Nor will you. Therefore you must be ready at all times. The point is surely simple enough. The schoolboy does not know which part of his Virgil lesson he will be made to translate: that is why he must be prepared to translate *any* passage. The sentry does not know at what time an enemy will attack, or an officer inspect, his post: that is why he must keep awake *all* the time. The return is wholly unpredictable. There will be wars and rumours of wars and all kinds of catastrophes, as there always are. Things will be, in that sense, normal, the hour before the heavens roll up like a scroll. You cannot guess it. If you could, one chief purpose for which it was foretold would be frustrated. And God's purposes are not so easily frustrated as that. One's ears should be closed against any future William Miller in advance. The folly of listening to him at all is almost equal to the folly of believing him. He *couldn't* know what he pretends, or thinks, he knows.

Of this folly George MacDonald has written well. 'Do those,' he asks, 'who say, Lo here or lo there are the signs of his coming, think to be too keen for him and spy his approach? When he tells them to watch lest he find them neglecting their work, they stare this way and that, and watch lest he should succeed in coming like a thief! Obedience is the one key of life.'

The doctrine of the second coming has failed, so far as we are concerned, if it does not make us realise that at every moment of every year in our lives Donne's question 'What if this present were the world's last night?' is equally relevant.

Sometimes this question has been pressed upon our minds with the purpose of exciting fear. I do not think that is its right use. I am, indeed, far from agreeing with those who think all religious fear barbarous and degrading and demand that it should be banished from the spiritual life. Perfect love, we know, casteth out fear. But so do several other things – ignorance, alcohol, passion, presumption, and stupidity. It is very desirable that we should all advance to that perfection of love in which we shall fear no longer; but it is very undesirable, until we have reached that stage, that we should allow any inferior agent to cast out our fear. The objection to any attempt at perpetual trepidation about the second coming is, in my view, quite a different one: namely, that it will certainly not succeed. Fear is an emotion: and it is quite impossible – even physically impossible – to maintain any emotion for very long. A perpetual excitement of hope about the second coming is impossible for the same reason. Crisis-feeling of any sort is essentially transitory. Feelings come and go, and when they come a good use can be made of them: they cannot be our regular spiritual diet.

What is important is not that we should always fear (or hope) about the End but that we should always remember, always take it into account. An analogy may help here. A man of seventy need not be always feeling (much less talking) about his approaching death: but a wise man of seventy should always take it into account. He would be foolish to embark on schemes which presuppose twenty more years of life: he would be criminally foolish not to make – indeed, not to have made long since – his will. Now, what death is to each man, the second coming is to the whole human race. We all believe, I suppose, that a man should 'sit loose' to his own individual life, should remember how short, precarious, temporary, and provisional a thing it is; should never give all his heart to anything which will end when his life ends. What modern Christians find it harder to remember is that the whole life of humanity in this world is also precarious, temporary, provisional.

Any moralist will tell you that the personal triumph of an athlete or of a girl at a ball is transitory: the point is to remember that an empire or a civilisation is also transitory. All achievements and triumphs, in so far as they are merely this-worldly achievements and triumphs, will come to nothing in the end. Most scientists here join hands with the theologians; the earth will not always be habitable. Man, though longer lived than men, is equally mortal. The difference is that whereas the scientists expect only a slow decay from within, we reckon with sudden interruption from without – at any moment. ('What if this present were the world's last night?')

Taken by themselves, these considerations might seem to invite a relaxation in our efforts for the good of posterity: but if we remember that what may be upon us at any moment is not merely an end but a judgement, they should have no such result. They may, and should, correct the tendency of some moderns to talk as though duties to posterity were the only duties we had. I can imagine no man who will look with more horror on the End than a conscientious revolutionary who has, in a sense sincerely, been justifying cruelties and injustices inflicted on millions of his contemporaries by the benefits which he hopes to confer on future generations: generations who, as one terrible moment now reveals to him, were never going to exist. Then he will see the massacres, the faked trials, the deportations, to be all ineffaceably real, an essential part, his part, in the drama that has just ended: while the future Utopia had never been anything but a fantasy.

Frantic administration of panaceas to the world is certainly discouraged by the reflection that 'this present' might be 'the world's last night'; sober work for the future, within the limits of ordinary morality and prudence, is not. For what comes is judgement: happy are those whom it finds labouring in their vocations, whether they were merely going out to feed the pigs or laying good plans to deliver humanity a hundred years hence from some great evil. The curtain has indeed now fallen. Those pigs will never in fact be fed, the great campaign against white slavery or governmental tyranny will never in fact proceed to victory. No matter; you were at your post when the inspection came.

Our ancestors had a habit of using the word 'judgement' in this context as if it meant simply 'punishment': hence the popular expression, 'It's a judgement on him.' I believe we can sometimes render the thing more vivid to ourselves by taking judgement in a stricter sense: not as the sentence or award, but as the verdict. Some day (and 'What if this present were the world's last night?') an absolutely correct verdict – if you like, a perfect critique – will be passed on what each of us is.

We have all encountered judgements or verdicts on ourselves in this life. Every now and then we discover what our fellow creatures really think of us. I don't of course mean what they tell us to our faces: that we usually have to discount. I am thinking of what we sometimes over-hear by accident or of the opinions about us which our neighbours or employees or subordinates unknowingly reveal in their actions: and of the terrible, or lovely, judgements artlessly betrayed by children or even animals. Such discoveries can be the bitterest or sweetest experiences we have. But of course both the bitter and the sweet are limited by our doubt as to the wisdom of those who judge. We always hope that those who so clearly think us cowards or bullies are ignorant and malicious; we always fear that those who trust us or admire us are misled by partiality. I suppose the experience of the final judgement (which may break in upon us at any moment) will be like these little experiences, but magnified to the Nth.

For it will be infallible judgement. If it is favourable we shall have no fear, if unfavourable, no hope that it is wrong. We shall not only believe, we shall know, beyond doubt in every fibre of our appalled or delighted being, that as the Judge has said, so we are: neither more nor less nor other. We shall perhaps even realise that in some dim fashion we could have known it all along. We shall know and all creation will know too: our ancestors, our parents, our wives or husbands, our children. The unanswerable and (by then) self-evident truth about each will be known to all.

I do not find that pictures of physical catastrophe – that sign in the clouds, those heavens rolled up like a scroll – help one so much as the naked idea of judgement. We cannot always be excited. We can, perhaps, train ourselves to ask more and more often how the thing which we are saying or doing (or failing to do) at each moment will look when the irre-sistible light streams in upon it; that light which is so different from the light of this world – and yet, even now, we know just enough of it to take it into account. Women sometimes have the problem of trying to judge by artificial light how a dress will look by daylight. That is very like the problem of all of us: to dress our souls not for the electric lights of the present world but for the daylight of the next. The good dress is the one that will face that light. For that light will last longer.

[7]
IS THEISM IMPORTANT?

First published in The Socratic (Digest), *No. 5 (1952) and reproduced in* Undeceptions *(1971) and* Timeless at Heart *(1991), this essay was also in* Compelling Reason *(1998).*

I have lost the notes of what I originally said in replying to Professor Price's paper and cannot now remember what it was, except that I welcomed most cordially his sympathy with the Polytheists. I still do. When grave persons express their fear that England is relapsing into Paganism, I am tempted to reply, 'Would that she were!' For I do not think it at all likely that we shall ever see Parliament opened by the slaughtering of a garlanded white bull in the House of Lords, or Cabinet Ministers leaving sandwiches in Hyde Park as an offering for the Dryads. If such a state of affairs came about, then the Christian apologist would have something to work on. For a Pagan, as history shows, is a man eminently convertible to Christianity. He is essentially, the pre-Christian, or sub-Christian, religious man. The post-Christian man of our own day differs from him as much as a *divorcée* differs from a virgin. The Christian and the Pagan have much more in common with one another than either has with the writers of the *New Statesman*; and those writers would of course agree with me. For the rest, what now occurs to me after re-reading Professors Price's paper is something like this.

(1) I think we must introduce into the discussion a distinction between two senses of the word *Faith*. This may mean (a) a settled intellectual assent. In that sense faith (or 'belief') in God hardly differs from faith in the uniformity of nature or in the consciousness of other people. This is what, I think, has sometimes been called a 'notional' or 'intellectual' or 'carnal' faith. It may also mean (b) a trust, or confidence, in the God whose existence is thus assented to. This involves an attitude of the will. It is more like our confidence in a friend. It would be generally agreed that Faith in sense A is not a religious state. The devils who 'believe and tremble' (James 2:19) have Faith-A. A man who curses or ignores God

may have Faith-A. Philosophical arguments for the existence of God are presumably intended to produce Faith-A. No doubt those who construct them are anxious to produce Faith-A because it is a necessary precondition of Faith-B, and in that sense their ultimate intention is religious. But their immediate object, the conclusion they attempt to prove, is not. I therefore think they cannot be justly accused of trying to get a religious conclusion out of non-religious premises. I agree with Professor Price that this cannot be done: but I deny that the religious philosophers are trying to do it.

I also think that in some ages, what claim to be Proofs of Theism have had much more efficacy in producing Faith-A than Professor Price suggests. Nearly everyone I know who has embraced Christianity in adult life has been influenced by what seemed to him to be at least probable arguments for Theism. I have known some who were completely convinced by Descartes' Ontological Proof:[1] that is, they received Faith-A from Descartes first and then went on to seek, and to find, Faith-B. Even quite uneducated people who have been Christians all their lives not infrequently appeal to some simplified form of the Argument from Design. Even acceptance of tradition implies an argument which sometimes becomes explicit in the form 'I reckon all those wise men wouldn't have believed in it if it weren't true.'

Of course Faith-A usually involves a degree of subjective certitude which goes beyond the logical certainty, or even the supposed logical certainty, of the arguments employed. It may retain this certitude for a long time, I expect, even without the support of Faith-B. This excess of certitude in a settled assent is not at all uncommon. Most of those who believe in Uniformity of Nature, Evolution, or the Solar System, share it.

(2) I doubt whether religious people have ever supposed that Faith-B follows automatically on the acquisition of Faith-A. It is described as a 'gift' (e.g. 1 Corinthians 12:1–11; Ephesians 2:8). As soon as we have Faith-A in the existence of God, we are instructed to ask from God Himself the gift of Faith-B. An odd request, you may say, to address to a First Cause, an *Ens Realissimum*, or an *Unmoved Mover*. It might be argued, and I think I would argue myself, that even such an aridly philosophical God rather fails to invite than actually repels a personal approach. It would, at any rate, do no harm to try it. But I fully admit that most of those who, having reached Faith-A, pray for Faith-B, do so because they have already had something like religious experience. Perhaps the best way of putting

---

[1] This is briefly summed up in René Descartes, *Discours de la Méthode*, Part iv, in which he says 'I think, therefore I am'.

it would be to say that Faith-A converts into religious experience what was hitherto only potentially or implicitly religious. In this modified form I would accept Professor Price's view that philosophical proofs never, by themselves, lead to religion. Something at least *quasi*-religious uses them before, and the 'proofs' remove an inhibition which was preventing their development into religion proper.

This is not exactly *fides quaerens intellectum*,[2] for these quasi-religious experiences were not *fides*. In spite of Professor Price's rejection I still think Otto's account of the Numinous[3] is the best analysis of them we have. I believe it is a mistake to regard the Numinous as merely an affair of 'feeling'. Admittedly, Otto can describe it only by referring to the emotions it arouses in us; but then nothing can be described except in terms of its effects in consciousness. We have in English an exact name for the emotion aroused by the Numinous, which Otto, writing in German, lacked; we have the word Awe – an emotion very like fear, with the important difference that it need imply no estimate of danger. When we fear a tiger, we fear that it may kill us: when we fear a ghost – well, we just fear the ghost, not this or that mischief which it may do us. The Numinous or Awful is that of which we have this, as it were, objectless or disinterested fear – this awe. And 'the Numinous' is not a name for our own feeling of Awe any more than 'the Contemptible' is a name for contempt. It is the answer to the question 'Of what do you feel awe?' And what we feel awe of is certainly not itself awe.

With Otto and, in a sense, with Professor Price, I would find the seed of religious experience in our experience of the Numinous. In an age like our own such experience does occur but, until religion comes and retrospectively transforms it, it usually appears to the subject to be a special form of aesthetic experience. In ancient times I think experience of the Numinous developed into the Holy only in so far as the Numinous (not in itself at all necessarily moral) came to be connected with the morally good. This happened regularly in Israel, sporadically elsewhere. But even in the higher Paganism, I do not think this process led to anything exactly like *fides*. There is nothing credal in Paganism. In Israel we do get *fides* but this is always connected with certain historical affirmations. Faith is not simply in the numinous *Elohim*, nor even simply in the holy Jahweh, but in the God 'of our fathers', the God who called Abraham and brought Israel out of Egypt. In Christianity this historical element is strongly

---

[2] Faith seeking understanding.
[3] Rudolph Otto, *The Idea of the Holy*, trans. John W. Harvey (London, 1923).

reaffirmed. The object of faith is at once the *ens entium*[4] of the philosophers, the Awful Mystery of Paganism, the Holy Law given of the moralists, and Jesus of Nazareth who was crucified under Pontius Pilate and rose again on the third day.

Thus we must admit that Faith, as we know it, does not flow from philosophical argument alone; nor from experience of the Numinous alone; nor from moral experience alone; nor from history alone; but from historical events which at once fulfil and transcend the moral category, which link themselves with the most numinous elements in Paganism, and which (as it seems to us) demand as their presupposition the existence of a Being who is more, but not less, than the God whom many reputable philosophers think they can establish.

Religious experience, as we know it, really involves all these elements. We may, however, use the word in a narrower sense to denote moments of mystical, or devotional, or merely numinous experience; and we may then ask, with Professor Price, how such moments, being a kind of *visio*, are related to faith, which by definition is 'not sight'. This does not seem to me one of the hardest questions. 'Religious experience' in the narrower sense comes and goes: especially goes. The operation of Faith is to retain, so far as the will and intellect are concerned, what is irresistible and obvious during the moments of special grace. By faith we believe always what we hope hereafter to see always and perfectly and have already seen imperfectly and by flashes. In relation to the philosophical premises a Christian's faith is of course excessive: in relation to what is sometimes shown him, it is perhaps just as often defective. My faith even in an earthly friend goes beyond all that could be demonstratively proved; yet in another sense I may often trust him less than he deserves.

[4] Being of beings.

[8]

THE SEEING EYE

First published in the American periodical Show, *Volume III (February 1963), the editor entitled it 'Onward, Christian Spacemen', a title which Lewis so disliked that it was renamed for publication in* Christian Reflections *(1998).*

The Russians, I am told, report that they have not found God in outer space. On the other hand, a good many people in many different times and countries claim to have found God, or been found by God, here on earth.

The conclusion some want us to draw from these data is that God does not exist. As a corollary, those who think they have met Him on earth were suffering from a delusion.

But other conclusions might be drawn:

1 We have not yet gone far enough in space. There had been ships on the Atlantic for a good time before America was discovered.
2 God does exist but is locally confined to this planet.
3 The Russians did find God in space without knowing it, because they lacked the requisite apparatus for detecting Him.
4 God does exist but is not an object either located in a particular part of space nor diffused, as we once thought 'ether' was, throughout space.

The first two conclusions do not interest me. The sort of religion for which they could be a defence would be a religion for savages: the belief in a local deity who can be contained in a particular temple, island or grove. That, in fact, seems to be the sort of religion about which the Russians – or some Russians, and a good many people in the West – are being irreligious. It is not in the least disquieting that no astronauts have discovered a god of that sort. The really disquieting thing would be if they had.

The third and fourth conclusions are the ones for my money.

Looking for God – or Heaven – by exploring space is like reading or seeing all Shakespeare's plays in the hope that you will find Shakespeare as one of the characters or Stratford as one of the places. Shakespeare is in one sense present at every moment in every play. But he is never present in the same way as Falstaff or Lady Macbeth. Nor is he diffused through the play like a gas.

If there were an idiot who thought plays existed on their own, without an author (not to mention actors, producer, manager, stage-hands and what not), our belief in Shakespeare would not be much affected by his saying, quite truly, that he had studied all the plays and never found Shakespeare in them.

The rest of us, in varying degrees according to our perceptiveness, 'found Shakespeare' in the plays. But it is a quite different sort of 'finding' from anything our poor friend has in mind.

Even he has in reality been in some way affected by Shakespeare, but without knowing it. He lacked the necessary apparatus for detecting Shakespeare.

Now of course this is only an analogy. I am not suggesting at all that the existence of God is as easily established as the existence of Shakespeare. My point is that, if God does exist, He is related to the universe more as an author is related to a play than as one object in the universe is related to another.

If God created the universe, He created space-time, which is to the universe as the metre is to a poem or the key is to music. To look for Him as one item within the framework which He Himself invented is nonsensical.

If God – such a God as any adult religion believes in – exists, mere movement in space will never bring you any nearer to Him or any farther from Him than you are at this very moment. You can neither reach Him nor avoid Him by travelling to Alpha Centauri or even to other galaxies. A fish is no more, and no less, in the sea after it has swum a thousand miles than it was when it set out.

How, then, it may be asked, can we either reach or avoid Him?

The avoiding, in many times and places, has proved so difficult that a very large part of the human race failed to achieve it. But in our own time and place it is extremely easy. Avoid silence, avoid solitude, avoid any train of thought that leads off the beaten track. Concentrate on money, sex, status, health and (above all) on your own grievances. Keep the radio on. Live in a crowd. Use plenty of sedation. If you must read books, select them very carefully. But you'd be safer to stick to the papers. You'll find the advertisements helpful; especially those with a sexy or a snobbish appeal.

About the reaching, I am a far less reliable guide. That is because I never had the experience of looking for God. It was the other way round; He was the hunter (or so it seemed to me) and I was the deer. He stalked me like a redskin, took unerring aim, and fired. And I am very thankful that that is how the first (conscious) meeting occurred. It forearms one against subsequent fears that the whole thing was only wish fulfilment. Something one didn't wish for can hardly be that.

But it is significant that this long-evaded encounter happened at a time when I was making a serious effort to obey my conscience. No doubt it was far less serious than I supposed, but it was the most serious I had made for a long time.

One of the first results of such an effort is to bring your picture of yourself down to something nearer life-size. And presently you begin to wonder whether you are yet, in any full sense, a person at all; whether you are entitled to call yourself 'I' (it is a sacred name). In that way, the process is like being psycho-analysed, only cheaper – I mean, in dollars; in some other ways it may be more costly. You find that what you called yourself is only a thin film on the surface of an unsounded and dangerous sea. But not merely dangerous. Radiant things, delights and inspirations, come to the surface as well as snarling resentments and nagging lusts.

One's ordinary self is, then, a mere façade. There's a huge area out of sight behind it.

And then, if one listens to the physicists, one discovers that the same is true of all the things around us. These tables and chairs, this magazine, the trees, clouds and mountains are façades. Poke (scientifically) into them and you find the unimaginable structure of the atom. That is, in the long run, you find mathematical formulas.

There are you (whatever YOU means) sitting reading. Out there (whatever THERE means) is a white page with black marks on it. And both are façades. Behind both lies – well, Whatever-it-is. The psychologists, and the theologians, though they use different symbols, equally use symbols when they try to probe the depth behind the façade called YOU. That is, they can't really say 'It is this', but they can say 'It is in some way like this'. And the physicists, trying to probe behind the other façade, can give you only mathematics. And the mathematics may be true about the reality, but it can hardly be the reality itself, any more than contour lines are real mountains.

I am not in the least blaming either set of experts for this state of affairs. They make progress. They are always discovering things. If governments make a bad use of the physicists' discoveries, or if novelists and biographers make a bad use of the psychologists' discoveries, the experts are not to blame. The point, however, is that every fresh discovery, far from dissipating, deepens the mystery.

Presently, if you are a person of a certain sort, if you are one who has to believe that all things which exist must have unity it will seem to you irresistibly probable that what lies ultimately behind the one façade also lies ultimately behind the other. And then – again, if you are that sort of person – you may come to be convinced that your contact with that mystery in the area you call yourself is a good deal closer than your contact through what you call matter. For in the one case I, the ordinary, conscious I, am continuous with the unknown depth.

And after that, you may come (some do) to believe that that voice – like all the rest, I must speak symbolically – that voice which speaks in your conscience and in some of your intensest joys, which is sometimes so obstinately silent, sometimes so easily silenced, and then at other times so loud and emphatic, is in fact the closest contact you have with the mystery; and therefore finally to be trusted, obeyed, feared and desired more than all other things. But still, if you are a different sort of person, you will not come to this conclusion.

I hope everyone sees how this is related to the astronautical question from which we started. The process I have been sketching may equally well occur, or fail to occur, wherever you happen to be. I don't mean that all religious and all irreligious people have either taken this step or refused to take it. Once religion and its opposite are in the world – and they have both been in it for a very long time – the majority in both camps will be simply conformists. Their belief or disbelief will result from their upbringing and from the prevailing tone of the circles they live in. They will have done no hunting for God and no flying for God on their own. But if no minorities who did these things on their own existed I presume that the conforming majorities would not exist either. (Don't imagine I'm despising these majorities. I am sure the one contains better Christians than I am; the other, nobler atheists than I was.)

Space-travel really has nothing to do with the matter. To some, God is discoverable everywhere; to others, nowhere. Those who do not find Him on earth are unlikely to find Him in space. (Hang it all, we're in space already; every year we go a huge circular tour in space.) But send a saint up in a spaceship and he'll find God in space as he found God on earth. Much depends on the seeing eye.

And this is especially confirmed by my own religion, which is Christianity. When I said a while ago that it was nonsensical to look for God as one item within His own work, the universe, some readers may have wanted to protest. They wanted to say, 'But surely, according to

Christianity, that is just what did once happen? Surely the central doctrine is that God became man and walked about among other men in Palestine? If that is not appearing as an item in His own work, what is it?'

The objection is much to the point. To meet it, I must readjust my old analogy of the play. One might imagine a play in which the dramatist introduced himself as a character into his own play and was pelted off the stage as an impudent impostor by the other characters. It might be rather a good play; if I had any talent for the theatre I'd try my hand at writing it. But since (as far as I know) such a play doesn't exist, we had better change to a narrative work; a story into which the author puts himself as one of the characters.

We have a real instance of this in Dante's *Divine Comedy*. Dante is (1) the muse outside the poem who is inventing the whole thing, and (2) a character inside the poem, whom the other characters meet and with whom they hold conversations. Where the analogy breaks down is that everything the poem contains is merely imaginary, in that the characters have no free will. They (the characters) can say to Dante only what Dante (the poet) has decided to put into their mouths. I do not think we humans are related to God in that way. I think God can make things which not only – like a poet's or novelist's characters – *seem* to have a partially independent life, but really have it. But the analogy furnishes a crude model of the Incarnation in two respects: (1) Dante the poet and Dante the character are in a sense one, but in another sense two. This is a faint and far-off suggestion of what theologians mean by the 'union of the two natures' (divine and human) in Christ. (2) The other people in the poem meet and see and hear Dante; but they have not even the faintest suspicion that he is making the whole world in which they exist and has a life of his own, outside it, independent of it.

It is the second point which is most relevant. For the Christian story is that Christ was perceived to be God by very few people indeed; perhaps, for a time only by St Peter, who would also, and for the same reason, have found God in space. For Christ said to Peter, 'Flesh and blood have not taught you this.' The methods of science do not discover facts of that order.

Indeed the expectation of finding God by astronautics would be very like trying to verify or falsify the divinity of Christ by taking specimens of His blood or dissecting Him. And in their own way they did both. But they were no wiser than before. What is required is a certain faculty of recognition.

If you do not at all know God, of course you will not recognize Him, either in Jesus or in outer space.

The fact that we have not found God in space does not, then, bother me in the least. Nor am I much concerned about the 'space race' between America and Russia. The more money, time, skill and zeal they both spend on that rivalry, the less, we may hope, they will have to spend on armaments. Great powers might be more usefully, but are seldom less dangerously, employed than in fabricating costly objects and flinging them, as you might say, overboard. Good luck to it! It is an excellent way of letting off steam.

But there are three ways in which space-travel will bother me if it reaches the stage for which most people are hoping.

The first is merely sentimental, or perhaps aesthetic. No moon-lit night will ever be the same to me again if, as I look up at that pale disc, I must think 'Yes: up there to the left is the Russian area, and over there to the right is the American bit. And up at the top is the place which is now threatening to produce a crisis.' The immemorial Moon – the Moon of the myths, the poets, the lovers – will have been taken from us for ever. Part of our mind, a huge mass of our emotional wealth, will have gone. Artemis, Diana, the silver planet belonged in that fashion to all humanity: he who first reaches it steals something from us all.

Secondly, a more practical issue will arise when, if ever, we discover rational creatures on other planets. I think myself, this is a very remote contingency. The balance of probability is against life on any other planet of the solar system. We shall hardly find it nearer than the stars. And even if we reach the Moon we shall be no nearer to stellar travel than the first man who paddled across a river was to crossing the Pacific.

This thought is welcome to me because, to be frank, I have no pleasure in looking forward to a meeting between humanity and any alien rational species. I observe how the white man has hitherto treated the black, and how, even among civilised men, the stronger have treated the weaker. If we encounter in the depth of space a race, however innocent and amiable, which is technologically weaker than ourselves, I do not doubt that the same revolting story will be repeated. We shall enslave, deceive, exploit or exterminate; at the very least we shall corrupt it with our vices and infect it with our diseases.

We are not fit yet to visit other worlds. We have filled our own with massacre, torture, syphilis, famine, dust bowls and with all that is hideous to ear or eye. Must we go on to infect new realms?

Of course we might find a species stronger than ourselves. In that case we shall have met, if not God, at least God's judgement in space. But once more the detecting apparatus will be inadequate. We shall think it just our bad luck if righteous creatures rightly destroy those who come to reduce them to misery.

It was in part these reflections that first moved me to make my own small contributions to science fiction. In those days writers in that genre almost automatically represented the inhabitants of other worlds as monsters and the terrestrial invaders as good. Since then the opposite set-up has become fairly common. If I could believe that I had in any degree contributed to this change, I should be a proud man.[1]

The same problem, by the way, is beginning to threaten us as regards the dolphins. I don't think it has yet been proved that they are rational. But if they are, we have no more right to enslave them than to enslave our fellow-men. And some of us will continue to say this, but we shall be mocked.

The third thing is this. Some people are troubled, and others are delighted, at the idea of finding not one, but perhaps innumerable rational species scattered about the universe. In both cases the emotion arises from a belief that such discoveries would be fatal to Christian theology. For it will be said that theology connects the Incarnation of God with the Fall and Redemption of man. And this would seem to attribute to our species and to our little planet a central position in cosmic history which is not credible if rationally inhabited planets are to be had by the million.

Older readers will, with me, notice the vast change in astronomical speculation which this view involves. When we were boys all astronomers, so far as I know, impressed upon us the antecedent improbabilities of life in any part of the universe whatever. It was not thought unlikely that this earth was the solitary exception to a universal reign of the inorganic. Now Professor Hoyle, and many with him, say that in so vast a universe, life must have occurred in times and places without number. The interesting thing is that I have heard both these estimates used as arguments against Christianity.

Now it seems to me that we must find out more than we can at present know – which is nothing – about hypothetical rational species before we can say what theological corolaries or difficulties their discovery would raise.

We might, for example, find a race which was, like us, rational but, unlike us, innocent – no wars nor any other wickedness among them; all

---

[1] The reference is to Lewis's interplanetary novels, *Out of the Silent Planet*, *Perelandra* and *That Hideous Strength*. He was probably the first writer to introduce the idea of having *fallen* terrestrial invaders discover on other planets – in his own books, Mars (*Out of the Silent Planet*) and Venus (*Perelandra*) – *unfallen* rational beings who were in no need of redemption and with nothing to learn from us. See also his essay, 'Religion and Rocketry' (p. 231).

peace and good fellowship. I don't think any Christian would be puzzled to find that they knew no story of an Incarnation or Redemption, and might even find our story hard to understand or accept if we told it to them. There would have been no Redemption in such a world because it would not have needed redeeming. 'They that are whole need not the physician.' The sheep that has never strayed need not be sought for. We should have much to learn from such people and nothing to teach them. If we were wise, we should fall at their feet. But probably we should be unable to 'take it'. We'd find some reason for exterminating them.

Again, we might find a race which, like ours, contained both good and bad. And we might find that for them, as for us, something had been done: that at some point in their history some great interference for the better, believed by some of them to be supernatural, had been recorded, and that its effects, though often impeded and perverted, were still alive among them. It need not, as far as I can see, have conformed to the pattern of Incarnation, Passion, Death and Resurrection. God may have other ways – how should I be able to imagine them? – of redeeming a lost world. And Redemption in that alien mode might not be easily recognisable by our missionaries, let alone by our atheists.

We might meet a species which, like us, needed Redemption but had not been given it. But would this fundamentally be more of a difficulty than any Christian's first meeting with a new tribe of savages? It would be our duty to preach the Gospel to them. For if they are rational, capable both of sin and repentance, they are our brethren, whatever they look like. Would this spreading of the Gospel from earth, through man, imply a pre-eminence for earth and man? Not in any real sense. If a thing is to begin at all, it must begin at some particular time and place; and any time and place raises the question: 'Why just then and just there?' One can conceive an extraterrestrial development of Christianity so brilliant that earth's place in the story might sink to that of a prologue.

Finally, we might find a race which was strictly diabolical – no tiniest spark felt in them from which any goodness could ever be coaxed into the feeblest glow; all of them incurably perverted through and through. What then? We Christians had always been told that there were creatures like that in existence. True, we thought they were all incorporeal spirits. A minor readjustment thus becomes necessary.

But all this is in the realm of fantastic speculation. We are trying to cross a bridge, not only before we come to it, but even before we know there is a river that needs bridging.

MUST OUR IMAGE OF GOD GO?

Taken from The Observer *(24 March 1963), this article was reprinted in* The Honest to God Debate: Some Reactions to the Book 'Honest to God' *with a new chapter by its author, J.A.T. Robinson, Bishop of Woolwich, edited by David L. Edwards (SCM Press, 1963). It was reproduced in* Undeceptions *(1971) and* God in the Dock *(1998).*

The Bishop of Woolwich will disturb most of us Christian laymen less than he anticipates. We have long abandoned belief in a God who sits on a throne in a localised Heaven. We call that belief anthropomorphism, and it was officially condemned before our time. There is something about this in Gibbon. I have never met any adult who replaced 'God up there' by 'God out there' in the sense 'spatially external to the universe'. If I said God is 'outside' or 'beyond' space-time, I should mean 'as Shakespeare is outside *The Tempest*'; i.e., its scenes and persons do not exhaust his being. We have always thought of God as being not only 'in' and 'above', but also 'below' us: as the depth of ground. We can imaginatively speak of 'Father in Heaven' yet also of the everlasting arms that are 'beneath'. We do not understand why the Bishop is so anxious to canonise the one image and forbid the other. We admit his freedom to use which he prefers. We claim our freedom to use both.

His view of Jesus as a 'window' seems wholly orthodox ('he that hath seen me hath seen the Father' [John 14:9]). Perhaps the real novelty is in the Bishop's doctrine about God. But we can't be certain, for here he is very obscure. He draws a sharp distinction between asking 'Does God exist as a person?' and asking whether ultimate reality is personal. But surely he who says yes to the second question has said yes to the first? Any entity describable without gross abuse of language as God must be ultimate reality, and if ultimate reality is personal, then God is personal. Does the Bishop mean that something which is not 'a person' could yet be 'personal'? Even this could be managed if 'not a person' were taken to mean 'a person and more' – as is provided for by the doctrine of the Trinity. But the Bishop does not mention this.

Thus, though sometimes puzzled, I am not shocked by his article. His heart, though perhaps in some danger of bigotry, is in the right place. If he has failed to communicate why the things he is saying move him so deeply as they obviously do, this may be primarily a literary failure. If I were briefed to defend his position I should say 'The image of the Earth-Mother gets in something which that of the Sky-Father leaves out. Religions of the Earth-Mother have hitherto been spiritually inferior to those of the Sky-Father, but, perhaps, it is now time to readmit some of their elements.' I shouldn't believe it very strongly, but some sort of case could be made out.

PART 2

ASPECTS OF FAITH

[10]

CHRISTIANITY AND CULTURE

This collection of three articles was Lewis's part in a series of five papers first published in Theology, *Volumes XL and XLI (March–December 1940), and later in* Christian Reflections *(1998). The other writers were S.L. Bethell and E.F. Carritt ('Replies to Mr Lewis'), and George Every ('In Defence of Criticism').*

If the heavenly life is not grown up in you, it signifies nothing what you have chosen in the stead of it, or why you have chosen it.

William Law

I

At an early age I came to believe that the life of culture (that is, of intellectual and aesthetic activity) was very good for its own sake, or even that it was good for man. After my conversion, which occurred in my later twenties, I continued to hold this belief without consciously asking how it could be reconciled with my new belief that the end of human life was salvation in Christ and the glorifying of God. I was awakened from this confused state of mind by finding that the friends of culture seemed to me to be exaggerating. In my reaction against what seemed exaggerated I was driven to the other extreme, and began, in my own mind, to belittle the claims of culture. As soon as I did this I was faced with the question, 'If it is a thing of so little value, how are you justified in spending so much of your life on it?'

The present inordinate esteem of culture by the cultured began, I think, with Matthew Arnold – at least if I am right in supposing that he first popularised the use of the English word *spiritual* in the sense of German *geistlich*. This was nothing less than the identification of levels of life hitherto usually distinguished. After Arnold came the vogue of Croce, in whose philosophy the aesthetic and logical activities were made autonomous forms of 'the spirit' co-ordinate with the ethical. There followed the poetics of Dr I.A. Richards. This great atheist critic found in a good poetical taste the means of attaining psychological adjustments which improved a man's power of effective and satisfactory living all round, while bad taste resulted in a corresponding loss. Since this theory of value was a purely psychological one, this amounted to giving poetry a kind of soteriological function; it held the keys of the only heaven that Dr Richards believed in. His work (which I respect profoundly) was continued, though not always in directions that he accepted, by the editors of *Scrutiny*,[1] who believe in 'a necessary relationship between the quality of the individual's response to art and his general fitness for humane living'. Finally, as might have been expected, a somewhat similar view was expressed by a Christian writer: in fact by Brother Every in *Theology* for March 1939. In an article entitled 'The Necessity of *Scrutiny*' Brother Every inquired what Mr Eliot's admirers were to think of a Church where those who seemed to be theologically equipped preferred Housman, Mr Charles Morgan, and Miss Sayers, to Lawrence, Joyce and Mr E.M. Forster; he spoke (I think with sympathy) of the 'sensitive questioning individual' who is puzzled at finding the same judgements made by Christians as by 'other conventional people'; and he talked of 'testing' theological students as regards their power to evaluate a new piece of writing on a secular subject.

As soon as I read this there was the devil to pay. I was not sure that I understood – I am still not sure that I understand – Brother Every's position. But I felt that some readers might easily get the notion that 'sensitivity' or good taste were among the *notes* of the true Church, or that coarse, unimaginative people were less likely to be saved than refined and poetic people. In the heat of the moment I rushed to the opposite extreme. I felt, with some spiritual pride, that I had been saved in the nick of time from being 'sensitive'. The 'sentimentality and cheapness' of much Christian hymnody had been a strong point in my own resistance to conversion. Now I felt almost thankful for the bad hymns.[2] It was good that we should have to lay down our precious refinement at the very doorstep of the church; good that we should be cured at the outset of our inveterate confusion between *psyche* and *pneuma*, nature and supernature.

---

[1] I take *Scrutiny* throughout as it is represented in Brother Every's article. An independent criticism of that periodical is no part of my purpose. – C.S.L.
[2] We should be cautious of assuming that we know what their most banal expressions actually stand for in the minds of uneducated, holy persons. Of a saint's conversation Patmore says: 'He will most likely dwell with reiteration on commonplaces with which you were perfectly acquainted before you were twelve years old; but you must … remember that the knowledge which is to you a superficies is to him a solid' (*Rod, Root and Flower, Magna Moralia*, xiv). — C.S.L.

A man is never so proud as when striking an attitude of humility. Brother Every will not suspect me of being still in the condition I describe, nor of still attributing to him the preposterous beliefs I have just suggested. But there remains, none the less, a real problem which his article forced upon me in its most acute form. No one, presumably, is really maintaining that a fine taste in the arts is a condition of salvation. Yet the glory of God, and, as our only means to glorifying Him, the salvation of human souls, is the real business of life. What, then, is the value of culture? It is, of course, no new question; but as a living question it was new to me.

I naturally turned first to the New Testament. Here I found, in the first place, a demand that whatever is most highly valued on the natural level is to be held, as it were, merely on sufferance, and to be abandoned without mercy the moment it conflicts with the service of God. The organs of sense (Matthew 5:29) and of virility (Matthew 19:12) may have to be sacrificed. And I took it that the least these words could mean was that a life, by natural standards, crippled and thwarted was not only no bar to salvation, but might easily be one of its conditions. The text about hating father and mother (Luke 14:26) and our Lord's apparent belittling even of His own natural relation to the Blessed Virgin (Matthew 12:48) were even more discouraging. I took it for granted that anyone in his senses would hold it better to be a good son than a good critic, and that whatever was said of natural affection was implied *a fortiori* of culture. The worst of all was Philippians 3:8, where something obviously more relevant to spiritual life than culture can be – 'blameless' conformity to the Jewish Law – was described as 'muck'.

In the second place I found a number of emphatic warnings against every kind of superiority. We were told to become as children (Matthew 18:3), not to be called Rabbi (Matthew 23:8), to dread reputation (Luke 6:26). We were reminded that few of the σοφοὶ κατὰ σάρκα – which, I suppose, means precisely the intelligentsia – are called (1 Corinthians 1:26); that a man must become a fool by secular standards before he can attain real wisdom (1 Corinthians 3:18).

Against all this I found some passages that could be interpreted in a sense more favourable to culture. I argued that secular learning might be embodied in the Magi; that the Talents in the parable might conceivably include 'talents' in the modern sense of the word; that the miracle at Cana in Galilee by sanctifying an innocent, sensuous pleasure[3] could be taken to

---

[3] On a possible deeper significance in this miracle, see F. Mauriac, *Vie de Jésus*, ch. 5, ad fin.

sanctify at least a recreational use of culture – mere 'entertainment'; and that aesthetic enjoyment of nature was certainly hallowed by our Lord's praise of the lilies. At least some use of science was implied in St Paul's demand that we should perceive the Invisible through the visible (Romans 1:20). But I was more than doubtful whether his exhortation, 'Be not children in mind' (1 Corinthians 14:20), and his boast of 'wisdom' among the initiate, referred to anything that we should recognise as secular culture.

On the whole, the New Testament seemed, if not hostile, yet unmistakably cold to culture. I think we can still believe culture to be innocent after we have read the New Testament; I cannot see that we are encouraged to think it important.

It might be important none the less, for Hooker has finally answered the contention that Scripture must contain everything important or even everything necessary. Remembering this, I continued my researches. If my selection of authorities seems arbitary, that is due not to a bias but to my ignorance. I used such authors as I happened to know.

Of the great pagans Aristotle is on our side. Plato will tolerate no culture that does not directly or indirectly conduce either to the intellectual vision of the good or the military efficiency of the commonwealth. Joyce and D.H. Lawrence would have fared ill in the Republic. The Buddha was, I believe, anti-cultural, but here especially I speak under correction.

St Augustine regarded the liberal education which he had undergone in his boyhood as a *dementia*, and wondered why it should be considered *honestior et uberior* than the really useful 'primary' education which preceded it (*Conf.* I, xiii). He is extremely distrustful of his own delight in church music (ibid., X, xxxiii). Tragedy (which for Dr Richards is 'a great exercise of the spirit')[4] is for St Augustine a kind of sore. The spectator suffers, yet loves his suffering, and this is a *miserabilis insania ... quid autem mirum cum infelix pecus aberrans a grege tuo et inpatiens custodiae tuae turpi scabie foedarer* (ibid., III, ii).

St Jerome, allegorising the parable of the Prodigal Son, suggests that the husks with which he was fain to fill his belly may signify *cibus daemonum ... carmina poetarum, saecularis sapientia, rhetoricorum pompa verborum* (Ep. xxi, 4).

Let none reply that the Fathers were speaking of polytheistic literature at a time when polytheism was still a danger. The scheme of values presupposed in most imaginative literature has not become very much

---

[4] *Principles of Literary Criticism* (1930), p. 69.

more Christian since the time of St Jerome. In *Hamlet* we see everything questioned *except* the duty of revenge. In all Shakespeare's works the conception of good really operative – whatever the characters may say – seems to be purely worldly. In medieval romance, honour and sexual love are the true values; in nineteenth-century fiction, sexual love and material prosperity. In romantic poetry, either the enjoyment of nature (ranging from pantheistic mysticism at one end of the scale to mere innocent sensuousness at the other) or else the indulgence of a *Sehnsucht* awakened by the past, the distant, and the imagined, but not believed, supernatural. In modern literature, the life of liberated instinct. There are, of course, exceptions: but to study these exceptions would not be to study literature as such, and as a whole. 'All literatures,' as Newman has said,[5] 'are one; they are the voices of the natural man ... if Literature is to be made a study of human nature, you cannot have a Christian Literature. It is a contradiction in terms to attempt a sinless Literature of sinful man.' And I could not doubt that the sub-Christian or anti-Christian values implicit in most literature did actually infect many readers. Only a few days ago I was watching, in some scholarship papers, the results of this infection in a belief that the crimes of such Shakespearian characters as Cleopatra and Macbeth were somehow compensated for by a quality described as their 'greatness'. This very morning I have read in a critic the remark that if the wicked lovers in Webster's *White Devil* had repented we should hardly have forgiven them. And many people certainly draw from Keats's phrase about negative capability or 'love of good and evil' (if the reading which attributes to him such meaningless words is correct) a strange doctrine that experience *simpliciter* is good. I do not say that the sympathetic reading of literature must produce such results, but that it may and often does. If we are to answer the Fathers' attack on pagan literature we must not ground our answer on a belief that literature as a whole has become, in any important sense, more Christian since their days.

In Thomas Aquinas I could not find anything directly bearing on my problem; but I am very poor Thomist and shall be grateful for correction on this point.

Thomas à Kempis I take to be definitely on the anti-cultural side.

In the *Theologia Germanica* (ch. xx) I found that nature's refusal of the life of Christ 'happeneth most of all where there are high natural gifts of reason, for that soareth upwards in its own light and by its own power, till at last it cometh to think itself the true Eternal Light.' But in a later chapter (xlii) I found the evil of the false light identified with its tendency

[5] *Scope and Nature of University Education* (1852), Discourse 8.

75

to love knowledge and discernment more than the object known and discerned. This seemed to point to the possibility of a knowledge which avoided that error.

The cumulative effect of all this was very discouraging to culture. On the other side – perhaps only through the accidental distribution of my ignorance – I found much less.

I found the famous saying, attributed to Gregory, that our use of secular culture was comparable to the action of the Israelites in going down to the Philistines to have their knives sharpened. This seems to me a most satisfactory argument as far as it goes, and very relevant to modern conditions. If we are to convert our heathen neighbours, we must understand their culture. We must 'beat them at their own game'. But of course, while this would justify Christian culture (at least for some Christians whose vocation lay in that direction) at the moment, it would come very far short of the claims made for culture in our modern tradition. On the Gregorian view culture is a weapon; and a weapon is essentially a thing we lay aside as soon as we safely can.

In Milton I found a disquieting ally. His *Areopagitica* troubled me just as Brother Every's article had troubled me. He seemed to make too little of the difficulties; and his glorious defence of freedom to explore all good and evil seemed, after all, to be based on an aristocratic preoccupation with great souls and a contemptuous indifference to the mass of mankind which, I suppose, no Christian can tolerate.

Finally I came to that book of Newman's from which I have already quoted, the lectures on *University Education*. Here at last I found an author who seemed to be aware of both sides of the question; for no one ever insisted so eloquently as Newman on the beauty of culture for its own sake, and no one ever so sternly resisted the temptation to confuse it with things spiritual. The cultivation of the intellect, according to him, is 'for this world':[6] between it and 'genuine religion' there is a 'radical difference';[7] it makes 'not the Christian ... but the gentleman', and looks like virtue 'only at a distance',[8] he 'will not for an instant allow' that it makes men better.[9] The 'pastors of the Church' may indeed welcome culture because it provides innocent distraction at those moments of spiritual relaxation which would otherwise very likely lead to sin; and in this way it

---

[6] Op. cit., VIII, p. 227, in Everyman Edition.
[7] VII, pp. 184–5.
[8] IV, p. 112.
[9] IV, p. 111.

often 'draws the mind off from things which will harm it to subjects worthy of a rational being'. But even in so doing 'it does not raise it above nature, nor has any tendency to make us pleasing to our Maker'.[10] In some instances the cultural and the spiritual value of an activity may even be in inverse ratio. Theology, when it ceases to be part of liberal knowledge, and is pursued for purely pastoral ends, gain in 'meritoriousness' but loses in liberality 'just as a face worn by tears and fasting loses its beauty'.[11] On the other hand Newman is certain that liberal knowledge is an end in itself; the whole of the fourth Discourse is devoted to this theme. The solution of this apparent antinomy lies in his doctrine that everything, including, of course, the intellect, 'has its own perfection. Things animate, inanimate, visible, invisible, all are good in their kind, and have a *best* of themselves, which is an object of pursuit.'[12] To perfect the mind is 'an object as intelligible as the cultivation of virtue, while, at the same time, it is absolutely distinct from it'.[13]

Whether because I am too poor a theologian to understand the implied doctrine of grace and nature, or for some other reason, I have not been able to make Newman's conclusion my own. I can well understand that there is a kind of goodness which is not moral; as a well-grown healthy toad is 'better' or 'more perfect' than a three-legged toad, or an archangel is 'better' than an angel. In this sense a clever man is 'better' than a dull one, or any man than any chimpanzee. The trouble comes when we start asking how much of our time and energy God wants us to spend in becoming 'better' or 'more perfect' in this sense. If Newman is right in saying that culture has *no* tendency 'to make us pleasing to our Maker', then the answer would seem to be, 'None.' And that is a tenable view: as though God said, 'Your *natural* degree of perfection, your place in the chain of being, is my affair: do you get on with what I have explicitly left as your task – righteousness.' But if Newman had thought this he would not, I suppose, have written the discourse on 'Liberal Knowledge its Own End'. On the other hand, it would be possible to hold (perhaps it is pretty generally held) that one of the moral duties of a rational creature was to attain to the highest non-moral perfection it could. But if this were so, then (a) The perfecting of the mind would not be 'absolutely distinct' from virtue but part of the content of virtue; and (b) It would be very odd that Scripture and the tradition of the Church have little or nothing to

10 VII, p. 180.
11 IV, p. 100.
12 IV, p. 113.
13 IV, p. 114.

say about this duty. I am afraid that Newman has left the problem very much where he found it. He has clarified our minds by explaining that culture gives us a non-moral 'perfection'. But on the real problem – that of relating such non-moral values to the duty or interest of creatures who are every minute advancing either to heaven or hell – he seems to help little. 'Sensitivity' may be a perfection: but if by becoming sensitive I neither please God nor save my soul, why should I become sensitive? Indeed, what exactly is meant by a 'perfection' compatible with utter loss of the end for which I was created?

My researches left me with the impression that there could be no question of restoring to culture the kind of status which I had given it before my conversion. If any constructive case for culture was to be built up it would have to be of a much humbler kind; and the whole tradition of educated infidelity from Arnold to *Scrutiny* appeared to me as but one phase in that general rebellion against God which began in the eighteenth century. In this mood I set about construction.

1. I begin at the lowest and least ambitious level. My own professional work, though conditioned by taste and talents, is immediately motivated by the need for earning my living. And on earning one's living I was relieved to note that Christianity, in spite of its revolutionary and apocalyptic elements, can be delightfully humdrum. The Baptist did not give the tax-gatherers and soldiers lectures on the immediate necessity of turning the economic and military system of the ancient world upside down; he told them to obey the moral law – as they had presumably learned it from their mothers and nurses – and sent them back to their jobs. St Paul advised the Thessalonians to stick to their work (1 Thessalonians 4:11) and not to become busybodies (2 Thessalonians 3:11). The need for money is therefore *simpliciter* an innocent, though by no means a splendid, motive for any occupation. The Ephesians are warned to work professionally at something that is 'good' (Ephesians 4:28). I hoped that 'good' here did not mean much more than 'harmless', and I was certain it did not imply anything very elevated. Provided, then, that there was a demand for culture, and that culture was not actually deleterious, I concluded I was justified in making my living by supplying that demand – and that all others in my position (dons, schoolmasters, professional authors, critics, reviewers) were similarly justified; especially if, like me, they had few or no talents for any other career – if their 'vocation' to a cultural profession consisted in the brute fact of not being fit for anything else.

2. But is culture even harmless? It certainly can be harmful and often is. If a Christian found himself in the position of one inaugurating a new

society *in vacuo* he might well decide not to introduce something whose abuse is so easy and whose use is, at any rate, not necessary. But that is not our position. The abuse of culture is already there, and will continue whether Christians cease to be cultured or not. It is therefore probably better that the ranks of the 'culture-sellers' should include some Christians – as an antidote. It may even be the duty of some Christians to be culture-sellers. Not that I have yet said anything to show that even the lawful use of culture stands very high. The lawful use might be no more than innocent pleasure; but if the abuse is common, the task of resisting that abuse might be not only lawful but obligatory. Thus people in my position might be said to be 'working the thing which is good' in a stronger sense than that reached in the last paragraph.

In order to avoid misunderstanding, I must add that when I speak of 'resisting the abuse of culture' I do not mean that a Christian should take money for supplying one thing (culture) and use the opportunity thus gained to supply a quite different thing (homiletics and apologetics). That is stealing. The mere presence of Christians in the ranks of the culture-sellers will inevitably provide an antidote.

It will be seen that I have now reached something very like the Gregorian view of culture as a weapon. Can I now go a step further and find any intrinsic goodness in culture for its own sake?

3. When I ask what culture has done to me personally, the most obviously true answer is that it has given me quite an enormous amount of pleasure. I have no doubt at all that pleasure is in itself a good and pain in itself an evil; if not, then the whole Christian tradition about heaven and hell and the passion of our Lord seems to have no meaning. Pleasure, then, is good; a 'sinful' pleasure means a good offered, and accepted, under conditions which involve a breach of the moral law. The pleasures of culture are not intrinsically bound up with such conditions – though of course they can very easily be so enjoyed as to involve them. Often, as Newman saw, they are an excellent diversion from guilty pleasures. We may, therefore, enjoy them ourselves, and lawfully, even charitably, teach others to enjoy them.

This view gives us some ease, though it would go a very little way towards satisfying the editors of *Scrutiny*. We should, indeed, be justified in propagating good taste on the ground that cultured pleasure in the arts is more varied, intense, and lasting, than vulgar or 'popular' pleasure.[14] But we should not regard it as meritorious. In fact, much as we should

[14] If this is true, as I should gladly believe but have never seen proved. — C.S.L.

differ from Bentham about value in general, we should have to be Benthamites on the issue between pushpin and poetry.

4. It was noticed above that the values assumed in literature were seldom those of Christianity. Some of the principal values actually implicit in European literature were described as (a) honour, (b) sexual love, (c) material prosperity, (d) pantheistic contemplation of nature, (e) *Sehnsucht* awakened by the past, the remote, or the (imagined) supernatural, (f) liberation of impulses. These were called 'sub-Christian'. This is a term of disapproval if we are comparing them with Christian values: but if we take 'sub-Christian' to mean 'immediately sub-Christian' (i.e. the highest level of merely natural value lying immediately below the lowest level of spiritual value) it may be a term of relative approval. Some of the six values I have enumerated may be sub-Christian in this (relatively) good sense. For (c) and (f) I can make no defence; whenever they are accepted by the reader with anything more than a 'willing suspension of disbelief' they must make him worse. But the other four are all two-edged. I may symbolise what I think of them all by the aphorism 'Any road out of Jerusalem must also be a road into Jerusalem.' Thus:

(a) To the perfected Christian the ideal of honour is simply a temptation. His courage has a better root, and, being learned in Gethsemane, may have no honour about it. But to the man coming up from below, the ideal of knighthood may prove a schoolmaster to the ideal of martyrdom. Galahad is the *son* of Launcelot.

(b) The road described by Dante and Patmore is a dangerous one. But mere animalism, however disguised as 'honesty', 'frankness', or the like, is not dangerous, but fatal. And not all are qualified to be, even in sentiment, eunuchs for the Kingdom's sake. For some souls romantic love also has proved a schoolmaster.[15]

(d) There is any easy transition from Theism to Pantheism; but there is also a blessed transition in the other direction. For some souls I believe, for my own I remember, Wordsworthian contemplation can be the first and lowest form of recognition that there is something outside ourselves which demands reverence. To return to Pantheistic errors about the nature of this something would, for a Christian, be very bad. But once again, for 'the man coming up from below' the Wordsworthian experience is an advance. Even if he goes no further he has escaped the worst arrogance of materialism: if he goes on he will be converted.

(e) The dangers of romantic *Sehnsucht* are very great. Eroticism and even occultism lie in wait for it. On this subject I can only give my own

[15] See Charles Williams, *He Came Down from Heaven* (1938).

experience for what it is worth. When we are first converted I suppose we think mostly of our recent sins; but as we go on, more and more of the terrible past comes under review. In this process I have not (or not yet) reached a point at which I can honestly repent of my earlier experiences of romantic *Sehnsucht*. That they were occasions to much that I do repent, is clear; but I still cannot help thinking that this was my abuse of them, and that the experiences themselves contained, from the very first, a wholly good element. Without them my conversion would have been more difficult.[16]

I have dwelt chiefly on certain kinds of literature, not because I think them the only elements in culture that have this value as schoolmasters, but because I know them best; and on literature rather than art and knowledge for the same reason. My general case may be stated in Richardian terms – that culture is a storehouse of the best (sub-Christian) values. These values are in themselves of the soul, not the spirit. But God created the soul. Its values may be expected, therefore, to contain some reflection or antepast of the spiritual values. They will save no man. They resemble the regenerate life only as affection resembles charity, or honour resembles virtue, or the moon the sun. But though 'like is not the same', it is better than unlike. Imitation may pass into initiation. For some it is a good beginning. For others it is not; culture is not everyone's road into Jerusalem, and for some it is a road out.

There is another way in which it may predispose to conversion. The difficulty of converting an uneducated man nowadays lies in his complacency. Popularised science, the conventions or 'unconventions' of his immediate circle, party programmes, etc., enclose him in a tiny window-less universe which he mistakes for the only possible universe. There are no distant horizons, no mysteries. He thinks everything has been settled. A cultured person, on the other hand, is almost compelled to be aware that reality is very odd and that the ultimate truth, whatever it may be, *must* have the characteristics of strangeness – *must* be something that would seem remote and fantastic to the uncultured. Thus some obstacles to faith have been removed already.

On these grounds I conclude that culture has a distinct part to play in bringing certain souls to Christ. Not all souls – there is a shorter, and safer, way which has always been followed by thousands of simple

[16] I am quite ready to describe *Sehnsucht* as 'spilled religion' provided it is not forgotten that the spilled drops may be full of blessing to the unconverted man who licks them up, and therefore begins to search for the cup whence they were spilled. For the drops will be taken by some whose stomachs are not yet sound enough for the full draught. — C.S.L.

affectional natures who begin, where we hope to end, with devotion to the person of Christ.

Has it any part to play in the life of the converted? I think so, and in two ways. (a) If all the cultural values, on the way up to Christianity, were dim antepasts and ectypes of the truth, we can recognise them as such still. And since we must rest and play, where can we do so better than here – in the suburbs of Jerusalem? It is lawful to rest our eyes in moonlight – especially now that we know where it comes from, that it is only sunlight at second hand. (b) Whether the purely contemplative life is, or is not, desirable for any, it is certainly not the vocation of all. Most men must glorify God by doing to His glory something which is not *per se* an act of glorifying but which becomes so by being offered. If, as I now hope, cultural activities are innocent and even useful, then they also (like the sweeping of the room in Herbert's poem) can be done to the Lord. The work of a charwoman and the work of a poet become spiritual in the same way and on the same condition. There must be no return to the Arnoldian or Richardian view. Let us stop giving ourselves airs.

If it is argued that the 'sensitivity' which Brother Every desires is something different from my 'culture' or 'good taste', I must reply that I have chosen those words as the most general terms for something which is differently conceived in every age – 'wit', 'correctness', 'imagination' and (now) 'sensitivity'. These names, of course, record real changes of opinion about it. But if it were contended that the latest conception is so different from all its predecessors that we now have a radically new situation – that while 'wit' was not necessary for a seventeenth-century Christian, 'sensitivity' is necessary for a twentieth-century Christian – I should find this very hard to believe. 'Sensitivity' is a potentiality, therefore neutral. It can no more be an end to Christians than 'experience'. If Philippians 1:9 is quoted against me, I reply that delicate discriminations are there traced to charity, not to critical experience of books. Every virtue is a *habitus* – i.e. a *good* stock response. Dr Richards very candidly recognises this when he speaks of people 'hag-ridden by their vices *or their virtues*' (op. cit., p. 52, italics mine). But we want to be so ridden. I do not want a sensitivity which will show me how different each temptation to lust or cowardice is from the last, how unique, how unamenable to general rules. A stock response is precisely what I need to acquire. Moral theologians, I believe, tell us to fly at sight from temptations to faith or chastity. If that is not (in Dr Richards's words) a 'stock', 'stereotyped', 'conventional' response, I do not know what is. In fact, the new ideal of 'sensitivity' seems to me to present culture to Christians in a somewhat less favourable light than its predecessors. Sidney's poetics would be better. The whole school of critical thought which descends from Dr Richards bears such deep marks of its anti-Christian origins that I question if it can ever be baptized.

II

To the Editor of *Theology*:

Sir,

Mr Bethell's main position is so important that I hope you will allow me at some future date to deal with it in a full-length argument. For the moment, therefore, I will only say: (1) That I made no reference to his previous paper for the worst of reasons and the best of causes – namely, that I had forgotten it. For this negligence I ask his pardon. On looking back at the relevant number of *Theology*, I see from marginalia in my own hand that I must have read his contribution with great interest; for my forgetfulness I can only plead that a great many things have happened to us all since then. I am distressed that Mr Bethell should suppose himself deliberately slighted. I intended no disrespect to him. (2) That my position 'logically implies … total depravity' I deny simply. How any logician could derive the proposition 'Human nature is totally depraved' from the proposition 'Cultural activities do not in themselves improve our spiritual condition', I cannot understand. Even if I had said (which I did not), 'Man's aesthetic nature is totally depraved', no one could infer 'Man's whole nature is totally depraved' without a glaring transference from *secundum quid* to *simpliciter*. I put it to Mr Bethell that he has used 'logically implies' to mean 'may without gross uncharity rouse the suspicion of' – and that he ought not to use words that way.

To Mr Carritt I reply that my argument assumed the divinity of Christ, the truth of the creeds, and the authority of the Christian tradition, because I was writing in an Anglican periodical. That is why Dominical and patristic sayings have for me more than an antiquarian interest. But though my attribution of authority to Christ or the Fathers may depend on premises which Mr Carritt does not accept, my belief that it is proper to combine my own reasonings with the witness of authority has a different ground, prior to any decision on the question, 'Who is authoritative?' One of the things my reason tells me is that I ought to check the results of my own thinking by the opinions of the wise. I go to authority because reason sends me to it – just as Mr Carritt, after adding up a column of figures, might ask a friend, known to be a good calculator, to check it for him, and might distrust his own result if his friend got a different one.

I said that culture was a storehouse of the best sub-Christian *values*, not the best sub-Christian *virtues*. I meant by this that culture recorded man's striving for those ends which, though not the true end of man (the fruition of God), have nevertheless some degree of similarity to it, and are not so grossly inadequate to the nature of man as, say, physical pleasure, or money. This similarity, of course, while making it less evil to rest in them, makes the danger of resting in them greater and more subtle.

The salvation of souls in a means to the glorifying of God because only saved souls can duly glorify Him. The thing to which, on my view, culture must be subordinated, is not (though it includes) moral virtue, but the conscious direction of all will and desire to a transcendental Person in whom I believe all values to reside, and the reference to Him in every thought and act. Since that Person 'loves righteousness' this total surrender to Him involves Mr Carritt's 'conscientiousness'. It would therefore be impossible to 'glorify God by doing what we thought wrong'. Doing what we think right, on the other hand, is not the same as glorifying God. I fully agree with Mr Carritt that *a priori* we might expect the production of whatever is 'good' to be one of our duties. If God had never spoken to man, we should be justified in basing the conduct of life wholly on such *a priori* grounds. Those who think God has spoken will naturally listen to what He has to say about the where, how, to what extent, and in what spirit any 'good' is to be pursued. This does not mean that our own 'conscience' is simply negated. On the contrary, just as reason sends me to authority, so conscience sends me to obedience: for one of the things my conscience tells me is that if there exists an absolutely wise and good Person (Aristotle's φρόνιμος raised to the nth) I owe Him obedience, specially when that Person, as the ground of my existence, has a kind of paternal claim on me, and, as a benefactor, has a claim on my gratitude. What would happen if there were an absolute clash between God's will and my own conscience – i.e. if *either* God could be bad *or* I were an incurable moral idiot – I naturally do not know, any more than Mr Carritt knows what would happen if he found absolutely demonstrative evidence for two contradictory propositions.

I mentioned Hooker, not because he simply denied that Scripture contains all things necessary, but because he advanced a proof that it cannot – which proof, I supposed, most readers of *Theology* would remember. 'Text-hunting' is, of course, 'Puritanical', but also scholastic, patristic, apostolic, and Dominical. To *that* kind of charge I venture, presuming on an indulgence which Mr Carritt has extended to me for nearly twenty years, to reply with homely saws: as that an old trout can't be caught by tickling, and they know a trick worth two of that where I come from. Puritan, quotha!

Yours faithfully,
C.S. Lewis

III
Peace Proposals for Brother Every and Mr Bethell

I believe there is little real disagreement between my critics (Brother Every and Mr Bethell) and myself. Mr Carritt, who does not accept the Christian premises, must here be left out of account, though with all the respect and affection I feel for my old tutor and friend.

The conclusion I reached in *Theology*, March 1940, was that culture, though not in itself meritorious, was innocent and pleasant, might be a vocation for some, was helpful in bringing certain souls to Christ, and could be pursued to the glory of God. I do not see that Brother Every and Mr Bethell really want me to go beyond this position.

The argument of Mr Bethell's paper in *Theology*, July 1939 (excluding its historical section, which does not here concern us), was that the deepest, and often unconscious, beliefs of a writer were implicit in his work, even in what might seem the minor details of its style, and that, unless we were Croceans, such beliefs must be taken into account in estimating the value of that work. In *Theology*, May 1940, Mr Bethell reaffirmed this doctrine, with the addition that the latent beliefs in much modern fiction were naturalistic, and that we needed trained critics to put Christian readers on their guard against this pervasive influence.

Brother Every, in *Theology*, September 1940, maintained that our tastes are symptomatic of our real standards of value, which may differ from our professed standards; and that we needed trained critics to show us the real latent standards in literature – in fact 'to teach us how to read'.

I cannot see that my own doctrine and those of my critics come into direct contradiction at any point. My fear was lest excellence in reading and writing were being elevated into a spiritual value, into something meritorious *per se*; just as other things excellent and wholesome in themselves, like conjugal love (in the sense of *eros*) or physical cleanliness, have at some times and in some circles been confused with virtue itself or esteemed necessary parts of it. But it now appears that my critics never intended to make any such claim. Bad Taste for them is not itself spiritual evil but the symptom which betrays, or the 'carrier' which circulates, spiritual evil. And the spiritual evil thus betrayed or carried turns out not to be any specifically cultural or literary kind of evil, but false beliefs or standards – that is, intellectual error or moral baseness; and as I never intended to deny that error and baseness were evils nor that literature could imply and carry them, I think that all three of us may shake hands and say we are agreed. I do not mean to suggest that my critics have *merely* restated a platitude which neither I nor anyone else ever disputed. The value of their contribution lies in their insistence that the real beliefs may differ from the professed and may lurk in the turn of a phrase or the choice of an epithet; with the result that many preferences which seem to the ignorant to be simply 'matters of taste' are visible to the trained critic as choices between good and evil, or truth and error. And I fully admit that this important point had been neglected in my essay of March 1940. Now that it has been made, I heartily accept it. I think this is agreement.

But to test the depth of agreement I would like my critics to consider the following positions. By agreement I mean only agreement in our doctrines. Differences of temper and emphasis between Christian critics are inevitable and probably desirable.

1. Is it the function of the 'trained critic' to discover the latent beliefs and standards in a book, or to pass judgement on them when discovered, or both? I think Brother Every confines the critic's function to discovery. About Mr Bethell I am not so sure. When he says (*Theology*, May 1940, p. 360) that we need a minority of trained critics to 'lay bare the false values of contemporary culture' this might mean two things: (a) 'To expose the falsity of the values of contemporary culture'; (b) 'To reveal what the values of contemporary culture actually are – and, by the way, I personally think those values false.' It is necessary to clear this up before we know what is meant by a 'trained critic'. Trained in what? A man who has had a literary training may be an expert in disengaging the beliefs and values latent in literature; but the judgement on those beliefs and values (that is, the judgement on all possible human thoughts and moralities) belongs either to a quite different set of experts (theologians, philosophers, casuists, scientists) or else not to experts at all but to the unspecialised 'good and wise man', the φρόνιμος. Now I for my part have no objection to our doing both when we criticise, but I think it very important to keep the two operations distinct. In the discovery of the latent belief we have had a special training, and speak as experts; in the judgement of the beliefs, once they have been discovered, we humbly hope that we are being trained, like everyone else, by reason and ripening experience, under the guidance of the Holy Ghost, as long as we live, but we speak on them simply as men, on a level with all our even-Christians, and indeed with less authority than any illiterate man who happens to be

older, wiser, and purer, than we. To transfer to these judgements any specialist authority which may belong to us as 'trained critics' is charlatanism, if the attempt is conscious, and confusion if it is not. If Brother Every (see *Theology*, September 1940, p. 161) condemns a book because of 'English Liberal' implications he is really saying two things: (a) This book has English Liberal implications; (b) English Liberalism is an evil. The first he utters with authority because he is a trained critic. In the second, he may be right or he may be wrong; but he speaks with no more authority than any other man. Failure to observe this distinction may turn literary criticism into a sort of stalking horse from behind which a man may shoot all his personal opinions on any and every subject, without ever really arguing in their defence and under cover of a quite irrelevant specialist training in literature. I do not accuse Brother Every of this. But a glance at any modern review will show that it is an ever-present danger.

2. In *Theology*, May 1940 (p. 359), Mr Bethell speaks of 'some form of biological or economic naturalism' as the unconscious attitude in most popular fiction of today, and cities, as straws that show the wind, the popularity of 'urges' and 'overmastering passions'. Now, fortunately, I agree with Mr Bethell in thinking naturalism an erroneous philosophy: and I am ready to grant, for the purposes of argument, that those who talk about 'urges' do so because they are unconsciously naturalistic. But when all this has been granted, can we honestly say that the *whole* of our dislike of 'urges' is explained, without remainder, by our disagreement with naturalism? Surely not. Surely we object to that way of writing for another reason *as well* – because it is so worn, so facile, so obviously attempting to be impressive, so associated in our minds with dullness and pomposity.[17] In other words, there are two elements in our reaction. One is the detection of an attitude in the writer which, as instructed Christians and amateur philosophers, we disapprove; the other is really, and strictly, an affair of taste. Now these, again, require to be kept distinct. Being fallen creatures we tend to resent offences against our taste, at least as much as, or even more than, offences against our conscience or reason; and we would dearly like to be able – if only we can find any plausible argument for doing so – to inflict upon the man whose writing (perhaps for reasons utterly unconnected with good and evil) has afflicted us like a bad smell, the same kind of condemnation which we can inflict on him

---

[17] Pomp is at times a literary virtue. Pomposity (the unsuccessful attempt at pomp) may, of course, spring from an evil (pride); it may also be the maladroit effort of a humble writer to 'rise' to a subject which he honestly feels to be great. — C.S.L.

who has uttered the false and the evil. The tendency is easily observed among children; friendship wavers when you discover that a hitherto trusted playmate actually *likes* prunes. But even for adults it is 'sweet, sweet, sweet poison' to feel able to imply 'thus saith the Lord' at the end of every expression of our pet aversions. To avoid this horrible danger we must perpetually try to distinguish, however closely they get entwined both by the subtle nature of the facts and by the secret importunity of our passions, those attitudes in a writer which we can honestly and confidently condemn as real evils, and those qualities in his writing which simply annoy and offend us as men of taste. This is difficult, because the latter are often so much more obvious and provoke such a very violent response. The only safe course seems to me to be this: to reserve our condemnation of attitudes for attitudes universally acknowledged to be bad by the Christian conscience speaking in agreement with Scripture and ecumenical tradition. A bad book is to be deemed a real evil in so far as it can be shown to prompt to sensuality, or pride, or murder, or to conflict with the doctrine of Divine Providence, or the like. The other dyslogistic terms dear to critics (vulgar, derivative, cheap, precious, academic, affected, bourgeois, Victorian, Georgian, 'literary', etc.) had better be kept strictly on the taste side of the account. In discovering what attitudes are present you can be as subtle as you like. But in your theological and ethical condemnation (as distinct from your dislike of the taste) you had better be very unsubtle. You had better reserve it for plain mortal sins, and plain atheism and heresy. For our passions are always urging us in the opposite direction, and if we are not careful criticism may become a mere excuse for taking revenge on books whose smell we dislike by erecting our temperamental antipathies into pseudo-moral judgements.

3. In practical life a certain amount of 'reading between the lines' is necessary: if we took every letter and every remark simply at its face value we should soon find ourselves in difficulties. On the other hand, most of us have known people with whom 'reading between the lines' became such a mania that they overlooked the obvious truth of every situation and lived in the perpetual discovery of mares' nests; and doctors tell us of a form of lunacy in which the simplest remark uttered in the patient's presence becomes to him evidence of a conspiracy and the very furniture of his cell takes on an infinitely sinister significance. Will my critics admit that the subtle and difficult task of digging out the latent beliefs and values, however necessary, is attended with some danger of our neglecting the obvious and surface facts about a book, whose importance, even if less than that of the latent facts, is certainly much higher

than zero? Suppose two books A and B. Suppose it can be truly said of A: 'The very style of this book reveals great sensitivity and honesty, and a readiness for total commitments; excellent raw material for sanctity if ever the author were converted.' And suppose it can be truly said of B: 'The very style of this book betrays a woolly, compromising state of mind, knee-deep entangled in the materialistic values which the author thinks he has rejected.' But might it not also be true to say of book A, 'Despite its excellent latent implications, its ostensible purpose (which will corrupt thousands of readers) is the continued glorification of mortal sin'; and of B, 'Despite its dreadful latent materialism, it does set courage and fidelity before the reader in an attractive light, and thousands of readers will be edified (though much less edified than they suppose) by reading it'? And is there not a danger of this second truth being neglected? We want the abstruse knowledge *in addition* to the obvious: not *instead* of it.

4. It is clear that the simple and ignorant are least able to resist, by reason, the influence of latent evil in the books they read. But is it not also true that this is often balanced by a kind of protection which comes to them through ignorance itself? I base this on three grounds: (a) Adults often disquiet themselves about the effect of a work upon children – for example, the effect of the bad elements in *Peter Pan*, such as the desire not to grow up or the sentimentalities about Wendy. But if I may trust my own memory, childhood simply does not receive these things. It rightly wants and enjoys the flying, the Indians, and the pirates (not to mention the pleasure of being in a theatre at all), and just accepts the rest as part of the meaningless 'roughage' which occurs in all books and plays; for at that age we never expect any work of art to be interesting all through. (When I began writing stories in exercise books I tried to put off all the things I really wanted to write about till at least the second page – I thought it wouldn't be like a real grown-up book if it became interesting at once.) (b) I often find expressions in my pupils' essays which seem to me to imply a great deal of latent error and evil. Now, since it would, in any case, be latent, one does not expect them to own up to it when challenged. But one does expect that a process of exploration would dicover the mental atmosphere to which the expression belonged. But in my experience exploration often produces a conviction that it had, in my pupils' minds, no evil associations, because it had no associations at all. They just thought it was the ordinary way of translating thought into what they suppose to be 'literary English'. Thousands of people are no more corrupted by the implications of 'urges', 'dynamism', and 'progressive' than they are edified by the implications of 'secular', 'charity', and

Platonic'.[18] The same process of attrition which empties good language of its virtue does, after all, empty bad language of much of its vice.[19] (c) If one speaks to an uneducated man about some of the worst features in a film or a book, does he not often reply unconcernedly, 'Ah ... they always got to bring a bit of that into a film,' or, 'I reckon they put that in to wind it up like'? And does this not mean that he is aware, even to excess, of the difference between art and life? He *expects* a certain amount of meaningless nonsense – which expectation, though very regrettable from the cultural point of view, largely protects him from the consequences of which we, in our sophisticated naivety, are afraid.

5. Finally, I agree with Brother Every that our leisure, even our play, is a matter of serious concern. There is no neutral ground in the universe: every square inch, every split second, is claimed by God and counterclaimed by Satan. But will Brother Every agree in acknowledging a real difficulty about merely recreational reading (I do not include all reading under this head), as about games? I mean that they are serious, and yet, to do them at all, we must somehow do them as if they were not. It is a serious matter to choose wholesome recreations: but they would no longer be recreations if we pursued them seriously. When Mr Bethell speaks of the critic's 'working hours' (May 1940, p. 360) I hope he means his hours of criticism, not his hours of reading. For a great deal (not all) of our literature was made to be read lightly for entertainment. If we do not read it, in a sense, 'for fun' and with our feet on the fender, we are not using it as it was meant to be used, and all our criticism of it will be pure illusion. For you cannot judge any artefact except by using it as it was intended. It is no good judging a butter-knife by seeing whether it will saw logs. Much bad criticism, indeed, results from the efforts of critics to get a work-time result out of something that never aimed at producing more than pleasure. There is a real problem here, and I do not see my way through it. But I should be disappointed if my critics denied the existence of the problem.

If any real disagreement remains between us, I anticipate that it will be about my third point – about the distinction there drawn between the real spiritual evil carried or betrayed in a book and its mere faults of taste.

[18] For example, God forbid that when Mr Bethell (May 1940, p. 361) uses 'old-fashioned' as a dyslogistic term we should immediately conclude that he really had the garage or dressmaking philosophy (Madam would like the *latest* model) which his words suggest. We know it slipped out by a sort of accident, for which *veniam petimus damusque vicissim*. — C.S.L.

[19] This applies also to 'bad language' in the popular sense, obscenity or profanity. The custom of such language has its origin in sin, but to the individual speaker it may be mere meaningless noise. — C.S.L.

And on this subject I confess that my critics can present me with a very puzzling dilemma. They can ask me whether the statement, 'This is tawdry writing', is an objective statement describing something bad in a book and capable of being true or false, or whether it is merely a statement about the speaker's own feelings – different in form, but fundamentally the same, as the proposition 'I don't like oysters.' If I choose the latter, then most criticism becomes purely subjective – which I don't want. If I choose the former then they can ask me, 'What are these qualities in a book which you admit to be in some sense good and bad but which, you keep on warning us, are not "really" or "spiritually" good and bad? Is there a kind of good which is not good? Is there any good that is not pleasing to God or any bad which is not hateful to Him?' And if you press me along these lines I end in doubts. But I will not get rid of those doubts by falsifying the little light I already have. That little light seems to compel me to say that there are two kinds of good and bad. The first, such as virtue and vice or love and hatred, besides being good or bad themselves make the possessor good or bad. The second do not. They include such things as physical beauty or ugliness, the possession or lack of a sense of humour, strength or weakness, pleasure or pain. But the two most relevant for us are the two I mentioned at the beginning of this essay, conjugal *eros* (as distinct from *agape*, which, of course, is a good of the first class) and physical cleanliness. Surely we have all met people who said, indeed, that the latter was *next* to godliness, but whose unconscious attitude made it a *part* of godliness, and no small part? And surely we agree that any good of this second class, however good on its own level, becomes an enemy when it thus assumes demonic pretensions and erects itself into a quasi-spiritual value. As M. de Rougemont has recently told us, the conjugal *eros* 'ceases to be a devil only when it ceases to be a god'. My whole contention is that in literature, in addition to the spiritual good and evil which it carries, there is also a good and evil of this second class, a properly cultural or literary good and evil, which must not be allowed to masquerade as good and evil of the first class. And I shall feel really happy about all the minor differences between my critics and me when I find in them some recognition of this danger – some admission that they and I, and all of the like education, are daily tempted to a kind of idolatry.

I am not pretending to know how this baffling phenomenon – the two kinds or levels of good and evil – is to be fitted into a consistent philosophy of values. But it is one thing to be unable to explain a phenomenon, another to ignore it. And I admit that all of these lower goods ought to be encouraged, that, as pedagogues, it is our duty to try to make our pupils happy and beautiful, to give them cleanly habits and good taste; and the discharge of that duty is, of course, a good of the first class. I will admit, too, that evils of this second class are often the result and symptom of real spiritual evil; dirty fingernails, a sluggish liver, boredom, and a bad English style, may often in a given case result from disobedience, laziness, arrogance, or intemperance. But they may also result from poverty or other misfortune. They may even result from virtue. The man's ears may be unwashed behind or his English style borrowed from the jargon of the daily press, because he has given to good works the time and energy which others use to acquire elegant habits or good language. Gregory the Great, I believe, vaunted the barbarity of his style. Our Lord ate with unwashed hands.

I am stating, not solving, a problem. If my critics want to continue the discussion I think they can do so most usefully by taking it right away from literature and the arts to some other of these mysterious 'lower goods' – where, probably, all our minds will work more coolly. I should welcome an essay from Brother Every or Mr Bethell on conjugal *eros* or personal cleanliness. My dilemma about literature is that I admit bad taste to be, in some sense, 'a bad thing', but do not think it *per se* 'evil'. My critics will probably say the same of physical dirt. If we could thrash the problem out on the neutral ground of clean and dirty fingers, we might return to the battlefield of literature with new lights.

I hope it is now unnecessary to point out that in denying 'taste' to be a spiritual value, I am not for a moment suggesting, as Mr Bethell thought (May 1940, p. 357), that it comes 'under God's arbitrary condemnation'. I enjoyed my breakfast this morning, and I think that was a good thing and do not think it was condemned by God. But I do not think myself a good man for enjoying it. The distinction does not seem to me a very fine one.

[11]

EVIL AND GOD

Published in The Spectator, *Volume CLXVI (7 February 1941) after an article by C.E.M. Joad under the same title in the previous issue (31 January), and then in* Undeceptions *(1971) and* Christian Reunion *(1990).*

Dr Joad's article on 'God and Evil' last week suggests the interesting conclusion that since neither 'mechanism' nor 'emergent evolution' will hold water, we must choose in the long run between some monotheistic philosophy, like the Christian, and some such dualism as that of the Zoroastrians. I agree with Dr Joad in rejecting mechanism and emergent evolution. Mechanism, like all materialist systems, breaks down at the problem of knowledge. If thought is the undesigned and irrelevant product of cerebral motions, what reason have we to trust it? As for emergent evolution, if anyone insists on using the word *God* to mean 'whatever the universe happens to be going to do next', of course we cannot prevent him. But nobody would in fact so use it unless he had a secret belief that what is coming next will be an improvement. Such a belief, besides being unwarranted, presents peculiar difficulties to an emergent evolutionist. If things can improve, this means that there must be some absolute standard of good above and outside the cosmic process to which that process can approximate. There is no sense in talking of 'becoming better' if better means simply 'what we are becoming' – it is like congratulating yourself on reaching your destination and defining destination as 'the place you have reached'. Mellontolatry, or the worship of the future, is a *fuddled* religion.

We are left then to choose between monotheism and dualism – between a single, good, almighty source of being, and two equal uncreated, antagonistic Powers, one good and the other bad. Dr Joad suggests that the latter view stands to gain from the 'new urgency' of the fact of evil. But *what* new urgency? Evil may seem more urgent to us that it did to the Victorian philosophers – favoured members of the happiest class in the happiest country of the world at the world's happiest period. But it is no more urgent for us than for the great majority of monotheists all down the ages. The classic expositions of the doctrine that the world's miseries are compatible with its creation and guidance by a wholly good Being come from Boethius waiting in prison to be beaten to death, and from St Augustine meditating on the sack of Rome. The present state of the world is normal; it was the last century that was the abnormality.

This drives us to ask why so many generations rejected Dualism. Not, assuredly, because they were unfamiliar with suffering; and not because its obvious *prima facie* plausibility escaped them. It is more likely that they saw its two fatal difficulties, the one metaphysical and the other moral.

The metaphysical difficulty is this. The two Powers, the good and the evil, do not explain each other. Neither Ormuzd nor Ahriman can claim to be the Ultimate. More ultimate than either of them is the inexplicable fact of their being there together. Neither of them chose this *tête-à-tête*. Each of them, therefore, is *conditioned* – finds himself willy nilly in a situation; and either that situation itself, or some unknown force which produced that situation, is the real Ultimate. Dualism has not yet reached the ground of being. You cannot accept two conditioned and mutually independent beings as the self-grounded, self-comprehending Absolute. On the level of picture thinking this difficulty is symbolised by our inability to think of Ormuzd and Ahriman without smuggling in the idea of a common *space* in which they can be together, and thus confessing that we are not yet dealing with the source of the universe but only with two members contained in it. Dualism is a truncated metaphysic.

The moral difficulty is that Dualism gives evil a positive, substantive, self-consistent nature, like that of good. If this were true, if Ahriman existed in his own right no less than Ormuzd, what could we mean by calling Ormuzd good except that we happened to prefer *him?* In what sense can the one party be said to be right and the other wrong? If evil has the same kind of reality as good, the same autonomy and completeness, our allegiance to good becomes the arbitrarily chosen loyalty of a partisan. A sound theory of value demands something very different. It demands that good should be original and evil a mere perversion; that good should be the tree and evil the ivy; that good should be able to see all round evil (as when sane men understand lunacy) while evil cannot retaliate in kind; that good should be able to exist on its own while evil requires the good on which it is parasitic in order to continue its parasitic existence.

The consequences of neglecting this are serious. It means believing that bad men like badness as such, in the same way in which good men like goodness. At first this denial of any common nature between us and our enemies seems gratifying. We call them fiends and feel that we need not forgive them. But, in reality, along with the power to forgive, we have lost the power to condemn. If a taste for cruelty and a taste for kindness were equally ultimate and basic, by what common standard could the one reprove the other? In reality, cruelty does not come from desiring evil as such, but from perverted sexuality, inordinate resentment, or lawless ambition and avarice. That is precisely why it can be judged and condemned from the standpoint of innocent sexuality, righteous anger, and ordinate acquisitiveness. The master can correct a boy's sums because they are blunders in arithmetic – in the same arithmetic which he does and does better. If they were not even attempts at arithmetic – if they were not in the arithmetical world at all – they could not be arithmetical mistakes.

Good and evil, then, are not on all fours. Badness is not even bad *in the same way* in which goodness is good. Ormuzd and Ahriman cannot be equals. In the long run, Ormuzd must be original and Ahriman derivative. The first hazy idea of *devil* must, if we begin to think, be analysed into the more precise ideas of 'fallen' and 'rebel' angel. But only in the long run. Christianity can go much further with the Dualist than Dr Joad's article seems to suggest. There was never any question of tracing *all* evil to man; in fact, the New Testament has a good deal more to say about dark superhuman powers than about the fall of Adam. As far as this world is concerned, a Christian can share most of the Zoroastrian outlook; we all live between the 'fell, incensed points' of Michael and Satan. The difference between the Christian and the Dualist is that the Christian thinks one stage further and sees that if Michael is really in the right and Satan really in the wrong this must mean that they stand in two different relations to somebody or something far further back, to the ultimate ground of reality itself. All this, of course, has been watered down in modern times by the theologians who are afraid of 'mythology', but those who are prepared to reinstate Ormuzd and Ahriman are presumably not squeamish on that score.

Dualism can be a manly creed. In the Norse form ('The giants will beat the gods in the end, but I am on the side of the gods') it is nobler by many degrees than most philosophies of the moment. But it is only a half-way house. Thinking along these lines you can avoid Monotheism, and remain a Dualist, only be refusing to follow your thoughts home. To revive Dualism would be a real step backwards and a bad omen (though not the worst possible) for civilisation.

[12]
THE WEIGHT OF GLORY

A sermon given in the Church of St Mary the Virgin, Oxford, and first published in Theology, *Volume XLIII (November 1941). It was reproduced as a pamphlet by SPCK and later appeared in* Transposition and Other Addresses *(1949),* They Asked for a Paper *(1962) and then in* Screwtape Proposes a Toast *(1998).*

If you asked twenty good men today what they thought the highest of the virtues, nineteen of them would reply, Unselfishness. But if you had asked almost any of the great Christians of old he would have replied, Love. You see what has happened? A negative term has been substituted for a positive, and this is of more than philological importance. The negative idea of Unselfishness carries with it the suggestion not primarily of securing good things for others, but of going without them ourselves, as if our abstinence and not their happiness was the important point. I do not think this is the Christian virtue of Love. The New Testament has lots to say about self-denial, but not about self-denial as an end in itself. We are told to deny ourselves and to take up our crosses in order that we may follow Christ; and nearly every description of what we shall ultimately find if we do so contains an appeal to desire. If there lurks in most modern minds the notion that to desire our own good and earnestly to hope for the enjoyment of it is a bad thing, I submit that this notion has crept in from Kant and the Stoics and is no part of the Christian faith. Indeed, if we consider the unblushing promises of reward and the staggering nature of the rewards promised in the Gospels, it would seem that Our Lord finds our desires, not too strong, but too weak. We are half-hearted creatures, fooling about with drink and sex and ambition when infinite joy is offered us, like an ignorant child who wants to go on making mud pies in a slum because he cannot imagine what is meant by the offer of a holiday at the sea. We are far too easily pleased.

We must not be troubled by unbelievers when they say that this promise of reward makes the Christian life a mercenary affair. There are different kinds of reward. There is the reward which has no natural connection with the things you do to earn it, and is quite foreign to the desires that ought to accompany those things. Money is not the natural reward of love, that is why we call a man mercenary if he marries a woman for the sake of her money. But marriage is the proper reward for a real lover, and he is not mercenary for desiring it. A general who fights well in order to get a peerage is mercenary; a general who fights for victory is not, victory being the proper reward of battle as marriage is the proper reward of love. The proper rewards are not simply tacked on to the activity for which they are given, but are the activity itself in consummation. There is also a third case, which is more complicated. An enjoyment of Greek poetry is certainly a proper, and not a mercenary, reward for learning Greek; but only those who have reached the stage of enjoying Greek poetry can tell from their own experience that this is so. The schoolboy beginning Greek grammar cannot look forward to his adult enjoyment of Sophocles as a lover looks forward to marriage or a general to victory. He has to begin by working for marks, or to escape punishment, or to please his parents, or, at best, in the hope of a future good which he cannot at present imagine or desire. His position, therefore, bears a certain resemblance to that of the mercenary; the reward he is going to get will, in actual fact, be a natural or proper reward, but he will not know that till he has got it. Of course, he gets it gradually; enjoyment creeps in upon the mere drudgery, and nobody could point to a day or an hour when the one ceased and the other began. But it is just in so far as he approaches the reward that he becomes able to desire it for its own sake; indeed, the power of so desiring it is itself a preliminary reward.

The Christian, in relation to heaven, is in much the same position as this schoolboy. Those who have attained everlasting life in the vision of God doubtless know very well that it is no mere bribe, but the very consummation of their earthly discipleship; but we who have not yet attained it cannot know this in the same way, and cannot even begin to know it at all except by continuing to obey and finding the first reward of our obedience in our increasing power to desire the ultimate reward. Just in proportion as the desire grows, our fear lest it should be a mercenary desire will die away and finally be recognised as an absurdity. But probably this will not, for most of us, happen in a day; poetry replaces grammar, gospel replaces law, longing transforms obedience, as gradually as the tide lifts a grounded ship.

But there is one other important similarity between the schoolboy and ourselves. If he is an imaginative boy he will, quite probably, be revelling in the English poets and romancers suitable to his age some time before he begins to suspect that Greek grammar is going to lead him to more and more enjoyments of this same sort. He may even be neglecting his Greek to read Shelley and Swinburne in secret. In other words, the desire which Greek is really going to gratify already exists in him and is attached to objects which seem to him quite unconnected with Xenophon and the verbs in μι. Now, if we are made for heaven, the desire for our proper place will be already in us, but not yet attached to the true object, and will even appear as the rival of that object. And this, I think, is just what we find. No doubt there is one point in which my analogy of the schoolboy breaks down. The English poetry which he reads when he ought to be doing Greek exercises may be just as good as the Greek poetry to which the exercises are leading him, so that in fixing on Milton instead of journeying on to Aeschylus his desire is not embracing a false object. But our case is very different. If a transtemporal, transfinite good is our real destiny, then any other good on which our desire fixes must be in some degree fallacious, must bear at best only a symbolical relation to what will truly satisfy.

In speaking of this desire for our own far-off country, which we find in ourselves even now, I feel a certain shyness. I am almost committing an indecency. I am trying to rip open the inconsolable secret in each one of you – the secret which hurts so much that you take your revenge on it by calling it names like Nostalgia and Romanticism and Adolescence; the secret also which pierces with such sweetness that when, in very intimate conversation, the mention of it becomes imminent, we grow awkward and affect to laugh at ourselves; the secret we cannot hide and cannot tell, though we desire to do both. We cannot tell it because it is a desire for something that has never actually appeared in our experience. We cannot hide it because our experience is constantly suggesting it, and we betray ourselves like lovers at the mention of a name. Our commonest expedient is to call it beauty and behave as if that had settled the matter. Wordsworth's expedient was to identify it with certain moments in his own past. But all this is a cheat. If Wordsworth had gone back to those moments in the past, he would not have found the thing itself, but only the reminder of it; what he remembered would turn out to be itself a remembering. The books or the music in which we thought the beauty was located will betray us if we trust to them; it was not *in* them, it only came *through* them, and what came through them was longing. These things – the beauty, the memory of our own past – are good images of what we really desire; but if they are mistaken for the thing itself they turn into dumb idols, breaking the hearts of their worshippers. For they are not the thing itself; they are only the scent of a flower we have not found, the echo of a tune we have not heard, news from a country we have never yet visited. Do you think I am trying to weave a spell? Perhaps I am; but remember your fairy tales. Spells are used for breaking enchantments as well as for inducing them. And you and I have need of the strongest spell that can be found to wake us from the evil enchantment of worldliness which has been laid upon us for nearly a hundred years. Almost our whole education has been directed to silencing this shy, persistent, inner voice; almost all our modern philosophies have been devised to convince us that the good of man is to be found on this earth. And yet it is a remarkable thing that such philosophies of Progress or Creative Evolution themselves bear reluctant witness to the truth that our real goal is elsewhere. When they want to convince you that earth is your home, notice how they set about it. They begin by trying to persuade you that earth can be made into heaven, thus giving a sop to your sense of exile in earth as it is. Next, they tell you that this fortunate event is still a good way off in the future, thus giving a sop to your knowledge that the fatherland is not here and now. Finally, lest your longing for the transtemporal should awake and spoil the whole affair, they use any rhetoric that comes to hand to keep out of your mind the recollection that even if all the happiness they promised could come to man on earth, yet still each generation would lose it by death, including the last generation of all, and the whole story would be nothing, not even a story, for ever and ever. Hence all the nonsense that Mr *Shaw* puts into the final speech of Lilith, and Bergson's remark that the *élan vital* is capable of surmounting all obstacles, perhaps even death – as if we could believe that any social or biological development on this planet will delay the senility of the sun or reverse the second law of thermodynamics.

Do what they will, then, we remain conscious of a desire which no natural happiness will satisfy. But is there any reason to suppose that reality offers any satisfaction to it? 'Nor does the being hungry prove that we have bread.' But I think it may be urged that this misses the point. A man's physical hunger does not prove that that man will get any bread; he may die of starvation on a raft in the Atlantic. But surely a man's hunger does prove that he comes of a race which repairs its body by eating and inhabits a world where eatable substances exist. In the same way, though I do not believe (I wish I did) that my desire for Paradise proves that I shall enjoy it, I think it a pretty good indication that such a thing exists and that some men will. A man may love a woman and not win her; but it would be very odd if the phenomenon called 'falling in love' occurred in a sexless world.

Here, then, is the desire, still wandering and uncertain of its object and still largely unable to see that object in the direction where it really lies. Our sacred books give us some account of the object. It is, of course, a symbolical account. Heaven is, by definition, outside our experience, but all intelligible descriptions must be of things within our experience. The scriptural picture of heaven is therefore just as symbolical as the picture which our desire, unaided, invents for itself; heaven is not really full of jewellery any more than it is really the beauty of Nature, or a fine piece of music. The difference is that the scriptural imagery has authority. It comes to us from writers who were closer to God than we, and it has stood the test of Christian experience down the centuries. The natural appeal of this authoritative imagery is to me, at first, very small. At first sight it chills, rather than awakes, my desire. And that is just what I ought to expect. If Christianity could tell me no more of the far-off land than my own temperament led me to surmise already, then Christianity would be no higher than myself. If it has more to give me, I must expect it to be less immediately attractive than 'my own stuff'. Sophocles at first seems dull and cold to the boy who has only reached Shelley. If our religion is something objective, then we must never avert our eyes from those elements in it which seem puzzling or repellent; for it will be precisely the puzzling or the repellent which conceals what we do not yet know and need to know.

The promises of Scripture may very roughly be reduced to five heads. It is promised, firstly, that we shall be with Christ; secondly, that we shall be like Him; thirdly, with an enormous wealth of imagery, that we shall have 'glory'; fourthly, that we shall, in some sense, be fed or feasted or entertained; and, finally, that we shall have some sort of official position in the universe – ruling cities, judging angels, being pillars of God's temple. The first question I ask about these promises is: 'Why any of them except the first?' Can anything be added to the conception of being with Christ? For it must be true, as an old writer says, that he who has God and everything else has no more than he who has God only. I think the answer turns again on the nature of symbols. For though it may escape our notice at first glance, yet it is true that any conception of being with Christ which most of us can now form will be not very much less symbolical than the other promises; for it will smuggle in ideas of proximity in space and loving conversation as we now understand conversation, and it will probably concentrate on the humanity of Christ to the exclusion of His deity. And, in fact, we find that those Christians who attend solely to this first promise always do fill it up with very earthly imagery indeed – in fact with hymeneal or erotic imagery. I am not for a moment condemning such imagery. I heartily wish I could enter into it more deeply than I do, and pray that I yet shall. But my point is that this also is only a symbol, like the reality in some respects, but unlike it in others, and therefore needs correction from the different symbols in the other promises. The variation of the promises does not mean that anything other than God will be our ultimate bliss; but because God is more than a Person, and lest we should imagine the joy of His presence too exclusively in terms of our present poor experience of personal love, with all its narrowness and strain and monotony, a dozen changing images correcting and relieving each other, are supplied.

I turn next to the idea of glory. There is no getting away from the fact that this idea is very prominent in the New Testament and in early Christian writings. Salvation is constantly associated with palms, crowns, white robes, thrones, and splendour like the sun and stars. All this makes no immediate appeal to me at all, and in that respect I fancy I am a typical modern. Glory suggests two ideas to me, of which one seems wicked and the other ridiculous. Either glory means to me fame, or it means luminosity. As for the first, since to be famous means to be better known than other people, the desire for fame appears to me as a competitive passion and therefore of hell rather than heaven. As for the second, who wishes to become a kind of living electric light bulb?

When I began to look into this matter I was shocked to find such different Christians as Milton, Johnson and Thomas Aquinas taking heavenly glory quite frankly in the sense of fame or good report. But not fame conferred by our fellow creatures – fame with God, approval or (I might say) 'appreciation' by God. And then, when I had thought it over, I saw that this view was scriptural; nothing can eliminate from the parable the divine *accolade*, 'Well done, thou good and faithful servant'. With that, a good deal of what I had been thinking all my life fell down like a house of cards. I suddenly remembered that no one can enter heaven except as a child; and nothing is so obvious in a child – not in a conceited child, but in a good child – as its great and undisguised pleasure in being praised. Not only in a child, either, but even in a dog or a horse. Apparently what I had mistaken for humility had, all these years, prevented me from understanding what is in fact the humblest, the most childlike, the most creaturely of pleasures – nay, the specific pleasure of the inferior: the pleasure of a beast before men, a child before its father, a pupil before his teacher, a creature before its Creator. I am not forgetting how horribly this most innocent desire is parodied in our human ambitions, or how very quickly, in my own experience, the lawful pleasure of praise from those whom it was my duty to please turns into the deadly poison of self-admiration. But I thought I could detect a moment – a very, very short moment – before this happened, during which the satisfaction of having pleased those whom I rightly loved and rightly feared was pure. And that is enough to raise our thoughts to what may happen when the redeemed soul, beyond all hope and nearly beyond belief, learns at last that she has pleased Him whom she was created to please. There will be no room for vanity then. She will be free from the miserable illusion that it is her doing. With no taint of what we should now call self-approval she will most innocently rejoice in the thing that God has made her to be, and the moment which heals her old inferiority complex for ever will also drown her pride deeper than Prospero's book. Perfect humility dispenses with modesty. If God is satisfied with the work, the work may be satisfied with itself; 'it is not for her to bandy compliments with her Sovereign'. I can imagine someone saying that he dislikes my idea of heaven as a place where we are patted on the back. But proud misunderstanding is behind that dislike. In the end that Face which is the delight or the terror of the universe must be turned upon each of us either with one expression or with the other, either conferring glory inexpressible or inflicting shame that can never be cured or disguised. I read in a periodical the other day that the fundamental thing is how we think of God. By God Himself, it is not! How God thinks of us is not only more important, but infinitely more important. Indeed, how we think of Him is of no importance except in so far as it is related to how He thinks of us. It is written that we shall 'stand before' Him, shall appear, shall be inspected. The promise of glory is the promise, almost incredible and only possible by the work of Christ, that some of us, that any of us who really chooses, shall actually survive that examination, shall find approval, shall please God. To please God ... to be a real ingredient in the divine happiness ... to be loved by God, not merely pitied, but delighted in as an artist delights in his work or a father in a son – it seems impossible, a weight or burden of glory which our thoughts can hardly sustain. But so it is.

And now notice what is happening. If I had rejected the authoritative and scriptural image of glory and stuck obstinately to the vague desire which was, at the outset, my only pointer to heaven, I could have seen no connection at all between that desire and the Christian promise. But now, having followed up what seemed puzzling and repellent in the sacred books, I find, to my great surprise, looking back, that the connection is perfectly clear. Glory, as Christianity teaches me to hope for it, turns out to satisfy my original desire and indeed to reveal an element in that desire which I had not noticed. By ceasing for a moment to consider my own wants I have begun to learn better what I really wanted. When I attempted, a few minutes ago, to describe our spiritual longings, I was omitting one of their most curious characteristics. We usually notice it just as the moment of vision dies away, as the music ends or as the landscape loses the celestial light. What we feel then has been well described by Keats as 'the journey homeward to habitual self'. You know what I mean. For a few minutes we have had the illusion of belonging to that world. Now we wake to find that it is no such thing. We have been mere spectators. Beauty has smiled, but not to welcome us; her face was turned in our direction, but not to see us. We have not been accepted, welcomed, or taken into the dance. We may go when we please, we may stay if we can: 'Nobody marks us.' A scientist may reply that since most of the things we call beautiful are inanimate, it is not very surprising that they take no notice of us. That, of course, is true. It is not the physical objects that I am speaking of, but that indescribable something of which they become for a moment the messengers. And part of the bitterness which mixes with the sweetness of that message is due to the fact that it so seldom seems to be a message intended for us, but rather something we have overheard. By bitterness I mean pain, not resentment. We should hardly dare to ask that any notice be taken of ourselves. But we pine. The sense that in this universe we are treated as strangers, the longing to be acknowledged, to meet with some response, to bridge some chasm that yawns between us and reality, is part of our inconsolable secret. And surely, from this point of view, the promise of glory, in the sense described, becomes highly relevant to our deep desire. For glory means good report with God, acceptance by God, response, acknowledgement, and welcome into the heart of things. The door on which we have been knocking all our lives will open at last.

Perhaps it seems rather crude to describe glory as the fact of being 'noticed' by God. But this is almost the language of the New Testament. St Paul promises to those who love God not, as we should expect, that they will know Him, but that they will be known by Him (1 Corinthians 8:3). It is a strange promise. Does not God know all things at all times? But it is dreadfully re-echoed in another passage of the New Testament. There we are warned that it may happen to any one of us to appear at last before the face of God and hear only the appalling words: 'I never knew you. Depart from Me.' In some sense, as dark to the intellect as it is unendurable to the feelings, we can be both banished from the presence of Him who is present everywhere and erased from the knowledge of Him who knows all. We can be left utterly and absolutely *outside* – repelled, exiled, estranged, finally and unspeakably ignored. On the other hand, we can be called in, welcomed, received, acknowledged. We walk every day on the razor edge between these two incredible possibilities. Apparently, then, our lifelong nostalgia, our longing to be reunited with something in the universe from which we now feel cut off, to be on the inside of some door which we have always seen from the outside, is no mere neurotic fancy, but the truest index of our real situation. And to be at last summoned inside would be both glory and honour beyond all our merits and also the healing of that old ache.

And this brings me to the other sense of glory – glory as brightness, splendour, luminosity. We are to shine as the sun, we are to be given the Morning Star. I think I begin to see what it means. In one way, of course, God has given us the Morning Star already: you can go and enjoy the gift on many fine mornings if you get up early enough. What more, you may ask, do we want? Ah, but we want so much more – something the books on aesthetics take little notice of. But the poets and the mythologies know all about it. We do not want merely to *see* beauty, though, God knows, even that is bounty enough. We want something else which can hardly be put into words – to be united with the beauty we see, to pass into it, to receive it into ourselves, to bathe in it, to become part of it. That is why we have peopled air and earth and water with gods and goddesses and nymphs and elves – that, though we cannot, yet these projections can, enjoy in themselves that beauty, grace, and power of which Nature is the image. That is why the poets tell us such lovely falsehoods. They talk as if the west wind could really sweep into a human soul; but it can't. They tell us that 'beauty born of murmuring sound' will pass into a human face; but it won't. Or not yet. For if we take the imagery of Scripture seriously, if we believe that God will one day *give* us the Morning Star and cause us to *put on* the splendour of the sun, then we may surmise that both the ancient myths and the modern poetry, so false as history, may be very near the truth as prophecy. At present we are on the outside of the world, the wrong side of the door. We discern the freshness and purity of morning, but they do not make us fresh and pure. We cannot mingle with the splendours we see. But all the leaves of the New Testament are rustling with the rumour that it will not always be so. Some day, God willing, we shall get *in*. When human souls have become as perfect in voluntary obedience as the inanimate creation is in its lifeless obedience, then they will put on its glory, or rather that greater glory of which Nature is only the first sketch. For you must not think that I am putting forward any heathen fancy of being absorbed into Nature. Nature is mortal; we shall outlive her. When all the suns and nebulae have passed away, each one of you will still be alive. Nature is only the image, the symbol; but it is the symbol Scripture invites me to use. We are summoned to pass in through Nature, beyond her, into that splendour which she fitfully reflects.

And in there, in beyond Nature, we shall eat of the tree of life. At present, if we are reborn in Christ, the spirit in us lives directly on God; but the mind, and still more the body, receives life from Him at a thousand removes – through our ancestors, through our food, through the elements. The faint, far-off results of those energies which God's creative rapture implanted in matter when He made the worlds are what we now call physical pleasures; and even thus filtered, they are too much for our present management. What would it be to taste at the fountain-head that stream of which even these lower reaches prove so intoxicating? Yet that, I believe, is what lies before us. The whole man is to drink joy from the fountain of joy. As St Augustine said, the rapture of the saved soul will 'flow over' into the glorified body. In the light of our present specialised and depraved appetites we cannot imagine this *torrens voluptatis*, and I warn everyone most seriously not to try. But it must be mentioned, to drive out thoughts even more misleading – thoughts that what is saved is a mere ghost, or that the risen body lives in numb insensibility. The body was made for the Lord, and these dismal fancies are wide of the mark.

Meanwhile the cross comes before the crown and tomorrow is a Monday morning. A cleft has opened in the pitiless walls of the world, and we are invited to follow our great Captain inside. The following Him is, of course, the essential point. That being so, it may be asked what practical use there is in the speculations which I have been indulging. I can think of at least one such use. It may be possible for each to think too much of his own potential glory hereafter; it is hardly possible for him to think too often or too deeply about that of his neighbour. The load, or weight, or burden of my neighbour's glory should be laid daily on my back, a load so heavy that only humility can carry it, and the backs of the proud will be broken. It is a serious thing to live in a society of possible gods and goddesses, to remember that the dullest and most uninteresting person you can talk to may one day be a creature which, if you saw it now, you would be strongly tempted to worship, or else a horror and a corruption such as you now meet, if at all, only in a nightmare. All day long we are, in some degree, helping each other to one or other of these destinations. It is in the light of these overwhelming possibilities, it is with the awe and the circumspection proper to them, that we should conduct all our dealings with one another, all friendships, all loves, all play, all politics. There are no *ordinary* people. You have never talked to a mere mortal. Nations, cultures, arts, civilisations – these are mortal, and their life is to ours as the life of a gnat. But it is immortals whom we joke with, work with, marry, snub, and exploit – immortal horrors or everlasting splendours. This does not mean that we are to be perpetually solemn. We must play. But our merriment must be of that kind (and it is, in fact, the merriest kind) which exists between people who have, from the outset, taken each other seriously – no flippancy, no superiority, no presumption. And our charity must be a real and costly love, with deep feeling for the sins in spite of which we love the sinner – no mere tolerance, or indulgence which parodies love as flippancy parodies merriment. Next to the Blessed Sacrament itself, your neighbour is the holiest object presented to your senses. If he is your Christian neighbour he is holy in almost the same way, for in him Christ *vere latitat* – the glorifier and the glorified, Glory Himself – is truly hidden.

[13]

MIRACLES

First published in The Guardian *(2 October 1942), the text was expanded and preached as a sermon in St Jude on the Hill Church, London, subsequently appearing in* St Jude's Gazette, *No. 73 (October 1942). It was later published in* Undeceptions *(1971) and* God in the Dock *(1998).*

I have known only one person in my life who claimed to have seen a ghost. It was a woman; and the interesting thing is that she disbelieved in the immortality of the soul before seeing the ghost and still disbelieves after having seen it. She thinks it was a hallucination. In other words, seeing is not believing. This is the first thing to get clear in talking about miracles. Whatever experiences we may have, we shall not regard them as miraculous if we already hold a philosophy which excludes the supernatural. Any event which is claimed as a miracle is, in the last resort, an experience received from the senses; and the senses are not infallible. We can always say we have been the victims of an illusion; if we disbelieve in the supernatural this is what we always shall say. Hence, whether miracles have really ceased or not, they would certainly appear to cease in Western Europe as materialism became the popular creed. For let us make no mistake. If the end of the world appeared in all the literal trappings of the Apocalypse,[1] the modern materialist saw with his own eyes the heavens rolled up (6:14) and the great white throne appearing (20:11), if he had the sensation of being himself hurled into the Lake of Fire (19:20; 20:10, 14–15; 21:8), he would continue forever, in that lake itself, to regard his experience as an illusion and to find the explanation of it in psycho-analysis, or cerebral pathology. Experience by itself proves nothing. If a man doubts whether he is dreaming or waking, no experiment can solve his doubt, since every experiment may itself be part of the dream. Experience proves this, or that, or nothing, according to the preconceptions we bring to it.

---

[1] The Book of Revelation.

This fact that the interpretation of experience depends on preconceptions, is often used as an argument against miracles. It is said that our ancestors, taking the supernatural for granted and greedy of wonders, read the miraculous into events that were really not miracles. And in a sense I grant it. That is to say, I think that just as our preconceptions would prevent us from apprehending miracles if they really occurred, so their preconceptions would lead them to imagine miracles even if they did not occur. In the same way, the doting man will think his wife faithful when she is not and the suspicious man will not think her faithful when she is: the question of her actual fidelity remains meanwhile to be settled, if at all, on other grounds. But there is one thing often said about our ancestors which we must *not* say. We must not say 'They believed in miracles because they did not know the laws of nature.' This is nonsense. When St Joseph discovered that his bride was pregnant, he was 'minded to put her away' (Matthew 1:19). He knew enough biology for that. Otherwise, of course, he would not have regarded pregnancy as a proof of infidelity. When he accepted the Christian explanation, he regarded it as a miracle precisely because he knew enough of the laws of nature to know that this was a suspension of them. When the disciples saw Christ walking on the water (Matthew 14:26; Mark 6:49; John 6:19) they were frightened: they would not have been frightened unless they had known the laws of nature and known that this was an exception. If a man had no conception of a regular order in nature, then of course he could not notice departures from that order: just as a dunce who does not understand the normal metre of a poem is also unconscious of the poet's variations from it. Nothing is wonderful except the abnormal and nothing is abnormal until we have grasped the norm. Complete ignorance of the laws of nature would preclude the perception of the miraculous just as rigidly as complete disbelief in the supernatural precludes it, perhaps even more so. For while the materialist would have at least to explain miracles away, the man wholly ignorant of nature would simply not notice them.

The experience of a miracle in fact requires two conditions. First we must believe in a normal stability of nature, which means we must recognise that the data offered by our senses recur in regular patterns. Secondly, we must believe in some reality beyond nature. When both beliefs are held, and not till then, we can approach with an open mind the various reports which claim that this super- or extra-natural reality has sometimes invaded and disturbed the sensuous content of space and time which makes our 'natural' world. The belief in such a supernatural reality itself can neither be proved nor disproved by experience. The arguments for its existence are metaphysical, and to me conclusive. They turn on the fact that even to think and act in the natural world we have to assume something beyond it and even assume that we partly belong to that something. In order to think we must claim for our own reasoning a validity which is not credible if our thought is merely a function of our brain, and our brains a by-product of irrational physical processes. In order to act, above the level of mere impulse, we must claim a similar validity for our judgements of good and evil. In both cases we get the same disquieting result. The concept of nature itself is one we have reached only tacitly by claiming a sort of *super*-natural status for ourselves.

If we frankly accept this position and then turn to the evidence, we find, of course, that accounts of the supernatural meet us on every side. History is full of them – often in the same documents which we accept wherever they do not report miracles. Respectable missionaries report them not infrequently. The whole Church of Rome claims their continued occurrence. Intimate conversation elicits from almost every acquaintance at least one episode in his life which is what he would call 'queer' or 'rum'. No doubt most stories of miracles are unreliable; but then, as anyone can see by reading the papers, so are most stories of all events. Each story must be taken on its merits: what one must not do is to rule out the supernatural as the one impossible explanation. Thus you may disbelieve in the Mons Angels[2] because you cannot find a sufficient number of sensible people who say they saw them. But if you found a sufficient number, it would, in my view, be unreasonable to explain this by collective hallucination. For we know enough of psychology to know that spontaneous unanimity in hallucination is very improbable, and we do not know enough of the supernatural to know that a manifestation of angels is equally improbable. The supernatural theory is the less improbable of the two. When the Old Testament says that Sennacherib's invasion was stopped by angels (2 Kings 19:35), and Herodotus says it was stopped by a lot of mice who came and ate up all the bowstrings of his army,[3] an open-minded man will be on the side of the angels. Unless you start by begging the question, there is nothing intrinsically unlikely in the existence of angels or in the action ascribed to them. But mice just don't do these things.

A great deal of scepticism now current about the miracles of Our Lord does not, however, come from disbelief of all reality beyond nature. It

---

[2] Lewis is referring to the story that angels appeared, protecting British troops in their retreat from Mons, France, on 26 August 1914. A summary of the event by Jill Kitson, 'Did Angels appear to British troops at Mons?' is found in *History Makers*, No. 3 (1969), pp. 132–3.

[3] Herodotus, Bk. II, Sect. 141.

comes from two ideas which are respectable but I think mistaken. In the first place, modern people have an almost aesthetic dislike of miracles. Admitting that God can, they doubt if He would. To violate the laws He Himself has imposed on His creation seems to them arbitrary, clumsy, a theatrical device only fit to impress savages – a solecism against the grammar of the universe. In the second place, many people confuse the laws of nature with the laws of thought and imagine that their reversal or suspension would be a contradiction in terms – as if the resurrection of the dead were the same sort of thing as two and two making five.

I have only recently found the answer to the first objection. I found it first in George MacDonald and then later in St Athanasius. This is what St Athanasius says in his little book *On the Incarnation*: 'Our Lord took a body like to ours and lived as a man in order that those who had refused to recognise Him in His superintendence and captaincy of the whole universe might come to recognise from the works He did here below in the body that what dwelled in this body was the Word of God.' This accords exactly with Christ's own account of His miracles: 'The Son can do nothing of Himself, but what He seeth the Father do.' (John 5:19). The doctrine, as I understand it, is something like this:

There is an activity of God displayed throughout creation, a wholesale activity let us say which men refuse to recognise. The miracles done by God incarnate, living as a man in Palestine, perform the very same things as this wholesale activity, but at a different speed and on a smaller scale. One of their chief purposes is that men having seen a thing done by personal power on the small scale, may recognise, when they see the same thing done on the large scale, that the power behind it is also personal – is indeed the very same person who lived among us two thousand years ago. The miracles in fact are a retelling in small letters of the very same story which is written across the whole world in letters too large for some of us to see. Of that larger script part is already visible, part is still unsolved. In other words, some of the miracles do locally what God has already done universally: others do locally what he has not yet done, but will do. In that sense, and from our human point of view, some are reminders and others prophecies.

God creates the vine and teaches it to draw up water by its roots and, with the aid of the sun, to turn that water into a juice which will ferment and take on certain qualities. Thus every year, from Noah's time till ours, God turns water into wine. That, men fail to see. Either like the Pagans they refer the process to some finite spirit, Bacchus or Dionysus: or else, like the moderns, they attribute real and ultimate causality to the chemical and other material phenomena which are all that our senses can discover in it. But when Christ at Cana makes water into wine, the mask is off (John 2:1–11). The miracle has only half its effect if it only convinces us that Christ is God: it will have its full effect if whenever we see a vineyard or drink a glass of wine we remember that here works He who sat at the wedding party in Cana. Every year God makes a little corn into much corn: the seed is sown and there is an increase, and men, according to the fashion of their age, say 'It is Ceres, it is Adonis, it is the Corn King,' or else 'It is the laws of nature.' The close-up, the translation, of this annual wonder is the feeding of the five thousand (Matthew 14:15–21; Mark 6:34–44; Luke 9:12–17; John 6:1–11). Bread is not made there of nothing. Bread is not made of stones, as the Devil once suggested to Our Lord in vain (Matthew 4:3; Luke 4:3). A little bread is made into much bread. The Son will do nothing but what He sees the Father do. There is, so to speak, a family *style*. The miracles of healing fall into the same pattern. This is sometimes obscured for us by the somewhat magical view we tend to take of ordinary medicine. The doctors themselves do not take this view. The magic is not in the medicine but in the patient's body. What the doctor does is to stimulate nature's functions in the body, or to remove hindrances. In a sense, though we speak for convenience of healing a cut, every cut heals itself; no dressing will make skin grow over a cut on a corpse. That same mysterious energy which we call gravitational when it steers the planets and biochemical when it heals a body is the efficient cause of all recoveries, and if God exists, that energy, directly or indirectly, is His. All who are cured are cured by Him, the healer within. But once He did it visibly, a Man meeting a man. Where He does not work within in this mode, the organism dies. Hence Christ's one miracle of destruction is also in harmony with God's wholesale activity. His bodily hand held out in symbolic wrath blasted a single fig tree (Matthew 21:19; Mark 11:13–20); but no tree died that year in Palestine, or any year, or in any land, or even ever will, save because He has done something, or (more likely) ceased to do something, to it.

When He fed the thousands he multiplied fish as well as bread. Look in every bay and almost every river. This swarming, pulsating fecundity shows He is still at work. The ancients had a god called Genius – the god of animal and human fertility, the presiding spirit of gynaecology, embryology, or the marriage bed – the 'genial bed' as they called it after its god Genius.[4] As the miracles of wine and bread and healing showed who Bacchus really was, who Ceres, who Apollo, and that all were one, so this

---

[4] For further information on this subject see the chapter on 'Genius and Genius' in Lewis's *Studies in Medieval and Renaissance Literature*, ed. Walter Hooper (Cambridge, 1966), pp. 169–74.

miraculous multiplication of fish reveals the real Genius. And with that we stand at the threshold of the miracle which for some reason most offends modern ears. I can understand the man who denies the miraculous altogether; but what is one to make of the people who admit some miracles but deny the Virgin Birth? Is it that for all their lip service to the laws of nature there is only one law of nature that they really believe? Or is it that they see in this miracle a slur upon sexual intercourse which is rapidly becoming the one thing venerated in a world without veneration? No miracle is in fact more significant. What happens in ordinary generation? What is a father's function in the act of begetting? A microscopic particle of matter from his body fertilises the female: and with that microscopic particle passes, it may be, the colour of his hair and his great grandfather's hanging lip, and the human form in all its complexity of bones, liver, sinews, heart, and limbs, and prehuman form which the embryo will recapitulate in the womb. Behind every spermatozoon lies the whole history of the universe: locked within it is no small part of the world's future. That is God's normal way of making a man – a process that takes centuries, beginning with the creation of matter itself, and narrowing to one second and one particle at the moment of begetting. And once again men will mistake the sense impressions which this creative act throws off for the act itself or else refer it to some finite being such as Genius. Once, therefore, God does it directly, instantaneously; without a spermatozoon, without the millenniums of organic history behind the spermatozoon. There was of course another reason. This time He was creating not simply a man, but the man who was to be Himself: the only true Man. The process which leads to the spermatozoon has carried down with it through the centuries much undesirable silt; the life which reaches us by that normal route is tainted. To avoid that taint, to give humanity a fresh start, He once short-circuited the process. There is a vulgar anti-God paper which some anonymous donor sends me every week. In it recently I saw the taunt that we Christians believe in a God who committed adultery with the wife of a Jewish carpenter. The answer to that is that if you describe the action of God in fertilising Mary as 'adultery', then, in that sense, God would have committed adultery with every woman who ever had a baby. For what He did once without a human father, He does always even when He uses a human father as His instrument. For the human father in ordinary generation is only a carrier, sometimes an unwilling carrier, always the last in a long line of carriers, of life that comes from the supreme life. Thus the filth that our poor, muddled, sincere, resentful enemies fling at the Holy One, either does not stick, or, sticking, turns into glory.

So much for the miracles which do small and quick what we have already seen in the large letters of God's universal activity. But before I go on to the second class – those which foreshadow parts of the universal activity we have not yet seen – I must guard against a misunderstanding. Do not imagine I am trying to make the miracles less miraculous. I am not arguing that they are more probable because they are less unlike natural events: I am trying to answer those who think them arbitrary, theatrical, unworthy of God, meaningless interruptions of universal order. They remain in my view wholly miraculous. To do instantly with dead and baked corn what ordinarily happens slowly with live seed is just as great a miracle as to make bread of stones. Just as great, but a different *kind* of miracle. That is the point. When I open Ovid,[5] or Grimm, I find the sort of miracles which really would be arbitrary. Trees talk, houses turn into trees, magic rings raise tables richly spread with food in lonely places, ships become goddesses, and men are changed into snakes or birds or bears. It is fun to read about: the least suspicion that it had really happened would turn that fun into nightmare. You find no miracles of that kind in the Gospels. Such things, if they could be, would prove that some alien power was invading nature; they would not in the least prove that it was the same power which had made nature and rules her every day. But the true miracles express not simply a god, but God: that which is outside nature, not as a foreigner, but as her sovereign. They announce not merely that a King has visited our town, but that it is *the* King, *our* King.

The second class of miracles, on this view, foretell what God has not yet done, but will do, universally. He raised one man (the man who was Himself) from the dead because He will one day raise all men from the dead. Perhaps not only men, for there are hints in the New Testament that all creation will eventually be rescued from decay, restored to shape and subserve the splendour of re-made humanity.[6] The Transfiguration (Matthew 17:1–9; Mark 9:2–10) and the walking on the water (Matthew 14:26; Mark 6:49; John 6:19) are glimpses of the beauty and the effortless power over all matter which will belong to men when they are really waked by God. Now resurrection certainly involves 'reversal' of natural process in the sense that it involves a series of changes moving in the opposite direction to those we see. At death, matter which has been organic, falls back gradually into the inorganic, to be finally scattered and

---

[5] The reference is to Ovid's (43 BC–AD 18) *Metamorphoses*.
[6] E.g. Romans 8:22: 'We know that the whole creation groaneth and travaileth in pain together until now.'

used perhaps in other organisms. Resurrection would be the reverse process. It would not of course mean the restoration to each personality of those very atoms, numerically the same, which had made its first or 'natural' body. There would not be enough to go round, for one thing; and for another, the unity of the body even in this life was consistent with a slow but perplexed change of its actual ingredients. But it certainly does mean matter of some kind rushing towards organism as now we see it rushing away. It means, in fact, playing backwards a film we have already seen played forwards. In that sense it is reversal of nature. But, of course, it is a further question whether reversal in this sense is necessarily contradiction. Do we know that the film cannot be played backwards?

Well, in one sense, it is precisely the teaching of modern physics that the film never works backwards. For modern physics, as you have heard before, the universe is 'running down'. Disorganisation and chance are continually increasing. There will come a time, not infinitely remote, when it will be wholly run down or wholly disorganised, and science knows of no possible return from that state. There must have been a time, not infinitely remote, in the past when it was wound up, though science knows of no winding-up process. The point is that for our ancestors the universe was a picture: for modern physics it is a story. If the universe is a picture these things either appear in that picture or not; and if they don't, since it is an infinite picture, one may suspect that they are contrary to the nature of things. But a story is a different matter; specially if it is an incomplete story. And the story told by modern physics might be told briefly in the words 'Humpty Dumpty was falling.' That is, it proclaims itself an incomplete story. There must have been a time before he fell, when he was sitting on the wall; there must be a time after he has reached the ground. It is quite true that science knows of no horses and men who can put him together again once he has reached the ground and broken. But then she also knows of no means by which he could originally have been put on the wall. You wouldn't expect her to. All science rests on observation: all our observations are taken *during* Humpty Dumpty's fall, because we were born after he lost his seat on the wall and shall be extinct long before he reaches the ground. But to assume from observations taken while the clock is running down that the unimaginable winding-up which must have preceded this process cannot occur when the process is over is the merest dogmatism. From the very nature of the case the laws of degradation and disorganisation which we find in matter at present, cannot be the ultimate and eternal nature of things. If they were, there would have been nothing to degrade and disorganise. Humpty Dumpty can't fall off a wall that never existed.

Obviously, an event which lies outside the falling or disintegrating process which we know as nature, is not imaginable. If anything is clear from the records of Our Lord's appearances after His resurrection, it is that the risen body was very different from the body that died and that it lives under conditions quite unlike those of natural life. It is frequently not recognised by those who see it (Luke 24:13–31; 36–37; John 20:14–16): and it is not related to space in the same way as our bodies. The sudden appearances and disappearances (Mark 16:14); Luke 24:31, 36; John 20:19, 26) suggest the ghost of popular tradition: yet He emphatically insists that He is not merely a spirit and takes steps to demonstrate that the risen body can still perform animal operations, such as eating (Luke 24:42–43; John 21:13). What makes all this baffling to us is our assumption that to pass beyond what we call nature – beyond the three dimensions and the five highly specialised and limited senses – is immediately to be in a world of pure negative spiritually, a world where space of any sort and sense of any sort have no function. I know no grounds for believing this. To explain even an atom Schrödinger wants seven dimensions: and give us new senses and we should find a new nature. There may be natures piled upon natures, each supernatural to the one beneath it, before we come to the abyss of pure spirit; and to be in that abyss, at the right hand of the Father, may not mean being absent from any of these natures – may mean a yet more dynamic presence on all levels. That is why I think it very rash to assume that the story of the Ascension is mere allegory. I know it sounds like the work of people who imagined an absolute up and down and a local heaven in the sky. But to say this is after all to say 'Assuming that the story is fake, we could thus explain how it arose.' Without that assumption we find ourselves 'moving about in worlds unrealised'[7] with no probability – or improbability – to guide us. For if the story is true then a being still in some mode, though not our mode, corporeal, withdrew at His own will from the Nature presented by our three dimensions and five senses, not necessarily into the non-sensuous and undimensioned but possibly into, or through, a world or worlds of super-sense and super-space. And He might choose to do it gradually. Who on earth knows what the spectators might see? If they say they saw a momentary movement along the vertical plane – then an indistinct mass – then nothing – who is to pronounce this improbable?

My time is nearly up and I must be very brief with the second class of people whom I promised to deal with: those who mistake the laws of nature for laws of thought and, therefore, think that any departure from

<hr />

[7] This is probably a misquotation of Wordsworth's 'Moving about in worlds not realized'. *Intimations of Immortality*, ix, 149. — W.H.

them is a self-contradiction, like a square circle or two and two making five. To think this is to imagine that the normal processes of nature are transparent to the intellect, that we can say why she behaves as she does. For, of course, if we cannot see why a thing is so, then we cannot see any reason why it should not be otherwise. But in fact the actual course of nature is wholly inexplicable. I don't mean that science has not yet explained it, but may do so some day. I mean that the very nature of explanation makes it impossible that we should even explain why matter has the properties it has. For explanation, by its very nature, deals with a world of 'ifs and ands'. Every explanation takes the form 'Since A, there-fore B' or 'If C, then D'. In order to explain any event you have to assume the universe as a going concern, a machine working in a particular way. Since this particular way of working is the basis of all explanation, it can never be itself explained. We can see no reason why it should not have worked a different way.

To say this is not only to remove the suspicion that miracle is self-contradictory, but also to realise how deeply right St Athanasius was when he found an essential likeness between the miracles of Our Lord and the general order of nature. Both are a full stop for the explaining intellect. If the 'natural' means that which can be fitted into a class, that which obeys a norm, that which can be paralleled, that which can be explained by refer-ence to other events, then nature herself as a whole is *not* natural. If a miracle means that which must simply be accepted, the unanswerable actuality which gives no account of itself but simply *is*, then the universe is one great miracle. To direct us to that great miracle is one main object of the earthly acts of Christ: they are, as He Himself said, Signs (Matthew 12:39; 16:4; 24:24, 30; Mark 13:22; 16:17, 20; Luke 21:11, 25). They serve to remind us that the explanations of particular events which we derive *from* the given, the unexplained, the almost wilful character of the actual universe, are not explanations of that character. These Signs do not take us away from reality; they recall us to it – recall us from our dream world of 'ifs and ands' to the stunning actuality of everything that is real. They are focal points at which more reality becomes visible than we ordinarily see at once. I have spoken of how He made miraculous bread and wine and of how, when the Virgin conceived, He had shown Himself the true Genius whom men had ignorantly worshipped long before. It goes deeper than that. Bread and wine were to have an even more sacred significance for Christians and the act of generation was to be the chosen symbol among all mystics for the union of the soul with God. These things are no acci-dents. With Him there are no accidents. When He created the vegetable world He knew already what dreams the annual death and resurrection of the corn would cause to stir in pious Pagan minds, He knew already that He Himself must so die and live again and in what sense, including and far transcending the old religion of the Corn King. He would say 'This is my Body' (Matthew 26:26; Mark 14:22; Luke 22:19; I Corinthians 11:24). *Common* bread, miraculous bread, sacramental bread – these three are distinct, but not to be separated. Divine reality is like a fugue. All His acts are different, but they all rhyme or echo to one another. It is this that makes Christianity so difficult to talk about. Fix your mind on any one story or any one doctrine and it becomes at once a magnet to which truth and glory come rushing from all levels of being. Our featureless panthe-istic unities and glib rationalist distinctions are alike defeated by the seamless, yet ever-varying, texture of reality, the liveness, the elusiveness, the intertwined harmonies of the multi-dimensional fertility of God. But if this is the difficulty, it is also one of the firm grounds of our belief. To think that this was a fable, a product of our own brains as they are a product of matter would be to believe that this vast symphonic splendour had come out of something much smaller and emptier than itself. It is not so. We are nearer to the truth in the vision seen by Julian of Norwich, when Christ appeared to her holding in His hand a little thing like a hazel nut and saying, 'This is all that is created.'[8] And it seemed to her so small and weak that she wondered how it could hold together at all.

[8] *Sixteen Revelations of Divine Love*, ed. Roger Hudleston (London, 1927), ch. 5, p. 9.

DOGMA AND THE UNIVERSE

This essay was originally published in two parts ('Dogma and the Universe' and 'Dogma and Science') in The Guardian *(19 and 26 March 1943). It was reprinted in* Undeceptions *(1971) and* God in the Dock *(1998).*

It is a common reproach against Christianity that its dogmas are unchanging, while human knowledge is in continual growth. Hence, to unbelievers, we seem to be always engaged in the hopeless task of trying to force the new knowledge into moulds which it has outgrown. I think this feeling alienates the outsider much more than any particular discrepancies between this or that doctrine and this or that scientific theory. We may, as we say, 'get over' dozens of isolated 'difficulties', but that does not alter his sense that the endeavour as a whole is doomed to failure and perverse: indeed, the more ingenious, the more perverse. For it seems to him clear that, if our ancestors had known what we know about the universe, Christianity would never have existed at all: and, however we patch and mend, no system of thought which claims to be immutable can, in the long run, adjust itself to our growing knowledge.

That is the position I am going to try to answer. But before I go on to what I regard as the fundamental answer, I would like to clear up certain points about the actual relations between Christian doctrine and the scientific knowledge we already have. That is a different matter from the continual growth of knowledge we imagine, whether rightly or wrongly, in the future and which, as some think, is bound to defeat us in the end.

In one respect, as many Christians have noticed, contemporary science has recently come into line with Christian doctrine, and parted company with the classical forms of materialism. If anything emerges clearly from modern physics, it is that nature is not everlasting. The universe had a beginning, and will have an end. But the great materialistic systems of the past all believed in the eternity, and thence in the self-existence of matter.

As Professor Whittaker said in the Riddell Lectures of 1942, 'It was never possible to oppose seriously the dogma of the Creation except by maintaining that the world has existed from all eternity in more or less its present state.'[1] This fundamental ground for materialism has now been withdrawn. We should not lean too heavily on this, for scientific theories change. But at the moment it appears that the burden of proof rests, not on us, but on those who deny that nature has some cause beyond herself.

In popular thought, however, the origin of the universe has counted (I think) for less than its character – its immense size and its apparent indifference, if not hostility, to human life. And very often this impresses people all the more because it is supposed to be a modern discovery – an excellent example of those things which our ancestors did not know and which, if they had known them, would have prevented the very beginnings of Christianity. Here there is a simple historical falsehood. Ptolemy knew just as well as Eddington[2] that the earth was infinitesimal in comparison with the whole content of space.[3] There is no question here of knowledge having grown until the frame of archaic thought is no longer able to contain it. The real question is why the spatial insignificance of the earth, after being known for centuries, should suddenly in the last century have become an argument against Christianity. I do not know why this has happened; but I am sure it does not mark an increased clarity of thought, for the argument from size is, in my opinion, very feeble.

When the doctor at a post-mortem diagnoses poison, pointing to the state of the dead man's organs, his argument is rational because he has a clear idea of that opposite state in which the organs would have been found if no poison were present. In the same way, if we use the vastness of space and the smallness of earth to disprove the existence of God, we ought to have a clear idea of the sort of universe we should expect if God did exist. But have we? Whatever space may be in itself – and, of course, some moderns think it finite – we certainly perceive it as three-dimensional, and to three-dimensional space we can conceive no boundaries. By the very forms of our perceptions, therefore, we must feel as if we lived somewhere in infinite space. If we discovered no objects in this infinite space except those which are of use to man (our own sun and moon), then this vast emptiness would certainly be used as a strong argument against the existence of God. If we discover other bodies, they must be

---

[1] Sir Edmund Taylor Whittaker, *The Beginning and End of the World*, Riddell Memorial Lectures, Fourteenth Series (Oxford, 1942), p. 40.

[2] Sir Arthur Stanley Eddington (1882–1944).

[3] Ptolemy lived at Alexandria in the second century AD. The reference is to his *Almagest*, Bk. I, ch. 5. — W.H.

habitable or uninhabitable: and the odd thing is that both these hypotheses are used as grounds for rejecting Christianity. If the universe is teeming with life, this, we are told, reduces to absurdity the Christian claim – or what is thought to be the Christian claim – that man is unique, and the Christian doctrine that to this one planet God came down and was incarnate for us men and our salvation. If, on the other hand, the earth is really unique, then that proves that life is only an accidental by-product in the universe, and so again disproves our religion. Really, we are hard to please. We treat God as the police treat a man when he is arrested; whatever He does will be used in evidence against Him. I do not think this is due to our wickedness. I suspect there is something in our very mode of thought which makes it inevitable that we should always be baffled by actual existence, *whatever* character actual existence may have. Perhaps a finite and contingent creature – a creature that might not have existed – will always find it hard to acquiesce in the brute fact that it is, here and now, attached to an actual order of things.

However that may be, it is certain that the whole argument from size rests on the assumption that differences of size ought to coincide with differences of value: for unless they do, there is, of course, no reason why the minute earth and the yet smaller human creatures upon it should not be the most important things in a universe that contains the spiral nebulae. Now, is this assumption rational or emotional? I feel, as well as anyone else, the absurdity of supposing that the galaxy could be of less moment in God's eyes than such an atom as a human being. But I notice that I feel no similar absurdity in supposing that a man of five-feet high may be more important than another man who is five-feet three and a half – nor that a man may matter more than a tree, or a brain more than a leg. In other words, the feeling of absurdity arises only if the differences of size are very great. But where a relation is perceived by reason it holds good universally. If size and value had any real connection, small differences in size would accompany small differences in value as surely as large differences in size accompany large differences in value. But no sane man could suppose that this is so. I don't think the taller man *slightly* more valuable than the shorter one. I don't allow a slight superiority to trees over men, and then neglect it because it is too small to bother about. I perceive, as long as I am dealing with the small differences of size, that they have no connection with value whatsoever. I therefore conclude that the importance attached to the great differences of size is an affair, not of reason but of emotion – of that peculiar emotion which superiorities in size produce only after a certain point of absolute size has been reached.

We are inveterate poets. When a quantity is very great, we cease to regard it as mere quantity. Our imaginations awake. Instead of mere quantity, we now have a quality – the sublime. Unless this were so, the merely arithmetical greatness of the galaxy would be no more impressive than the figures in a telephone directory. It is thus, in a sense, from ourselves that the material universe derives its power to over-awe us. To a mind which did not share our emotions, and lacked our imaginative energies, the argument from size would be sheerly meaningless. Men look on the starry heavens with reverence: monkeys do not. The silence of the eternal spaces terrified Pascal,[4] but it was the greatness of Pascal that enabled them to do so. When we are frightened by the greatness of the universe, we are (almost literally) frightened by our own shadows: for these light years and billions of centuries are mere arithmetic until the shadow of man, the poet, the maker of myth, falls upon them. I do not say we are wrong to tremble at his shadow; it is a shadow of an image of God. But if ever the vastness of matter threatens to overcross our spirits, one must remember that it is matter spiritualized which does so. To puny man, the great nebula in Andromeda owes in a sense its greatness.

And this drives me to say yet again that we are hard to please. If the world in which we found ourselves were not vast and strange enough to give us Pascal's terror, what poor creatures we should be! Being what we are, rational but also animate, amphibians who start from the world of sense and proceed through myth and metaphor to the world of spirit, I do not see how we could have come to know the greatness of God without that hint furnished by the greatness of the material universe. Once again, what sort of universe do we demand? If it were small enough to be cosy, it would not be big enough to be sublime. If it is large enough for us to stretch our spiritual limbs in, it must be large enough to baffle us. Cramped or terrified, we must, in any conceivable world, be one or the other. I prefer terror. I should be suffocated in a universe that I could see to the end of. Have you never, when walking in a wood, turned back deliberately for fear you should come out at the other side and thus make it ever after in your imagination a mere beggarly strip of trees?

I hope you do not think I am suggesting that God made the spiral nebulae solely or chiefly in order to give me the experience of awe and bewilderment. I have not the faintest idea why He made them; on the whole, I think it would be rather surprising if I had. As far as I understand the matter, Christianity is not wedded to an anthropocentric view of the

[4] Blaise Pascal, *Pensées*, No. 206.

universe as a whole. The first chapters of Genesis, no doubt, give the story of creation in the form of a folk-tale – a fact recognised as early as the time of St Jerome – and if you take them alone you might get that impression. But it is not confirmed by the Bible as a whole. There are few places in literature where we are more sternly warned against making man the measure of all things than in the Book of Job: 'Canst thou draw out leviathan with an hook? Will he make a covenant with thee? Wilt thou take him for a servant? Shall not one be cast down even at the sight of him?' (Job 41:1, 4, 9). In St Paul, the powers of the skies seem usually to be hostile to man. It is, of course, the essence of Christianity that God loves man and for his sake became man and died. But that does not prove that man is the sole end of Nature. In the parable (Matthew 18:12; Luke 15:4), it was the one lost sheep that the shepherd went in search of: it was not the only sheep in the flock, and we are not told that it was the most valuable – save in so far as the most desperately in need has, while the need lasts, a peculiar value in the eyes of Love. The doctrine of the Incarnation would conflict with what we know of this vast universe only if we knew also that there were other rational species in it who had, like us, fallen, and who needed redemption in the same mode, and that they had not been vouchsafed it. But we know none of these things. It may be full of life that needs no redemption. It may be full of life that has been redeemed. It may be full of things quite other than life which satisfy the Divine Wisdom in fashions one cannot conceive. We are in no position to draw up maps of God's psychology, and prescribe limits to His interests. We would not do so even for a man whom we knew to be greater than ourselves. The doctrine that God is Love and that He delights in men, are positive doctrines, not limiting doctrines. He is not less than this. What more He may be, we do not know; we know only that He must be more than we can conceive. It is to be expected that His creation should be, in the main, unintelligible to us.

Christians themselves have been much to blame for the misunderstanding on these matters. They have a bad habit of talking as if revelation existed to gratify curiosity by illuminating all creation so that it becomes self-explanatory and all questions are answered. But revelation appears to me to be purely practical, to be addressed to the particular animal, Fallen Man, for the relief of his urgent necessities – not to the spirit of inquiry in man for the gratification of his liberal curiosity. We know that God has visited and redeemed His people, and that tells us just as much about the general character of the creation as a dose given to one sick hen on a big farm tells us about the general character of farming in England. What we must do, which road we must take to the fountain of life, we know, and none who has seriously followed the directions complains that he has been deceived. But whether there are other creatures like ourselves, and how they are dealt with: whether inanimate matter exists only to serve living creatures or for some other reason: whether the immensity of space is a means to some end, or an illusion, or simply the natural mode in which infinite energy might be expected to create – on all these points I think we are left to our own speculations.

No. It is not Christianity which need fear the giant universe. It is those systems which place the whole meaning of existence in biological or social evolution on our own planet. It is the creative evolutionist, the Bergsonian or Shavian, or the Communist, who should tremble when he looks up at the night sky. For he really is committed to a sinking ship. He really is attempting to ignore the discovered nature of things, as though by concentrating on the possibly upward trend in a single planet he could make himself forget the inevitable downward trend in the universe as a whole, the trend to low temperatures and irrevocable disorganisation. For entropy is the real cosmic wave, and evolution only a momentary tellurian ripple within it.

On these grounds, then, I submit that we Christians have as little to fear as anyone from the knowledge actually acquired. But, as I said at the beginning, that is not the fundamental answer. The endless fluctuations of scientific theory which seem today so much friendlier to us than in the last century may turn against us tomorrow. The basic answer lies elsewhere.

Let me remind you of the question we are trying to answer. It is this: How can an unchanging system survive the continual increase of knowledge? Now, in certain cases we know very well how it can. A mature scholar reading a great passage in Plato, and taking in at one glance the metaphysics, the literary beauty, and the place of both in the history of Europe, is in a very different position from a boy learning the Greek alphabet. Yet through that unchanging system of the alphabet all this vast mental and emotional activity is operating. It has not been broken by the new knowledge. It is not outworn. If it changed, all would be chaos. A great Christian statesman, considering the morality of a measure which will affect millions of lives, and which involves economic, geographical and political considerations of the utmost complexity, is in a different position from a boy first learning that one must not cheat or tell lies, or hurt innocent people. But only in so far as that first knowledge of the great moral platitudes survives unimpaired in the statesman will his deliberation be moral at all. If that goes, then there has been no progress, but only mere change. For change is not progress unless the core remains unchanged. A small oak grows into a big oak; if it became a beech, that would not be growth, but mere change. And thirdly, there is a great difference between counting apples and arriving at the mathematical formulae of modern physics. But the multiplication table is used in both and does not grow out of date.

In other words, wherever there is real progress in knowledge, there is some knowledge that is not superseded. Indeed, the very possibility of progress demands that there should be an unchanging element. New bottles for new wine, by all means: but not new palates, throats and stomachs, or it would not be, for us, 'wine' at all. I take it we should all agree to find this sort of unchanging element in the simple rules of mathematics. I would add to these the primary principles of morality. And I would also add the fundamental doctrines of Christianity. To put it in rather more technical language, I claim that the positive historical statements made by Christianity have the power, elsewhere found chiefly in formal principles, of receiving, without intrinsic change, the increasing complexity of meaning which increasing knowledge puts into them.

For example, it may be true (though I don't for a moment suppose it is) that when the Nicene Creed said 'He came down from Heaven', the writers had in mind a local movement from a local heaven to the surface of the earth – like a parachute descent. Others since may have dismissed the idea of a spatial heaven altogether. But neither the significance nor the credulity of what is asserted seems to be in the least affected by the change. On either view, the thing is miraculous: on either view, the mental images which attend the act of belief are inessential. When a Central African convert and a Harley Street specialist both affirm that Christ rose from the dead, there is, no doubt, a very great difference between their thoughts. To one, the simple picture of a dead body getting up is sufficient; the other may think of a whole series of biochemical and even physical processes beginning to work backwards. The Doctor knows that, in his experience, they never have worked backwards; but the Negro knows that dead bodies don't get up and walk. Both are faced with miracle, and both know it. If both think miracle impossible, the only difference is that the Doctor will expound the impossibility in much greater detail, will give an elaborate gloss on the simple statement that dead men don't walk about. If both believe, all the Doctor says will merely analyse and explicate the words 'He rose.' When the author of Genesis says that God made man in His own image, he may have pictured a vaguely corporeal God making man as a child makes a figure out of plasticine. A modern Christian philosopher may think of a process lasting from the first creation of matter to the final appearance on this planet of an organism fit to receive spiritual as well as biological life. But both mean essentially the same thing. Both are denying the same thing – the doctrine that matter by some blind power inherent in itself has produced spirituality.

Does this mean that Christians on different levels of general education conceal radically different beliefs under an identical form of words? Certainly not. For what they agree on is the substance, and what they differ about is the shadow. When one imagines his God seated in a local heaven above a flat earth, where another sees God and creation in terms of Professor Whitehead's philosophy,[5] this difference touches precisely what does not matter. Perhaps this seems to you an exaggeration. But is it? As regards material reality, we are now being forced to the conclusion that we know nothing about it save its mathematics. The tangible beach and pebbles of our first calculators, the imaginable atoms of Democritus, the plain man's picture of space, turn out to be the shadow: numbers are the substance of our knowledge, the sole liaison between mind and things. What nature is in herself evades us; what seem to naive perception to be the evident things about her, turn out to be the most phantasmal. It is something the same with our knowledge of spiritual reality. What God is in Himself, how He is to be conceived by philosophers, retreats continually from our knowledge. The elaborate world-pictures which accompany religion and which look each so solid while they last, turn out to be only shadows. It is religion itself – prayer and sacrament and repentance and adoration – which is here, in the long run, our sole avenue to the real. Like mathematics, religion can grow from within, or decay. The Jew knows more than the Pagan, the Christian more than the Jew, the modern vaguely religious man less than any of the three. But, like mathematics, it remains simply itself, capable of being applied to any new theory of the material universe and outmoded by none.

When any man comes into the presence of God he will find, whether he wishes it or not, that all those things which seemed to make him so different from the men of other times, or even from his earlier self, have fallen off him. He is back where he always was, where every man always is. *Eadem sunt omnia semper* (Everything is always the same). Do not let us deceive ourselves. No possible complexity which we can give to our picture of the universe can hide us from God: there is no copse, no forest, no jungle thick enough to provide cover. We read in Revelation (20:11) of Him that sat on the throne 'from whose face the earth and the heaven fled

[5] Alfred North Whitehead (1861–1947).

away'. It may happen to any of us at any moment. In the twinkling of an eye, in a time too small to be measured, and in any place, all that seems to divide us from God can flee away, vanish, leaving us naked before Him, like the first man, like the only man, as if nothing but He and I existed. And since that contact cannot be avoided for long, and since it means either bliss or horror, the business of life is to learn to like it. That is the first and great commandment.

[15]
'HORRID RED THINGS'

First published in The Church of England Newspaper, *Volume LI (6 October 1944) and reproduced in* Undeceptions *(1971) and* Compelling Reason *(1998).*

Many theologians and some scientists are now ready to proclaim that the nineteenth-century 'conflict between science and religion' is over and done with. But even if this is true, it is a truth known only to real theologians and real scientists – that is, to a few highly educated men. To the man in the street the conflict is still perfectly real, and in his mind it takes a form which the learned hardly dream of.

The ordinary man is not thinking of particular dogmas and particular scientific discoveries. What troubles him is an all-pervading difference of atmosphere between what he believes Christianity to be and that general picture of the universe which he has picked up from living in a scientific age. He gathers from the Creed that God has a 'Son' (just as if God were a god, like Odin or Jupiter): that this Son 'came down' (like a parachutist) from 'Heaven', first to earth and later to some land of the dead situated beneath the earth's surface: that, still later, He ascended into the sky and took His seat in a decorated chair placed a little to the right of His Father's throne. The whole thing seems to imply a local and material heaven – a palace in the stratosphere – a flat earth and all the rest of those archaic misconceptions.

The ordinary man is well aware that we should deny all the beliefs he attributes to us and interpret our Creed in a different sense. But this by no means satisfies him. 'No doubt,' he thinks, 'once those articles of belief are there, they can be allegorised or spiritualised away to any extent you please. But is it not plain that they would never have been there at all if the first generation of Christians had had any notion of what the real universe is like? A historian who has based his work on the misreading of a document, may afterwards (when his mistake had been exposed) exercise great ingenuity in showing that his account of a certain battle can still be reconciled with what the document records. But the point is that none of these ingenious explanations would ever have come into existence if he had read his documents correctly at the outset. They are therefore really a waste of labour; it would be manlier of him to admit his mistake and begin over again.'

I think there are two things that Christians must do if they wish to convince this 'ordinary' modern man. In the first place, they must make it quite clear that what will remain of the Creed after all their explanations and reinterpretations will still be something quite unambiguously super-natural, miraculous, and shocking. We may not believe in a flat earth and a sky-palace. But we must insist from the beginning that we believe, as firmly as any savage or theosophist, in a spirit-world which can, and does, invade the natural or phenomenal universe. For the plain man suspects that when we start explaining, we are going to explain away: that we have mythology for our ignorant hearers and are ready, when cornered by educated hearers, to reduce it to innocuous moral platitudes which no one ever dreamed of denying. And there are theologians who justify this suspicion. From them we must part company absolutely. If nothing remains except what would be equally well stated without Christian formulae, then the honest thing is to admit that Christianity is untrue and to begin over again without it.

In the second place, we must try to teach something about the difference between thinking and imagining. It is, of course, a historical error to sup-pose that all, or even most, early Christians believed in the sky-palace in the same sense in which we believe in the solar system. Anthropomorphism was condemned by the Church as soon as the question was explicitly before her. But some early Christians may have done this; and probably thousands never thought of their faith without anthropomorphic imagery. That is why we must distinguish the core of belief from the attendant imagining.

When I think of London I always see a picture of Euston Station. But I do not believe that London *is* Euston Station. That is a simple case, because there the thinker *knows* the imagery to be false. Now let us take a more complex one. I once heard a lady tell her daughter that if you ate too many aspirin tablets you would die. 'But why?' asked the child. 'If you squash them you don't find any horrid red things inside them.' Obviously, when this child thought of poison she not only had an atten-dant image of 'horrid red things', but she actually believed that poison was red. And this is an error. But how far does it invalidate her thinking about poison? She learned that an overdose of aspirin would kill you; her belief was true. She knew, within limits, which of the substances in her mother's house were poisonous. If I, staying in the house, had raised a glass of what looked like water to my lips, and the child had said, 'Don't drink that. Mummie says it's poisonous,' I should have been foolish to disregard the warning on the ground that 'This child has an archaic and mythological idea of poison as horrid red things.'

There is thus a distinction not only between thought and imagination in general, but even between thought and those images which the thinker (falsely) believes to be true. When the child learned later that poison is not always red, she would not have felt that anything essential in her beliefs about poison had been altered. She would still know, as she had always known, that poison is what kills you if you swallow it. That is the essence of poison. The erroneous beliefs about colour drop away without affecting it.

In the same way an early peasant Christian might have thought that Christ's sitting at the right hand of the Father really implied two chairs of state, in a certain spatial relation, inside a sky-palace. But if the same man afterwards received a philosophical education and discovered that God has no body, parts, or passions, and therefore neither a right hand nor a palace, he would not have felt that the essentials of his belief had been altered. What had mattered to him, even in the days of his simplicity, had not been supposed details about celestial furniture. It had been the assurance that the once crucified Master was now the supreme Agent of the unimaginable Power on whom the whole universe depends. And he would recognise that in this he had never been deceived.

The critic may still ask us why the imagery – which we admit to be untrue – should be used at all. But he has not noticed that any language we attempt to substitute for it would involve imagery that is open to all the same objections. To say that God 'enters' the natural order involves just as much spatial imagery as to say that He 'comes down'; one has simply substituted horizontal (or undefined) for vertical movement. To say that he is 're-absorbed' into the Noumenal is better than to say He 'ascended' into Heaven, only if the picture of something dissolving in warm fluid, or being sucked into a throat, is less misleading than the picture of a bird, or a balloon, going up. All language, except about objects of sense, is metaphorical through and through. To call God a 'Force' (that is, something like a wind or a dynamo) is as metaphorical as to call Him a Father or a King. On such matters we can make our language more polysyllabic and duller: we cannot make it more literal. The difficulty is not peculiar to theologians. Scientists, poets, psychoanalysts and metaphysicians are all in the same boat: 'Man's reason is in such deep insolvency to sense'.[1]

---

[1] Robert Bridges, *The Testament of Beauty*, Book I, line 57.

Where, then, do we draw the line between explaining and 'explaining away'? I do not think there is much difficulty. All that concerns the un-incarnate activities of God – His operation on that plane of being where sense cannot enter – must be taken along with imagery which we know to be, in the literal sense, untrue. But there can be no defence for applying the same treatment to the miracles of the Incarnate God. They are recorded as events on this earth which affected human senses. They are the sort of thing we can describe literally. If Christ turned water into wine, and we had been present, we could have seen, smelled, and tasted. The story that He did so is not of the same order as His 'sitting at the right hand of the Father'. It is either fact, or legend, or lie. You must take it or leave it.

[16]
RELIGION: REALITY OR SUBSTITUTE?

Most of this essay was originally printed in World Dominion, *Volume XIX (September–October 1943), but paragraph 4 and part of paragraph 9 were added some years later. It was published in* Christian Reflections *by Geoffrey Bles in 1967.*

Hebrews 10:1: 'The Law having a shadow of good things to come.'

We are all quite familiar with this idea, that the old Jewish priesthood was a mere symbol and that Christianity is the reality which it symbolised. It is important, however, to notice what an astonishing, even impudent, claim it must have seemed as long as the temple at Jerusalem was still standing. In the temple you saw real sacrifice being offered – real animals really had their throats cut and their actual flesh and blood were used in the ritual; in Christian assemblies a ceremony with wine and bits of bread was conducted. It must have been all but impossible to resist the conviction that the Jewish service was the reality and the Christian one a mere substitute – wine is so obviously a substitute for blood and bread for flesh! Yet the Christians had the audacity to maintain that it was the other way round – that their innocuous little ritual meal in private houses was the real sacrifice and that all the slaughtering, incense, music, and shouting in the temple was merely the shadow.

In considering this we touch upon the very central region where all doubts about our religion live. Things do look so very much as if our whole faith were a substitute for the real well-being we have failed to achieve on earth. It seems so very likely that our rejection of the World is only the disappointed fox's attempt to convince himself that unattainable grapes are sour. After all, we do not usually think much about the next world till our hopes in this have been pretty well flattened out – and when they are revived we not infrequently abandon our religion. And does not all that talk of celestial love come chiefly from monks and nuns, starved celibates consoling themselves with a compensatory hallucination? And the worship of the Christ child – does it not also come to us from centuries of lonely old maids? There is no good ignoring these disquieting thoughts. Let us admit from the outset that the psychologists have a good *prima facie* case. The theory that our religion is a substitute has a great deal of plausibility.

Faced with this, the first thing I do is to try to find out what I know about substitutes, and the realities for which they are substituted, in general. And I find that I don't know so much as I thought I did. Until I considered the matter I had a sort of impression that one could recognise the difference by mere inspection if one was really honest – that the substitute would somehow betray itself by the mere taste, would ring false. And this impression was, in fact, one of the sources from which the doubts I mentioned were drawing their strength. What made it seem so likely that religion was a substitute was not any general philosophical argument about the existence of God, but rather the experienced fact that for the most of us at most times the spiritual life *tasted* so thin, or insipid, compared with the natural. And I thought that was just what a substitute might be expected to taste like. But after reflection, I discovered that this was not only not an obvious truth but was even contradicted by some of my own experience.

I once knew two bad boys who smoked secretly and stole their father's tobacco. Their father had cigarettes, which he really smoked himself, and cigars – a great many cigars – which he kept for visitors. The boys liked cigarettes very much better than cigars. But every now and then there would come a day when their father had let his supply of cigarettes get so low that the boys thought the theft of even one or two would inevitably be detected. On such days they took cigars instead; and one of them would say to the other: 'I'm afraid we'll have to put up with cigars today', and the other would reply: 'Well, I suppose a cigar is better than nothing.' This is not a fable I'm inventing, but a historical fact that I can vouch for. And here, surely, we have a very good instance of the value to be attached to anyone's first hasty ideas about a reality and a substitute. To these children, a cigar was simply an inferior substitute for a cigarette, a *pis aller*. And, of course, the boys, at that stage, were quite right about their own feelings: but they would have become ludicrously wrong if they had therefore inferred that cigars, in their own nature, were merely a kind of makeshift cigarette. On that question their own childish experience offered them no evidence: they had to learn the answer from quite different sources, or else to wait until their palates were grown up. And may I add the important moral of the story? One of these boys has been permanently punished by a lifelong inability to appreciate cigars.

Here is another example. When I was a boy, gramophone records were not nearly so good as they are now. In the old recording of an orchestral piece you could hardly hear the separate instrument at all, but only a single undifferentiated sound. That was the sort of music I grew up on. And when, at a somewhat later age, I began to hear real orchestras, I was actually disappointed with them, just because you didn't get that single sound. What one got in a concert room seemed to me to lack the unity I had grown to expect, to be not an orchestra but merely a number of individual musicians on the same platform. In fact, I felt it 'wasn't the Real Thing'. This is an even better example than the former one. For a gramophone record is precisely a substitute, and an orchestra the reality. But owing to my musical miseducation the reality appeared to be a substitute and the substitute a reality.

'Substitutes' suggest wartime feeding. Well, there too I have an example. During the last war, as at present, we had to eat margarine instead of butter. When I began doing so I couldn't tell the difference between them. For the first week or so, I would have said, 'you may call the margarine a substitute if you like, but it is actually just as good as the real thing'. But by the end of the war I could never again have mistaken one for the other and I never wanted to see margarine again. This is different from the previous examples because here I started knowing which, in fact, was the substitute. But the point is that mere immediate taste did not at first confirm this bit of knowledge. It was only after long experience that the margarine revealed itself to my senses as the inferior.

But enough of my own experiences. I will turn to a better man, to Milton, and to that scene which I used to think the most grotesque, but now think one of the most profound, in *Paradise Lost*. I mean the part where Eve, a few minutes after her creation, sees herself in a pool of water, and falls in love with her own reflection. Then God makes her look up, and she sees Adam. But the interesting point is that the first sight of Adam is a disappointment; he is a much less immediately attractive object than herself. Being divinely guided, Eve gets over this difficult *pons asinorum* and lives to learn that being in love with Adam is more inexhaustible, more fruitful, and even better fun, than being in love with herself. But if she had been a sinner, like ourselves, she would not have made the transition so easily; she also would have passed through the stage of finding the real, external lover a second best. Indeed the region from which this example is drawn illustrates my theme better than almost any other. To the pervert, normal love, when it does not appear simply repulsive, appears at best a mere milk and water substitute for that ghastly world of impossible fantasies which have become to him the 'real thing'. But every department of life furnishes us with examples. The ears that are delighted with jazz cannot quite believe that 'classical music' is anything but a sort of 'vegetarian jazz' (to quote my friend Barfield), and great literature seems to vulgar taste at first a pale reflection of the 'thrillers' or 'triangle dramas' which it prefers.

From all this I want to draw the following conclusion. Introspection is of no use at all in deciding which of two experiences is a substitute or a second best. At a certain stage all those sensations which we should expect to find accompanying the proper satisfaction of a fundamental need will actually accompany the substitute, and *vice versa*. And I want to insist that if we are once convinced of this principle, we should then hold it quite unflinchingly from this moment to the end of our lives. When a witness has once been proved unreliable, turn him out of the court. It is mere waste of time to go sneaking back to his evidence and thinking 'After all' and 'He *did* say'. If immediate feeling has shown itself quite worthless in this matter, then let us never listen to immediate feeling again. In our criterion between a real, and a substituted, satisfaction must be sought somewhere else, then in God's name, seek it somewhere else.

When I say 'somewhere else' I am not yet speaking of Faith or a supernatural gift. What I mean can be shown by an example. If those two bad boys had really wanted to find out whether their view of cigars and cigarettes were correct, there were various things they might have done. They might have asked a grown-up, who would have told them that cigars were actually regarded as the greater luxury of the two, and thus had their error corrected by authority. Or they might have found out by their own researches – that is by buying their smokes instead of stealing them – that cigars were more expensive than cigarettes and thence inferred that they could not in reality be a mere substitute for them. This would have been correction by reason. Finally, they might have practised obedience, honesty, and truthfulness and waited till an age at which they were allowed to smoke – in which case they would have arrived at a more reasonable view about these two ways of preparing tobacco by experience. Authority, reason, experience; on these three, mixed in varying proportions, all our knowledge depends. The authority of many wise men in many different times and places forbids me to regard the spiritual world as an illusion. My reason, showing me the apparently insoluble difficulties of materialism and proving that the hypothesis of a spiritual world covers far more of the facts with far fewer assumptions, forbids me again. My experience even of such feeble attempts as I have made to live the spiritual life does not lead to the results which the pursuit of an illusion ordinarily leads to, and therefore forbids me yet again. I am not now saying that no one's reason and no one's experience produce different results. I am only trying to put the whole problem the right way round, to make it clear that the value given to the testimony of any feeling must depend on our whole philosophy, not our whole philosophy on a feeling. If those who deny the spiritual world prove their case on general grounds, then, indeed, it will follow that our apparently spiritual experiences *must* be an illusion; but equally, if we are right, it will follow that they are the prime reality and that our natural experiences are a second best. And let us note that whichever view we embrace, mere feeling will continue to assault our conviction. Just as the Christian has his moments when the clamour of this visible and audible world is so persistent and the whisper of the spiritual world so faint that faith and reason can hardly stick to their guns, as I well remember, the atheist too has his moments of shuddering misgiving, of an all but irresistible suspicion that old tales may after all be true, that something or someone from outside may at any moment break into his neat, explicable, mechanical universe. Believe in God and you will have to face hours when it seems *obvious* that this material world is the only reality: disbelieve in Him and you must face hours when this material world seems to shout at you that it is *not* all. No conviction, religious or irreligious, will, of itself, end once and for all this fifth-columnist in the soul. Only the practice of Faith resulting in the habit of Faith will gradually do that.

Have we now got to a position from which we can talk about Faith without being misunderstood? For in general we are shy of speaking plain about Faith as a virtue. It looks so like praising an intention to believe what you want to believe in the face of evidence to the contrary: the American in the old story defined Faith as 'the power of believing what we know to be untrue'. Now I define Faith as the power of continuing to believe what we once honestly thought to be true until cogent reasons for honestly changing our minds are brought before us. The difficulty of such continuing to believe is constantly ignored or misunderstood in discussions of this subject. It is always assumed that the difficulties of faith are intellectual difficulties, that a man who has once accepted a certain proposition will automatically go on believing it till real grounds for disbelief occur. Nothing could be more superficial. How many of the freshmen who come up to Oxford from religious homes and lose their Christianity in the first year have been honestly *argued* out of it? How many of our own sudden temporary losses of faith have a rational basis which would stand examination for a moment? I don't know how it is with others, but I find that mere change of scene always has a tendency to decrease my faith at first – God is less credible when I pray in a hotel bedroom than when I am in College. The society of unbelievers makes Faith harder even when they are people whose opinions, on any other subject, are known to be worthless.

These irrational fluctuations in belief are not peculiar to religious belief. They are happening about all our beliefs all day long. Haven't you noticed it with our thoughts about the war? Some days, of course, there is really good or really bad news, which gives us rational grounds for increased optimism or pessimism. But everyone must have experienced days in which we are caught up in a great wave of confidence or down into a trough of anxiety though there are no new grounds either for the one or the other. Of course, once the mood is on us, we *find* reasons soon enough. We say that we've been 'thinking it over': but it is pretty plain that the mood has created the reasons and not *vice versa*. But there are examples closer to the Christian problem even than these. There are things, say in learning to swim or to climb, which look dangerous and aren't. Your instructor tells you it's safe. You have good reason from past experience to trust him. Perhaps you can even see for yourself, by your own reason, that it is safe. But the crucial question is, will you be able to go on believing this when you actually see the cliff edge below you or actually feel yourself unsupported in the water? You will have no *rational* grounds for disbelieving. It is your senses and your imagination that are going to attack belief. Here, as in the New Testament, the conflict is not between faith and sight. We can face things which we *know* to be dangerous if they don't look or sound too dangerous; our real trouble is often with things we *know* to be safe but which look dreadful. Our faith in Christ wavers not so much when real arguments come against it as when it *looks* improbable – when the whole world takes on that desolate *look* which really tells us much more about the state of our passions and even our digestion than about reality.

When we exhort people to Faith as a virtue, to the settled intention of continuing to believe certain things, we are not exhorting them to fight against reason. The intention of continuing to believe is required because, though Reason is divine, human reasoners are not. When once passion takes part in the game, the human reason, unassisted by Grace, has about as much chance of retaining its hold on truths already gained as a snowflake has of retaining its consistency in the mouth of a blast furnace. The sort of arguments against Christianity which our reason can be persuaded to accept at the moment of yielding to temptation are often preposterous. Reason may win truths; without Faith she will retain them just so long as Satan pleases. There is nothing we cannot be made to believe or disbelieve. If we wish to be rational, not now and then, but constantly, we must pray for the gift of Faith, for the power to go on believing not in the teeth of reason but in the teeth of lust and terror and jealousy and boredom and indifference that which reason, authority, or experience, or all three, have once delivered to us for truth. And the answer to that prayer, will, perhaps, surprise us when it comes. For I am not sure, after all, whether one of the causes of our weak faith is not a secret wish that our faith should *not* be very strong. Is there some reservation in our minds? Some fear of what it might be like if our religion became *quite* real? I hope not. God help us all, and forgive us.

MYTH BECAME FACT

This essay first appeared in World Dominion, *Volume XXII (September–October 1944) and was reproduced in* Undeceptions *(1971) and* God in the Dock *(1998).*

My friend Corineus has advanced the charge that none of us are in fact Christians at all. According to him historic Christianity is something so barbarous that no modern man can really believe it: the moderns who claim to do so are in fact believing a modern system of thought which retains the vocabulary of Christianity and exploits the emotions inherited from it while quietly dropping its essential doctrines. Corineus compared modern Christianity with the modern English monarchy: the forms of kingship have been retained, but the reality has been abandoned.

All this I believe to be false, except of a few 'modernist' theologians who, by God's grace, become fewer every day. But for the moment let us assume that Corineus is right. Let us pretend, for purposes of argument, that *all* who now call themselves Christians have abandoned the historic doctrines. Let us suppose that modern 'Christianity' reveals a system of names, rituals, formulae and metaphors which persists although the thoughts behind it have changed. Corineus ought to be able to *explain* the persistence.

Why, on his view, do all these educated and enlightened pseudo-Christians insist on expressing their deepest thoughts in terms of an archaic mythology which must hamper and embarrass them at every turn? Why do they refuse to cut the umbilical cord which binds the living and flourishing child to its moribund mother? For, if Corineus is right, it should be a great relief to them to do so. Yet the odd thing is that even those who seem most embarrassed by the sediment of 'barbaric' Christianity in their thought become suddenly obstinate when you ask them to get rid of it altogether. They will strain the cord almost to breaking point, but they refuse to cut it. Sometimes they will take every step except the last one.

If all who professed Christianity were clergymen, it would be easy (though uncharitable) to reply that their livelihood depends on *not* taking that last step. Yet even if this were the true cause of their behaviour, even if all clergymen are intellectual prostitutes who preach for pay – and usually starvation pay – what they secretly believe to be false, surely so widespread a darkening of conscience among thousands of men not otherwise known to be criminal, itself demands explanation? And of course the profession of Christianity is not confined to the clergy. It is professed by millions of lay men and women who earn thereby contempt, unpopularity, suspicion, and the hostility of their own families. How does this come to happen?

Obstinacies of this sort are interesting. 'Why not cut the cord?' asks Corineus. 'Everything would be much easier if you would free your thought from this vestigial mythology.' To be sure: far easier. Life would be far easier for the mother of an invalid child if she put it into an Institution and adopted someone else's healthy baby instead. Life would be far easier to many a man if he abandoned the woman he has actually fallen in love with and married someone else because she is more suitable. The only defect of the healthy baby and the suitable woman is that they leave out the patient's only reason for bothering about a child or wife at all. 'Would not conversation be much more rational than dancing?' said Jane Austen's Miss Bingley. 'Much more rational,' replied Mr Bingley, 'but much less like a ball.'[1]

In the same way, it would be much more rational to abolish the English monarchy. But how if, by doing so, you leave out the one element in our State which matters most? How if the monarchy is the channel through which all the *vital* elements of citizenship – loyalty, the consecration of secular life, the hierarchical principle, splendour, ceremony, continuity – still trickle down to irrigate the dust-bowl of modern economic Statecraft?

The real answer of even the most 'modernist' Christianity to Corineus is the same. Even assuming (which I most constantly deny) that the doctrines of historic Christianity are merely mythical, it is the myth which is the vital and nourishing element in the whole concern. Corineus wants us to move with the times. Now, we know where times move. They move *away*. But in religion we find something that does not move away. It is what Corineus calls the myth, that abides; it is what he calls the modern and living thought that moves away. Not only the thought

[1] *Pride and Prejudice*, ch. 11.

of theologians, but the thought of anti-theologians. Where are the predecessors of Corineus? Where is the epicureanism of Lucretius,[2] the pagan
revival of Julian the Apostate?[3] Where are the Gnostics, where is the
monism of Averroës,[4] the deism of Voltaire, the dogmatic materialism of
the great Victorians? They have moved with the times. But the thing they
were all attacking remains: Corineus finds it still there to attack. The
myth (to speak his language) has outlived the thoughts of all its defenders
and of all its adversaries. It is the myth that gives life. Those elements even
in modernist Christianity which Corineus regards as vestigial, are the
substance: what he takes for the 'real modern belief' is the shadow.

To explain this we must look a little closer at myth in general, and at this
myth in particular. Human intellect is incurably abstract. Pure mathematics is the type of successful thought. Yet the only realities we experience
are concrete – this pain, this pleasure, this dog, this man. While we are
loving the man, bearing the pain, enjoying the pleasure, we are not intellectually apprehending Pleasure, Pain or Personality. When we begin to
do so, on the other hand, the concrete realities sink to the level of mere
instances or examples: we are no longer dealing with them, but with that
which they exemplify. This is our dilemma – either to taste and not to
know or to know and not to taste – or, more strictly, to lack one kind of
knowledge because we are in an experience or to lack another kind because
we are outside it. As thinkers we are cut off from what we think about;
as tasting, touching, willing, loving, hating, we do not clearly understand.
The more lucidly we think, the more we are cut off: the more deeply we
enter into reality, the less we can think. You cannot *study* Pleasure in the
moment of the nuptial embrace, nor repentance while repenting, nor
analyse the nature of humour while roaring with laughter. But when else
can you really know these things? 'If only my toothache would stop, I
could write another chapter about Pain.' But once it stops, what do I know
about pain?

Of this tragic dilemma myth is the partial solution. In the enjoyment
of a great myth we come nearest to experiencing as a concrete what can
otherwise be understood only as an abstraction. At this moment, for
example, I am trying to understand something very abstract indeed – the
fading, vanishing of tasted reality as we try to grasp it with the discursive
reason. Probably I have made heavy weather of it. But if I remind you,

[2] Titus Lucretius Carus (c. 99–55 BC) the Roman poet.
[3] Roman emperor AD 361–3.
[4] Averroës (1126–98) of Cordova, believed that only one intellect exists for the whole human race in
  which every individual participates, to the exclusion of personal immortality.

instead, of Orpheus and Eurydice, how he was suffered to lead her by the hand but, when he turned round to look at her, she disappeared, what was merely a principle becomes imaginable. You may reply that you never till this moment attached that 'meaning' to that myth. Of course not. You are not looking for an abstract 'meaning' at all. If that was what you were doing the myth would be for you no true myth but a mere allegory. You were not knowing, but tasting; but what you were tasting turns out to be a universal principle. The moment we *state* this principle, we are admittedly back in the world of abstraction. It is only while receiving the myth as a story that you experience the principle concretely.

When we translate we get abstraction – or rather, dozens of abstractions. What flows into you from the myth is not truth but reality (truth is always *about* something, but reality is that *about which* truth is), and, therefore, every myth becomes the father of innumerable truths on the abstract level. Myth is the mountain whence all the different streams arise which become truths down here in the valley; *in hac valle abstractionis*.[5] Or, if you prefer, myth is the isthmus which connects the peninsular world of thought with that vast continent we really belong to. It is not, like truth, abstract; nor is it, like direct experience, bound to the particular.

Now as myth transcends thought, Incarnation transcends myth. The heart of Christianity is a myth which is also a fact. The old myth of the Dying God, *without ceasing to be myth*, comes down from the heaven of legend and imagination to the earth of history. It *happens* – at a particular date, in a particular place, followed by definable historical consequences. We pass from a Balder or an Osiris, dying nobody knows when or where, to a historical Person crucified (it is all in order) *under Pontius Pilate*. By becoming fact it does not cease to be myth: that is the miracle. I suspect that men have sometimes derived more spiritual sustenance from myths they did not believe than from the religion they professed. To be truly Christian we must both assent to the historical fact and also receive the myth (fact though it has become) with the same imaginative embrace which we accord to all myths. The one is hardly more necessary than the other.

A man who disbelieved the Christian story as fact but continually fed on it as myth would, perhaps, be more spiritually alive than one who assented and did not think much about it. The modernist – the extreme modernist, infidel in all but name – need not be called a fool or hypocrite because he obstinately retains, even in the midst of his intellectual atheism, the language, rites, sacraments, and story of the Christians. The poor man

---

[5] In this valley of separation.

may be clinging (with a wisdom he himself by no means understands) to that which is his life. It would have been better that Loisy[6] should have remained a Christian: it would not necessarily have been better that he should have purged his thought of vestigial Christianity.

Those who do not know that this great myth became fact when the Virgin conceived are, indeed, to be pitied. But Christians also need to be reminded – we may thank Corineus for reminding us – that what became fact was a myth, that it carries with it into the world of fact all the properties of a myth. God is more than a god, not less; Christ is more than Balder, not less. We must not be ashamed of the mythical radiance resting on our theology. We must not be nervous about 'parallels' and 'Pagan Christs': they *ought* to be there – it would be a stumbling block if they weren't. We must not, in false spirituality, withhold our imaginative welcome. If God chooses to be mythopoeic – and is not the sky itself a myth? – shall we refuse to be *mythopathic*? For this is the marriage of heaven and earth: Perfect Myth and Perfect Fact: claiming not only our love and our obedience, but also our wonder and delight, addressed to the savage, the child, and the poet in each one of us no less than to the moralist, the scholar, and the philosopher.

[6] Alfred Loisy (1857–1940), a French theologian and founder of the Modernist movement.

[18]

RELIGION AND SCIENCE

First published in The Coventry Evening Telegraph *(3 January 1945)*
and reproduced in Undeceptions *(1971) and* God in the Dock *(1998)*.

'Miracles,' said my friend. 'Oh, come. Science has knocked the bottom out of all that. We know now that Nature is governed by fixed laws.'

'Didn't people always know that?' said I.

'Good Lord, no,' said he. 'For instance, take a story like the Virgin Birth. We know now that such a thing couldn't happen. We know there *must* be a male spermatozoon.'

'But look here,' said I. 'St Joseph –'

'Who's he?' asked my friend.

'He was the husband of the Virgin Mary. If you'll read the story in the Bible you'll find that when he saw his fiancée was going to have a baby he decided to cry off the marriage. Why did he do that?'

'Wouldn't most men?'

'Any man would,' said I, 'provided he knew the laws of nature – in other words, provided he knew that a girl doesn't ordinarily have a baby unless she's been sleeping with a man. But according to your theory people in the old days didn't know that nature was governed by fixed laws. I'm pointing out that the story shows that St Joseph knew *that* law just as well as you do.'

'But he came to believe in the Virgin Birth afterwards, didn't he?'

'Quite. But he didn't do so because he was under any illusion as to where babies came from in the ordinary course of nature. He believed in the Virgin Birth as something *super*-natural. He knew nature works in fixed, regular ways: but he also believed that there existed something *beyond* nature which could interfere with her workings – from outside, so to speak.'

'But modern science has shown there's no such thing.'

'Really,' said I. 'Which of the sciences?'

'Oh, well, that's a matter of detail,' said my friend. 'I can't give you chapter and verse from memory.'

'But, don't you see,' said I, 'that science never could show anything of the sort?'

'Why on earth not?'

'Because science studies nature. And the question is whether anything *besides* nature exists – anything "outside". How could you find that out by studying simply nature?'

'But don't we find out that nature *must* work in an absolutely fixed way? I mean, the laws of nature tell us not merely how things *do* happen, but how they *must* happen. No power could possibly alter them.'

'How do you mean?' said I.

'Look here,' said he. 'Could this "something outside" that you talk about make two and two five?'

'Well, no,' said I.

'All right,' said he. 'Well, I think the laws of nature are really like two and two making four. The idea of their being altered is as absurd as the idea of altering the laws of arithmetic.'

'Half a moment,' said I. 'Suppose you put sixpence into a drawer today, and sixpence into the same drawer tomorrow. Do the laws of arithmetic make it certain you'll find a shilling's worth there the day after?'

'Of course,' said he, 'provided no one's been tampering with your drawer.'

'Ah, but that's the whole point,' said I. 'The laws of arithmetic can tell you what you'll find, with absolute certainty, *provided that* there's no interference. If a thief has been at the drawer of course you'll get a different result. But the thief won't have broken the laws of arithmetic – only the laws of England. Now, aren't the laws of nature much in the same boat? Don't they all tell you what will happen *provided* there's no interference?'

'How do you mean?'

'Well, the laws will tell you how a billiard ball will travel on a smooth surface if you hit it in a particular way – but only provided no one interferes. If, after it's already in motion, someone snatches up a cue and gives it a biff on one side – why, then, you won't get what the scientists predicted.'

'No, of course not. He can't allow for monkey-tricks like that.'

'Quite, and in the same way, if there was anything outside nature, and if it interfered – then the events which the scientist expected wouldn't follow. That would be what we call a miracle. In one sense it wouldn't break the laws of nature. The laws tell you what will happen if nothing interferes. They can't tell you whether something *is* going to interfere. I mean, it's not the expert at arithmetic who can tell you how likely someone is to interfere with the pennies in my drawer; a detective would be more use. It isn't the physicist who can tell you how likely I am to catch up a cue and spoil his experiment with the billiard ball; you'd better ask a psychologist. And it isn't the scientist who can tell you how likely nature is to be interfered with from outside. You must go to the metaphysician.'

'These are rather niggling points,' said my friend. 'You see, the real objection goes far deeper. The whole picture of the universe which science has given us makes it such rot to believe that the Power at the back of it all could be interested in us tiny little creatures crawling about on an unimportant planet! It was all so obviously invented by people who believed in a flat earth with the stars only a mile or two away.'

'When did people believe that?'

'Why, all those old Christian chaps you're always talking about did. I mean Boethius and Augustine and Thomas Aquinas and Dante.'

'Sorry,' said I, 'but this is one of the few subjects I do know something about.'

I reached out my hand to a bookshelf. 'You see this book,' I said, 'Ptolemy's *Almagest*. You know what it is?'

'Yes,' said he. 'It's the standard astronomical handbook used all through the Middle Ages.'

'Well, just read that,' I said, pointing to Book I, chapter 5.

'The earth,' read out my friend, hesitating a bit as he translated the Latin, 'the earth, in relation to the distance of the fixed stars, has no appreciable size and must be treated as a mathematical point!'

There was another short silence.

'Did they really know that *then?*' said my friend. 'But – but none of the histories of science – none of the modern encyclopedias ever mentions the fact.'

'Exactly,' said I. 'I'll leave you to think out the reason. It almost looks as if someone was anxious to hush it up, doesn't it? I wonder why.'

There was another short silence.

'At any rate,' said I, 'we can now state the problem accurately. People usually think the problem is how to reconcile what we now know about the size of the universe with our traditional ideas of religion. That turns out not to be the problem at all. The real problem is this. The enormous size of the universe and the insignificance of the earth were known for centuries, and no one ever dreamed that they had any bearing on the religious question. Then, less than a hundred years ago, they are suddenly trotted out as an argument against Christianity. And the people who trot them out carefully hush up the fact that they were known long ago. Don't you think that all you atheists are strangely unsuspicious people?'

[19]
CHRISTIAN APOLOGETICS

*This was read to the (Anglican) Carmarthen Conference for Youth
Leaders and Junior Clergy at Easter 1945. It was subsequently
published in* Undeceptions *(1971) and later in* Compelling Reason
(1998).

Some of you are priests and some are leaders of youth organisations. I
have little right to address either. It is for priests to teach me, not for me to
teach them. I have never helped to organise youth, and while I was young
myself I successfully avoided being organised. If I address you it is in
response to a request so urged that I came to regard compliance as a
matter of Obedience.

I am to talk about Apologetics. Apologetics means of course Defence.
The first question is – what do you propose to defend? Christianity, of
course: and Christianity as understood by the Church in Wales. And here
at the outset I must deal with an unpleasant business. It seems to the
layman that in the Church of England we often hear from our priests
doctrine which is not Anglican Christianity. It may depart from Anglican
Christianity in either of two ways: (1) It may be so 'broad' or 'liberal' or
'modern' that it in fact excludes any real Supernaturalism and thus ceases
to be Christian at all. (2) It may, on the other hand, be Roman. It is not,
of course, for me to define to you what Anglican Christianity is – I am
your pupil, not your teacher. But I insist that wherever you draw the lines,
bounding lines must exist, beyond which your doctrine will cease either
to be Anglican or to be Christian: and I suggest also that the lines come a
great deal sooner than many modern priests think. I think it is your duty
to fix the lines clearly in your own minds: and if you wish to go beyond
them you must change your profession.

This is your duty not specially as Christians or as priests but as honest
men. There is a danger here of the clergy developing a special professional
conscience which obscures the very plain moral issue. Men who have
passed beyond these boundary lines in either direction are apt to protest

that they have come by their unorthodox opinions honestly. In defence of these opinions they are prepared to suffer obloquy and to forfeit professional advancement. They thus come to feel like martyrs. But this simply misses the point which so gravely scandalises the layman. We never doubted that the unorthodox opinions were honestly held: what we complain of is your continuing your ministry after you have come to hold them. We always knew that a man who makes his living as a paid agent of the Conservative Party may honestly change his views and honestly become a Communist. What we deny is that he can honestly continue to be a Conservative agent and to receive money from one party while he supports the policy of another.

Even when we have thus ruled out teaching which is in direct contradiction to our profession, we must define our task still further. We are to defend Christianity itself – the faith preached by the Apostles, attested by the Martyrs, embodied in the Creeds, expounded by the Fathers. This must be clearly distinguished from the whole of what any one of us may think about God and Man. Each of us has his individual emphasis: each holds, in addition to the Faith, many opinions which seem to him to be consistent with it and true and important. And so perhaps they are. But as apologists it is not our business to defend *them*. We are defending Christianity; not 'my religion'. When we mention our personal opinions we must always make quite clear the difference between them and the Faith itself. St Paul has given us the model in 1 Corinthians 7:25: on a certain point he has 'no commandment of the Lord' but gives 'his judgement'. No one is left in doubt as to the difference in *status* implied.

This distinction, which is demanded by honesty, also gives the apologist a great tactical advantage. The great difficulty is to get modern audiences to realise that you are preaching Christianity solely and simply because you happen to think it *true*; they always suppose you are preaching it because you like it or think it good for society or something of that sort. Now a clearly maintained distinction between what the Faith actually says and what you would like it to have said, or what you understand or what you personally find helpful or think probable, forces your audience to realise that you are tied to your data just as the scientist is tied by the results of the experiments; that you are not just saying what you like. This immediately helps them to realise that what is being discussed is a question about objective fact – not gas about ideals and points of view.

Secondly, this scrupulous care to preserve the Christian message as something distinct from one's own ideas, has one very good effect upon the apologist himself. It forces him, again and again, to face up to those elements in original Christianity which he personally finds obscure or repulsive. He is saved from the temptation to skip or slur or ignore what he finds disagreeable. And the man who yields to that temptation will, of course, never progress in Christian knowledge. For obviously the doctrines which one finds easy are the doctrines which give Christian sanction to truths you already knew. The new truth which you do not know and which you need, must, in the very nature of things, be hidden precisely in the doctrines you least like and least understand. It is just the same here as in science. The phenomenon which is troublesome, which doesn't fit in with the current scientific theories, is the phenomenon which compels reconsideration and thus leads to new knowledge. Science progresses because scientists, instead of running away from such trouble-some phenomena or hushing them up, are constantly seeking them out. In the same way, there will be progress in Christian knowledge only as long as we accept the challenge of the difficult or repellent doctrines. A 'liberal' Christianity which considers itself free to alter the Faith whenever the Faith looks perplexing or repellent *must* be completely stagnant. Progress is made only into a *resisting* material.

From this there follows a corollary about the Apologist's private reading. There are two questions he will naturally ask himself. (1) Have I been 'keeping up', keeping abreast of recent movements in theology? (2) Have I *stood firm* (*super monstratas vias*) [1] amidst all these 'winds of doctrine' (Ephesians 4:14)? I want to say emphatically that the second question is far the more important of the two. Our upbringing and the whole atmosphere of the world we live in make it certain that our main temptation will be that of yielding to winds of doctrine, not that of ignoring them. We are not at all likely to be hidebound: we are very likely indeed to be the slaves of fashion. If one has to choose between reading the new books and reading the old, one must choose the old: not because they are necessarily better but because they contain precisely those truths of which our own age is neglectful. The standard of permanent Christianity must be kept clear in our minds and it is against that stan-dard that we must test all contemporary thought. In fact, we must at all costs *not* move with the times. We serve One who said, 'Heaven and Earth shall move with the times, but my words shall not move with the times' (Matthew 24:35; Mark 13:31; Luke 21:33).

---

[1] The source of this is, I believe, Jeremiah 6:16, '*State super vias et videte, et interrogate de semitis antiquis quae sit via bona, et ambulate in ea*', which is translated, 'Stand ye in the ways, and see, and ask for the old paths, where is the good way, and walk therein.'

I am speaking, so far, of theological reading. Scientific reading is a different matter. If you know any science it is very desirable that you should keep it up. We have to answer the current scientific attitude towards Christianity, not the attitude which scientists adopted one hundred years ago. Science is in continual change and we must try to keep abreast of *it*. For the same reason, we must be very cautious of snatching at any scientific theory which, for the moment, seems to be in our favour. We may *mention* such things; but we must mention them lightly and without claiming that they are more than 'interesting'. Sentences beginning 'Science has now proved' should be avoided. If we try to base our apologetic on some recent development in science, we shall usually find that just as we have put the finishing touches to our argument science has changed its mind and quietly withdrawn the theory we have been using as our foundation stone. *Timeo Danaos et dona ferentes*[2] is a sound principle.

While we are on the subject of science, let me digress for a moment. I believe that any Christian who is qualified to write a good popular book on any science may do much more good by that than by any directly apologetic work. The difficulty we are up against is this. We can make people (often) attend to the Christian point of view for half an hour or so; but the moment they have gone away from our lecture or laid down our article, they are plunged back into a world where the opposite position is taken for granted. Every newspaper, film, novel and text book undermines our work. As long as that situation exists, widespread success is simply impossible. We must attack the enemy's line of communication. What we want is not more little books about Christianity, but more little books by Christians on other subjects – with their Christianity *latent*. You can see this most easily if you look at it the other way round. Our Faith is not very likely to be shaken by any book on Hinduism. But if whenever we read an elementary book on Geology, Botany, Politics or Astronomy, we found that its implications were Hindu, that would shake us. It is not the books written in direct defence of Materialism that make the modern man a materialist; it is the materialistic assumptions in all the other books. In the same way, it is not books on Christianity that will really trouble him. But he would be troubled if, whenever he wanted a cheap popular introduction to some science, the best work on the market was always by a Christian. The first step to the reconversion of the country is a series, produced by Christians, which can beat the *Penguins*

[2] 'I fear the Greeks even when they bear gifts.' Virgil, *Aeneid*, Bk. II, line 49.

and the *Thinkers' Library* on their own ground. Its Christianity would have to be latent, not explicit: and *of course* its science perfectly honest. Science *twisted* in the interests of apologetics would be sin and folly. But I must return to my immediate subject.

Our business is to present that which is timeless (the same yesterday, today and tomorrow – Hebrews 8:8) in the particular language of our own age. The bad preacher does exactly the opposite: he takes the ideas of our own age and tricks them out in the traditional language of Christianity. Thus, for example, he may think about the Beveridge Report [3] and *talk* about the coming of the Kingdom. The core of his thought is merely contemporary; only the superficies is traditional. But your teaching must be timeless at its heart and wear a modern dress.

This raises the question of Theology and Politics. The nearest I can get to a settlement of the frontier problem between them is this: that Theology teaches us what ends are desirable and what means are lawful, while Politics teaches what means are effective. Thus Theology tells us that every man ought to have a decent wage. Politics tells by what means this is likely to be attained. Theology tells us which of these means are consistent with justice and charity. On the political question guidance comes not from Revelation but from natural prudence, knowledge of complicated facts and ripe experience. If we have these qualifications we may, of course, state our political opinions: but then we must make it quite clear that we are giving our personal judgement and have no command from the Lord. Not many priests have these qualifications. Most political sermons teach the congregation nothing except what newspapers are taken at the Rectory.

Our great danger at present is lest the Church should continue to practise a merely missionary technique in what has become a missionary situation. A century ago our task was to edify those who had been brought up in the Faith: our present task is chiefly to convert and instruct infidels. Great Britain is as much part of the mission field as China. Now if you were sent to the Bantus you would be taught their language and traditions. You need similar teaching about the language and mental habits of your own uneducated and unbelieving fellow countrymen. Many priests are quite ignorant on this subject. What I know about it I have learned from talking in RAF camps. They were mostly inhabited by Englishmen

---

[3] Sir William H. Beveridge, *Social Insurance and Allied Services*, Command Paper 6404, Parliamentary Session 1942–3 (London: H.M. Stationery Office, 1942). The 'Beveridge Report' was a plan for the Social Security system in Britain.

and, therefore, some of what I shall say may be irrelevant to the situation in Wales. You will sift out what does not apply.

(1) I find that the uneducated Englishman is an almost total sceptic about History. I had expected he would disbelieve the Gospels because they contain miracles: but he really disbelieves them because they deal with things that happened 2,000 years ago. He would disbelieve equally in the battle of Actium if he heard of it. To those who have had our kind of education, his state of mind is very difficult to realise. To us the Present has always appeared as one section in a huge continuous process. In his mind the Present occupies almost the whole field of vision. Beyond it, isolated from it, and quite unimportant, is something called 'The Old Days' – a small, comic jungle in which highwaymen, Queen Elizabeth, knights-in-armour, etc., wander about. Then (strangest of all) beyond The Old Days comes a picture of 'Primitive Man'. He is 'science', not 'history', and is therefore felt to be much more real than The Old Days. In other words, the Prehistoric is much more believed in than the Historic.

(2) He has a distrust (very rational in the state of his knowledge) of ancient texts. Thus a man has sometimes said to me, 'These records were written in the days before printing, weren't they? and you haven't got the original bit of paper, have you? So what it comes to is that someone wrote something and someone else copied it and someone else copied *that* and so on. Well, by the time it comes to us, it won't be in the least like the original.' This is a difficult objection to deal with because one cannot, there and then, start teaching the whole science of textual criticism. But at this point their real religion (i.e. faith in 'science') has come to my aid. The assurance that there is a 'science' called 'Textual Criticism' and that its results (not only as regards the New Testament, but as regards ancient texts in general) are generally accepted, will usually be received without objection. (I need hardly point out that the word 'text' must not be used, since to your audience it means only 'a scriptural quotation'.)

(3) A sense of sin is almost totally lacking. Our situation is thus very different from that of the Apostles. The Pagans (and still more the *metuentes*[4]) to whom they preached were haunted by a sense of guilt and to them the gospel was, therefore, 'good news'. We address people who have been trained to believe that whatever goes wrong in the world is

---

[4] The *metuentes* or 'god-fearers' were a class of Gentiles who worshipped God without submitting to circumcision and the other ceremonial obligations of the Jewish Law. See Psalm 118:4 and Acts 10:2.

someone else's fault – the Capitalists', the Government's, the Nazis', the Generals', etc. They approach God Himself as His *judges*. They want to know, not whether they can be acquitted for sin, but whether He can be acquitted for creating such a world.

In attacking this fatal insensibility it is useless to direct attention (a) to sins your audience do not commit, or (b) to things they do, but do not regard as sins. They are usually not drunkards. They are mostly fornicators, but then they do not feel fornication to be wrong. It is, therefore, useless to dwell on either of these subjects. (Now that contraceptives have removed the obviously *uncharitable* element in fornication I do not myself think we can expect people to recognise it as a sin until they have accepted Christianity as a whole.)

I cannot offer you a water-tight technique for awaking the sense of sin. I can only say that, in my experience, if one begins from the sin that has been one's own chief problem during the last week, one is very often surprised at the way this shaft goes home. But whatever method we use, our continual effort must be to get their minds away from public affairs and 'crime' and bring them down to brass tacks – to the whole network of spite, greed, envy, unfairness and conceit in the lives of 'ordinary decent people' like themselves (and ourselves).

(4) We must learn the language of our audience. And let me say at the outset that it is no use at all laying down *a priori* what the 'plain man' does or does not understand. You have to find out by experience. Thus most of us would have supposed that the change from 'may truly and indifferently minister justice' to 'may truly and impartially'[5] made that place easier to the uneducated; but a priest of my acquaintance discovered that his sexton saw no difficulty in *indifferently* ('It means making no difference between one man and another' he said) but had no idea what *impartially* meant.

On this question of language the best thing I can do is to make a list of words which are used by the people in a sense different from ours.

ATONEMENT. Does not really exist in a spoken modern English, though it would be recognised as 'a religious word'. In so far as it conveys any meaning to the uneducated I think it means *compensation*. No one word will express to them what Christians mean by *Atonement*: you must paraphrase.

---

[5] The first quotation is from the prayer for the 'Whole state of Christ's Church' in the service of Holy Communion, Prayer Book (1662). The second is the revised form of that same phrase as found in the 1928 Prayer Book.

BEING (noun). Never means merely 'entity' in popular speech. Often it means what we should call a 'personal being' (e.g. a man said to me 'I believe in the Holy Ghost but I don't think He is a being').

CATHOLIC means Papistical.

CHARITY. Means (a) alms, (b) a 'charitable organisation', (c) much more rarely – indulgence (i.e. a 'charitable' attitude towards a man is conceived as one that denies or condones his sins, not as one that loves the sinner in spite of them).

CHRISTIAN. Has come to include almost no idea of *belief.* Usually a vague term of approval. The question 'What do you call a Christian?' has been asked of me again and again. The answer they *wish* to receive is 'A Christian is a decent chap who's unselfish, etc.'

CHURCH. Means (a) sacred building, (b) the clergy. Does *not* suggest to them the 'company of all faithful people'.[6] Generally used in a bad sense. Direct defence of the Church is part of our duty: but use of the word *Church* where there is no time to defend it alienates sympathy and should be avoided where possible.

CREATIVE. Now means merely 'talented', 'original'. The idea of creation in the theological sense is absent from their minds.

CREATURE. Means 'beast', 'irrational animal'. Such an expression as 'We are only creatures' would almost certainly be misunderstood.

CRUCIFIXION, CROSS, ETC. Centuries of hymnody and religious cant have so exhausted these words that they now very faintly – if at all – convey the idea of execution by torture. It is better to paraphrase; and, for the same reason to say *flogged* for New Testament *scourged* (Matthew 27:26; Mark 15:15; John 19:1).

DOGMA. Used by the people only in a bad sense to mean 'unproved assertion delivered in an arrogant manner'.

IMMACULATE CONCEPTION. In the mouth of an uneducated speaker *always* means *Virgin Birth*.

MORALITY means *chastity*.

PERSONAL. I had argued for at least 10 minutes with a man about the existence of a 'personal devil' before I discovered that *personal* meant to him *corporeal.* I suspect this of being widespread. When they say they don't believe in a 'personal' God they may often mean only that they are not anthropomorphists.

POTENTIAL. When used at all is used in an engineering sense: *never* means 'possible'.

---

[6] A phrase which occurs in the prayer of 'Thanksgiving' at the end of the service of Holy Communion in the Book of Common Prayer (1662).

PRIMITIVE. Means crude, clumsy, unfinished, inefficient. 'Primitive Christianity' would not mean to them at all what it does to you.

SACRIFICE. Has no associations with temple and altar. They are familiar with this word only in the journalistic sense ('The Nation must be prepared for heavy sacrifices').

SPIRITUAL. Means primarily *immaterial, incorporeal,* but with serious confusions from the Christian uses of πνεῦμα.[7] Hence the idea that whatever is 'spiritual' in the sense of 'non-sensuous' is somehow *better* than anything sensuous: e.g. they don't really believe that envy could be as bad as drunkenness.

VULGARITY. Usually means obscenity or 'smut'. There are bad confusions (and not only in uneducated minds) between:

(a) The obscene or lascivious: what is calculated to provoke lust.
(b) The indecorous: what offends against good taste or propriety.
(c) The vulgar proper: what is socially 'low'.

'Good' people tend to think (b) as sinful as (a), with the result that others feel (a) to be just as innocent as (b).

To conclude – you must translate every bit of your Theology into the vernacular. This is very troublesome and it means you can say very little in half an hour, but it is essential. It is also of the greatest service to your own thought. I have come to the conviction that if you cannot translate your thoughts into uneducated language, then your thoughts were confused. Power to translate is the test of having really understood one's own meaning. A passage from some theological work for translation into the vernacular ought to be a compulsory paper in every Ordination examination.

I turn now to the question of the actual attack. This may be either emotional or intellectual. If I speak only of the intellectual kind, that is not because I undervalue the other but because, not having been given the gifts necessary for carrying it out, I cannot give advice about it. But I wish to say most emphatically that where a speaker has that gift, the direct evangelical appeal of the 'Come to Jesus' type can be as overwhelming today as it was a hundred years ago. I have seen it done, preluded by a religious film and accompanied by hymn singing, and with very remarkable effect. I cannot do it: but those who can ought to do it with all their might. I am not sure that the ideal missionary team ought not to consist

---

[7] Which means 'spirit', as in 1 Corinthians 14:12.

of one who argues and one who (in the fullest sense of the word) preaches. Put up your arguer first to undermine their intellectual prejudices; then let the evangelist proper launch his appeal. I have seen this done with great success. But here I must concern myself only with the intellectual attack. *Non omnia possumus omnes.*[8]

And first, a word of encouragement. Uneducated people are not irrational people. I have found that they will endure, and can follow, quite a lot of sustained argument if you go slowly. Often, indeed, the novelty of it (for they have seldom met it before) delights them.

Do not attempt to water Christianity down. There must be no pretence that you can have it with the Supernatural left out. So far as I can see Christianity is precisely the one religion from which the miraculous cannot be separated. You must frankly argue for supernaturalism from the very outset.

The two popular 'difficulties' you will probably have to deal with are these.

1. 'Now that we know how huge the universe is and how insignificant the Earth, it is ridiculous to believe that the universal God should be specially interested in our concerns.' In answer to this you must first correct their error about *fact*. The insignificance of Earth in relation to the universe is not a modern discovery: nearly 2,000 years ago Ptolemy (*Almagest*, Bk. 1, ch. v) said that in relation to the distance of the fixed stars Earth must be treated as a mathematical point without magnitude. Secondly, you should point out that Christianity says what God has done for Man; it doesn't say (because it doesn't know) what He has or has not done in other parts of the universe. Thirdly, you might recall the parable of the one lost sheep (Matthew 18:11–14; Luke 15:4–7). If Earth has been specially sought by God (which we don't know) that may not imply that it is the most important thing in the universe, but only that it has *strayed*. Finally, challenge the whole tendency to identify size and importance. Is an elephant more important than a man, or a man's leg than his brain?

2. 'People believed in miracles in the Old Days because they didn't then know that they were contrary to the Laws of Nature.' But they did. If St Joseph didn't know that a virgin birth was contrary to Nature (i.e. if he didn't yet know the normal origin of babies) why, on discovering his wife's pregnancy, was he 'minded to put her away' (Matthew 1:19)? Obviously, no event would be recorded as a wonder *unless* the recorders knew the natural order and saw that this was an exception. If people

---

[8] 'Not all things can we all do.' Virgil, *Eclogues*, Bk. VIII, line 63.

didn't know that the Sun rose in the East they wouldn't be even interested in its once rising in the West. They would not record it as a *miraculum* – nor indeed record it at all. The very idea of 'miracle' presupposes knowledge of the Laws of Nature; you can't have the idea of an exception until you have the idea of a rule.

It is very difficult to produce arguments on the popular level for the existence of God. And many of the most popular arguments seem to me invalid. Some of these may be produced in discussion by friendly members of the audience. This raises the whole problem of the 'embarrassing supporter'. It is brutal (and dangerous) to repel him; it is often dishonest to agree with what he says. I usually try to avoid saying anything about the validity of his argument in *itself* and reply, 'Yes. That may do for you and me. But I'm afraid if we take that line our friend here on my left might say, etc., etc.'

Fortunately, though very oddly, I have found that people are usually disposed to hear the divinity of Our Lord discussed *before* going into the existence of God. When I began I used, if I were giving two lectures, to devote the first to mere Theism; but I soon gave up this method because it seemed to arouse little interest. The number of clear and determined Atheists is apparently not very large.

When we come to the Incarnation itself, I usually find that some form of the *aut Deus aut malus homo*[9] can be used. The majority of them started with the idea of the 'great human teacher' who was deified by His superstitious followers. It must be pointed out how very improbable this is among Jews and how different to anything that happened with Plato, Confucius, Buddha, Muhammad. The Lord's own words and claims (of which many are quite ignorant) must be forced home. (The whole case, on a popular level, is very well put indeed in Chesterton's *Everlasting Man*.)

Something will usually have to be said about the historicity of the Gospels. You who are trained theologians will be able to do this in ways which I could not. My own line was to say that I was a professional literary critic and I thought I did know the difference between legend and historical writing: that the Gospels were certainly not legends (in one sense they're not *good* enough): and that if they are not history then they are realistic prose fiction of a kind which actually never existed before the eighteenth century. Little episodes such as Jesus writing in the dust (John 8:3–8) when they brought Him the woman taken in adultery (which have no *doctrinal* significance at all) are the mark.

[9] 'Either God or a bad man.'

One of the great difficulties is to keep before the audience's mind the question of Truth. They always think you are recommending Christianity not because it is *true* but because it is *good*. And in the discussion they will at every moment try to escape from the issue 'True – or False' into stuff about a good society, or morals, or the incomes of Bishops, or the Spanish Inquisition, or France, or Poland – or anything whatever. You have to keep forcing them back, and again back, to the real point. Only thus will you be able to undermine (a) Their belief that a certain amount of 'religion' is desirable but one mustn't carry it too far. One must keep on pointing out that Christianity is a statement which, if false, is of *no* importance, and, if true, of infinite importance. The one thing it cannot be is moderately important. (b) Their firm belief of Article XVIII.[10] Of course it should be pointed out that, though all salvation is through Jesus, we need not conclude that He cannot save those who have not explicitly accepted Him in this life. And it should (at least in my judgement) be made clear that we are not pronouncing all other religions to be totally false, but rather saying that in Christ whatever is true in all religions is consummated and perfected. But, on the other hand, I think we must attack wherever we meet it the nonsensical idea that mutually exclusive propositions about God can both be true.

For my own part, I have sometimes told my audience that the only two things really worth considering are Christianity and Hinduism. (Islam is only the greatest of the Christian heresies, Buddhism only the greatest of the Hindu heresies. Real Paganism is dead. All that was best in Judaism and Platonism survives in Christianity.) There isn't really, for an adult mind, this infinite variety of religions to consider. We may *salva reverentia*[11] divide religions, as we do soups, into 'thick' and 'clear'. By Thick I mean those which have orgies and ecstasies and mysteries and local attachments: Africa is full of Thick religions. By Clear I mean those which are philosophical, ethical and universalising: Stoicism, Buddhism and the Ethical Church are Clear religions. Now if there is a true religion it must be both Thick and Clear: for the true God must have made both the child and the man, both the savage and the citizen, both the head and the belly. And the only two religions that fulfil this condition are Hinduism and Christianity. But Hinduism fulfils it imperfectly. The

[10] Article XVIII in the Prayer Book: *Of obtaining eternal Salvation only by the Name of Christ*, which says, 'They also are to be had accursed that presume to say, That every man shall be saved by the Law or Sect which he professeth, so that he be diligent to frame his life according to that Law, and the light of Nature. For holy Scripture doth set out unto us only the Name of Jesus Christ, whereby men must be saved.'

[11] Without outraging reverence.

Clear religion of the Brahmin hermit in the jungle and the Thick religion of the neighbouring temple go on *side by side*. The Brahmin hermit doesn't bother about the temple prostitution, nor the worshipper in the temple about the hermit's metaphysic. But Christianity really breaks down the middle wall of the partition. It takes a convert from central Africa and tells him to obey an enlightened universalist ethic: it takes a twentieth-century academic prig like me and tells me to go fasting to a Mystery, to drink the blood of the Lord. The savage convert has to be Clear: I have to be Thick. That is how one knows one has come to the real religion.

One last word. I have found that nothing is more dangerous to one's own faith than the work of an apologist. No doctrine of that Faith seems to me so spectral, so unreal as one that I have just successfully defended in a public debate. For a moment, you see, it has seemed to rest on oneself: as a result, when you go away from that debate, it seems no stronger than that weak pillar. That is why we apologists take our lives in our hands and can be saved only by falling back continually from the web of our own arguments, as from our intellectual counters, into the Reality – from Christian apologetics into Christ Himself. That also is why we need one another's continual help – *oremus pro invicem*.[12]

[12] Let us pray for each other.

WORK AND PRAYER

Published in The Coventry Evening Telegraph *(28 May 1945) and reproduced in* Undeceptions *(1971), this essay also appeared in* First and Second Things *(1985).*

'Even if I grant your point and admit that answers to prayer are theoretically possible, I shall still think they are infinitely improbable. I don't think it at all likely that God requires the ill-informed (and contradictory) advice of us humans as to how to run the world. If He is all-wise, as you say He is, doesn't He know already what is best? And if He is all-good won't He do it whether we pray or not?'

This is the case against prayer which has, in the last hundred years, intimidated thousands of people. The usual answer is that it applies only to the lowest sort of prayer, the sort that consists in asking for things to happen. The higher sort, we are told, offers no advice to God; it consists only of 'communion' or intercourse with Him; and those who take this line seem to suggest that the lower kind of prayer really is an absurdity and that only children or savages would use it.

I have never been satisfied with this view. The distinction between the two sorts of prayer is a sound one; and I think on the whole (I am not quite certain) that the sort which asks for nothing is the higher or more advanced. To be in the state in which you are so at one with the will of God that you wouldn't want to alter the course of events even if you could is certainly a very high or advanced condition.

But if one simply rules out the lower kind two difficulties follow. In the first place, one has to say that the whole historical tradition of Christian prayer (including the Lord's Prayer itself) has been wrong: for it has always admitted prayers for our daily bread, for the recovery of the sick, for protection from enemies, for the conversion of the outside world and the like. In the second place, though the other kind of prayer may be 'higher' if you restrict yourself to it because you have got beyond the desire to use any other, there is nothing specially 'high' or 'spiritual' about abstaining from prayers that make requests simply because you think they're no good. It might be a very pretty thing (but, again, I'm not absolutely certain) if a little boy never asked for cake because he was so high-minded and spiritual that he didn't want any cake. But there's nothing specially pretty about a little boy who doesn't ask because he has learned that it is no use asking. I think that the whole matter needs reconsideration.

The case against prayer (I mean the 'low' or old-fashioned kind) is this. The thing you ask for is either good – for you and for the world in general – or else it is not. If it is, then a good and wise God will do it anyway. If it is not, then He won't. In neither case can your prayer make any differ-ence. But if this argument is sound, surely it is an argument not only against praying, but against doing anything whatever?

In every action, just as in every prayer, you are trying to bring about a certain result; and this result must be good or bad. Why, then, do we not argue as the opponents of prayer argue, and say that if the intended result is good, God will bring it to pass without your interference, and that if it is bad He will prevent it happening whatever you do? Why wash your hands? If God intends them to be clean, they'll come clean without your washing them. If He doesn't, they'll remain dirty (as Lady Macbeth found)[1] however much soap you use. Why ask for the salt? Why put on your boots? Why do anything?

We know that we can act and that our actions produce results. Everyone who believes in God must therefore admit (quite apart from the question of prayer) that God has not chosen to write the whole of history with His own hand. Most of the events that go on in the universe are indeed out of our control, but not all. It is like a play in which the scene and the general outline of the story is fixed by the author, but certain minor details are left for the actors to improvise. It may be a mystery why He should have allowed us to cause real events at all; but it is no odder that He should allow us to cause them by praying than by any other method.

Pascal says that God 'instituted prayer in order to allow His creatures the dignity of causality'. It would perhaps be truer to say that He invented both prayer and physical action for that purpose. He gave us small crea-tures the dignity of being able to contribute to the course of events in two different ways. He made the matter of the universe such that we can (in those limits) do things to it; that is why we can wash our own hands and feed or murder our fellow creatures. Similarly, He made His own plan or

---

[1] *Macbeth*, V, i, 34–57.

plot of history such that it admits a certain amount of free play and can be modified in response to our prayers. If it is foolish and impudent to ask for victory in a war (on the ground that God might be expected to know best), it would be equally foolish and impudent to put on a mackintosh – does not God know best whether you ought to be wet or dry?

The two methods by which we are allowed to produce events may be called work and prayer. Both are alike in this respect – that in both we try to produce a state of affairs which God has not (or at any rate not yet) seen fit to provide 'on His own'. And from this point of view the old maxim *laborare est orare* (work is prayer) takes on a new meaning. What we do when we weed a field is not quite different from what we do when we pray for a good harvest. But there is an important difference all the same.

You cannot be sure of a good harvest whatever you do to a field. But you can be sure that if you pull up one weed that one weed will no longer be there. You can be sure that if you drink more than a certain amount of alcohol you will ruin your health or that if you go on for a few centuries more wasting the resources of the planet on wars and luxuries you will shorten the life of the whole human race. The kind of causality we exercise by work is, so to speak, divinely guaranteed, and therefore ruthless. By it we are free to do ourselves as much harm as we please. But the kind which we exercise by prayer is not like that; God has left Himself a discretionary power. Had He not done so, prayer would be an activity too dangerous for man and we should have the horrible state of things envisaged by Juvenal: 'Enormous prayers which Heaven in anger grants'.[2]

Prayers are not always – in the crude, factual sense of the word – 'granted'. This is not because prayer is a weaker kind of causality, but because it is a stronger kind. When it 'works' at all it works unlimited by space and time. That is why God has retained a discretionary power of granting or refusing it; except on that condition prayer would destroy us. It is not unreasonable for a headmaster to say, 'Such and such things you may do according to the fixed rules of this school. But such and such other things are too dangerous to be left to general rules. If you want to do them you must come and make a request and talk over the whole matter with me in my study. And then – we'll see.'

[2] *Satires*, Book IV, Satire x, line III.

[21]
RELIGION WITHOUT DOGMA?

Read to the Socratic Club on 20 May 1946 in answer to a paper by Professor H.H. Price on 'The Grounds of Modern Agnosticism' (20 October 1944), this essay was published under the title 'A Christian Reply to Professor Price' in The Phoenix Quarterly, *Volume I, No. i (Autumn 1946) and was then reprinted under the current title in* The Socratic Digest, *No. 4 (1948). It appeared in* Compelling Reason *(1998), together with a 'Reply' to an article by Miss G.E.M. Anscombe, 'A Reply to Mr C.S. Lewis's Argument that "Naturalism is Self-refuting" ' . (Lewis's argument is to be found in the original third chapter of his* Miracles *(1947).)*

In his paper on 'The Grounds of Modern Agnosticism', Professor Price maintains the following positions: (1) That the essence of religion is belief in God and immortality; (2) that in most actual religions the essence is found in connection with 'accretions of dogma and mythology' which have been rendered incredible by the progress of science; (3) that it would be very desirable, if it were possible, to retain the essence purged of the accretions; but (4) that science has rendered the essence almost as hard to believe as the accretions. For the doctrine of immortality involves the dualistic view that man is a composite creature, a soul in a state of symbiosis with a physical organism. But in so far as science can successfully regard man monistically, as a single organism whose psychological properties all arise from his physical, the soul becomes an indefensible hypothesis. In conclusion, Professor Price found our only hope in certain empirical evidence for the soul which appears to him satisfactory; in fact, in the findings of Psychical Research.

My disagreement with Professor Price begins, I am afraid, at the threshold. I do not define the essence of religion as belief in God and immortality. Judaism in its earlier stages had no belief in immortality, and for a long time no belief which was religiously relevant. The shadowy existence of the ghost in Sheol was one of which Jehovah took no account and which took no account of Jehovah. In Sheol all things are forgotten. The religion was centred on the ritual and ethical demands of Jehovah in the present life, and also, of course, on benefits expected from Him. These benefits are often merely worldly benefits (grandchildren, and peace upon Israel), but a more specifically religious note is repeatedly struck. The Jew is athirst for the living God (Psalm 42:2), he delights in His Laws as in honey or treasure (Psalm 19:10), he is conscious of himself in Jehovah's presence as unclean of lips and heart (Isaiah 6:5). The glory or splendour of the god is worshipped for its own sake. In Buddhism, on the other hand, we find that a doctrine of immortality is central, while there is nothing specifically religious. Salvation from immortality, deliverance from reincarnation, is the very core of its message. The existence of the gods is not necessarily decried, but it is of no religious significance. In Stoicism again both the religious quality and the belief in immortality are variables, but they do not vary in direct ratio. Even within Christianity itself we find a striking expression, not without influence from Stoicism, of the subordinate position of immortality. When Henry More ends a poem on the spiritual life by saying that if, after all, he should turn out to be mortal he would be:

> *... Satisfide*
> *A lonesome mortal God t' have dide.*[1]

From my own point of view, the examples of Judaism and Buddhism are of immense importance. The system which is meaningless without a doctrine of immortality regards immortality as a nightmare, not as a prize. The religion which, of all ancient religions, is most specifically religious, that is, at once most ethical and most numinous, is hardly interested in the question. Believing as I do, that Jehovah is a real being, indeed the *ens realissimum*, I cannot sufficiently admire the divine tact of thus training the chosen race for centuries in a religion before even hinting the shining secret of eternal life. He behaves like the rich lover in a romance who woos the maiden on his own merits, disguised as a poor man, and only when he has won her reveals that he has a throne and palace to offer. For I cannot help thinking that any religion which begins with a thirst for immortality is damned, as a religion, from the outset. Until a certain spiritual level has been reached, the promise of immortality will always operate as a bribe which vitiates the whole religion and infinitely inflames

---

[1] 'Resolution', *The Complete Poems of Dr Henry More*, ed. Alexander B. Grosart (Edinburgh, 1878), line 117, p. 176.

those very self-regards which religion must cut down and uproot. For the essence of religion, in my view, is the thirst for an end higher than natural ends; the finite self's desire for, and acquiescence in, and self-rejection in favour of, an object wholly good and wholly good for it. That the self-rejection will turn out to be also a self-finding, that bread cast upon the waters will be found after many days, that to die is to live – these are sacred paradoxes of which the human race must not be told too soon.

Differing from Professor Price about the essence of religion, I naturally cannot, in a sense, discuss whether the essence as he defines it co-exists with accretions of dogma and mythology. But I freely admit that the essence as I define it always co-exists with other things; and that some of these other things even I would call mythology. But my list of things mythological would not coincide with his, and our views of mythology itself probably differ. A great many different views on it have, of course, been held. Myths have been accepted as literally true, then as allegorically true (by the Stoics), as confused history (by Euhemerus),[2] as priestly lies (by the philosophers of the Enlightenment), as imitative agricultural ritual mistaken for propositions (in the days of Frazer).[3] If you start from a naturalistic philosophy, then something like the view of Euhemerus or the view of Frazer is likely to result. But I am not a naturalist. I believe that in the huge mass of mythology which has come down to us a good many different sources are mixed – true history, allegory, ritual, the human delight in story telling, etc. But among these sources I include the supernatural, both diabolical and divine. We need here concern ourselves only with the latter. If my religion is erroneous then occurrences of similar motifs in pagan stories are, of course, instances of the same, or a similar, error. But if my religion is true, then these stories may well be a *preparatio evangelica*, divine hinting in poetic and ritual form at the same central truth which was later focused and (so to speak) historicised in the Incarnation. To me, who first approached Christianity from a delighted interest in, and reverence for, the best pagan imagination, who loved Balder before Christ and Plato before St Augustine, the anthropological argument against Christianity has never been formidable. On the contrary, I could not believe Christianity if I were forced to say that there were a thousand religions in the world of which 999 were pure nonsense and the thousandth (fortunately) true. My conversion, very largely, depended on recognising Christianity as the completion, the actualisation,

---

[2] A Sicilian writer (c. 315 BC) who developed the theory that the ancient beliefs about the gods originated from the elaboration of traditions of actual historical persons.

[3] James George Frazer, *The Golden Bough* (London, 1922).

the entelechy, of something that had never been wholly absent from the mind of man. And I still think that the agnostic argument from similarities between Christianity and paganism works only if you know the answer. If you start by knowing on other grounds that Christianity is false, then the pagan stories may be another nail in its coffin: just as if you started by knowing that there were no such things as crocodiles then the various stories about dragons might help to confirm your disbelief. But if the truth or falsehood of Christianity is the very question you are discussing, then the argument from anthropology is surely a *petitio*.

There are, of course, many things in Christianity which I accept as fact and which Professor Price would regard as mythology. In a word, there are miracles. The contention is that science has proved that miracles cannot occur. According to Professor Price 'a Deity who intervened miraculously and suspended natural law could never be accepted by Science';[4] whence he passes on to consider whether we cannot still believe in Theism without miracles. I am afraid I have not understood why the miracles could never be accepted by one who accepted science.

Professor Price bases his view on the nature of scientific method. He says that that method is based on two assumptions. The first is that all events are subject to laws, and he adds: 'It does not matter for our purpose whether the laws are "deterministic" or only "statistical".'[5] But I submit that it matters to the scientist's view of the miraculous. The notion that natural laws may be merely statistical results from the modern belief that the individual unit of matter obeys no laws. Statistics were introduced to explain why, despite the lawlessness of the individual unit, the behaviour of gross bodies was regular. The explanation was that, by a principle well known to actuaries, the law of averages levelled out the individual eccentricities of the innumerable units contained in even the smallest gross body. But with this conception of the lawless units the whole impregnability of nineteenth-century Naturalism has, as it seems to me, been abandoned. What is the use of saying that all events are subject to laws if you also say that every event which befalls the individual unit of matter is *not* subject to laws. Indeed, if we define nature as the system of events in space-time governed by interlocking laws, then the new physics has really admitted that something other than nature exists. For if nature means the interlocking system then the behaviour of the individual unit is outside nature. We have admitted what may be called the sub-natural. After that

---

[4] H.H. Price, 'The Grounds of Modern Agnosticism', *Phoenix Quaterly*, Vol. 1, No. 1 (Autumn 1946), p. 20.
[5] Ibid.

admission what confidence is left us that there may not be a supernatural as well? It may be true that the lawlessness of the little events fed into nature from the sub-natural is always ironed out by the law of averages. It does not follow that great events could not be fed into her by the supernatural: nor that they also would allow themselves to be ironed out.

The second assumption which Professor Price attributes to the scientific method is 'that laws can only be discovered by the study of publicly observable regularities'.[6] Of course they can. This does not seem to me to be an assumption so much as a self-evident proposition. But what is it to the purpose? If a miracle occurs it is by definition an interruption of regularity. To discover a regularity is by definition not to discover its interruptions, even if they occur. You cannot discover a railway accident from studying Bradshaw: only by being there when it happens or hearing about it afterwards from someone who was. You cannot discover extra half-holidays by studying a school timetable: you must wait till they are announced. But surely this does not mean that a student of Bradshaw is logically forced to deny the possibility of railway accidents. This point of scientific method merely shows (what no one to my knowledge ever denied) that if miracles *did* occur, science, as science, would not prove, or disprove, their occurrence. What cannot be trusted to recur is not material for science: that is why history is not one of the sciences. You cannot find out what Napoleon did at the battle of Austerlitz by asking him to come and fight it again in a laboratory with the same combatants, the same terrain, the same weather, and in the same age. You have to go to the records. We have not, in fact, proved that science excludes miracles: we have only proved that the question of miracles, like innumerable other questions, excludes laboratory treatment.

[7] [If I thus hand over miracles from science to history (but not, of course, to historians who beg the question by beginning with materialistic assumptions) Professor Price thinks I shall not fare much better. Here I must speak with caution, for I do not profess to be a historian or a textual critic. I would refer you to Sir Arnold Lunn's book *The Third Day*.[8] If Sir Arnold is right, then the biblical criticism which began in the nineteenth century has already shot its bolt, and most of its conclusions have been successfully disputed, though it will, like nineteenth-century

---

[6] Ibid.

[7] In order that nothing should be lost to the reader, I have included between square brackets those portions from the *Socratic* version of this paper which Lewis omitted in revising it for the *Phoenix Quarterly*. See footnote 9.

[8] London, 1945.

materialism, long continue to dominate popular thought. What I can say with more certainty is that that *kind* of criticism – the kind which discovers that every old book was made by six anonymous authors well provided with scissors and paste, and that every anecdote of the slightest interest is unhistorical, has already begun to die out in the studies I know best. The period of arbitrary scepticism about the canon and text of Shakespeare is now over: and it is reasonable to expect that this method will soon be used only on Christian documents and survive only in the *Thinkers' Library* and the theological colleges.]

I find myself, therefore, compelled to disagree with Professor Price's second point. I do not think that science has shown, or, by its nature, could ever show that the miraculous element in religion is erroneous. I am not speaking, of course, about the psychological effects of science on those who practise it or read its results. That the continued application of scientific methods breeds a temper of mind unfavourable to the miraculous, may well be the case, but even here there would seem to be some difference among the sciences. Certainly, if we think, not of the miraculous in particular, but of religion in general, there is such a difference. Mathematicians, astronomers and physicists are often religious, even mystical; biologists much less often; economists and psychologists very seldom indeed. It is as their subject matter comes nearer to man himself that their anti-religious bias hardens.

And that brings me to Professor Price's fourth point – for I would rather postpone consideration of his third. His fourth point, it will be remembered, was that science had undermined not only what he regards as the mythological accretions of religion, but also what he regards as its essence. That essence is for him Theism and immortality. In so far as natural science can give a satisfactory account of man as a purely biological entity, it excludes the soul and therefore excludes immortality. That, no doubt, is why the scientists who are most, or most nearly, concerned with man himself are the most anti-religious.

Now most assuredly if naturalism is right then it is at this point, at the study of man himself, that it wins its final victory and overthrows all our hopes: not only our hope of immortality, but our hope of finding significance in our lives here and now. On the other hand, if naturalism is wrong, it will be here that it will reveal its fatal philosophical defect, and that is what I think it does.

On the fully naturalistic view all events are determined by laws. Our logical behaviour, in other words our thoughts, and our ethical behaviour, including our ideals as well as our acts of will, are governed by biochemical laws; these, in turn, by physical laws which are themselves actuarial statements about the lawless movements of matter. These units never intended to produce the regular universe we see: the law of averages (successor to Lucretius's *exiguum clinamen*)[9] has produced it out of the collision of these random variations in movement. The physical universe never intended to produce organisms. The relevant chemicals on earth, and the sun's heat, thus juxtaposed, gave rise to this disquieting disease of matter: organisation. Natural selection, operating on the minute differences between one organism and another, blundered into that sort of phosphorescence or mirage which we call consciousness – and that, in some cortexes beneath some skulls, at certain moments, still in obedience to physical laws, but to physical laws now filtered through laws of a more complicated kind, takes the form we call thought. Such, for instance, is the origin of this paper: such was the origin of Professor Price's paper. What we should speak of as his 'thoughts' were merely the last link of a causal chain in which all the previous links were irrational. He spoke as he did because the matter of his brain was behaving in a certain way: and the whole history of the universe up to that moment had forced it to behave in that way. What we called his thought was essentially a phenomenon of the same sort as his other secretions – the form which the vast irrational process of nature was bound to take at a particular point of space and time.

Of course it did not feel like that to him or to us while it was going on. He appeared to himself to be studying the nature of things, to be in some way aware of the realities, even supersensuous realities, outside his own head. But if strict naturalism is right, he was deluded: he was merely enjoying the conscious reflection of irrationally determined events in his own head. It appeared to him that his thoughts (as he called them) could have to outer realities that wholly immaterial relation which we call truth or falsehood: though, in fact, being but the shadow of cerebral events, it is not easy to see that they could have any relations to the outer world except causal relations. And when Professor Price defended scientists, speaking of their devotion to truth and their constant following of the best light they knew, it seemed to him that he was choosing an attitude in obedience to an ideal. He did not feel that he was merely suffering a reaction determined by ultimately amoral and irrational sources, and no more capable of rightness or wrongness than a hiccup or a sneeze.

It would have been impossible for Professor Price to have written, or us to have read, his paper with the slightest interest if he and we had consciously held the position of strict naturalism throughout. But we can

---

[9] 'Small inclination.' *De Rerum Natura*, Bk. II, line 292.

go further. It would be impossible to accept naturalism itself if we really and consistently believed naturalism. For naturalism is a system of thought. But for naturalism all thoughts are mere events with irrational causes. It is, to me at any rate, impossible to regard the thoughts which make up naturalism in that way and, at the same time, to regard them as a real insight into external reality. Bradley distinguished *idea-event* from *idea-making*,[10] but naturalism seems to me committed to regarding ideas simply as events. For meaning is a relation of a wholly new kind, as remote, as mysterious, as opaque to empirical study, as soul itself.

Perhaps this may be even more simply put in another way. Every particular thought (whether it is a judgement of fact or a judgement of value) is always and by all men discounted the moment they believe that it can be explained, without remainder, as the result of irrational causes. Whenever you know what the other man is saying is wholly due to his complexes or to a bit of bone pressing on his brain, you cease to attach any importance to it. But if naturalism were true then all thoughts whatever would be wholly the result of irrational causes. Therefore, all thoughts would be equally worthless. Therefore, naturalism is worthless. If it is true, then we can know no truths. It cuts its own throat.

[I remember once being shown a certain kind of knot which was such that if you added one extra complication to make assurance doubly sure you suddenly found that the whole thing had come undone in your hands and you had only a bit of string. It is like that with naturalism. It goes on claiming territory after territory: first the inorganic, then the lower organisms, then man's body, then his emotions. But when it takes the final step and we attempt a naturalistic account of thought itself, suddenly the whole thing unravels. The last fatal step has invalidated all the preceding ones: for they were all reasoning and reason itself has been discredited. We must, therefore, either give up thinking altogether or else begin over again from the ground floor.]

There is no reason, at this point, to bring in either Christianity or spiritualism. We do not need them to refute naturalism. It refutes itself. Whatever else we may come to believe about the universe, at least we cannot believe naturalism. The validity of rational thought, accepted in an utterly non-naturalistic, transcendental (if you will), supernatural sense, is the necessary presupposition of all other theorising. There is simply no sense in beginning with a view of the universe and trying to fit the claims of thought in at a later stage. By thinking at all we have claimed

---

[10] 'Spoken and Written English', *The Collected Papers of Henry Bradley*, ed. Robert Bridges (Oxford, 1928), pp. 168–93.

that our thoughts are more than mere natural events. All other propositions must be fitted in as best they can round that primary claim.

Holding that science has not refuted the miraculous element in religion,
much less that naturalism, rigorously taken, can refute anything except
itself, I do not, of course, share Professor Price's anxiety to find a religion
which can do without what he calls the mythology. What he suggests is
simple Theism, rendered credible by a belief in immortality which, in its
turn, is guaranteed by Psychical Research. Professor Price is not, of course,
arguing that immortality would of itself prove Theism: it would merely
remove an obstacle to Theism. The positive source of Theism he finds in
religious experience.

At this point it is very important to decide which of two questions we
are asking. We may be asking: (1) whether this purged minimal religion
suggested by Professor Price is capable, as a historical, social and psychological entity, of giving fresh heart to society, strengthening the moral
will, and producing all those other benefits which, it is claimed, the
old religions have sometimes produced. On the other hand, we may be
asking: (2) whether this minimal religion will be the true one; that is,
whether it contains the only true propositions we can make about ultimate questions.

The first question is not a religious question but a sociological one. The
religious mind as such, like the older sort of scientific mind as such, does
not care a rap about socially useful propositions. Both are athirst for
reality, for the utterly objective, for that which is what it is. The 'open
mind' of the scientist and the emptied and silenced mind of the mystic
are both efforts to eliminate what is our own in order that the Other may
speak. And if, turning aside from the religious attitude, we speak for
a moment as mere sociologists, we must admit that history does not
encourage us to expect much invigorating power in a minimal religion.
Attempts at such a minimal religion are not new – from Akhenaton[11] and
Julian the Apostate[12] down to Lord Herbert of Cherbury[13] and the late
H.G. Wells. But where are the saints, the consolations, the ecstasies? The
greatest of such attempts was that simplification of Jewish and Christian

[11] Akhenaton (Amenhotep IV), king of Egypt, who came to the throne about 1375 BC and introduced
a new religion, in which the sun-god Ra (designated as 'Aton') superseded Amon.
[12] Roman emperor AD 361–3, who was brought up compulsorily as a Christian, but who on attaining
the throne proclaimed himself a pagan. He made a great effort to revive the worship of the old gods.
[13] Edward Herbert (1583–1648). He is known as the 'Father of Deism', for he maintained that among
the 'common notions' apprehended by instinct are the existence of God, the duty of worship and
repentance, and future rewards and punishment. This 'natural religion', he maintained, had been
vitiated by superstition and dogma.

traditions which we call Islam. But it retained many elements which Professor Price would regard as mythical and barbaric, and its culture is by no means one of the richest or most progressive.

Nor do I see how such a religion, if it became a vital force, would long be preserved in its freedom from dogma. Is its God to be conceived pantheistically, or after the Jewish, Platonic, Christian fashion? If we are to retain the minimal religion in all its purity, I suppose the right answer would be: 'We don't know, and we must be content not to know.' But that is the end of the minimal religion as a practical affair. For the question is of pressing practical importance. If the God of Professor Price's religion is an impersonal spirituality diffused through the whole universe, equally present, and present in the same mode, at all points of space and time, then He – or It – will certainly be conceived as being beyond good and evil, expressed equally in the brothel or the torture chamber and in the model factory or the university common room. If, on the other hand, He is a personal Being standing outside His creation, commanding this and prohibiting that, quite different consequences follow. The choice between these two views affects the choice between courses of action at every moment both in private and public life. Nor is this the only such question that arises. Does the minimal religion know whether its god stands in the same relation to all men, or is he related to some as he is not related to others? To be true to its undogmatic character it must again say: 'Don't ask.' But if that is the reply, then the minimal religion cannot exclude the Christian view that He was present in a special way in Jesus, nor the Nazi view that He is present in a special way in the German race, nor the Hindu view that He is specially present in the Brahmin, nor the central African view that He is specially present in the thigh-bone of a dead English Tommy.

All these difficulties are concealed from us as long as the minimal religion exists only on paper. But suppose it were somehow established all over what is left of the British Empire, and let us suppose that Professor Price has (most reluctantly and solely from a sense of duty) become its supreme head on earth. I predict that one of two things must happen: (1) In the first month of his reign he will find himself uttering his first dogmatic definition – he will find himself saying, for example: 'No. God is not an amoral force diffused through the whole universe to whom suttee and temple prostitution are no more and no less acceptable than building hospitals and teaching children; he is a righteous creator, separate from his creation, who demands of you justice and mercy'; or (2) Professor Price will not reply. In the second case is it not clear what will happen? Those who have come to his minimal religion from Christianity will conceive God in the Jewish, Platonic, Christian way; those who have come from Hinduism will conceive Him pantheistically; and the plain men who have come from nowhere will conceive Him as a righteous Creator in their moments of moral indignation, and as a pantheistic God in their moments of self-indulgence. And the ex-Marxist will think He is specially present in the Proletariat, and the ex-Nazi will think he is specially present in the German people. And they will hold world conferences at which they all speak the same language and reach the most edifying agreement: but they will all mean totally different things. The minimal religion in fact cannot, while it remains minimal, be acted on. As soon as you *do* anything you have assumed one of the dogmas. In practice it will not be a religion at all; it will be merely a new colouring given to all the different things people were doing already.

[I submit it to Professor Price, with great respect, that when he spoke of mere Theism, he was all the time unconsciously assuming a particular conception of God: that is, he was assuming a dogma about God. And I do not think he was deducing it solely, or chiefly, from his own religious experience or even from a study of religious experience in general. For religious experience can be made to yield almost any sort of God. I think Professor Price assumed a certain sort of God because he has been brought up in a certain way: because Bishop Butler and Hooker and Thomas Aquinas and Augustine and St Paul and Christ and Aristotle and Plato are, as we say, 'in his blood'. He was not really starting from scratch. Had he done so, had God meant in his mind a being about whom no dogma whatever is held, I doubt whether he would have looked for even social salvation in such an empty concept. All the strength and value of the minimal religion, for him as for all others who accept it, is derived not from it, but from the tradition which he imports into it.]

The minimal religion will, in my opinion, leave us all doing what we were doing before. Now it, in itself, will not be an objection from Professor Price's point of view. He was not working for unity, but for some spiritual dynamism to see us through the black night of civilisation. If Psychical Research has the effect of enabling people to continue, or to return to, all the diverse religions which naturalism has threatened, and if they can thus get power and hope and discipline, he will, I fancy, be content. But the trouble is that if this minimal religion leaves Buddhists still Buddhists, and Nazis still Nazis, then it will, I believe, leave us – as Western, mechanised, democratic, secularised men – exactly where we were. In what way will a belief in the immortality vouched for by Psychical Research, and in an unknown God, restore to us the virtue and energy of our ancestors? It seems to me that both beliefs, unless reinforced by something else, will be to modern man very shadowy and inoperative. If indeed we knew that God were righteous, that He had purposes for us, that He was the leader in a cosmic battle and that some real issue hung on our conduct in the field, then it would be something to the purpose. Or if, again, the utterances which purport to come from the other world ever had the accent which really *suggests* another world, ever spoke (as even the inferior actual religions do) with that voice before which our mortal nature trembles with awe or joy, then that also would be to the purpose. But the god of minimal Theism remains powerless to excite either fear or love: can be given power to do so only from those traditional resources to which, in Professor Price's conception, science will never permit our return. As for the utterances of the mediums ... I do not wish to be offensive. But will even the most convinced spiritualist claim that one sentence from that source has ever taken its place among the golden sayings of mankind, has ever approached (much less equalled) in power to elevate, strengthen or correct even the second rank of such sayings? Will anyone deny that the vast majority of spirit messages sink pitiably below the best that has been thought and said even in this world? – that in most of them we find a banality and provincialism, a paradoxical union of the prim with the enthusiastic, of flatness and gush, which would suggest that the souls of the moderately respectable are in the keeping of Annie Besant[14] and Martin Tupper?[15]

I am not arguing from the vulgarity of the messages that their claim to come from the dead is false. If I did the spiritualist would reply that this quality is due to imperfections in the medium of communication. Let it be so. We are not here discussing the truth of spiritualism, but its power to become the starting point of a religion. And for that purpose I submit that the poverty of its contents disqualifies it. A minimal religion compounded of spirit messages and bare Theism has no power to touch any of the deepest chords in our nature, or to evoke any response which will raise us even to a higher secular level – let alone to the spiritual life. The god of whom no dogmas are believed is a mere shadow. He will not produce that fear of the Lord in which wisdom begins, and, therefore, will not produce that love in which it is consummated. The immortality

---

[14] Annie Besant (1847–1933) was an ardent supporter of Liberal causes and became a member of the Theosophical Society in 1889.

[15] Martin Tupper (1810–89) is probably best known for his *Proverbial Philosophy* – commonplace maxims and reflections couched in a rhythmical form.

which the messages suggest can produce in mediocre spirits only a vague comfort for our unredeemedly personal hankerings, a shadowy sequel to the story of this world in which all comes right (but right in how pitiable a sense!), while the more spiritual will feel that it has added a new horror to death – the horror of mere endless succession, of indefinite imprisonment in that which binds us all, *das Gemeine*.[16] There is in this minimal religion nothing that can convince, convert, or (in the higher sense) console; nothing, therefore, which can restore vitality to our civilisation. It is not costly enough. It can never be a controller or even a rival to our natural sloth and greed. A flag, a song, an old school tie, is stronger than it; much more, the pagan religions. Rather than pin my hopes on it I would almost listen again to the drum-beat in my blood (for the blood is at least in some sense the life) and join in the song of the Maenads:

> *Happy they whom the Daimons*
> *Have befriended, who have entered*
> *The divine orgies, making holy*
> *Their life-days, till the dance throbs*
> *In their heart-beats, while they romp with*
> *Dionysus on the mountains ...*[17]

Yes, almost; almost I'd sooner be a pagan suckled in a creed outworn.

Almost, but not, of course, quite. If one is forced to such an alternative, it is perhaps better to starve in a wholly secularised and meaningless universe than to recall the obscenities and cruelties of paganism. They attract because they are a distortion of the truth, and therefore, retain some of its flavour. But with this remark I have passed into our second question. I shall not be expected at the end of this paper to begin an apologetic for the truth of Christianity. I will only say something which in one form or another I have said perhaps too often already. If there is no God then we have no interest in the minimal religion or any other. We will not make a lie even to save civilisation. But if there is, then it is so probable as to be almost axiomatic that the initiative lies wholly on His side. If He can be known it will be by self-revelation on His part, not by speculation on ours. We, therefore, look for Him where it is claimed that He has revealed Himself by miracle, by inspired teachers, by enjoined ritual. The traditions conflict, yet the longer and more sympathetically

---

[16] Johann Wolfgang Goethe, *Epilog zu Schillers Glocke*, l. 32. '*Das Gemeine*' means something like 'that which dominates us all'.
[17] Euripides, *Bacchae*, line 74.

we study them the more we become aware of a common element in many of them: the theme of sacrifice, of mystical communion through the shed blood, of death and rebirth, of redemption, is too clear to escape notice. We are fully entitled to use moral and intellectual criticism. What we are not, in my opinion, entitled to do is simply to abstract the ethical element and set that up as a religion on its own. Rather in that tradition which is at once more completely ethical and most transcends mere ethics – in which the old themes of the sacrifice and rebirth recur in a form which transcends, though there it no longer revolts, our conscience and our reason – we may still most reasonably believe that we have the consummation of all religion, the fullest message from the wholly other, the living creator, who, if He is at all, must be the God not only of the philosophers, but of mystics and savages, not only of the head and heart, but also of the primitive emotions and the spiritual heights beyond all emotion. We may still reasonably attach ourselves to the Church, to the only concrete organisation which has preserved down to this present time the core of all the messages, pagan and perhaps pre-pagan, that have ever come from beyond the world, and begin to practise the only religion which rests not upon some selection of certain supposedly 'higher' elements in our nature, but on the shattering and rebuilding, the death and rebirth, of that nature in every part: neither Greek nor Jew nor barbarian, but a new creation.

[Note: *The debate between Lewis and Professor Price did not end here. In* The Socratic Digest, *No. 4 [1948], there follows a 'Reply' to Lewis's 'Religion Without Dogma?' by Professor Price (pp. 94–102). Then, at a meeting of the Socratic Club on 2 February 1948, Miss G.E.M. Anscombe read a paper entitled 'A Reply to Mr C.S. Lewis's Argument that "Naturalism is Self-refuting"', afterwards published in the same issue of the* Digest *(pp. 7–15) as Professor Price's 'Reply'. Miss Anscombe criticised the argument found on pp. 91–4 of the paper printed above as well as Chapter III, 'The Self-Contradiction of the Naturalist', of Lewis's book* Miracles *(London, 1947). The two short pieces that follow are (A) the Socratic minute-book account of Lewis's reply to Miss Anscombe, and (B) a reply written by Lewis himself – both reprinted from the same issue of the* Digest *mentioned above (pp. 15–16). Aware that the third chapter of his* Miracles *was ambiguous, Lewis revised this chapter for the Fontana (1960) issue of* Miracles *in which Chapter III is retitled 'The Cardinal Difficulty of Naturalism'.*]

A

In his reply Mr C.S. Lewis agreed that the words 'cause' and 'ground' were far from synonymous but said that the recognition of a ground could be the cause of assent, and that assent was only rational when such was its cause. He denied that such words as 'recognition' and 'perception' could be properly used of a mental act among whose causes the thing perceived or recognised was not one.

Miss Anscombe said that Mr Lewis had misunderstood her, and thus the first part of the discussion was confined to the two speakers who attempted to clarify their positions and their differences. Miss Anscombe said that Mr Lewis was still not distinguishing between 'having reasons' and 'having reasoned' in the casual sense. Mr Lewis understood the speaker to be making a tetrachotomy thus: (1) logical reasons; (2) having reasons (i.e. psychological); (3) historical causes; (4) scientific causes or observed regularities. The main point in his reply was that an observed regularity was only the symptom of a cause, and not the cause itself, and in reply to an interruption by the Secretary he referred to his notion of cause as 'magical'. An open discussion followed, in which some members tried to show Miss Anscombe that there was a connection between ground and cause, while others contended against the President [Lewis] that the test for the validity of reason could never in any event be such a thing as the state of the bloodstream. The President finally admitted that the word 'valid' was an unfortunate one. From the discussion in general it appeared that Mr Lewis would have to turn his argument into a rigorous analytic one, if his notion of 'validity' as the effect of causes were to stand the test of all the questions put to him.

B

I admit that *valid* was a bad word for what I meant; *veridical* (or *verific* or *veriferous*) would have been better. I also admit that the cause and effect relation between events and the ground and consequent relations between propositions are distinct. Since English uses the word *because* of both, let us here use *Because* CE for the cause and effect relation ('This doll always falls on its feet *because* CE its feet are weighted'), and *Because* GC for the ground and consequent relation ('A equals C *because* GC they both equal B'). But the sharper this distinction becomes the more my difficulty increases. If an argument is to be verific the conclusion must be related to the premises as consequent to ground, i.e. the conclusion is there *because* GC certain other propositions are true. On the other hand, our thinking the conclusion is an event and must be related to previous events as effect to cause, i.e. this act of thinking must occur *because* CE previous events have occurred. It would seem, therefore, that we never think the conclusion *because* GC it is the consequent of its grounds but only *because* CE certain previous events have happened. If so, it does not seem that the GC sequence makes us more likely to think the true conclusion than not. And this is very much what I meant by the difficulty in Naturalism.

[22]

THE DECLINE OF RELIGION

Taken from The Cherwell, *Oxford, Volume XXVI (29 November 1946), reproduced in* Undeceptions *(1971), then in* First and Second Things *(1985) and* Compelling Reason *(1998).*

From what I see of junior Oxford at present it would be quite easy to draw opposite conclusions about the religious predicament of what we call 'the rising generation', though in reality the undergraduate body includes men and women almost as much divided from one another in age, outlook and experience as they are divided from the dons. Plenty of evidence can be produced to show that religion is in its last decline among them, or that a revival of interest in religion is one of their most noticeable characteristics. And in fact something that may be called 'a decline' and something that may be called 'a revival' are both going on. It will be perhaps more useful to attempt to understand both than to try our luck at 'spotting the winner'.

The 'decline of religion' so often lamented (or welcomed) is held to be shown by empty chapels. Now it is quite true that chapels which were full in 1900 are empty in 1946. But this change was not gradual. It occurred at the precise moment when chapel ceased to be compulsory. It was not in fact a decline; it was a precipice. The sixty men who had come because chapel was a little later than 'rollers'[1] (its only alternative) came no more; the five Christians remained. The withdrawal of compulsion did not create a new religious situation, but only revealed the situation which had long existed. And this is typical of the 'decline in religion' all over England.

In every class and every part of the country the visible practice of Christianity has grown very much less in the last fifty years. This is often taken to show that the nation as a whole has passed from a Christian to a secular outlook. But if we judge the nineteenth century from the books

---

[1] After there came to be a number of non-Anglican students in the Oxford colleges, those students who did not wish to attend the morning chapel service were required to report to the Dean five or ten minutes before the service and have their names put on his roll-call. Thus the 'rollers' who did not go to chapel had to be up before those who did go. Neither chapel service nor the Dean's roll-call is compulsory now.

it wrote, the outlook of our grandfathers (with a very few exceptions) was quite as secular as our own. The novels of Meredith, Trollope and Thackeray are not written either by or for men who see this world as the vestibule of eternity, who regard pride as the greatest of the sins, who desire to be poor in spirit, and look for a supernatural salvation. Even more significant is the absence from Dickens' *Christmas Carol* of any interest in the Incarnation. Mary, the Magi, and the Angels are replaced by 'spirits' of his own invention, and the animals present are not the ox and ass in the stable but the goose and turkey in the poulterer's shop. Most striking of all is the thirty-third chapter of *The Antiquary*, where Lord Glenallan forgives old Elspeth for her intolerable wrong. Glenallan has been painted by Scott as a life-long penitent and ascetic, a man whose every thought has been for years fixed on the supernatural. But when he has to forgive, no motive of a Christian kind is brought into play: the battle is won by 'the generosity of his nature'. It does not occur to Scott that his fasts, his solitudes, his beads and his confessor, however useful as romantic 'properties', could be effectively connected with a serious action which concerns the plot of the book.

I am anxious here not to be misunderstood. I do not mean that Scott was not a brave, generous, honourable man and a glorious writer. I mean that in his work, as in that of most of his contemporaries, only secular and natural values are taken seriously. Plato and Virgil are, in that sense, nearer to Christianity than they.

Thus the 'decline of religion' becomes a very ambiguous phenomenon. One way of putting the truth would be that the religion which has declined was not Christianity. It was a vague Theism with a strong and virile ethical code, which, far from standing over against the 'World', was absorbed into the whole fabric of English institutions and sentiment and therefore demanded churchgoing as (at best) a part of loyalty and good manners or (at worst) a proof of respectability. Hence a social pressure, like the withdrawal of the compulsion, did not create a new situation. The new freedom first allowed accurate observations to be made. When no man goes to church except because he seeks Christ the number of actual believers can at last be discovered. It should be added that this new freedom was partly caused by the very conditions which it revealed. If the various anti-clerical and anti-theistic forces at work in the nineteenth century had had to attack a solid phalanx of radical Christians the story might have been different. But mere 'religion' – 'morality tinged with emotion', 'what a man does with his solitude', 'the religion of all good men' – has little power of resistance. It is not good at saying No.

The decline of 'religion', thus understood, seems to me in some ways a blessing. At the very worst it makes the issue clear. To the modern undergraduate Christianity is, at least, one of the intellectual options. It is, so to speak, on the agenda: it can be discussed, and a conversion may follow. I can remember times when this was much more difficult. 'Religion' (as distinct from Christianity) was too vague to be discussed ('too sacred to be lightly mentioned') and so mixed up with sentiment and good form as to be one of the embarrassing subjects. If it had to be spoken of, it was spoken of in a hushed, medical voice. Something of the shame of the Cross is, and ought to be, irremovable. But the merely social and sentimental embarrassment is gone. The fog of 'religion' has lifted; the positions and numbers of both armies can be observed; and real shooting is now possible.

The decline of 'religion' is no doubt a bad thing for the 'World'. By it all the things that made England a fairly happy country are, I suppose, endangered: the comparative purity of her public life, the comparative humanity of her police, and the possibility of some mutual respect and kindness between political opponents. But I am not clear that it makes conversions to Christianity rarer or more difficult: rather the reverse. It makes the choice more unescapable. When the Round Table is broken every man must follow either Galahad or Mordred: middle things are gone.

So much for the Decline of Religion; now for a Christian Revival. Those who claim that there is such a Revival would point to the success (I mean success in the sense that it can be tested by sales) of several explicitly and even violently Christian writers, the apparent popularity of lectures on theological subjects, and the brisk atmosphere of not unfriendly discussion on them in which we live. They point, in fact, to what I have heard described as 'the high-brow Christian racket'. It is difficult to describe the phenomenon in quite neutral terms: but perhaps no one would deny that Christianity is now 'on the map' among the younger *intelligentsia* as it was not, say, in 1920. Only freshmen now talk as if the anti-Christian position were self-evident. The days of 'simple un-faith' are as dead as those of 'simple faith'.

At this those who are on the same side as myself are quite properly pleased. We have cause to give thanks: and the comments which I have to add proceed, I hope, not from a natural middle-aged desire to pour cold water into any soup within reach, but only from a desire to forestall, and therefore to disarm, possible disappointments.

In the first place, it must be admitted by anyone who accepts Christianity, that an increased interest in it, or even a growing measure of intellectual assent to it, is a very different thing from the conversion of England or even a single soul. Conversion requires an alteration of the will, and an alteration which, in the last resort, does not occur without the intervention of the supernatural. I do not in the least agree with those who therefore conclude that the spread of an intellectual (and imaginative) climate favourable to Christianity is useless. You do not prove munition workers useless by showing that they cannot themselves win battles, however proper this reminder would be if they attempted to claim the honour due to fighting men. If the intellectual climate is such that, when a man comes to the crisis at which he must either accept or reject Christ, his reason and imagination are not on the wrong side, then his conflict will be fought out under favourable conditions. Those who help to produce and spread such a climate are therefore doing useful work: and yet no such great matter after all. Their share is a modest one; and it is always possible that nothing – nothing whatever – may come of it. Far higher than they stands that character whom, to the best of my knowledge, the present Christian movement has not yet produced – the *Preacher* in the full sense, the Evangelist, the man on fire, the man who infects. The propagandist, the apologist, only represents John Baptist: the Preacher represents the Lord Himself. He will be sent – or else he will not. But unless he comes we mere Christian intellectuals will not effect very much. That does not mean we should down tools.

In the second place we must remember that a widespread and lively interest in a subject is precisely what we call a Fashion. And it is the nature of Fashions not to last. The present Christian movement may, or may not, have a long run ahead of it. But sooner or later it must lose the public ear; in a place like Oxford such changes are extraordinarily rapid. Bradley and the other idealists fell in a few terms, the Douglas scheme even more suddenly, the Vorticists overnight.[2] (Who now remembers Pogo?[3] Who now reads *Childermass*?[4]) Whatever in our present success mere fashion has given us, mere fashion will presently withdraw. The real conversions will remain: but nothing else will. In that sense we may be on the brink of a real and permanent Christian revival: but it will work slowly and obscurely and in small groups. The present sunshine (if I may so call it) is certainly temporary. The grain must be got into the barns before the wet weather comes.

---

[2] F.H. Bradley (1846–1924) was a Fellow of Merton College, Oxford, and the author of *Appearance and Reality* (London, 1893). Major C.H. Douglas, a socio-economist, wrote, among other works, *Social Credit* (London, 1933). The Vorticists were a school of artists of the 1920s.

[3] No one, practically. Pogo, or the Pogo-stick, which was invented in 1922, is a stilt with a spring on which the player jumps about.

[4] *Childermass* is by P. Wyndham Lewis (London, 1928).

This mutability is the fate of all movements, fashions, intellectual climates and the like. But a Christian movement is also up against something sterner than the mere fickleness of taste. We have not yet had (at least in junior Oxford) any really bitter opposition. But if we have many more successes, this will certainly appear. The enemy has not yet thought it worth while to fling his whole weight against us. But he soon will. This happens in the history of every Christian movement, beginning with the Ministry of Christ Himself. At first it is welcome to all who have no special reason for opposing it: at this stage he who is not against it is for it. What men notice is its difference from those aspects of the World which they already dislike. But later on, as the real meaning of the Christian claim becomes apparent, its demand for total surrender, the sheer chasm between Nature and Supernature, men are increasingly 'offended'. Dislike, terror, and finally hatred succeed: none who will not give it what it asks (and it asks all) can endure it: all who are not with it are against it. That is why we must cherish no picture of the present intellectual movement simply growing and spreading and finally reclaiming millions by sweet reasonableness. Long before it became as important as that the real opposition would have begun, and to be on the Christian side would be costing a man (at the least) his career. But remember, in England the opposition will quite likely be *called* Christianity (or Christo-democracy, or British Christianity, or something of that kind).

I think – but how should I know? – that all is going reasonably well. But it is early days. Neither our armour nor our enemies' is yet engaged. Combatants always tend to imagine that the war is further on than it really is.

[23]

ON FORGIVENESS

Written in 1947 but not found until much later, this essay was published in Fern-seed and Elephants *(1998).*

We say a great many things in church (and out of church too) without thinking of what we are saying. For instance, we say in the Creed 'I believe in the forgiveness of sins.' I had been saying it for several years before I asked myself why it was in the Creed. At first sight it seems hardly worth putting in. 'If one is a Christian,' I thought, 'of course one believes in the forgiveness of sins. It goes without saying.' But the people who compiled the Creed apparently thought that this was a part of our belief which we needed to be reminded of every time we went to church. And I have begun to see that, as far as I am concerned, they were right. To believe in the forgiveness of sins is not nearly so easy as I thought. Real belief in it is the sort of thing that very easily slips away if we don't keep on polishing it up.

We believe that God forgives us our sins; but also that he will not do so unless we forgive other people their sins against us. There is no doubt about the second part of this statement. It is in the Lord's Prayer: it was emphatically stated by our Lord. If you don't forgive you will not be forgiven. No part of his teaching is clearer: and there are no exceptions to it. He doesn't say that we are to forgive other people's sins provided they are not too frightful, or provided there are extenuating circumstances, or anything of that sort. We are to forgive them all, however spiteful, however mean, however often they are repeated. If we don't, we shall be forgiven none of our own.

Now it seems to me that we often make a mistake both about God's forgiveness of our sins and about the forgiveness we are told to offer to other people's sins. Take it first about God's forgiveness. I find that when I think I am asking God to forgive me I am often in reality (unless I watch myself very carefully) asking him to do something quite different. I am asking him not to forgive me but to excuse me. But there is all the difference in the world between forgiving and excusing. Forgiveness says 'Yes, you have done this thing, but I accept your apology, I will never hold it against you and everything between us two will be exactly as it was before.' But excusing says 'I see that you couldn't help it or didn't mean it, you weren't really to blame.' If one was not really to blame then there is nothing to forgive. In that sense forgiveness and excusing are almost opposites. Of course in dozens of cases, either between God and man, or between one man and another, there may be a mixture of the two. Part of what seemed at first to be the sins turns out to be really nobody's fault and is excused; the bit that is left over is forgiven. If you had a perfect excuse you would not need forgiveness: if the whole of your action needs forgiveness then there was no excuse for it. But the trouble is that what we call 'asking God's forgiveness' very often really consists in asking God to accept our excuses. What leads us into this mistake is the fact that there usually is some amount of excuse, some 'extenuating circumstances'. We are so very anxious to point these out to God (and to ourselves) that we are apt to forget the really important thing; that is, the bit left over, the bit which the excuses don't cover, the bit which is inexcusable but not, thank God, unforgivable. And if we forget this we shall go away imagining that we have repented and been forgiven when all that has really happened is that we have satisfied ourselves with our own excuses. They may be very bad excuses: we are all too easily satisfied about ourselves.

There are two remedies for this danger. One is to remember that God knows all the real excuses very much better than we do. If there are real 'extenuating circumstances' there is no fear that he will overlook them. Often he must know many excuses that we have never thought of, and therefore humble souls will, after death, have the delightful surprise of discovering that on certain occasions they sinned much less than they had thought. All the real excusing he will do. What we have got to take to him is the inexcusable bit, the sin. We are only wasting time by talking about all the parts which can (we think) be excused. When you go to a doctor, you show him the bit of you that is wrong – say, a broken arm. It would be a mere waste of time to keep on explaining that your legs and eyes and throat are all right. You may be mistaken in thinking so; and anyway, if they are really all right, the doctor will know that.

The second remedy is really and truly to believe in the forgiveness of sins. A great deal of our anxiety to make excuses comes from not really believing in it; from thinking that God will not take us to himself again unless he is satisfied that some sort of case can be made out in our favour. But that would not be forgiveness at all. Real forgiveness means looking steadily at the sin, the sin that is left over without any excuse, after all allowances have been made, and seeing it in all its horror, dirt, meanness and malice, and nevertheless being wholly reconciled to the man who has done it. That, and only that, is forgiveness; and that we can always have from God if we ask for it.

When it comes to a question of our forgiving other people, it is partly the same and partly different. It is the same because, here also, forgiving does not mean excusing. Many people seem to think it does. They think that if you ask them to forgive someone who has cheated or bullied them you are trying to make out that there was really no cheating or no bullying. But if that were so, there would be nothing to forgive. They keep on replying 'But I tell you the man broke a most solemn promise.' Exactly: that is precisely what you have to forgive. (This doesn't mean you must necessarily believe his next promise. It does mean that you must make every effort to kill every trace of resentment in your own heart – every wish to humiliate or hurt him or to pay him out.) The difference between this situation and the one in which you are asking God's forgiveness is this. In our own case we accept excuses too easily, in other people's we do not accept them easily enough. As regards my own sins it is a safe bet (though not a certainty) that the excuses are not really so good as I think: as regards other men's sins against me it is a safe bet (though not a certainty) that the excuses are better than I think. One must therefore begin by attending carefully to everything which may show that the other man was not so much to blame as we thought. But even if he is absolutely fully to blame we still have to forgive him; and even if ninety-nine per cent of his apparent guilt can be explained away by really good excuses, the problem of forgiveness begins with the one per cent of guilt which is left over. To excuse what can really produce good excuses is not Christian charity; it is only fairness. To be a Christian means to forgive the inexcusable, because God has forgiven the inexcusable in you.

This is hard. It is perhaps not so hard to forgive a single great injury. But to forgive the incessant provocations of daily life – to keep on forgiving the bossy mother-in-law, the bullying husband, the nagging wife, the selfish daughter, the deceitful son – how can we do it? Only, I think, by remembering where we stand, by meaning our words when we say in our prayers each night 'Forgive us our trespasses as we forgive those that trespass against us.' We are offered forgiveness on no other terms. To refuse it is to refuse God's mercy for ourselves. There is no hint of exceptions and God means what he says.

24

THE PAINS OF ANIMALS

A Problem in Theology

In his book The Problem of Pain, *one of the questions that Lewis
addressed was how to account for the occurrence of pain in a universe
which is the creation of an all-good God, and in creatures that are not
morally sinful. His chapter on 'Animal Pain' provoked a counter-
inquiry from C.E.M. Joad, Head of the Department of Philosophy in
the University of London. The resulting controversy, first published in*
The Month, *Volume CLXXXIX (February 1950), was published
in* Undeceptions *(1971),* Timeless at Heart *(1991) and* Compelling
Reason *(1998).*

The Inquiry by C.E.M. Joad

For many years the problem of pain and evil seemed to me to offer an
insuperable objection to Christianity. Either God could abolish them but
did not, in which case, since He deliberately tolerated the presence in the
universe of a state of affairs which was bad, I did not see how He could be
good; or He wanted to abolish them but could not, in which case I did
not see how He could be all-powerful. The dilemma is as old as St
Augustine, and nobody pretends that there is an easy way of escape.

Moreover, all the attempts to explain pain away, or to mitigate its stark
ferocity, or to present it as other than a very great evil, perhaps the greatest
of evils, are palpable failures. They are testimonies to the kindness of
men's hearts or perhaps to the queasiness of their consciences, rather than
to the sharpness of their wits.

And yet, granting pain to be an evil, perhaps the greatest of evils, I have
come to accept the Christian view of pain as not incompatible with the
Christian concept of the Creator and of the world that He has made.
That view I take to be briefly as follows: It was of no interest to God
to create a species consisting of virtuous automata, for the 'virtue' of
automata who can do no other than they do is a courtesy title only; it is
analogous to the 'virtue' of the stone that rolls downhill or of the water

that freezes at 32°. To what end, it may be asked, should God create such creatures? That He might be praised by them? But automatic praise is a mere succession of noises. That He might love them? But they are essentially unlovable; you cannot love puppets. And so God gave man free will that he might increase in virtue by his own efforts and become, as a free moral being, a worthy object of God's love. Freedom entails freedom to go wrong: man did, in fact, go wrong, misusing God's gift and doing evil. Pain is a by-product of evil; and so pain came into the world as a result of man's misuse of God's gift of free will.

So much I can understand; so much, indeed, I accept. It is plausible; it is rational; it hangs together.

But now I come to a difficulty, to which I see no solution; indeed, it is in the hope of learning of one that this article is written. This is the difficulty of animal pain, and, more particularly, of the pain of the animal world before man appeared upon the cosmic scene. What account do theologians give of it? The most elaborate and careful account known to me is that of C.S. Lewis.

He begins by making a distinction between sentience and consciousness. When we have the sensations a, b and c, the fact that we have them and the fact that we know that we have them imply that there is something which stands sufficiently outside them to notice that they occur and that they succeed one another. This is consciousness, the consciousness to which the sensations happen. In other words, the experience of succession, the succession of sensations, demands a self or soul which is other than the sensations which it experiences. (Mr Lewis invokes the helpful metaphor of the bed of a river along which the stream of sensations flows.) Consciousness, therefore, implies a continuing *ego* which recognises the succession of sensations; sentience is their mere succession. Now animals have sentience but not consciousness. Mr Lewis illustrates as follows:

> This would mean that if you give such a creature two blows with a whip, there are, indeed, two pains: but there is no co-ordinating self which can recognise that 'I have had two pains'. Even in the single pain there is no self to say 'I am in pain' – for if it could distinguish itself from the sensation – the bed from the stream – sufficiently to say 'I am in pain', it would also be able to connect the two sensations as *its* experience.[1]

(a) I take Mr Lewis's point – or, rather, I take it without perceiving its relevance. The question is how to account for the occurrence of pain (i) in a

---

[1] *The Problem of Pain*, ch. 9, p. 136 (Signature Classics edition).

universe which is the creation of an all-good God; (ii) in creatures who are not morally sinful. To be told that the creatures are not really creatures, since they are not conscious in the sense of consciousness defined, does not really help matters. If it be true, as Mr Lewis says, that the right way to put the matter is not 'This animal is feeling pain' but 'Pain is taking place in this animal',[2] pain is nevertheless taking place. Pain is felt even if there is no continuing *ego* to feel it and to relate it to past and to future pains. Now it is the fact that pain is felt, no matter who or what feels it, or whether any continuing consciousness feels it, in a universe planned by a good God, that demands explanation.

(b) Secondly, the theory of sentience as mere succession of sensations presupposes that there is no continuing consciousness. No continuing consciousness presupposes no memory. It seems to me to be nonsense to say that animals do not remember. The dog who cringes at the sight of the whip by which he has been constantly beaten *behaves* as if he remembers, and behaviour is all that we have to go by. In general, we all act upon the assumption that the horse, the cat, and the dog with which we are acquainted remember very well, remember sometimes better that we do. Now I do not see how it is possible to explain the fact of memory without a continuing consciousness.

Mr Lewis recognises this and concedes that the higher animals – apes, elephants, dogs, cats and so on – have a self which connects experiences; have, in fact what he calls a soul.[3] But this assumption presents us with a new set of difficulties.

(a) If animals have souls, what is to be done about their immortality? The question, it will be remembered, is elaborately debated in Heaven at the beginning of Anatole France's *Penguin Island* after the short-sighted St Mael has baptised the penguins, but no satisfactory solution is offered.

(b) Mr Lewis suggests that the higher domestic animals achieve immortality as members of a corporate society of which the head is man. It is, apparently, 'The-goodman-and-the-goodwife-ruling-their-children-and-their-beasts-in-the-good-homestead'[4] who survive. 'If you ask,' he writes, 'concerning an animal thus raised as a member of the whole Body of the homestead, where its personal identity resides, I answer, "Where its identity always did reside even in the earthly life – in its relation to the Body and, specially, to the master who is the head of

[2] Ibid., pp. 136.
[3] Ibid., p. 136.
[4] Ibid., p. 143.

that Body." In other words, the man will know his dog: the dog will know its master and, in knowing him, will *be* itself.'[5]

Whether this is good theology, I do not know, but to our present inquiry it raises two difficulties.

(i) It does not cover the case of the higher animals who do not know man – for example, apes and elephants – but who are yet considered by Mr Lewis to have souls.

(ii) If one animal may attain good immortal selfhood in and through a good man, he may attain bad immortal selfhood in and through a bad man. One thinks of the overnourished lapdogs of idle overnourished women. It is a little hard that when, through no fault of their own, animals fall to selfish, self-indulgent, or cruel masters, they should through eternity form part of selfish, self-indulgent, or cruel superpersonal wholes and perhaps be punished for their participation in them.

(c) If the animals have souls and, presumably, freedom, the same sort of explanation must be adopted for pain in animals as is offered for pain in men. Pain, in other words, is one of the evils consequent upon sin. The higher animals, then, are corrupt. The question arises, who corrupted them? There seem to be two possible answers: (1) The Devil; (2) Man.

1. Mr Lewis considers this answer. The animals, he says, may originally all have been herbivorous. They became carnivorous – that is to say, they began to prey upon, to tear, and to eat one another – because 'some mighty created power had already been at work for ill on the material universe, or the solar system, or, at least, the planet Earth, before ever man came on the scene ... If there is such a power ... it may well have corrupted the animal creation before man appeared.'[6]

I have three comments to make:

(i) I find the supposition of Satan tempting monkeys frankly incredible. This, I am well aware, is not a logical objection. It is one's imagination – or perhaps one's common sense? – that revolts against it.

(ii) Although most animals fall victims to the redness of nature's 'tooth and claw', many do not. The sheep falls down the ravine, breaks its leg, and starves; hundreds of thousands of migrating birds die every year of hunger; creatures are struck and not killed by lightning, and their seared bodies take long to die. Are these pains due to corruption?

[5] Ibid., p. 144.
[6] Ibid., pp. 138.

(iii) The case of animals without souls cannot, on Mr Lewis's own showing, be brought under the 'moral corruption' explanation. Yet consider just one instance of nature's arrangements. The wasps, *Ichneumonidae*, sting their caterpillar prey in such a way as to paralyse its nerve centres. They then lay their eggs on the helpless caterpillar. When the grubs hatch from the eggs, they immediately proceed to feed upon the living but helpless flesh of their incubators, the paralysed but still sentient caterpillars.

It is hard to suppose that the caterpillar feels no pain when slowly consumed; harder still to ascribe the pain to moral corruption; hardest of all to conceive how such an arrangement could have been planned by an all-good and all-wise Creator.

2. The hypothesis that the animals were corrupted by man does not account for animal pain during the hundreds of millions of years (probably about 900 million) when the earth contained living creatures but did not contain man.

In sum, either animals have souls or they have no souls. If they have none, pain is felt for which there can be no moral responsibility, and for which no misuse of God's gift of moral freedom can be invoked as an excuse. If they have souls, we can give no plausible account (a) of their immortality – how draw the line between animals with souls and men with souls? – or (b) of their moral corruption, which would enable Christian apologists to place them in respect of their pain under the same heading of explanation as that which is proposed and which I am prepared to accept for man?

It may well be that there is an answer to this problem. I would be grateful to anyone who would tell me what it is.

The Reply by C.S. Lewis

Though there is pleasure as well as danger in encountering so sincere and economical a disputant as Dr Joad, I do so with no little reluctance. Dr Joad writes not merely as a controversialist who demands, but as an inquirer who really desires, an answer. I come into the matter at all only because my answers have already failed to satisfy him. And it is embarrassing to me, and possibly depressing to him, that he should, in a manner, be sent back to the same shop which has once failed to supply the goods. If it were wholly a question of defending the original goods, I think I would let it alone. But it is not exactly that. I think he has perhaps slightly misunderstood what I was offering for sale.

Dr Joad is concerned with the ninth chapter of my *Problem of Pain*. And the first point I want to make is that no one would gather from his article how confessedly speculative that chapter was. This was acknowledged in my preface and repeatedly emphasised in the chapter itself. This, of course, can bring no ease to Dr Joad's difficulties; unsatisfactory answers do not become satisfactory by being tentative. I mention the character of the chapter to underline the fact that it stands on a rather different level from those which preceded it. And that difference suggests the place which my 'guess-work' about Beasts (so I called it at the time and call it still) had in my own thought, and which I would like this whole question to have in Dr Joad's thought too.

The first eight chapters of my book attempted to meet the *prima facie* case against Theism based on human pain. They were the fruit of a slow change of mind not at all unlike that which Dr Joad himself has undergone and to which, when it had been completed, he at once bore honourable and (I expect) costly witness. The process of his thought differed at many points (very likely for the better) from the process of mine. But we came out, more or less, at the same place. The position of which he says in his article 'So much I understand; so much, indeed, I accept' is very close to that which I reached in the first eight chapters of my *Problem*.

So far, so good. Having 'got over' the problem of human pain, Dr Joad and I both find ourselves faced with the problem of animal pain. We do not at once part company even then. We both (if I read him correctly) turn with distaste from 'the easy speeches that comfort cruel men',[7] from theologians who do not seem to see that there is a real problem, who are content to say that animals are, after all, only animals. To us, pain without guilt or moral fruit, however low and contemptible the sufferer may be, is a very serious matter.

I now ask Dr Joad to observe rather closely what I do at this point, for I doubt if it is exactly what he thinks. I do not advance a doctrine of animal sentience as proved and thence conclude, 'Therefore beasts are not sacrificed without recompense, and therefore God is just.' If he will look carefully at my ninth chapter he will see that it can be divided into two very unequal parts: Part One consisting of the first paragraph, and Part Two of all the rest. They might be summarised as follows:

Part One. The data which God has given us enable us in some degree to understand human pain. We lack such data about beasts. We know

---

[7] G.K. Chesterton, 'A Hymn', line 11. The first line begins 'O God of earth and altar'.

neither what they are nor why they are. All that we can say for certain is that if God is good (and I think we have grounds for saying that He is) then the appearance of divine cruelty in the animal world must be a false appearance. What the reality behind the false appearance may be we can only guess.

Part Two. And here are some of my own guesses.

Now it matters far more whether Dr Joad agrees with Part One than whether he approves any of the speculations in Part Two. But I will first deal, so far as I can, with his critique of the speculations.

1. Conceding (*positionis causa*)[8] my distinction between sentience and consciousness, Dr Joad thinks it irrelevant. 'Pain is felt,' he writes, 'even if there is no continuing *ego* to feel it and to relate it to past and future pain,' and 'it is the fact that pain is felt, no matter who or what feels it ... that demands explanation.' I agree that in one sense it does not (for the present purpose) matter 'who or what' feels it. That is, it does not matter how humble, or helpless, or small, or how removed from our spontaneous sympathies, the sufferer is. But it surely does matter how far the sufferer is capable of what we can recognise as misery, how far the genuinely pitiable is consistent with its mode of existence. It will hardly be denied that the more coherently conscious the subject is, the more pity and indignation its pains deserve. And this seems to me to imply that the less coherently conscious, the less they deserve. I still think it possible for there to be a pain so instantaneous (through the absence of all perception of succession) that its 'unvalue', if I may coin the word, is indistinguishable from zero. A correspondent has instanced shooting pains in our own experience on those occasions when they are unaccompanied by fear. They may be intense: but they are gone as we recognise their intensity. In my own case I do not find anything in them which demands pity; they are, rather, comical. One tends to laugh. A series of such pains is, no doubt, terrible; but then the contention is that the series could not exist for sentience without consciousness.

2. I do not think that behaviour 'as if from memory' proves memory in the conscious sense. A non-human observer might suppose that if we blink our eyes at the approach of an object we are 'remembering' pains received on previous occasions. But no memories, in the full sense, are involved. (It is, of course, true that the behaviour of the organism is modified by past experiences, and we may thus by metonymy say that the

---

[8] For the sake of argument.

nerves remember what the mind forgets; but that is not what Dr Joad and I are talking of.) If we are to suppose memory in all cases where behaviour adapts itself to a probable recurrence of past events, shall we not have to assume in some insects an inherited memory of their parents' breeding habits? And are we prepared to believe this?

3. Of course my suggested theory of the tame animals' resurrection 'in' its human (and therefore, indirectly, divine) context does not cover wild animals or ill-treated tame ones. I had made the point myself, and added 'it is intended only as an illustration ... of the general principles to be observed in framing a theory of animal resurrection'.[9] I went on to make an alternative suggestion, observing, I hope, the same principles. My chief purpose at this stage was at once to liberate imagination and to confirm a due agnosticism about the meaning and destiny of brutes. I had begun by saying that if our previous assertion of divine goodness was sound, we might be sure that *in some way or other* 'all would be well, and all manner of thing would be well'.[10] I wanted to reinforce this by indicating how little we knew and, therefore, how many things one might keep in mind as possibilities.

4. If Dr Joad thinks I pictured Satan 'tempting monkeys', I am myself to blame for using the word 'encouraged'. I apologise for the ambiguity. In fact, I had not supposed that 'temptation' (that is, solicitation of the will) was the only mode in which the Devil could corrupt or impair. It is probably not the only mode in which he can impair even human beings; when Our Lord spoke of the deformed woman as one 'bound by Satan' (Luke 13:16), I presume He did not mean that she had been tempted into deformity. Moral corruption is not the only kind of corruption. But the word *corruption* was perhaps ill-chosen and invited misunderstanding. *Distortion* would have been safer.

5. My correspondent writes 'That even the severest injuries in most invertebrate animals are almost if not quite painless is the view of most biologists. Loeb collected much evidence to show that animals without cerebral hemispheres were indistinguishable from plants in every psychological respect. The instance readily occurs of the caterpillars which serenely go on eating though their interiors are being devoured by the larvae of some ichneumon fly. The Vivisection Act does not apply to invertebrates; which indicates the views of those who framed it.'

6. Though Dr Joad does not raise the point, I cannot forbear adding some most interesting suggestions about animal fear from the same

---

[9] *The Problem of Pain*, p. 144.
[10] Lady Julian of Norwich, *Sixteen Revelations of Divine Love*, ch. 29.

correspondent. He points out that human fear contains two elements: (a) the physical sensations, due to the secretions, etc.; (b) the mental images of what will happen if one loses hold, or if the bomb falls here, or if the train leaves the rails. Now (a), in itself, is so far from being an unmixed grief, that when we can get it without (b), or with unbelieved (b), or even with subdued (b), vast numbers of people like it: hence switchbacks, water-shoots, fast motoring, mountain climbing.

But all this is nothing to a reader who does not accept Part One in my ninth chapter. No man in his senses is going to start building up a theodicy with speculations about the minds of beasts as his foundation. Such speculations are in place only, as I said, to open the imagination to possibilities and to deepen and confirm our inevitable agnosticism about the reality, and only after the ways of God *to Man* have ceased to seem unjustifiable. We do not know the answer: these speculations were guesses at what it might possibly be. What really matters is the argument that there must be an answer: the argument that if, in our own lives, where alone (if at all) we know Him, we come to recognise the *pulchritudo tam antiqua et tam nova*,[11] then, in other realms where we cannot know Him (*connaître*), though we may know (*savoir*) some few things about Him – then, despite appearances to the contrary, He cannot be a power of darkness. For there were appearances to the contrary in our own realm too; yet, for Dr Joad as for me, they have somehow been got over.

I know that there are moments when the incessant continuity and desperate helplessness of what at least seems to be animal suffering makes every argument for Theism sound hollow, and when (in particular) the insect world appears to be Hell itself visibly in operation around us. Then the old indignation, the old pity arises. But how strangely ambivalent this experience is: I need not expound the ambivalence at much length, for I think I have done so elsewhere, and I am sure that Dr Joad had long discerned it for himself. If I regard this pity and indignation simply as subjective experiences of my own with no validity beyond their strength at the moment (which next moment will change), I can hardly use them as standards whereby to arraign the creation. On the contrary, they become strong as arguments against God just in so far as I take them to be transcendent illuminations to which creation must conform or be condemned. They are arguments against God only if they are themselves the voice of God. The more Shelleyan, the more Promethean my revolt, the more surely it claims a divine sanction. That the mere contingent

[11] 'Beauty so ancient and so new.' St Augustine, *Confessions*, Bk. X, ch. 27.

Joad or Lewis, born in an era of secure and liberal civilisation and imbibing from it certain humanitarian sentiments, should happen to be offended by suffering – what is that to the purpose? How will one base an argument for or against God on such an historical accident?

No. Not in so far as we feel these things, but in so far as we claim to be right in feeling them, in so far as we are sure that these standards have an empire *de jure* over all possible worlds, so far, and so far only, do they become a ground for disbelief – and at the same moment, for belief. God within us steals back at the moment of our condemning the apparent God without. Thus in Tennyson's poem the man who had become convinced that the God of his inherited creed was evil exclaimed: 'If there be such a God, may the Great God curse him and bring him to nought.'[12] For if there is no 'Great God' behind the curse, who curses? Only a puppet of the little apparent 'God'. His very curse is poisoned at the root: it is just the same sort of event as the very cruelties he is condemning, part of the meaningless tragedy.

From this I see only two exits: either that there is a Great God, and also a 'God of this world' (2 Corinthians 4:4), a prince of the powers of the air, whom the Great God does curse, and sometimes curse through us; or else that the operations of the Great God are not what they seem to me to be.

[12] 'Despair', 19, 106.

25

PETITIONARY PRAYER:

A Problem Without an Answer

Read to the Oxford Clerical Society on 8 December 1953, this essay was first published in Christian Reflections *(1998).*

The problem I am submitting to you arises not about prayer in general but only about that kind of prayer which consists of request or petition. I hope no one will think that he is helping to solve my problem by reminding me that there are many other and perhaps higher sorts of prayer. I agree that there are. I here confine myself to petitionary prayer not because I think it the only, or the best, or the most characteristic, form of prayer, but because it is the form which raises the problem. However low a place we may decide to give it in the life of prayer, we must give it some place, unless we are prepared to reject both Our Lord's precept in telling us to pray for our daily bread and His practice in praying that the cup might pass from Him. And as long as it holds any place at all, I have to consider my problem.

Let me make clear at once where that problem does not lie. I am not at all concerned with the difficulty which unbelievers sometimes raise about the whole conception of petitioning God, on the ground that absolute wisdom cannot need to be informed of our desires, or that absolute good-ness cannot need to be prompted to beneficence, or that the immutable and impassible cannot be affected by us, cannot be to us as patient to agent. All these difficulties are, no doubt, well worth most serious discus-sion, but I do not propose to discuss them here. Still less am I asking why petitions, and even the fervent petitions of holy men, are sometimes not granted. That has never seemed to me to be, in principle, a difficulty at all. That wisdom must sometimes refuse what ignorance may quite inno-cently ask seems to be self-evident.

My problem arises from one fact and one only; the fact that Christian teaching seems at first sight to contain two different patterns of peti-tionary prayer which are inconsistent: perhaps inconsistent in their theological implications, but much more obviously and pressingly inconsistent in the practical sense that no man, so far as I can see, could possibly follow them both at the same moment. I shall call them the A Pattern and the B Pattern.

The A Pattern is given in the prayer which Our Lord Himself taught us. The clause 'Thy will be done' by its very nature must modify the sense in which the following petitions are made. Under the shadow – or perhaps I should rather say, in the light – of that great submission nothing can be asked save conditionally, save in so far as the granting of it may be in accordance with God's will. I do not of course mean that the words 'Thy will be done' are merely a submission. They should, and if we make progress they will increasingly, be the voice of joyful desire, free of hunger and thirst, and I argue very heartily that to treat them simply as a clause of submission or renunciation greatly impoverishes the prayer. But though they should be something far more and better than resigned or submissive, they must not be less: they must be that *at least*. And as such they necessarily discipline all the succeeding clauses. The other specimen of the A Pattern comes from Our Lord's own example in Gethsemane. A particular event is asked for with the reservation, 'Nevertheless, not my will but thine.'

It would seem from these passages that we are directed both by Our Lord's command and by His example to make all our petitionary prayers in this conditional form; well aware that God in His wisdom may not see fit to give us what we ask and submitting our wills in advance to a possible refusal which, if it meets us, we shall know to be wholly just, merciful, and salutary. And this, I suppose, is how most of us do try to pray and how most spiritual teachers tell us to pray. With this pattern of prayer – the A Pattern – I myself would be wholly content. It is in accordance both with my heart and my head. It presents no theoretical difficulties. No doubt my rebellious will and my turbulent hopes and fears will find plenty of practical difficulty in following it. But as far as my intellect goes it is all easy. The road may be hard but the map is clear.

You will notice that in the A Pattern, whatever faith the petitioner has in the existence, the goodness, and the wisdom of God, what he obviously, even as it were by definition, has not got is a sure and unwavering belief that God will give him the particular thing he asks for. When Our Lord in Gethsemane asks that the cup may be withdrawn His words, far from implying a certainty or even a strong expectation that it will in fact be withdrawn, imply the possibility that it will not be; a possibility, or even a probability, so fully envisaged that a preparatory submission to that event is already being made.

We need not, so far as I can see, here concern ourselves with any special problems raised by the unique and holy Person of Him who prayed. It is enough to point out that if we are expected to imitate Him in our prayers, then, though we are doubtless to pray with faith in one sense, we are not to pray with any assurance that we shall receive what we ask. For real assurance that we shall receive it seems to be incompatible with the act of preparing ourselves for a denial. Men do not prepare for an event which they think impossible. And unless we think refusal impossible, how can we believe granting to be certain?

And, once again, if this were the only pattern of prayer, I should be quite content. If the faith which is demanded of us were always a faith in the goodness of God, a faith that whether granting or denying He equally gave us the best, and never a faith that He would give precisely what we ask, I should have no problem. Indeed, such a submissive faith would seem to me, if I were left to my own thoughts, far better than any confidence that our own necessarily ignorant petitions would prevail. I should be thankful that we were safe from that cruel mercy which the wiser Pagans had to dread, *numinibus vota exaudita malignis*. Even as it is I must often be glad that certain past prayers of my own were not granted.

But of course this is not the actual situation. Over against the A Pattern stands the B Pattern. Again and again in the New Testament we find the demand not for faith in such a general and (as it would seem to me) spiritual sense as I have described but for faith of a far more particular and (as it would seem to me) cruder sort: faith that the particular thing the petitioner asks will be given him. It is as if God demanded of us a faith which the Son of God in Gethsemane did not possess, and which if He had possessed it, would have been erroneous.

What springs first to mind is, of course, the long list of passages in which faith is required of those whom Our Lord healed. Some of these may be, for our present purpose, ambiguous. Thus in Matthew 9:22, the words 'Your faith has healed you' to the woman with the haemorrhage will be interpreted by some as a proposition not in theology but in medicine. The woman was cured by auto-suggestion: faith in any charm or quack remedy would on that view have done as well as faith in Christ – though, of course, the power in Christ to evoke faith even of that kind might have theological implications in the long run. But such a view, since it will not cover all the instances, had better not be brought in for any, on the principle of Occam's razor. And surely it can be stretched only by extreme efforts to cover instances where the faith is, so to speak, vicarious. Thus the relevant faith in the case of the sick servant (Matthew 8:13) is not his own but that of his master the Centurion; the healing of the Canaanite child (Matthew 15:28) depends on her mother's faith.

Again, it might perhaps be maintained that in some instances the faith in question is not a faith that this particular healing will take place but a deeper, more all-embracing faith in the Person of Christ Himself; not, of course, that the petitioners can be supposed to have believed in His deity but that they recognised and accepted His holy, or at the very least, His numinous, character. I think there is something in this view; but sometimes the faith seems to be very definitely attached to the particular gift. Thus in Matthew 9:28, the blind men are asked not 'Do you believe in Me?' but 'Do you believe that I can do this?' Still, the words are 'that I can' not 'that I will', so we may pass that example over. But what are we to say of Matthew 14:31, where Peter is called ὀλιγόπιστε, because he lost his faith and sank in the waves. I should perhaps say, at this point, that I find no difficulty in accepting the walking on the water as historical. I suspect that the distinction often made between 'Nature' miracles and others seems plausible only because most of us know less about pathology and psychology than about gravitation. Perhaps if we knew all, the Divine suggestion of a single new thought to my mind would appear neither more nor less a 'Nature' miracle than stilling the storm or feeding the five thousand. But that is not a point I wish to raise. I am concerned only with the implications of ὀλιγόπιστε. For it would seem that St Peter might have had any degree of faith in the goodness and power of God and even in the Deity of Christ and yet been wholly uncertain whether he could continue walking on the water. For in that case his faith would surely have told him that whether he walked or whether he sank he was equally in God's hands, and, submitting himself in the spirit of the Gethsemane prayer, he would have prepared himself, so far as infirmity allowed, to glorify God either by living or by drowning, and his failure, if he failed, would have been due to an imperfect mortification of instinct but not to a lack (in that sense) of faith. The faith which he is accused of lacking must surely be faith in the particular event: the continued walking on water.

All these examples, however, might be dismissed on the ground that they are not, in one strict sense of the word, examples of prayer. Let us then turn to those that are.

Whether you will agree to include Matthew 21:21, I don't know. Our Lord there says ἐὰν ἔχητε πίστιν καὶ μὴ διακριθῆτε, 'If you have faith with no hesitations or reservations, you can tell a mountain to throw itself into the sea and it will.' I very much hope that no one will solemnly remind us that Our Lord, according to the flesh, was an Oriental and that Orientals use hyperboles, and think that this has disposed of the passage. Of course Orientals, and Occidentals, use hyperboles, and of course Our

Lord's first hearers did not suppose Him to mean that large and highly mischievous disturbances of the landscape would be common or edifying operations of faith. But a sane man does not use hyperbole to mean nothing: by a great thing (which is not literally true) he suggests a great thing which is. When he says that someone's heart is broken he does not mean that this organ is literally fractured, but he does mean that the person in question is in very great anguish. Only a windbag says 'His heart is broken' when he means 'He is somewhat depressed'. And if all Orientals were doomed by the mere fact of being Orientals to be wind-bags (which of course they are not) the Truth Himself, the Wisdom of the Father, would not and could not have been united with the human nature of an Oriental. (The point is worth making. Some people make allowances for local and temporary conditions in the speeches of Our Lord on a scale which really implies that God chose the time and place of the Incarnation very injudiciously.) Our Lord need not mean the words about the mountain literally; but at the very least they must mean doing some mighty work. The point is that the condition of doing such a mighty work is unwavering, unhesitating faith. Indeed He goes on in the very next sentence to make the same statement without any figures of speech at all: πάντα ὅσα ἂν ααἰτήσητε ἐν τῇ προσευχῇ πιστεύοντες λήψεσθε.[1]

Can we even here take πιστεύοντες to mean 'having a general faith in the power and goodness of God'? We cannot. The corresponding passage in Mark,[2] though it adds a new difficulty, makes this point at least embar-rassingly plain. The words are πάντα ὅσα προσεύχεσθε καὶ αἰτεῖσθε πιστεύετε ὅτι ἐλάβετε καὶ ἔσται ὑμῖν. The tense, present or (worse still) aorist, is of course perplexing. I hope someone will explain to us what either might represent in Aramaic. But there is no doubt at all that what we are to believe is precisely that we get 'all the things' we ask for. We are not to believe that we shall get either what we ask or else something far better: we are to believe that we shall get those very things. It is a faith, unwavering faith in that event, to which success is promised.

The same astonishing – and even, to my natural feelings, shocking – promise is repeated elsewhere with additions which may or may not turn out to be helpful for our present purpose.

---

[1] Matthew 21:22: 'And whatever you ask in prayer, you will receive, if you have faith.'

[2] Mark 11:23f: 'Truly, I say to you, whoever says to this mountain, "Be taken up and cast into the sea", and does not doubt in his heart, but believes that what he says will come to pass, it will be done for him. Therefore I tell you, whatever you ask in prayer, believe that you receive it, and you will.'

In Matthew 18:19, we learn that if two (or two or three) agree in a petition it will be granted. Faith is not explicitly mentioned here but is no doubt assumed: if it were not, the promise would be only the more startling and the further (I think) from the pattern of Gethsemane. The reason for the promise follows: 'For where two or three are gathered together εἰς τὸ ἐμὸν ὄνομα, there am I in their midst.' With this goes John 14:13, 'Whatever you ask in my name, I will do this': not this or something far better, but 'whatever you ask'.

I have discovered that some people find in these passages a solution of the whole problem. For here we have the prayer of the Church (as soon as two or three are gathered together in that Name) and the presence of Christ in the Church: so that the prayer which is granted by the Father is the prayer of the Son, and prayer and answer alike are an operation within the Deity.

I agree that this makes the promises less startling; but does it reconcile them with the A Pattern? And does it reconcile them with the facts? For surely there have been occasions on which the whole Church prays and is refused? I suppose that at least twice in this century the whole Church prayed for peace and no peace was given her. I think, however, we define the Church, we must say that the whole Church prayed: popes in Italy and peasants in Russian villages, elders at Peebles, Anglicans in Cambridge, Congregationalists in Liverpool, Salvationists in East London. You may say (though I would not) that some who prayed were not in the Church; but it would be hard to find any in the Church who did not pray. But the cup did not pass from them. I am not, in principle, puzzled by the fact of the refusal: what I am puzzled by is the promise of granting.

And this at once raises a question which shows how frighteningly practical the problem is. *How* did the Church pray? Did she use the A Pattern or the B? Did she pray with unwavering confidence that peace would be given, or did she humbly follow the example of Gethsemane, adding 'If it be Thy will ... not as I will, but as Thou wilt', preparing herself in advance for a refusal of that particular blessing and putting all her faith into the belief that even if it were denied, the denial would be full of mercy? I am disposed to believe that she did the latter. And was that, conceivably, her ghastly mistake? Was she like the διακρινόμενος, the man of doubtful faith who, as St James tells us,[3] must not suppose that he will receive

---

[3] James 1:6–8: 'But let him ask in faith, with no doubting, for he who doubts is like a wave of the sea that is driven and tossed by the wind. For that person must not suppose that a double-minded man, unstable in all his ways, will receive anything from the Lord.'

anything? Have all my own intercessory prayers for years been mistaken? For I have always prayed that the illnesses of my friends might be healed 'if it was God's will', very clearly envisaging the possibility that it might not be. Perhaps this has all been a fake humility and a false spirituality for which my friends owe me little thanks; perhaps I ought never to have dreamed of refusal, μηδὲν διακρινόμενος?

Again, if the true prayer is joined with the prayer of the Church and hers with the prayer of Christ, and is therefore irresistible, was not it Christ who prayed in Gethsemane, using a different method and meeting with denial?

Another attempted solution runs something like this. The promise is made to prayers in Christ's name. And this of course means not simply prayers which end with the formula 'Through Jesus Christ Our Lord' but prayers prayed in the spirit of Christ, prayers uttered by us when, and in so far as, we are 'in' Him. Such prayers are the ones that can be made with unwavering faith that the blessing we ask for will be given us. And this may be supported (though I suspect it had better not be) from 1 John 5:14, 'Whatever we ask Him according to His will, He will hear us.' But how are we to hold this view and yet avoid the implication (*quod nefas dicere*) that Christ Himself in Gethsemane failed to pray in the spirit of Christ, since He neither used the form which that spirit is held to justify nor received the answer which that spirit is held to insure? As for the Johannine passage, would we dare to produce it in this context before an audience of intelligent but simple inquirers. They come to us (this often happens) saying that they have been told that those who pray in faith to the Christian God will get what they ask: that they have tried it and not got what they asked: and what, please, is our explanation? Dare we say that when God promises 'You shall have what you ask' He secretly means 'You shall have it if you ask for something I wish to give you'? What should we think of an earthly father who promised to give his son whatever he chose for his birthday and, when the boy asked for a bicycle gave him an arithmetic book, then first disclosing the silent reservation with which the promise was made?

Of course the arithmetic book may be better for the son than the bicycle, and a robust faith may manage to believe so. That is not where the difficulty, the sense of cruel mockery, lies. The boy is tempted, not to complain that the bicycle was denied, but that the promise of 'anything he chose' was made. So with us.

It is possible that someone present may be wholly on the side of the B Pattern: someone who has seen many healed by prayer. Such a person will be tempted to reply that most of us are in fact grievously

wrong in our prayer-life: that miracles are accorded to unwavering faith: that if we dropped our disobedient lowliness and pseudo-spiritual timidity blessings we never dreamed of would be showered on us at every turn. I certainly would not hear such a person with scepticism, still less with mockery. I believe in miracles, here and now. But if this is the complete answer, then why was the A Pattern of prayer ever given at all?

I have no answer to my problem, though I have taken it to about every Christian I know, learned or simple, lay or clerical, within my own Communion or without. Before closing I have, however, one hesitant observation to make.

One thing seems to be clear to me. Whatever else faith may mean (that is, faith in the granting of the blessing asked, for with faith in any other sense we need not at this point be concerned) I feel quite sure that it does not mean any state of psychological certitude such as might be – I think it sometimes is – manufactured from within by the natural action of a strong will upon an obedient imagination. The faith that moves mountains is a gift from Him who created mountains. That being so, can I ease my problem by saying that until God gives me such a faith I have no practical decision to make; I must pray after the A Pattern because, in fact, I cannot pray after the B Pattern? If, on the other hand, God ever gave me such a faith, then again I should have no decision to make; I should find myself praying in the B Pattern. This would fall in with an old opinion of my own that we ought all of us to be ashamed of not performing miracles and that we do not feel this shame enough. We regard our own state as normal and theurgy as exceptional, whereas we ought perhaps to regard the worker of miracles, however rare, as the true Christian norm and ourselves as spiritual cripples. Yet I do not find this quite a satisfactory solution. I think we might get over the prayer in Gethsemane. We might say that in His tender humility Our Lord, just as He refused the narcotic wine mingled with myrrh, and just as He chose (I think) to be united to a human nature not of iron nerves but to a nature sensitive, shrinking, and unable not to live through torture in advance, so He chose on that night to plumb the depths of Christian experience, to resemble not the heroes of His army but the very weakest camp followers and unfits; or even that such a choice is implied in those unconsciously profound and involuntarily blessed words: 'He saved others, Himself He cannot save.' But some discomfort remains. I do not like to represent God as saying 'I will grant what you ask in faith' and adding, so to speak, 'Because I will not give you the faith – not that kind – unless you ask what I want to give you.' Once more, there is just a faint suggestion of mockery, of goods that look a little larger in the advertisement than they turn out to be. Not that we complain of any defect in the goods: it is the faintest suspicion of excess in the advertisement that is disquieting. But at present I have got no further. I come to you, reverend Fathers, for guidance. How am I to pray this very night?

[26]

ON OBSTINACY IN BELIEF

A paper read to the Socratic Club and subsequently published in The Socratic Digest *and* The Sewanee Review, *Volume LXIII (Autumn) in 1955. It later appeared in* The World's Last Night *(US, 1960) and* They Asked for a Paper *(1962), and then in* Screwtape Proposes a Toast *(1998).*

Papers have more than once been read to the Socratic Club at Oxford in which a contrast was drawn between a supposed Christian attitude and a supposedly scientific attitude to belief. We have been told that the scientist thinks it his duty to proportion the strength of his belief exactly to the evidence; to believe less as there is less evidence and to withdraw belief altogether when reliable adverse evidence turns up. We have been told that, on the contrary, the Christian regards it as positively praiseworthy to believe without evidence, or in excess of the evidence, or to maintain his belief unmodified in the teeth of steadily increasing evidence against it. Thus a 'faith that has stood firm', which appears to mean a belief immune from all the assaults of reality, is commended.

If this were a fair statement of the case, then the co-existence within the same species of such scientists and such Christians, would be a very staggering phenomenon. The fact that the two classes appear to overlap, as they do, would be quite inexplicable. Certainly all discussion between creatures so different would be hopeless. The purpose of this essay is to show that things are really not quite so bad as that. The sense in which scientists proportion their belief to the evidence and the sense in which Christians do not, both need to be defined more closely. My hope is that when this has been done, though disagreement between the two parties may remain, they will not be left staring at one another in wholly dumb and desperate incomprehension.

And first, a word about belief in general. I do not see that the state of 'proportioning belief to evidence' is anything like so common in the scientific life as has been claimed. Scientists are mainly concerned not with believing things but with finding things out. And no one, to the best of my knowledge, uses the word 'believe' about things he has found out. The doctor says he 'believes' a man was poisoned before he has examined the body; after the examination, he says the man was poisoned. No one says that he believes the multiplication table. No one who catches a thief red-handed says he believes that man was stealing. The scientist, when at work, that is, when he is a scientist, is labouring to escape from belief and unbelief into knowledge. Of course he uses hypotheses or supposals. I do not think these are beliefs. We must look, then, for the scientist's behaviour about belief not to his scientific life but to his leisure hours.

In actual modern English usage the verb 'believe', except for two special usages, generally expresses a very weak degree of opinion. 'Where is Tom?' 'Gone to London, I believe.' The speaker would be only mildly surprised if Tom had not gone to London after all. 'What was the date?' '430 BC, I believe.' The speaker means that he is far from sure. It is the same with the negative if it is put in the form 'I believe not'. ('Is Jones coming up this term?' 'I believe not.') But if the negative is put in a different form it then becomes one of the special usages I mentioned a moment ago. This is of course the form 'I don't believe it', or the still stronger 'I don't believe you'. 'I don't believe it' is far stronger on the negative side than 'I believe' is on the positive. 'Where is Mrs Jones?' 'Eloped with the butler, I believe.' 'I don't believe it.' This, especially if said with anger, may imply a conviction which in subjective certitude might be hard to distinguish from knowledge by experience. The other special usage is 'I believe' as uttered by a Christian. There is no great difficulty in making the hardened materialist understand, however little he approves, the sort of mental attitude which this 'I believe' expresses. The materialist need only picture himself replying, to some report of a miracle, 'I don't believe it', and then imagine this same degree of conviction on the opposite side. He knows that he cannot, there and then, produce a refutation of the miracle which would have the certainty of mathematical demonstration; but the formal possibility that the miracle might after all have occurred does not really trouble him any more than a fear that water might not be H and O. Similarly, the Christian does not necessarily claim to have demonstrative proof; but the formal possibility that God might not exist is not necessarily present in the form of the least actual doubt. Of course there are Christians who hold that such demonstrative proof exists, just as there may be materialists who hold that there is demonstrative disproof. But then, whichever of them is right (if either is) while he retained the proof or disproof would be not believing or disbelieving but knowing. We are speaking of belief and disbelief in the strongest degree but not of knowledge. Belief, in this sense, seems to me to be assent to a proposition which we think so overwhelmingly probable that there is a psychological exclusion of doubt, though not a logical exclusion of dispute.

It may be asked whether belief (and of course disbelief) of this sort ever attaches to any but theological propositions. I think that many beliefs approximate to it; that is, many probabilities seem to us so strong that the absence of logical certainty does not induce in us the least shade of doubt. The scientific beliefs of those who are not themselves scientists often have this character, especially among the uneducated. Most of our beliefs about other people are of the same sort. The scientist himself, or he who was a scientist in the laboratory, has beliefs about his wife and friends which he holds, not indeed without evidence, but with more certitude than the evidence, if weighed in the laboratory manner, would justify. Most of my generation had a belief in the reality of the external world and of other people – if you prefer it, a disbelief in solipsism – far in excess of our strongest arguments. It may be true, as they now say, that the whole thing arose from category mistakes and was a pseudo-problem; but then we didn't know that in the twenties. Yet we managed to disbelieve in solipsism all the same.

There is, of course, no question so far of belief without evidence. We must beware of confusion between the way in which a Christian first assents to certain propositions and the way in which he afterwards adheres to them. These must be carefully distinguished. Of the second it is true, in a sense, to say that Christians do recommend a certain discounting of apparent contrary evidence, and I will later attempt to explain why. But so far as I know it is not expected that a man should assent to these propositions in the first place without evidence or in the teeth of the evidence. At any rate, if anyone expects that, I certainly do not. And in fact, the man who accepts Christianity always thinks he has good evidence; whether, like Dante, *fisici e metafisici argomenti*, or historical evidence, or the evidence of religious experience, or authority, or all these together. For of course authority, however we may value it in this or that particular instance, is a kind of evidence. All of our historical beliefs, most of our geographical beliefs, many of our beliefs about matter that concern us in daily life, are accepted on the authority of other human beings, whether we are Christians, Atheists, Scientists, or Men-in-the-Street.

It is not the purpose of this essay to weigh the evidence, of whatever kind, on which Christians base their belief. To do that would be to write a full-dress *apologia*. All that I need do here is to point out that, at the very worst, this evidence cannot be so weak as to warrant the view that all whom it convinces are indifferent to evidence. The history of thought seems to make this quite plain. We know, in fact, that believers are not cut off from unbelievers by any portentous inferiority of intelligence or any perverse refusal to think. Many of them have been people of powerful minds. Many of them have been scientists. We may suppose them to have been mistaken, but we must suppose that their error was at least plausible. We might indeed, conclude that it was, merely from the multitude and diversity of the arguments against it. For there is not one case against religion, but many. Some say, like Capaneus in Statius, that it is a projection of our primitive fears, *primus in orbe deos fecit timor*: others, with Euhemerus, that it is all a 'plant' put up by wicked kings, priests, or capitalists; others, with Tylor, that it comes from dreams about the dead; others, with Frazer, that it is a by-product of agriculture; others, like Freud, that it is a complex; the moderns that it is a category mistake. I will never believe that an error against which so many and various defensive weapons have been found necessary was, from the outset, wholly lacking in plausibility. All this 'post haste and rummage in the land' obviously implies a respectable enemy.

There are of course people in our own day to whom the whole situation seems altered by the doctrine of the concealed wish. They will admit that men, otherwise apparently rational, have been deceived by the arguments for religion. But they will say that they have been deceived first by their own desires and produced the arguments afterwards as a rationalisation: that these arguments have never been intrinsically even plausible, but have seemed so because they were secretly weighted by our wishes. Now I do not doubt that this sort of thing happens in thinking about religion as in thinking about other things: but as a general explanation of religious assent it seems to me quite useless. On that issue our wishes may favour either side or both. The assumption that every man would be pleased, and nothing but pleased, if only he could conclude that Christianity is true, appears to me to be simply preposterous. If Freud is right about the Oedipus complex, the universal pressure of the wish that God should not exist must be enormous, and atheism must be an admirable gratification to one of our strongest suppressed impulses. This argument, in fact, could be used on the theistic side. But I have no intention of so using it. It will not really help either party. It is fatally ambivalent. Men wish on both sides: and again, there is fear-fulfilment as well as wish-fulfilment, and hypochondriac temperaments will always tend to think true what they most wish to be false. Thus instead of the one predicament on which our opponents sometimes concentrate there are in fact four. A man may be a Christian because he wants Christianity to be true. He may be an atheist because he wants atheism to be true. He may be an atheist because he wants Christianity to be true. He may be a Christian because he wants atheism to be true. Surely these possibilities cancel one another out? They may be of some use in analysing a particular instance of belief or disbelief, where we know the case history, but as a general explanation of either they will not help us. I do not think they overthrow the view that there is evidence both for and against the Christian propositions which fully rational minds, working honestly, can assess differently.

I therefore ask you to substitute a different and less tidy picture for that with which we began. In it, you remember, two different kinds of men, scientists, who proportioned their belief to the evidence, and Christians, who did not, were left facing one another across a chasm. The picture I should prefer is like this. All men alike, on questions which interest them, escape from the region of belief into that of knowledge when they can, and if they succeed in knowing, they no longer say they believe. The questions in which mathematicians are interested admit of treatment by a particularly clear and strict technique. Those of the scientist have their own technique, which is not quite the same. Those of the historian and the judge are different again. The mathematician's proof (at least so we laymen suppose) is by reasoning, the scientist's by experiment, the historian's by documents, the judge's by concurring sworn testimony. But all these men, as men, on questions outside their own disciplines, have numerous beliefs to which they do not normally apply the methods of their own disciplines. It would indeed carry some suspicion of morbidity and even of insanity if they did. These beliefs vary in strength from weak opinion to complete subjective certitude. Specimens of such beliefs at the strongest are the Christian's 'I believe' and the convinced atheist's 'I don't believe a word of it'. The particular subject-matter on which these two disagree does not, of course, necessarily involve such strength of belief and disbelief. There are some who moderately opine that there is, or is not, a God. But there are others whose belief or disbelief is free from doubt. And all these beliefs, weak or strong, are based on what appears to the holders to be evidence; but the strong believers or disbelievers of course think they have very strong evidence. There is no need to suppose stark unreason on either side. We need only suppose error. One side has estimated the evidence wrongly. And even so, the mistake cannot be supposed to be of a flagrant nature; otherwise the debate would not continue.

So much, then, for the way in which Christians come to assent to certain propositions. But we have now to consider something quite different; their adherence to their belief after it has once been formed. It is here that the charge of irrationality and resistance to evidence becomes really important. For it must be admitted at once that Christians do praise such an adherence as if it were meritorious; and even, in a sense, more meritorious the stronger the apparent evidence against their faith becomes. They even warn one another that such apparent contrary evidence – such 'trials to faith' or 'temptations to doubt' – may be expected to occur, and determine in advance to resist them. And this is certainly shockingly unlike the behaviour we all demand of the scientist or the historian in their own disciplines. There, to slur over or ignore the faintest evidence against a favourite hypothesis, is admittedly foolish and shameful. It must be exposed to every test; every doubt must be invited. But then I do not admit that a hypothesis is a belief. And if we consider the scientist not among his hypotheses in the laboratory but among the beliefs in his ordinary life, I think the contrast between him and the Christian would be weakened. If, for the first time, a doubt of his wife's fidelity crosses the scientist's mind, does he consider it his duty at once to entertain this doubt with complete impartiality, at once to evolve a series of experiments by which it can be tested, and to await the result with pure neutrality of mind? No doubt it may come to that in the end. There are unfaithful wives; there are experimental husbands. But is such a course what his brother scientists would recommend to him (all of them, I suppose, except one) as the first step he should take and the only one consistent with his honour as a scientist? Or would they, like us, blame him for a moral flaw rather than praise him for an intellectual virtue if he did so?

This is intended, however, merely as a precaution against exaggerating the difference between Christian obstinacy in belief and the behaviour of normal people about their non-theological beliefs. I am far from suggesting that the case I have supposed is exactly parallel to the Christian obstinacy. For of course evidence of the wife's infidelity might accumulate, and presently reach a point at which the scientist would be pitiably foolish to disbelieve it. But the Christians seem to praise an adherence to the original belief which holds out against any evidence whatever. I must now try to show why such praise is in fact a logical conclusion from the original belief itself.

This can be done best by thinking for a moment of situations in which the thing is reversed. In Christianity such faith is demanded of us; but there are situations in which we demand it of others. There are times when we can do all that a fellow creature needs if only he will trust us. In getting a dog out of a trap, in extracting a thorn from a child's finger, in teaching a boy to swim or rescuing one who can't, in getting a frightened beginner over a nasty place on a mountain, the one fatal obstacle may be their distrust. We are asking them to trust us in the teeth of their senses, their imagination, and their intelligence. We ask them to believe that what is painful will relieve their pain and that what looks dangerous is their only safety. We ask them to accept apparent impossibilities: that moving the paw farther back into the trap is the way to get it out – that hurting the finger very much more will stop the finger hurting – that water which is obviously permeable will resist and support the body – that holding on to the only support within reach is not the way to avoid sinking – that to go higher and on to a more exposed ledge is the way not to fall. To support all these *incredibilia* we can rely only on the other party's confidence in us – a confidence certainly not based on demonstration, admittedly shot through with emotion, and perhaps, if we are strangers, resting on nothing but such assurance as the look of our face and the tone of our voice can supply, or even, for the dog, on our smell. Sometimes, because of their unbelief, we can do no mighty works. But if we succeed, we do so because they have maintained their faith in us against apparently contrary evidence. No one blames us for demanding such faith. No one blames them for giving it. No one says afterwards what an unintelligent dog or child or boy that must have been to trust us. If the young mountaineer were a scientist, it would not be held against him, when he came up for a fellowship, that he had once departed from Clifford's rule of evidence by entertaining a belief with strength greater than the evidence logically obliged him to.

Now to accept the Christian propositions is *ipso facto* to believe that we are to God, always, as that dog or child or bather or mountain climber was to us, only very much more so. From this it is a strictly logical conclusion that the behaviour which was appropriate to them will be appropriate to us, only very much more. Mark: I am not saying that the strength of our original belief must by psychological necessity produce such behaviour. I am saying that the content of our original belief by logical necessity entails the proposition that such behaviour is appropriate. If human life is in fact ordered by a beneficent being whose knowledge of our real needs and of the way in which they can be satisfied infinitely exceeds our own, we must expect *a priori* that His operations will often appear to us far from beneficent and far from wise, and that it will be our highest prudence to give Him our confidence in spite of this. This expectation is increased by the fact that when we accept Christianity we are warned that apparent evidence against it will occur – evidence strong enough 'to deceive if possible the very elect'. Our situation is rendered tolerable by two facts. One is that we seem to ourselves, besides the apparently contrary evidence, to receive favourable evidence. Some of it is in the form of external events: as when I go to see a man, moved by what I felt to be a whim, and find he has been praying that I should come to him that day. Some of it is more like the evidence on which the mountaineer or the dog might trust his rescuer – the rescuer's voice, look, and smell. For it seems to us (though you, on your premises, must believe us deluded) that we have something like a knowledge-by-acquaintance of the Person we believe in, however imperfect and intermittent it may be. We trust not because 'a God' exists, but because *this* God exists. Or if we ourselves dare not claim to 'know' Him, Christendom does, and we trust at least some of its representatives in the same way: because of the sort of people they are. The second fact is this. We think we can see already why, if our original belief is true, such trust beyond the evidence, against much apparent evidence, has to be demanded of us. For the question is not about being helped out of one trap or over one difficult place in a climb. We believe that His intention is to create a certain personal relation between Himself and us, a relation really *sui generis* but analogically describable in terms of filial or of erotic love. Complete trust is an ingredient in that relation – such trust as could have no room to grow except where there is also room for doubt. To love involves trusting the beloved beyond the evidence, even against much evidence. No man is our friend who believes in our good intentions only when they are proved. No man is our friend who will not be very slow to accept evidence against them. Such confidence, between one man and another, is in fact almost universally praised as a moral beauty, not blamed as a logical error. And the suspicious man is blamed for a meanness of character, not admired for the excellence of his logic.

There is, you see, no real parallel between Christian obstinacy in faith and the obstinacy of a bad scientist trying to preserve a hypothesis although the evidence has turned against it. Unbelievers very pardonably get the impression that an adherence to our faith is like that, because they meet Christianity, if at all, mainly in apologetic works. And there, of course, the existence and beneficence of God must appear as a speculative question like any other. Indeed, it is a speculative question as long as it is a question at all. But once it has been answered in the affirmative, you get quite a new situation. To believe that God – at least *this* God – exists is to believe that you as a person now stand in the presence of God as a Person. What would, a moment before, have been variations in opinion, now becomes variations in your personal attitude to a Person. You are no longer faced with an argument which demands your assent, but with a Person who demands your confidence. A faint analogy would be this. It is one thing to discuss *in vacuo* whether So-and-so will join us tonight, and another to discuss this when So-and-so's honour is pledged to come and some great matter depends on his coming. In the first case it would be merely reasonable, as the clock ticked on, to expect him less and less. In the second, a continued expectation far into the night would be due to our friend's character if we had found him reliable before. Which of us would not feel slightly ashamed if one moment after we had given him up he arrived with a full explanation of his delay? We should feel that we ought to have known him better.

Now of course we see, quite as clearly as you, how agonisingly two-edged all this is. A faith of this sort, if it happens to be true, is obviously what we need, and it is infinitely ruinous to lack it. But there can be faith of this sort where it is wholly ungrounded. The dog may lick the face of the man who comes to take it out of the trap; but the man may only mean to vivisect it in South Parks Road when he has done so. The ducks who come to the call 'Dilly, dilly, come and be killed' have confidence in the farmer's wife, and she wrings their necks for their pains. There is that famous French story of the fire in the theatre. Panic was spreading, the spectators were just turning from an audience into a mob. At that moment a huge bearded man leaped through the orchestra on to the stage, raised his hand with a gesture full of nobility, and cried, '*Que chacun regagne sa place.*' Such was the authority of his voice and bearing that everyone obeyed him. As a result they were all burned to death, while the bearded man walked quietly out through the wings to the stage door, took a cab which was waiting for someone else, and went home to bed.

That demand for our confidence which a true friend makes of us is exactly the same that a confidence trickster would make. That refusal to trust, which is sensible in reply to a confidence trickster, is ungenerous and ignoble to a friend, and deeply damaging to our relation with him. To be forewarned and therefore forearmed against apparently contrary appearance is eminently rational if our belief is true; but if our belief is a delusion, this same forewarning and forearming would obviously be the method whereby the delusion rendered itself incurable. And yet again, to be aware of these possibilities and still to reject them is clearly the precise mode, and the only mode, in which our personal response to God can establish itself. In that sense the ambiguity is not something that conflicts with faith so much as a condition which makes faith possible. When you are asked for trust you may give it or withhold it; it is senseless to say that you will trust if you are given demonstrative certainty. There would be no room for trust if demonstration were given. When demonstration is given what will be left will be simply the sort of relation which results from having trusted, or not having trusted, before it was given.

The saying 'Blessed are those that have not seen and have believed' has nothing to do with our original assent to the Christian propositions. It was not addressed to a philosopher inquiring whether God exists. It was addressed to a man who already believed that, who already had long acquaintance with a particular Person, and evidence that that Person could do very odd things, and who then refused to believe one odd thing more, often predicted by that Person and vouched for by all his closest friends. It is a rebuke not to scepticism in the philosophic sense but to the psychological quality of being 'suspicious'. It says in effect, 'You should have known me better.' There are cases between man and man where we should all, in our different way, bless those who have not seen and have believed. Our relation to those who trusted us only after we were proved innocent in court cannot be the same as our relation to those who trusted us all through.

Our opponents, then, have a perfect right to dispute with us about the grounds of our original assent. But they must not accuse us of sheer insanity if, after the assent has been given, our adherence to it is no longer proportioned to every fluctuation of the apparent evidence. They cannot of course be expected to know on what our assurance feeds, and how it revives and is always rising from its ashes. They cannot be expected to see how the *quality* of the object which we think we are beginning to know by acquaintance drives us to the view that if this were a delusion then we should have to say that the universe had produced no real thing of comparable value and that all explanations of the delusion seemed somehow less important than the thing explained. That is knowledge we cannot communicate. But they can see how the assent, of necessity, moves us from the logic of speculative thought into what might perhaps be called the logic of personal relations. What would, up till then, have been variations simply of opinion become variations of conduct by a person to a Person. *Credere Deum esse* turns into *Credere in Deum*. And *Deum* here is this God, the increasingly knowable Lord.

[27]

WHAT CHRISTMAS MEANS TO ME

Published in Twentieth Century, *Volume CLXII (December 1957), and reproduced in* Undeceptions *(1971) and* Christian Reunion *(1990).*

Three things go by the name of Christmas. One is a religious festival. This is important and obligatory for Christians; but as it can be of no interest to anyone else, I shall naturally say no more about it here. The second (it has complex historical connections with the first, but we needn't go into them) is a popular holiday, an occasion for merry-making and hospitality. If it were my business to have a 'view' on this, I should say that I much approve of merry-making. But what I approve of much more is everybody minding his own business. I see no reason why I should volunteer views as to how other people should spend their own money in their own leisure among their own friends. It is highly probable that they want my advice on such matters as little as I want theirs. But the third thing called Christmas is unfortunately everyone's business.

I mean of course the commercial racket. The interchange of presents was a very small ingredient in the older English festivity. Mr Pickwick took a cod with him to Dingley Dell; the reformed Scrooge ordered a turkey for his clerk; lovers sent love gifts; toys and fruit were given to children. But the idea that not only all friends but even all acquaintances should give one another presents, or at least send one another cards, is quite modern and has been forced upon us by the shopkeepers. Neither of these circumstances is in itself a reason for condemning it. I condemn it on the following grounds.

1. It gives on the whole much more pain than pleasure. You have only to stay over Christmas with a family who seriously try to 'keep' it (in its third, or commercial aspect) in order to see that the thing is a nightmare. Long before 25th December everyone is worn out – physically worn out by weeks of daily struggle in overcrowded shops, mentally worn out by the effort to remember all the right recipients and to think out suitable

gifts for them. They are in no trim for merry-making; much less (if they should want to) to take part in a religious act. They look far more as if there had been a long illness in the house.

2. Most of it is involuntary. The modern rule is that anyone can force you to give him a present by sending you a quite unprovoked present of his own. It is almost a blackmail. Who has not heard the wail of despair, and indeed of resentment, when, at the last moment, just as everyone hoped that the nuisance was over for one more year, the unwanted gift from Mrs Busy (whom we hardly remember) flops unwelcomed through the letter box, and back to the dreadful shops one of us has to go?

3. Things are given as presents which no mortal ever bought for himself – gaudy and useless gadgets, 'novelties' because no one was ever fool enough to make their like before. Have we really no better use for materials and for human skill and time than to spend them on all this rubbish?

4. The nuisance. For after all, during the racket we still have all our ordinary and necessary shopping to do, and the racket trebles the labour of it.

We are told that the whole dreary business must go on because it is good for trade. It is in fact merely one annual symptom of that lunatic condition of our country, and indeed of the world, in which everyone lives by persuading everyone else to buy things. I don't know the way out. But can it really be my duty to buy and receive masses of junk every winter just to help the shopkeepers? If the worst comes to the worst I'd sooner give them money for nothing and write it off as a charity. For nothing? Why, better for nothing than for a nuisance.

[28]

THE PSALMS

Probably written shortly before Reflections on the Psalms *(1958), this two-part essay appeared in* Christian Reflections *(1991).*

I

The dominant impression I get from reading the Psalms is one of antiquity. I seem to be looking into a deep pit of time, but looking through a lens which brings the figures who inhabit that depth up close to my eye. In that momentary proximity they are almost shockingly alien; creatures of unrestrained emotion, wallowing in self-pity, sobbing, cursing, screaming in exultation, clashing uncouth weapons or dancing to the din of strange musical instruments. Yet, side by side with this, there is also a different image in my mind: Anglican choirs, well-laundered surplices, soapy boys' faces, hassocks, an organ, prayer-books, and perhaps the smell of new-mown graveyard grass coming in with the sunlight through an open door. Sometimes the one, sometimes the other, impression grows faint, but neither, perhaps, ever quite disappears. The irony reaches its height when a boy soloist sings in that treble which is so beautifully free from all personal emotion the words whereby ancient warriors lashed themselves with frenzy against their enemies; and does this in the service of the God of Love, and himself, meanwhile, perhaps thinks neither of that God nor of ancient wars but of 'bullseyes' and the Comics. This irony, this double or treble vision, is part of the pleasure. I begin to suspect that it is part of the profit too.

How old the Psalms, as we now have them, really are is a question for the scholars. I am told there is one (18) which might really have come down from the age of David himself; that is, from the tenth century BC. Most of them, however, are said to be 'post exilic'; the book was put together when the Hebrews, long exiled in Babylonia, were repatriated by that enlightened ruler, Cyrus of Persia. This would bring us down to the sixth century. How much earlier material the book took in is uncertain. Perhaps for our present purpose it does not greatly matter. The whole spirit and technique and the characteristic attitudes in the Psalms we have might be very like those of much older sacred poetry which is now lost. We know that they had such poetry; they must have been already famous for that art when their Babylonian conquerors (see 137) asked them for a specimen. And some very early pieces occur elsewhere in the Old Testament. Deborah's song of triumph over Sisera in Judges 5 might be as old as the battle that gave rise to it back in the thirteenth century. If the Hebrews were conservative in such matters then sixth-century poems may be very like those of their ancestors. And we know they were con-servative. One can see that by leaping forward six centuries into the New Testament and reading the *Magnificat*. The Virgin has something other (and more momentous) to say than the old psalmists; but what she utters is quite unmistakably a psalm. The style, the dwelling on Covenant, the delight in the vindication of the poor, are all perfectly true to the old model. So might the old model have been true to one yet older. For poetry of that sort did not, like ours, seek to express those things in which individuals differ, and did not aim at novelty. Even if the Psalms we read were all composed as late as the sixth century BC, in reading them I suspect that we have our hands on the near end of a living cord that stretches far back into the past.

In most moods the spirit of the Psalms feels to me more alien than that of the oldest Greek literature. But that is not an affair of dates. Distance in temper does not always coincide with distance in time. To most of us, perhaps to all of us at most times (unless we are either very uneducated or very holy or, as might be, both), the civilisation that descends from Greece and Rome is closer, more congenial, than what we inherit from ancient Israel. The very words and concepts which we use for science, philosophy, criticism, government, grammar, are all Graeco-Roman. It is this, and not Israel, that has made us, in the ordinary sense, 'civilised'. But no Christian can read the Bible without discovering that these ancient Hebrews, generally so remote, may at any moment turn out to be our brothers in a sense in which no Greek or Roman ever was. What a dull, remote thing, for example, the Book of Proverbs seems at a first glance: bearded Orientals uttering endless platitudes as if in a parody of the *Arabian Nights*. Compared with Plato or Aristotle – compared even with Xenophon – it is not *thought* at all. Then, suddenly, just as you are going to give it up, your eye falls on the words, 'If thine enemy be hungry, give him bread to eat, and if he be thirsty give him water to drink' (25:21). One rubs one's eyes. So they were saying that already. They knew that so long before Christ came. There is nothing like it in Greek, nor, if my memory serves me, in Confucius. And this is the sort of surprise we shall often get in the Psalms. These strange, alien figures may at any moment show that, in spiritual descent (as opposed to cultural) it is they, after all, who are our ancestors and the classical nations who are alien. Conversely, in reading the classics we sometimes have the opposite surprise. Those loved authors, so civilised, tolerant, humane, and enlightened, every now and then reveal that they are divided from us by a gulf. Hence the eternal, roguish tittering about pederasty in Plato or the hard pride that makes Aristotle's *Ethics* in places almost comic. We begin to doubt whether any one of them (even Virgil himself) if we could recall him from the dead might not, in the first hour's conversation, let out something that would utterly estrange us.

I do not at all mean that the Hebrews were just 'better' than the Greeks and the Romans. On the contrary we shall find in the Psalms expressions of a cruelty more vindictive and a self-righteousness more complete than anything in the classics. If we ignore such passages and read only a few selected favourite psalms, we miss the point. For the point is precisely this: that these same fanatic and homicidal Hebrews, and not the more enlightened peoples, again and again – for brief moments – reach a Christian level of spirituality. It is not that they are better or worse than the Pagans, but that they are both better and worse. One is forced to recognise that, in one respect, these alien poets are our predecessors, and the only predecessors we can find in all antiquity. They have something the Pagans have not. They know something of which Socrates was ignorant. This Something does not seem to us to arise at all naturally from what else we can see of their character. It looks like something that has been given them from outside; in fact, like what it professes to be, a revelation. Their claim to be the 'Chosen' people is strong.

We may, indeed, be surprised at the choice. If we had been allowed to see the world as it was, say, in the fifteenth century BC, and asked to guess which of the stocks then existing was going to be entrusted with the consciousness of God and with the transmission of that blood which would one day produce a body for the incarnation of God Himself, I do not think many of us would have guessed right. (I think the Egyptians would have been my own favourite.)

A similar strangeness meets us elsewhere. The raw material out of which a thing is made is not always that which would seem most promising to one who does not understand the process. There is nothing hard, brittle, or transparent about the ingredients of glass. Again, to come nearer to the present matter, do not our own personal ancestors, our family, seem at first rather improbable? Later, as we begin to recognise the heredity that works in us, we understand. But surely not at first. What young man feels 'These are exactly the sort of people whose son (or grandson, or descendant) I might be expected to be'? For usually, in early life, the people with whom one seems to have most in common, the people who share one's interests, the 'men of one's own totem', are not one's relatives, so that the idea of having been born into the wrong family is an attractive myth. (We are delighted when the hero, in *Siegfried*, forces the dwarf to confess that he is not his son.) The thing one is made out of is not necessarily like oneself (still less, like one's idea of that self) and looks at first even more unlike than it really is. It may be so with the origins of our species. The Evolutionists say we descend from 'anthropoids', creatures akin to apes. Is it (at first sight) the descent we would have chosen? If an intelligence such as ours had looked at the pre-human world and been told that one of the species then in existence was to be raised to rational and spiritual status and at last behold its Creator face to face, would he have picked the winner? Not unless it realised the importance of its hand-like paws; just as one would not guess the ingredients of glass unless one knew some chemistry. So we, because of something we do not know, are bewildered to find the ancient Hebrews 'chosen' as they were.

From this point of view there is no better psalm to begin with than No. 109. It ends with a verse which every Christian can at once make his own: the Lord is 'the prisoner's friend', standing by the poor (or friendless) to save him from unjust judges. This is one of the characteristic notes of the Psalms and one of the things for which we love them. It anticipates the temper of the *Magnificat*. It is hardly to be paralleled in Pagan literature (the Greek gods were very active in casting down the proud, but hardly in raising the humble). It will commend itself even to a modern unbeliever of good will; he may call it wishful thinking, but he will respect the wish. In a word, if we read only the last verse we should feel in full sympathy with this psalmist. But the moment we look back at what precedes that verse, he turns out to be removed from us by infinite distances; or, worse still, to be loathsomely akin to that in us which it is the main business of life to purge away. Psalm 109 is as unabashed a hymn of hate as was ever written. The poet has a detailed programme for his enemy which he hopes God will carry out. The enemy is to be placed under a wicked ruler. He is to have 'an accuser' perpetually at his side: whether an evil spirit, a 'Satan', as our Prayer Book version renders it, or merely a human accuser – a spy, an *agent provocateur*, a member of the secret police (v. 5). If the enemy attempts to have any religious life, this, far from improving his position, must make him even worse: 'let his prayer be turned into sin' (v. 6). And after his death – which had better, please, be early (v. 7) – his widow and children and descendants are to live in unrelieved misery (vv. 8–12). What makes our blood run cold, even more than the unrestrained vindictiveness, is the writer's untroubled conscience. He has no qualms, scruples, or reservations; no shame. He gives hatred free rein – encourages and spurs it on – in a sort of ghastly innocence. He offers these feelings, just as they are, to God, never doubting that they will be acceptable: turning straight from the maledictions to 'Deal thou with me, O Lord God, according unto thy Name: for sweet is thy mercy' (v. 20).

The man himself, of course, lived very long ago. His injuries may have been (humanly speaking) beyond endurance. He was doubtless a hot-blooded barbarian, more like a modern child than a modern man. And though we believe (and can even see from the last verse) that some knowledge of the real God had come to his race, yet he lived in the cold of the year, the early spring of Revelation, and those first gleams of knowledge were like snow drops, exposed to the frosts. For him, then, there may have been excuses. But we – what good can we find in reading such stuff?

One good, certainly. We have here an uninhibited expression of those feelings which oppression and injustice naturally produce. The psalm is a portrait: under it should be written: 'This is what you make of a man by ill-treating him.' In a modern child or savage the results might be exactly the same. In a modern, Western European adult – especially if he were a professing Christian – they would be more sophisticated; disguised as a disinterested love of justice, claiming to be concerned with the good of society. But under that disguise, and none the better for it in the sight of God, the feelings might still be there. (I am thinking of a total stranger who forwarded to me a letter written to her in denigration of myself by another total stranger, because, as she said, 'she felt it her duty'.) Now in a case of what we ordinarily call 'seduction' (that is, sexual seduction) we should think it monstrous to dwell on the guilt of the party who yielded to temptation and ignore that of the party who tempted. But every injury or oppression is equally a temptation, a temptation to hatred, and in that sense a seduction. Whenever we have wronged our fellow man, we have tempted him to be such a man as wrote Psalm 109. We may have repented of our wrong: we do not always know if he has repented of his hatred. How do accounts now stand between us if he has not?

I do not know the answer to that question. But I am inclined to think that we had better look unflinchingly at the sort of work we have done; like puppies, we must have 'our noses rubbed in it'. A man, now penitent, who has once seduced and abandoned a girl and then lost sight of her, had better not avert his eyes from the crude realities of the life she may now be living. For the same reason we ought to read the psalms that curse the oppressor; read them with fear. Who knows what imprecations of the same sort have been uttered against ourselves? What prayers have Red men, and Black, and Brown and Yellow, sent up against us to their gods or sometimes to God Himself? All over the earth the White Man's offence 'smells to heaven': massacres, broken treaties, theft, kidnappings, enslavement, deportation, floggings, lynchings, beatings-up, rape, insult, mockery, and odious hypocrisy make up that smell. But the thing comes nearer than that. Those of us who have little authority, who have few people at our mercy, may be thankful. But how if one is an officer in the army (or, perhaps worse, an NCO)? a hospital matron? a magistrate? a prison-warden? a school prefect? a trade-union official? a Boss of any sort? in a word, anyone who cannot be 'answered back'? It is hard enough, even with the best will in the world, to be just. It is hard, under the pressure of haste, uneasiness, ill-temper, self-complacency, and conceit, even to continue intending justice. Power corrupts; the 'insolence of office' will creep in. We see it so clearly in our superiors; is it unlikely that our inferiors see it in us? How many of those who have been over us did not sometimes (perhaps often) need our forgiveness? Be sure that we likewise need the forgiveness of those that are under us.

We may not always receive it. They may not be Christians at all. They may not be far enough on the way to master that hard work of forgiveness which we have set them. Bitter, chronic resentment, unsuccessfully resisted or not resisted at all, may be burning against us: the spirit, essentially, of Psalm 109.

I do not mean that God hears and will grant such prayers as that psalmist uttered. They are wicked. He condemns them. All resentment is sin. And we may hope that those things which our inferiors resent were not really half so bad as they imagine. The snub was unintentional; the high-handed behaviour on the bench was due to ignorance and an uneasy awareness of one's own incapacity; the seemingly unfair distribution of work was not really unfair, or not intended to be; the inexplicable personal dislike for one particular inferior, so obvious to him and to some of his fellows, is something of which we are genuinely unconscious (it appears in our conscious mind as discipline, or the need for making an example). Anyway, it is very wicked of them to hate us. Yes; but the folly consists in supposing that God sees the wickedness in them apart from the wickedness in us which provoked it. They sin by hatred because we tempted them. We have, in that sense, seduced, debauched them. They are, as it were, the mothers of this hatred: we are the fathers.

It is from this point of view that the *Magnificat* is terrifying. If there are two things in the Bible which should make our blood run cold, it is one; the other is that phrase in Revelation, 'The wrath of the lamb'. If there is not mildness in the Virgin Mother, if even the lamb, the helpless thing that bleats and has its throat cut, is not the symbol of the harmless, where shall we turn? The resemblance between the *Magnificat* and traditional Hebrew poetry which I noted above is no mere literary curiosity. There is, of course, a difference. There are no cursings here, no hatred, no self-righteousness. Instead, there is mere statement. He has scattered the proud, cast down the mighty, sent the rich empty away. I spoke just now of the ironic contrast between the fierce psalmists and the choir-boy's treble. The contrast is here brought up to a higher level. Once more we have the treble voice, a girl's voice, announcing without sin that the sinful prayers of her ancestors do not remain entirely unheard; and doing this, not indeed with fierce exultation, yet – who can mistake the tone? – in a calm and terrible gladness.

I am tempted here to digress for a moment into a speculation which may bring ease to us in one direction while it alarms us in another. Christians are unhappily divided about the kind of honour in which the Mother of the Lord should be held, but there is one truth about which no doubt seems admissible. If we believe in the Virgin Birth and if we believe in Our Lord's human nature, psychological as well as physical (for it is heretical to think Him a human body which had the Second Person of the Trinity *instead of* a human soul) we must also believe in a human heredity for that human nature. There is only one source for it (though in that source all the true Israel is summed up). If there is an iron element in Jesus may we not without irreverence guess whence, humanly speaking, it came? Did neighbours say, in His boyhood, 'He's His Mother's Son'? This might set in a new and less painful light the severity of some things He said to, or about, His Mother. We may suppose that she understood them very well.

I have called this a digression, but I am not sure that it is one. Two things link the psalms with us. One is the *Magnificat*, and one, Our Lord's continued quotations from them, though not, to be sure, from such psalms as 109. We cannot reject from our minds a book in which His was so steeped. The Church herself has followed Him and steeped our minds in the same book.

In a word, the psalmists and we are both in the Church. Individually they, like us, may be sometimes very bad members of it; tares, but tares that we have no authority to pull up. They may often be ignorant, as we (though perhaps in different ways) are ignorant, what spirit they are of. But we cannot excommunicate them, nor they us.

I do not at all mean (though if you watch, you will certainly find some critic who says I meant) that we are to make any concession to their ferocity. But we may learn to see the good thing which that ferocity is mixed with. Through all their excesses there runs a passionate craving for justice. One is tempted at first to say that such a craving, on the part of the oppressed, is no very great merit; that the wickedest men will cry out for fair play when you give them foul play. But unfortunately this is not true. Indeed at this very moment the spirit which cries for justice may be dying out.

Here is an alarming example. I had a pupil who was certainly a socialist, probably a Marxist. To him the 'collective', the State, was everything, the individual nothing; freedom, a bourgeois delusion. Then he went down and became a schoolmaster. A couple of years later, happening to be in Oxford, he paid me a visit. He said he had given up socialism. He was completely disillusioned about state-control. The interferences of the Ministry of Education with schools and schoolmasters were, he had found, arrogant, ignorant, and intolerable: sheer tyranny. I could take lots of this and the conversation went on merrily. Then suddenly the real purpose of his visit was revealed. He was so 'browned-off' that he wanted to give up schoolmastering; and could I – had I any influence – would I pull any wires to get him a job – *in the Ministry of Education*?

There you have the new man. Like the psalmists he can hate, but he does not, like the psalmists, thirst for justice. Having decided that there is oppression he immediately asks: 'How can I join the oppressors?' He has no objection to a world which is divided between tyrants and victims; the important thing is which of these two groups you are in. (The moral of the story remains the same whether you share his views about the Ministry or not.)

There is, then, mixed with the hatred in the psalmists, a spark which should be fanned, not trodden out. That spark God saw and fanned, till it burns clear in the *Magnificat*. The cry for 'judgement' was to be heard.

But the ancient Hebrew idea of 'judgement' will need an essay to itself.

II

The Day of Judgement is an idea very familiar, and very dreadful, to Christians. 'In all times of our tribulation, in all times of our wealth, in the hour of death, and in the day of judgement, Good Lord deliver us.' If there is any concept which cannot by any conjuring be removed from the teaching of Our Lord, it is that of the great separation; the sheep and the goats, the broad way and the narrow, the wheat and the tares, the winnowing fan, the wise and foolish virgins, the good fish and the refuse, the door closed on the marriage feast, with some inside and some outside in the dark. We may dare to hope – some dare to hope – that this is not the whole story, that, as Julian of Norwich said, 'All will be well and all manner of thing will be well.' But it is no use going to Our Lord's own words for that hope. Something we may get from St Paul: nothing, of that kind, from Jesus. It is from His own words that the picture of 'Doomsday' has come into Christianity.

One result of this is that the word 'judgement' in a religious context immediately suggests to us a criminal trial; the Judge on the bench, the accused in the dock, the hope of acquittal, the fear of conviction. But to the ancient Hebrews 'judgement' usually suggested something quite different.

In the Psalms judgement is not something that the conscience-stricken believer fears but something the downtrodden believer hopes for. God 'shall judge the world in righteousness' and 'be a defence for the oppressed' (9:8f). 'Judge me, O Lord', cries the poet of Psalm 35. More surprisingly, in 67 even the 'nations', the Gentiles, are told to 'rejoice and be glad' because God will 'judge the folk righteously'. (Our fear is precisely lest the judgement should be a good deal more righteous than we can bear.) In the jubilant 96th Psalm the very sky and earth are to 'be glad', the fields are to 'be joyful' and all the trees of the wood 'shall rejoice before the Lord' because 'He cometh to judge the earth'. At the prospect of that judgement which we dread there is such revelry as a Pagan poet might have used to herald the coming of Dionysus.

Though Our Lord, as I have said, imposed on us the modern, Christian conception of the Day of Judgement, yet His own words elsewhere illuminate the old Hebraic conception. I am thinking of the Unjust Judge in the parable. To most of us, unless we had that parable in mind, the mention of a wicked judge would instantly suggest someone like Judge Jeffreys: a roaring, interrupting, bloodthirsty brute, bent on hanging a prisoner, bullying the jury and the witnesses. Our hope is that we shall *not* be judged by him. Our Lord's Unjust Judge is a wholly different character. You want him to judge you, you pester him to judge you. The whole difficulty is to get your case heard. Obviously what Our Lord has in view is not a criminal trial at all but a civil trial. We are looking at 'justice' from the point of view not of a prisoner but of a plaintiff: a plaintiff with a watertight case, if only she could get the defendant into court.

The picture is strange to us only because we enjoy in our own country an unusually good legal profession. We take it for granted that judges do not need to be bribed and cannot be bribed. This is, however, no law of nature, but a rare achievement; we ourselves might lose it (shall certainly lose it if no pains are taken for its conservation); it does not inevitably go with the use of the English language. Over many parts of the world and in many periods the difficulty for poor and unimportant people has been not only to get their case fairly heard but to get it heard at all. It is their voices that speak in the continual hope of the Hebrews for 'judgement', the hope that some day, somehow, wrongs will be righted.

But the idea is not associated only with courts of law. The 'Judges' who give their name to a most interesting historical book in the Old Testament were not, I gather, so called only because they sometimes exercised what we should consider judicial functions. Indeed the book has very little to say about 'judging' in that sense. Its 'judges' are primarily heroes, fighting men, who deliver Israel from foreign tyrants: giant-killers. The name which we translate as 'judges' is apparently connected with a verb which means to vindicate, to avenge, to right the wrongs of. They might equally well be called champions, avengers. The knight errant of medieval romance who spends his days liberating, and securing justice for, distressed damsels, would almost have been, for the Hebrews, a 'judge'.

Such a Judge – He who will at last do us right, the deliverer, the protector, the queller of tyrants – is the dominant image in the Psalms. There are, indeed, some few passages in which a psalmist thinks of 'judgement' with trembling: 'Enter not into judgement with thy servant: for in thy sight shall no man living be justified' (143:2), or 'If thou, Lord, wilt be extreme to mark what is done amiss: O Lord, who may abide it?' (130:3). But the opposite attitude is far commoner: 'Hear the right, O Lord' (17:1), 'Be thou my Judge' (26:1), 'Plead thou my cause' (35:1), 'Give sentence with me, O God' (43:1), 'Arise, thou Judge of the world' (94:2). It is for justice, for a hearing, far more often than for pardon, that the psalmists pray.

We thus reach a very paradoxical generalisation. Ordinarily, and of course correctly, the Jewish and the Christian church, the reign of Moses and the reign of Christ, are contrasted as Law against Grace, justice against mercy, rigour against tenderness. Yet apparently those who live under the sterner dispensation hope for God's judgement while those who live under the milder fear it. How does this come about? The answer, by and large, will be plain to all who have read the Psalms with attention. The psalmists, with very few exceptions, are eager for judgement because they believe themselves to be wholly in the right. Others have sinned against them; their own conduct (as they frequently assure us) has been impeccable. They earnestly invite the divine inspection, certain that they will emerge from it with flying colours. The adversary may have things to hide, but they have not. The more God examines their case, the more unanswerable it will appear. The Christian, on the other hand, trembles because he knows he is a sinner.

Thus in one sense we might say that Jewish confidence in the face of judgement is a by-product of Jewish self-righteousness. But this is far too summary. We must consider the whole experience out of which the self-righteous utterances grow: and secondly, what, on a deeper level, those utterances really mean.

The experience is dark and dreadful. We must not call it the 'dark night of the soul' for that name is already appropriate to another darkness and another dread, encountered at a far higher level than (I suppose) any of the psalmists had reached. But we may well call it the Dark Night of the Flesh, understanding by 'the flesh' the natural man. For the experience is not in itself necessarily religious and thousands of unbelievers undergo it in our own time. It arises from natural causes; but it becomes religious in the psalmists because they are religious men.

It must be confessed at the outset that all those passages which paint this Dark Night can be regarded, if we wish, as the expressions of a neurosis. If we choose to maintain that several psalmists wrote in, or on the verge of, a nervous breakdown, our theory will cover all the facts. That is, the psalmists assert as true about their own situation all those things which a patient, in a certain neurotic condition, wrongly believes to be true of his. For our present purpose, I think this does not matter much. Neurosis is a thing that occurs; we may have passed, or may yet have to pass, through that valley. It concerns us to see how certain believers in God behaved in it before us. And neurosis is, after all, a relative term. Who can say that he never touches the fringes of it? Even if the Psalms were written by neurotics, that will not make them wholly irrelevant.

But of course we cannot be at all sure that they were. The neurotic wrongly believes that he is threatened by certain evils. But another man (or the neurotic himself at another time) may be really threatened with those same evils. It may be only the patient's nerves that make him so sure that he has cancer, or is financially ruined, or is going to hell; but this does not prove that there are no such things as cancer or bankruptcy or damnation. To suggest that the situation described in certain psalms must be imaginary seems to me to be wishful thinking. The situation does occur in real life. If anyone doubts this let him consider, while I try to present this Dark Night of the Flesh, how easily it might be, not the subjective impression, but the real situation of any one of the following:

1. A small, ugly, unathletic, unpopular boy in his second term at a thoroughly bad English public school. 2. An unpopular recruit in an army hut. 3. A Jew in Hitler's Germany. 4. A man in a bad firm or government office whom a group of rivals are trying to get rid of. 5. A Papist in sixteenth-century England. 6. A Protestant in sixteenth-century Spain. 7. An African in Malan's Africa. 8. An American socialist in the hands of Senator McCarthy or a Zulu, noxious to Chaka, during one of the old, savage witch-hunts.

The Dark Night of the Flesh can be objective; it is not even very uncommon.

One is alone. The fellow-recruit who seemed to be a friend on the first day, the boys who were your friends last term, the neighbours who were your friends before the Jew-baiting began (or before you attracted Senator McCarthy's attention), even your connections and relatives, have begun to give you a wide berth. No one wishes to be seen with you. When you pass acquaintances in the street they always happen to be looking the other way. 'They of mine acquaintance were afraid of me; and they that did see me without conveyed themselves from me' (31:13). Lovers, neighbours, kinsmen stand 'afar off' (38:11). 'I am become a stranger unto my brethren' (69:8). 'Thou hast put away mine acquaintance far from me: and made me to be abhorrred of them' (88:7). 'I looked also upon my right hand and saw there was no man that would know me' (142:4).

Sometimes it is not an individual but a group (a religious body or even a whole nation) that has this experience. Members fall off; allies desert; the huge combinations against us extend and harden daily. Harder even to bear than our dwindling numbers and growing isolation, is the increasing evidence that 'our side' is ineffective. The world is turned upside down by bad men and 'What hath the righteous done?', where are our counter-measures? (11:3). We are 'put to rebuke' (12:9). Once there were omens in our favour and great leaders on our side. But those days are gone: 'We see not our tokens, there is not one prophet more' (74:10). England in modern Europe and Christians in modern England often feel like this.

And all round the isolated man, every day, is the presence of the unbelievers. They know well enough what we are believing or trying to believe ('help thou my unbelief') and regard it as total illusion. 'Many one there be that say of my soul, There is no help for him in his God' (3:2). As if God, supposing He exists, had nothing to do but look after *us*! (10:14); but in fact, 'There is no God' (14:1). If the sufferer's God really exists 'let Him deliver him' now! (22:8). 'Where is now thy God?' (42:3).

The man in the Dark Night of the Flesh is in everyone else's eyes extremely funny; the stock joke of that whole school or hut or office.

They can't see him without laughing: they make faces at him (22:7). The drunks work his name into their comic songs (69:12). He is a 'by-word' (44:15). Unfortunately all this laughter is not exactly honest, spontaneous laughter such as a man with some oddity of voice or face might learn to bear and even, in the end, to join in. These mockers do not laugh *although* it hurts him nor even without caring whether it hurts or not; they laugh *because* it will hurt. Any humiliation or miscarriage of his is jam to them; they crow over him when he's down – 'when my foot slipped, they rejoiced greatly against me' (38:16).

If one had a certain sort of aristocratic and Stoic pride one might perhaps answer scorn with scorn and even (in a sense) rejoice, as Coventry Patmore rejoiced, to live 'in the high mountain air of public obloquy'. If so, one would not be completely in the Dark Night. But the sufferer, for better or worse, is not – or if he once was, is now no longer – that sort of man. The continual taunts, slights, and humiliations (partly veiled or brutally plain according to the *milieu*) get past his defences and under his skin. He is in his own eyes also the object they would make him. He has no comeback. Shame has covered his face (69:7). He might as well be a dumb man; in his mouth are no reproofs (38:13). He is 'a worm and no man' (22:6).

[29]
RELIGION AND ROCKETRY

This essay has had various titles and was first published as 'Will We Lose God in Outer Space?' in The Christian Herald, *Volume LXXXI (April 1958); then as a pamphlet entitled* Shall We Lose God in Outer Space? *by SPCK in 1959; and finally, under the title which Lewis originally gave it, in* The World's Last Night *(US, 1960) and* Fernseed and Elephants *(1998).*

In my time I have heard two quite different arguments against my religion put forward in the name of science. When I was a youngster, people used to say that the universe was not only not friendly to life but positively hostile to it. Life had appeared on this planet by a millionth chance, as if at one point there had been a breakdown of the elaborate defences generally enforced against it. We should be rash to assume that such a leak had occurred more than once. Probably life was a purely terrestrial abnormality. We were alone in an infinite desert. Which just showed the absurdity of the Christian idea that there was a creator who was interested in living creatures.

But then came Professor F.B. Hoyle, the Cambridge cosmologist, and in a fortnight or so everyone I met seemed to have decided that the universe was probably quite well provided with inhabitable globes and with livestock to inhabit them. Which just showed (equally well) the absurdity of Christianity with its parochial idea that Man could be important to God.

This is a warning of what we may expect if we ever do discover animal life (vegetable does not matter) on another planet. Each new discovery, even every new theory, is held at first to have the most wide-reaching theological and philosophical consequences. It is seized by unbelievers as the basis for a new attack on Christianity; it is often, and more embarrassingly, seized by injudicious believers as the basis for a new defence.

But usually, when the popular hubbub has subsided and the novelty has been chewed over by real theologians, real scientists and real philosophers, both sides find themselves pretty much where they were before. So it was with Copernican astronomy, with Darwinism, with biblical criticism, with the new psychology. So, I cannot help expecting, it will be with the discovery of 'life on other planets' – if that discovery is ever made.

The supposed threat is clearly directed against the doctrine of the Incarnation, the belief that God of God 'for us men and for our salvation came down from heaven and was ... made man.' Why for us men more than for others? If we find ourselves to be but one among a million races, scattered through a million spheres, how can we, without absurd arrogance, believe ourselves to have been uniquely favoured? I admit that the question could become formidable. In fact, it will become formidable when, if ever, we know the answer to five other questions.

1. Are there animals anywhere except on earth? We do not know. We do not know whether we ever shall know.

2. Supposing there were, have any of these animals what we call 'rational souls'? By this I include not merely the faculty to abstract and calculate, but the apprehension of values, the power to mean by 'good' something more than 'good for me' or even 'good for my species'. If instead of asking, 'Have they rational souls?' you prefer to ask, 'Are they spiritual animals?' I think we shall both mean pretty much the same. If the answer to either question should be No, then of course it would not be at all strange that our species should be treated differently from theirs.

There would be no sense in offering to a creature, however clever or amiable, a gift which that creature was by its nature incapable either of desiring or of receiving. We teach our sons to read but not our dogs. The dogs prefer bones. And of course, since we do not yet know whether there are extra-terrestrial animals at all, we are a long way from knowing that they are rational (or 'spiritual').

Even if we met them we might not find it so easy to decide. It seems to me possible to suppose creatures so clever that they could talk, though they were, from the theological point of view, really only animals, capable of pursuing or enjoying only natural ends. One meets humans – the machine-minded and materialistic urban type – who *look* as if they were just that. As Christians we must believe the appearance to be false; somewhere under that glib surface there lurks, however atrophied, a human soul. But in other worlds there might be things that really are what these seem to be. Conversely, there might be creatures genuinely spiritual, whose powers of manufacture and abstract thought were so humble that we should mistake them for mere animals. God shield them from us!

3. If there are species, and rational species, other than man, are any or all of them, like us, fallen? This is the point non-Christians always seem to forget. They seem to think that the Incarnation implies some particular merit or excellence in humanity. But of course it implies just the reverse: a particular demerit and depravity. No creature that deserved Redemption would need to be redeemed. They that are whole need not the physician. Christ died for men precisely because men are *not* worth dying for; to make them worth it. Notice what waves of utterly unwarranted hypothesis these critics of Christianity want us to swim through. We are now supposing the fall of hypothetically rational creatures whose mere existence is hypothetical!

4. If all of them (and surely *all* is a long shot) or any of them have fallen, have they been denied Redemption by the Incarnation and Passion of Christ? For of course it is no very new idea that the eternal Son may, for all we know, have been incarnate in other worlds than earth and so saved other races than ours. As Alice Meynell wrote in 'Christ in the Universe':

> ... in the eternities
> Doubtless we shall compare together, hear
> A million alien Gospels, in what guise
> He trod the Pleiades, the Lyre, the Bear.

I wouldn't go as far as 'doubtless' myself. Perhaps of all races *we* only fell. Perhaps Man is the only lost sheep; the one, therefore, whom the Shepherd came to seek. Or perhaps – but this brings us to the next wave of assumption. It is the biggest yet and will knock us head over heels, but I am fond of a tumble in the surf.

5. If we knew (which we don't) the answers to 1., 2. and 3. – and further, if we knew that Redemption by an Incarnation and Passion had been denied to creatures in need of it – is it certain that this is the only mode of Redemption that is possible? Here of course we ask for what is not merely unknown but, unless God should reveal it, wholly unknowable. It may be that the further we were permitted to see into his councils, the more clearly we should understand that thus and not otherwise – by the birth at Bethlehem, the cross on Calvary and the empty tomb – a fallen race could be rescued. There may be a necessity for this, insurmountable, rooted in the very nature of God and the very nature of sin. But we don't know. At any rate, I don't know. Spiritual as well as physical conditions might differ widely in different worlds. There might be different sorts and different degrees of fallenness. We must surely believe

that the divine charity is as fertile in resource as it is measureless in condescension. To different diseases, or even to different patients sick with the same disease, the great Physician may have applied different remedies: remedies which we should probably not recognise as such even if we ever heard of them.

It might turn out that the redemption of other species differed from ours by working through ours. There is a hint of something like this in St Paul (Romans 8:19–23) when he says that the whole creation is longing and waiting to be delivered from some kind of slavery, and that the deliverance will occur only when we, we Christians, fully enter upon our sonship to God and exercise our 'glorious liberty'.

On the conscious level I believe that he was thinking only of our own earth: of animal, and probably vegetable, life on earth being 'renewed' or glorified at the glorification of man in Christ. But it is perhaps possible – it is not necessary – to give his words a cosmic meaning. It may be that Redemption, starting with us, is to work from us and through us.

This would no doubt give man a pivotal position. But such a position need not imply any superiority in us or any favouritism in God. The general, deciding where to begin his attack, does not select the prettiest landscape or the most fertile field or the most attractive village. Christ was not born in a stable because a stable is, in itself, the most convenient or distinguished place for a maternity.

Only if we had some such function would a contact between us and such unknown races be other than a calamity. If indeed we were unfallen, it would be another matter.

It sets one dreaming – to interchange thoughts with beings whose thinking had an organic background wholly different from ours (other senses, other appetites), to be unenviously humbled by intellects possibly superior to our own yet able for that very reason to descend to our level, to descend lovingly ourselves if we met innocent and childlike creatures who could never be as strong or as clever as we, to exchange with the inhabitants of other worlds that especially keen and rich affection which exists between unlikes; it is a glorious dream. But make no mistake. It *is* a dream. We are fallen.

We know what our race does to strangers. Man destroys or enslaves every species he can. Civilised man murders, enslaves, cheats, and corrupts savage man. Even inanimate nature he turns into dust bowls and slagheaps. There are individuals who don't. But they are not the sort who are likely to be our pioneers in space. Our ambassador to new worlds will be the needy and greedy adventurer or the ruthless technical expert. They will do as their kind has always done. What that will be if they meet things weaker than themselves, the black man and the red man can tell. If they meet things stronger, they will be, very properly, destroyed.

It is interesting to wonder how things would go if they met an unfallen race. At first, to be sure, they'd have a grand time jeering at, duping, and exploiting its innocence: but I doubt if our half-animal cunning would long be a match for godlike wisdom, selfless valour, and perfect unanimity.

I therefore fear the practical, not the theoretical, problems which will arise if ever we meet rational creatures which are not human. Against them we shall, if we can, commit all the crimes we have already committed against creatures certainly human but differing from us in features and pigmentation; and the starry heavens will become an object to which good men can look up only with feelings of intolerable guilt, agonised pity, and burning shame.

Of course after the first debauch of exploitation we shall make some belated attempt to do better. We shall perhaps send missionaries. But can even missionaries be trusted? 'Gun and gospel' have been horribly combined in the past. The missionary's holy desire to save souls has not always been kept quite distinct from the arrogant desire, the busybody's itch, to (as he calls it) 'civilise' the (as he calls them) 'natives'. Would all our missionaries recognise an unfallen race if they met it? Could they? Would they continue to press upon creatures that did not need to be saved that plan of Salvation which God has appointed to Man? Would they denounce as sins mere differences of behaviour which the spiritual and biological history of these strange creatures fully justified and which God himself had blessed? Would they try to teach those from whom they had better learn? I do not know.

What I do know is that here and now, as our only possible practical preparation for such a meeting, you and I should resolve to stand firm against all exploitation and all theological imperialism. It will not be fun. We shall be called traitors to our own species. We shall be hated of almost all men; even of some religious men. And we must not give back one single inch. We shall probably fail, but let us go down fighting for the right side. Our loyalty is due not to our species but to God. Those who are, or can become, his sons, are our real brothers even if they have shells or tusks. It is spiritual, not biological, kinship that counts.

But let us thank God that we are still very far from travel to other worlds.

I have wondered before now whether the vast astronomical distances may not be God's quarantine precautions. They prevent the spiritual infection of a fallen species from spreading. And of course we are also very far from the supposed theological problem which contact with other rational species might raise. Such species may not exist. There is not at present a shred of empirical evidence that they do. There is nothing but what the logicians would call arguments from '*a priori* probability' – arguments that begin 'It is only natural to suppose', or 'All analogy suggests', or 'Is it not the height of arrogance to rule out –?' They make very good reading. But who except a born gambler ever risks five dollars on such grounds in ordinary life?

And, as we have seen, the mere existence of these creatures would not raise a problem. After that, we still need to know that they are fallen; then, that they have not been, or will not be, redeemed in the mode we know; and then, that no other mode is possible. I think a Christian is sitting pretty if his faith never encounters more formidable difficulties than these conjectural phantoms.

If I remember rightly, St Augustine raised a question about the theological position of satyrs, monopodes, and other semi-human creatures. He decided it could wait till we knew there were any. So can this.

'But supposing,' you say. 'Supposing all these embarrassing suppositions turned out to be true?' I can only record a conviction that they won't; a conviction which has for me become in the course of years irresistible. Christians and their opponents again and again expect that some new discovery will either turn matters of faith into matters of knowledge or else reduce them to patent absurdities. But it has never happened.

What we believe always remains intellectually possible; it never becomes intellectually compulsive. I have an idea that when this ceases to be so, the world will be ending. We have been warned that *all but* conclusive evidence against Christianity, evidence that would deceive (if it were possible) the very elect, will appear with Antichrist.

And after that there will be wholly conclusive evidence on the other side.

But not, I fancy, till then on either side.

[30]

THE EFFICACY OF PRAYER

This essay first appeared in The Atlantic Monthly, *CCIII (January 1959), then in* The World's Last Night *(US, 1960) and* Fern-seed and Elephants *(1998).*

Some years ago I got up one morning intending to have my hair cut in preparation for a visit to London, and the first letter I opened made it clear I need not go to London. So I decided to put the haircut off too. But then there began the most unaccountable little nagging in my mind, almost like a voice saying, 'Get it cut all the same. Go and get it cut.' In the end I could stand it no longer. I went. Now my barber at that time was a fellow-Christian and a man of many troubles whom my brother and I had sometimes been able to help. The moment I opened his shop door he said, 'Oh, I was praying you might come today.' And in fact if I had come a day or so later I should have been of no use to him.

It awed me; it awes me still. But of course one cannot rigorously prove a causal connection between the barber's prayers and my visit. It might be telepathy. It might be accident.

I have stood by the bedside of a woman whose thigh-bone was eaten through with cancer and who had thriving colonies of the disease in many other bones as well. It took three people to move her in bed. The doctors predicted a few months of life; the nurses (who often know better), a few weeks. A good man laid his hands on her and prayed. A year later the patient was walking (uphill, too, through rough woodland) and the man who took the last X-ray photos was saying, 'These bones are as solid as rock. It's miraculous.'

But once again there is no rigorous proof. Medicine, as all true doctors admit, is not an exact science. We need not invoke the supernatural to explain the falsification of its prophecies. You need not, unless you choose, believe in a causal connection between the prayers and the recovery.

The question then arises, 'What sort of evidence would prove the efficacy of prayer?' The thing we pray for may happen, but how can you ever know it was not going to happen anyway? Even if the thing were indisputably miraculous it would not follow that the miracle had occurred because of your prayers. The answer surely is that a compulsive empirical proof such as we have in the sciences can never be attained.

Some things are proved by the unbroken uniformity of our experiences. The law of gravitation is established by the fact that, in our experience, all bodies without exception obey it. Now even if all the things that people prayed for happened, which they do not, this would not prove what Christians mean by the efficacy of prayer. For prayer is request. The essence of request, as distinct from compulsion, is that it may or may not be granted. And if an infinitely wise Being listens to the requests of finite and foolish creatures, of course he will sometimes grant and sometimes refuse them. Invariable 'success' in prayer would not prove the Christian doctrine at all. It would prove something much more like magic – a power in certain human beings to control, or compel, the course of nature.

There are, no doubt, passages in the New Testament which may seem at first sight to promise an invariable granting of our prayers. But that cannot be what they really mean. For in the very heart of the story we meet a glaring instance to the contrary. In Gethsemane the holiest of all petitioners prayed three times that a certain cup might pass from him. It did not. After that the idea that prayer is recommended to us as a sort of infallible gimmick may be dismissed.

Other things are proved not simply by experience but by those artificially contrived experiences which we call experiments. Could this be done about prayer? I will pass over the objection that no Christian could take part in such a project, because he has been forbidden it: 'You must not try experiments on God, your Master.' Forbidden or not, is the thing even possible?

I have seen it suggested that a team of people – the more the better – should agree to pray as hard as they knew how, over a period of six weeks, for all the patients in Hospital A and none of those in Hospital B. Then you would tot up the results and see if A had more cures and fewer deaths. And I suppose you would repeat the experiment at various times and places so as to eliminate the influence of irrelevant factors.

The trouble is that I do not see how any real prayer could go on under such conditions. 'Words without thoughts never to heaven go,' says the King in *Hamlet*. Simply to say prayers is not to pray: otherwise a team of properly trained parrots would serve as well as men for our experiment. You cannot pray for the recovery of the sick unless the end you have in view is their recovery. But you can have no motive for desiring the recovery of all the patients in one hospital and none of those in another. You are not doing it in order that suffering should be relieved; you are doing it to find out what happens. The real purpose and the nominal purpose of your prayers are at variance. In other words, whatever your tongue and teeth and knees may do, you are not praying. The experiment demands an impossibility.

Empirical proof and disproof are, then, unobtainable. But this conclusion will seem less depressing if we remember that prayer is request and compare it with other specimens of the same thing.

We make requests of our fellow creatures as well as of God: we ask for the salt, we ask for a raise in pay, we ask a friend to feed the cat while we are on our holidays, we ask a woman to marry us. Sometimes we get what we ask for and sometimes not. But when we do, it is not nearly so easy as one might suppose to prove with scientific certainty a causal connection between the asking and the getting.

Your neighbour may be a humane person who would not have let your cat starve even if you had forgotten to make any arrangement. Your employer is never so likely to grant your request for a raise as when he is aware that you could get better money from a rival firm and is quite possibly intending to secure you by a raise in any case. As for the lady who consents to marry you – are you sure she had not decided to do so already? Your proposal, you know, might have been the result, not the cause, of her decision. A certain important conversation might never have taken place unless she had intended that it should.

Thus in some measure the same doubt that hangs about the causal efficacy of our prayers to God hangs also about our prayers to man. Whatever we get we might have been going to get anyway. But only, as I say, in some measure. Our friend, boss, and wife may tell us that they acted because we asked; and we may know them so well as to feel sure, first that they are saying what they believe to be true, and secondly that they understand their own motives well enough to be right. But notice that when this happens our assurance has not been gained by the methods of science. We do not try the control experiment of refusing the raise or breaking off the engagement and then making our request again under fresh conditions. Our assurance is quite different in kind from scientific knowledge. It is born out of our personal relation to the other parties; not from knowing things about them but from knowing *them*.

Our assurance – if we reach an assurance – that God always hears and sometimes grants our prayers, and that apparent grantings are not merely fortuitous, can only come in the same sort of way. There can be no question of tabulating successes and failures and trying to decide whether the successes are too numerous to be accounted for by chance. Those who best know a man best know whether, when he did what they asked, he did it because they asked. I think those who best know God will best know whether he sent me to the barber's shop because the barber prayed.

For up till now we have been tackling the whole question in the wrong way and on the wrong level. The very question 'Does prayer work?' puts us in the wrong frame of mind from the outset. 'Work': as if it were magic, or a machine – something that functions automatically. Prayer is either a sheer illusion or a personal contact between embryonic, incomplete persons (ourselves) and the utterly concrete Person. Prayer in the sense of petition, asking for things, is a small part of it; confession and penitence are its threshold, adoration its sanctuary, the presence and vision and enjoyment of God its bread and wine. In it God shows himself to us. That he answers prayers is a corollary – not necessarily the most important one – from that revelation. What he does is learned from what he is.

Petitionary prayer is, nonetheless, both allowed and commanded to us: 'Give us our daily bread.' And no doubt it raises a theoretical problem. Can we believe that God ever really modifies his action in response to the suggestions of men? For infinite wisdom does not need telling what is best, and infinite goodness needs no urging to do it. But neither does God need any of those things that are done by finite agents, whether living or inanimate. He could, if he chose, repair our bodies miraculously without food; or give us food without the aid of farmers, bakers, and butchers; or knowledge without the aid of learned men; or convert the heathen without missionaries. Instead, he allows soils and weather and animals and the muscles, minds, and wills of men to co-operate in the execution of his will. 'God,' said Pascal, 'instituted prayer in order to lend to his creatures the dignity of causality.' But not only prayer; whenever we act at all he lends us that dignity. It is not really stranger, nor less strange, that my prayers should affect the course of events than that my other actions should do so. They have not advised or changed God's mind – that is, his over-all purpose. But that purpose will be realised in different ways according to the actions, including the prayers, of his creatures.

For he seems to do nothing of himself which he can possibly delegate to his creatures. He commands us to do slowly and blunderingly what he could do perfectly and in the twinkling of an eye. He allows us to neglect what he would have us do, or to fail. Perhaps we do not fully realise the problem, so to call it, of enabling finite free will to co-exist with Omnipotence. It seems to involve at every moment almost a sort of divine abdication. We are not mere recipients or spectators. We are either privileged to share in the game or compelled to collaborate in the work, 'to wield our little tridents'. Is this amazing process simply Creation going on before our eyes? This is how (no light matter) God makes something – indeed, makes gods – out of nothing.

So at least it seems to me. But what I have offered can be, at the very best, only a mental model or symbol. All that we say on such subjects must be merely analogical and parabolic. The reality is doubtless not comprehensible by our faculties. But we can at any rate try to expel bad analogies and bad parables. Prayer is not a machine. It is not magic. It is not advice offered to God. Our act, when we pray, must not, any more than all our other acts, be separated from the continuous act of God himself, in which alone all finite causes operate.

It would be even worse to think of those who get what they pray for as sort of court favourites, people who have influence with the throne. The refused prayer of Christ in Gethsemane is answer enough to that. And I dare not leave out the hard saying which I once heard from an experienced Christian: 'I have seen many striking answers to prayer and more than one that I thought miraculous. But they usually come at the beginning: before conversion, or soon after it. As the Christian life proceeds, they tend to be rarer. The refusals, too, are not only more frequent; they become more unmistakable, more emphatic.'

Does God then forsake just those who serve him best? Well, he who served him best of all said, near his tortured death, 'Why hast thou forsaken me?' When God becomes man, that Man, of all others, is least comforted by God, at his greatest need. There is a mystery here which, even if I had the power, I might not have the courage to explore. Meanwhile, little people like you and me, if our prayers are sometimes granted, beyond all hope and probability, had better not draw hasty conclusions to our own advantage. If we were stronger, we might be less tenderly treated. If we were braver, we might be sent, with far less help, to defend far more desperate posts in the great battle.

[31]
FERN-SEED AND ELEPHANTS

Originally entitled 'Modern Theology and Biblical Criticism', Lewis read this essay at Westcott House, Cambridge, on 11 May 1959. Published under that title in Christian Reflections *(1981), it appeared most recently in* Fern-seed and Elephants *(1998).*

This paper arose out of a conversation I had with the Principal[1] one night last term. A book of Alec Vidler's happened to be lying on the table and I expressed my reaction to the sort of theology it contained. My reaction was a hasty and ignorant one, produced with the freedom that comes after dinner.[2] One thing led to another and before we were done I was saying a good deal more than I had meant about the type of thought which, so far as I could gather, is now dominant in many theological colleges. He then said, 'I wish you would come and say all this to my young men.' He knew of course that I was extremely ignorant of the whole thing. But I think his idea was that you ought to know how a certain sort of theology strikes the outsider. Though I may have nothing but misunderstandings to lay before you, you ought to know that such misunderstandings exist. That sort of thing is easy to overlook inside one's own circle. The minds you daily meet have been conditioned by the same studies and prevalent opinions as your own. That may mislead you. For of course as priests it is the outsiders you will have to cope with. You exist in the long run for no other purpose. The proper study of shepherds is sheep, not (save accidentally) other shepherds. And woe to you if you do not evangelise. I am not trying to teach my grandmother. I am a sheep,

---

[1] The Principal of Westcott House, Cambridge, now the Bishop of Edinburgh (the Rt Rev. Kenneth Carey).

[2] While the Bishop was out of the room, Lewis read 'The Sign at Cana' in Alec Vidler's *Windsor Sermons*. The Bishop recalls that when he asked him what he thought about it, Lewis 'expressed himself very freely about the sermon and said that he thought that it was quite incredible that we should have had to wait nearly 2,000 years to be told by a theologian called Vidler that what the Church has always regarded as a miracle was, in fact, a parable!'

telling shepherds what only a sheep can tell them. And now I start my bleating.

There are two sorts of outsiders: the uneducated, and those who are educated in some way but not in your way. How you are to deal with the first class, if you hold views like Loisy's or Schweitzer's or Bultmann's or Tillich's or even Alec Vidler's, I simply don't know. I see – and I'm told that you see – that it would hardly do to tell them what you really believe. A theology which denies the historicity of nearly everything in the Gospels to which Christian life and affections and thought have been fastened for nearly two millennia – which either denies the miraculous altogether or, more strangely, after swallowing the camel of the Resurrection strains at such gnats as the feeding of the multitudes – if offered to the uneducated man can produce only one or other of two effects. It will make him a Roman Catholic or an atheist. What you offer him he will not recognise as Christianity. If he holds to what he calls Christianity he will leave a Church in which it is no longer taught and look for one where it is. If he agrees with your version he will no longer call himself a Christian and no longer come to church. In his crude, coarse way, he would respect you much more if you did the same. An experienced clergyman told me that most liberal priests, faced with this problem, have recalled from its grave the late medieval conception of two truths: a picture-truth which can be preached to the people, and an esoteric truth for use among the clergy. I shouldn't think you will enjoy this conception much when you have to put it into practice. I'm sure if I had to produce picture-truths to a parishioner in great anguish or under fierce temptation, and produce them with that seriousness and fervour which his condition demanded, while knowing all the time that I didn't exactly – only in some Pickwickian sense – believe them myself, I'd find my forehead getting red and damp and my collar getting tight. But that is your headache, not mine. You have, after all, a different sort of collar. I claim to belong to the second group of outsiders: educated, but not theo-logically educated. How one member of that group feels I must now try to tell you.

The undermining of the old orthodoxy has been mainly the work of divines engaged in New Testament criticism. The authority of experts in that discipline is the authority in deference to whom we are asked to give up a huge mass of beliefs shared in common by the early Church, the Fathers, the Middle Ages, the Reformers, and even the nineteenth century. I want to explain what it is that makes me sceptical about this authority. Ignorantly sceptical, as you will all too easily see. But the scepticism is the father of the ignorance. It is hard to persevere in a close study when you can work up no *prima facie* confidence in your teachers.

First then, whatever these men may be as Biblical critics, I distrust them as critics. They seem to me to lack literary judgement, to be imperceptive about the very quality of the texts they are reading. It sounds a strange charge to bring against men who have been steeped in those books all their lives. But that might be just the trouble. A man who has spent his youth and manhood in the minute study of New Testament texts and of other people's studies of them, whose literary experience of those texts lacks any standard of comparison such as can only grow from a wide and deep and genial experience of literature in general, is, I should think, very likely to miss the obvious things about them. If he tells me that something in a Gospel is legend or romance, I want to know how many legends and romances he has read, how well his palate is trained in detecting them by the flavour; not how many years he has spent on that Gospel. But I had better turn to examples.

In what is already a very old commentary I read that the fourth Gospel is regarded by one school as a 'spiritual romance', 'a poem not a history', to be judged by the same canons as Nathan's parable, the book of Jonah, *Paradise Lost* 'or, more exactly, *Pilgrim's Progress*'.[3] After a man has said that, why need one attend to anything else he says about any book in the world? Note that he regards *Pilgrim's Progress*, a story which professes to be a dream and flaunts its allegorical nature by every single proper name it uses, as the closest parallel. Note that the whole epic panoply of Milton goes for nothing. But even if we leave out the grosser absurdities and keep to *Jonah*, the insensitiveness is crass – *Jonah*, a tale with as few even pretended historical attachments as *Job*, grotesque in incident and surely not without a distinct, though of course edifying, vein of typically Jewish humour. Then turn to *John*. Read the dialogues: that with the Samaritan woman at the well, or that which follows the healing of the man born blind. Look at its pictures: Jesus (if I may use the word) doodling with his finger in the dust; the unforgettable ἦν δὲ νύξ (13:30). I have been reading poems, romances, vision-literature, legends, myths all my life. I know what they are like. I know that not one of them is like this. Of this text there are only two possible views. Either this is reportage – though it may no doubt contain errors – pretty close up to the facts; nearly as close

---

[3] From 'The Gospel According to St John', by Walter Lock in *A New Commentary on Holy Scripture, including the Apocrypha*, ed. by Charles Gore, Henry Leighton Goudge, Alfred Guillaume (SPCK, 1928), p. 241. Lock, in turn, is quoting from James Drummond's *An Inquiry into the Character and Authorship of the Fourth Gospel* (London, 1903).

as Boswell. Or else, some unknown writer in the second century, without known predecessors or successors, suddenly anticipated the whole technique of modern, novelistic, realistic narrative. If it is untrue, it must be narrative of that kind. The reader who doesn't see this has simply not learned to read. I would recommend him to read Auerbach.[4]

Here, from Bultmann's *Theology of the New Testament* is another: 'Observe in what unassimilated fashion the prediction of the parousia (Mark 8:38) follows upon the prediction of the passion (8:31).'[5] What can he mean? Unassimilated? Bultmann believes that predictions of the parousia are older than those of the passion. He therefore wants to believe – and no doubt does believe – that when they occur in the same passage some discrepancy or 'unassimilation' must be perceptible between them. But surely he foists this on the text with shocking lack of perception. Peter has confessed Jesus to be the Anointed One. That flash of glory is hardly over before the dark prophecy begins – that the Son of Man must suffer and die. Then this contrast is repeated. Peter, raised for a moment by his confession, makes his false step: the crushing rebuff 'Get thee behind me' follows. Then, across that momentary ruin which Peter (as so often) becomes, the voice of the Master, turning to the crowd, generalises the moral. All his followers must take up the cross. This avoidance of suffering, this self-preservation, is not what life is really about. Then, more definitely still, the summons to martyrdom. You must stand to your tackling. If you disown Christ here and now, he will disown you later. Logically, emotionally, imaginatively, the sequence is perfect. Only a Bultmann could think otherwise.

Finally, from the same Bultmann: 'the personality of Jesus has no importance for the kerygma either of Paul or of John ... Indeed the tradition of the earliest Church did not even unconsciously preserve a picture of his personality. Every attempt to reconstruct one remains a play of subjective imagination.'[6]

So there is no personality of our Lord presented in the New Testament. Through what strange process has this learned German gone in order to make himself blind to what all men except him see? What evidence have we that he would recognise a personality if it were there? For it is Bultmann *contra mundum*. If anything whatever is common to all believers, and even to many unbelievers, it is the sense that in the Gospels

[4] Erich Auerbach's *Mimesis: The Representation of Reality in Western Literature*, translated by Willard R. Trask (Princeton, 1953).
[5] Rudolf Bultmann, *Theology of the New Testament*, translated by Kendrick Grobel, vol. I (SCM Press, 1952), p. 30.
[6] Ibid., p. 35.

they have met a personality. There are characters whom we know to be historical but of whom we do not feel that we have any personal knowledge – knowledge by acquaintance; such are Alexander, Attila, or William of Orange. There are others who make no claim to historical reality but whom, none the less, we know as we know real people: Falstaff, Uncle Toby, Mr Pickwick. But there are only three characters who, claiming the first sort of reality, also actually have the second. And surely everyone knows who they are: Plato's Socrates, the Jesus of the Gospels, and Boswell's Johnson. Our acquaintance with them shows itself in a dozen ways. When we look into the apocryphal gospels, we find ourselves constantly saying of this or that *logion*, 'No. It's a fine saying, but not his. That wasn't how he talked' – just as we do with all pseudo-Johnsoniana. We are not in the least perturbed by the contrasts within each character: the union in Socrates of silly and scabrous titters about Greek pederasty with the highest mystical fervour and the homeliest good sense; in Johnson, of profound gravity and melancholy with that love of fun and nonsense which Boswell never understood though Fanny Burney did; in Jesus of peasant shrewdness, intolerable severity, and irresistible tenderness. So strong is the flavour of the personality that, even while he says things which, on any other assumption than that of divine Incarnation in the fullest sense, would be appallingly arrogant, yet we – and many unbelievers too – accept him at his own valuation when he says 'I am meek and lowly of heart.' Even those passages in the New Testament which superficially, and in intention, are most concerned with the divine, and least with the human nature, bring us face to face with the personality. I am not sure that they don't do this more than any others. 'We beheld his glory, the glory as of the only begotten of the Father, full of graciousness and reality ... which we have looked upon and our hands have handled.' What is gained by trying to evade or dissipate this shattering immediacy of personal contact by talk about 'that significance which the early Church found that it was impelled to attribute to the Master'? This hits us in the face. Not what they were impelled to do but what impelled them. I begin to fear that by *personality* Dr Bultmann means what I should call impersonality: what you'd get in a Dictionary of National Biography article or an obituary or a Victorian *Life and Letters of Yeshua Bar-Yosef* in three volumes with photographs.

That then is my first bleat. These men ask me to believe they can read between the lines of the old texts; the evidence is their obvious inability to read (in any sense worth discussing) the lines themselves. They claim to see fern-seed and can't see an elephant ten yards away in broad daylight.

Now for my second bleat. All theology of the liberal type involves at some point – and often involves throughout – the claim that the real behaviour and purpose and teaching of Christ came very rapidly to be misunderstood and misrepresented by his followers, and has been recovered or exhumed only by modern scholars. Now long before I became interested in theology I had met this kind of theory elsewhere. The tradition of Jowett still dominated the study of ancient philosophy when I was reading Greats. One was brought up to believe that the real meaning of Plato had been misunderstood by Aristotle and wildly travestied by the neo-Platonists, only to be recovered by the moderns. When recovered, it turned out (most fortunately) that Plato had really all along been an English Hegelian, rather like T.H. Green. I have met it a third time in my own professional studies; every week a clever undergraduate, every quarter a dull American don, discovers for the first time what some Shakespearian play really meant. But in this third instance I am a privileged person. The revolution in thought and sentiment which has occurred in my own lifetime is so great that I belong, mentally, to Shakespeare's world far more than to that of these recent interpreters. I see – I feel it in my bones – I know beyond argument – that most of their interpretations are merely impossible; they involve a way of looking at things which was not known in 1914, much less in the Jacobean period. This daily confirms my suspicion of the same approach to Plato or the New Testament. The idea that any man or writer should be opaque to those who lived in the same culture, spoke the same language, shared the same habitual imagery and unconscious assumptions, and yet be transparent to those who have none of these advantages, is in my opinion preposterous. There is an *a priori* improbability in it which almost no argument and no evidence could counterbalance.

Thirdly, I find in these theologians a constant use of the principle that the miraculous does not occur. Thus any statement put into our Lord's mouth by the old texts, which, if he had really made it, would constitute a prediction of the future, is taken to have been put in after the occurrence which it seemed to predict. This is very sensible if we start by knowing that inspired prediction can never occur. Similarly in general, the rejection as unhistorical of all passages which narrate miracles is sensible if we start by knowing that the miraculous in general never occurs. Now I do not here want to discuss whether the miraculous is possible. I only want to point out that this is a purely philosophical question. Scholars, as scholars, speak on it with no more authority than anyone else. The canon 'If miraculous, unhistorical' is one they bring to their study of the texts, not one they have learned from it. If one is speaking of authority, the united authority of all the biblical critics in the world counts here for nothing. On this they speak simply as men; men obviously influenced by, and perhaps insufficiently critical of, the spirit of the age they grew up in.

But my fourth bleat – which is also my loudest and longest – is still to come.

All this sort of criticism attempts to reconstruct the genesis of the texts it studies; what vanished documents each author used, when and where he wrote, with what purposes, under what influences – the whole *Sitz im Leben* of the text. This is done with immense erudition and great ingenuity. And at first sight it is very convincing. I think I should be convinced by it myself, but that I carry about with me a charm – the herb *moly* – against it. You must excuse me if I now speak for a while of myself. The value of what I say depends on its being first-hand evidence.

What forearms me against all these reconstructions is the fact that I have seen it all from the other end of the stick. I have watched reviewers reconstructing the genesis of my own books in just this way.

Until you come to be reviewed yourself you would never believe how little of an ordinary review is taken up by criticism in the strict sense: by evaluation, praise, or censure, of the book actually written. Most of it is taken up with imaginary histories of the process by which you wrote it. The very terms which the reviewers use in praising or dispraising often imply such a history. They praise a passage as 'spontaneous' and censure another as 'laboured'; that is, they think they know that you wrote the one *currente calamo* and the other *invita Minerva*.

What the value of such reconstructions is I learned very early in my career. I had published a book of essays; and the one into which I had put most of my heart, the one I really cared about and in which I discharged a keen enthusiasm, was on William Morris.[7] And in almost the first review I was told that this was obviously the only one in the book in which I had felt no interest. Now don't mistake. The critic was, I now believe, quite right in thinking it the worst essay in the book; at least everyone agreed with him. Where he was totally wrong was in his imaginary history of the causes which produced its dullness.

Well, this made me prick up my ears. Since then I have watched with some care similar imaginary histories both of my own books and of books by friends whose real history I knew. Reviewers, both friendly and hostile, will dash you off such histories with great confidence; will tell you

[7] 'William Morris' first appeared in *Rehabilitations* (1939) and is reprinted in Lewis's *Selected Literary Essays*, ed. Walter Hooper (1969).

what public events had directed the author's mind to this or that, what other authors had influenced him, what his overall intention was, what sort of audience he principally addressed, why – and when – he did everything.

Now I must first record my impression; then, distinct from it, what I can say with certainty. My impression is that in the whole of my experience not one of these guesses has on any one point been right; that the method shows a record of 100 per cent failure. You would expect that by mere chance they would hit as often as they miss. But it is my impression that they do no such thing. I can't remember a single hit. But as I have not kept a careful record my mere impression may be mistaken. What I think I can say with certainty is that they are usually wrong.

And yet they would often sound – if you didn't know the truth – extremely convincing. Many reviewers said that the Ring in Tolkien's *The Lord of the Rings* was suggested by the atom bomb. What could be more plausible? Here is a book published when everyone was preoccupied by that sinister invention; here in the centre of the book is a weapon which it seems madness to throw away yet fatal to use. Yet in fact, the chronology of the book's composition makes the theory impossible. Only the other week a reviewer said that a fairy-tale by my friend Roger Lancelyn Green was influenced by fairy-tales of mine. Nothing could be more probable. I have an imaginary country with a beneficent lion in it: Green, one with a beneficent tiger. Green and I can be proved to read one another's works; to be indeed in various ways closely associated. The case for an affiliation is far stronger than many which we accept as conclusive when dead authors are concerned. But it's all untrue nevertheless. I know the genesis of that Tiger and that Lion and they are quite independent.[8]

Now this surely ought to give us pause. The reconstruction of the history of a text, when the text is ancient, sounds very convincing. But one is after all sailing by dead reckoning; the results cannot be checked by fact. In order to decide how reliable the method is, what more could you ask for than to be shown an instance where the same method is at work and we have facts to check it by? Well, that is what I have done. And we

---

[8] Lewis corrected this error in the following letter, 'Books for Children', in *The Times Literary Supplement* (28 November 1958), p. 689: 'Sir, – A review of Mr R.L. Green's *Land of the Lord High Tiger* in your issue of 21 November spoke of myself (in passing) with so much kindness that I am reluctant to cavil at anything it contained: but in justice to Mr Green I must. The critic suggested that Mr Green's Tiger owed something to my fairy-tales. In reality this is not so and is chronologically impossible. The Tiger was an old inhabitant, and his land a familiar haunt, of Mr Green's imagination long before I began writing. There is a moral here for all of us as critics. I wonder how much *Quellenforschung* in our studies of older literature seems solid only because those who knew the facts are dead and can't contradict it?'

find, that when this check is available, the results are either always, or else nearly always, wrong. The 'assured results of modern scholarship', as to the way in which an old book was written, are 'assured', we may conclude, only because the men who knew the facts are dead and can't blow the gaff. The huge essays in my own field which reconstruct the history of *Piers Plowman* or *The Faerie Queene* are most unlikely to be anything but sheer illusions.

Am I then venturing to compare every whipster who writes a review in a modern weekly with these great scholars who have devoted their whole lives to the detailed study of the New Testament? If the former are always wrong, does it follow that the latter must fare no better?

There are two answers to this. First, while I respect the learning of the great Biblical critics, I am not yet persuaded that their judgement is equally to be respected. But, secondly, consider with what overwhelming advantages the mere reviewers start. They reconstruct the history of a book written by someone whose mother-tongue is the same as theirs; a contemporary, educated like themselves, living in something like the same mental and spiritual climate. They have everything to help them. The superiority in judgement and diligence which you are going to attribute to the Biblical critics will have to be almost superhuman if it is to offset the fact that they are everywhere faced with customs, language, race-characteristics, class-characteristics, a religious background, habits of composition, and basic assumptions, which no scholarship will ever enable any man now alive to know as surely and intimately and instinctively as the reviewer can know mine. And for the very same reason, remember, the Biblical critics, whatever reconstructions they devise, can never be crudely proved wrong. St Mark is dead. When they meet St Peter there will be more pressing matters to discuss.

You may say, of course, that such reviewers are foolish in so far as they guess how a sort of book they never wrote themselves was written by another. They assume that you wrote a story as they would try to write a story; the fact that they would so try, explains why they have not produced any stories. But are the Biblical critics in this way much better off? Dr Bultmann never wrote a gospel. Has the experience of his learned, specialised, and no doubt meritorious, life really given him any power of seeing into the minds of those long dead men who were caught up into what, on any view, must be regarded as the central religious experience of the whole human race? It is no incivility to say – he himself would admit – that he must in every way be divided from the evangelists by far more formidable barriers – spiritual as well as intellectual – than any that could exist between my reviewers and me.

My picture of one layman's reaction – and I think it is not a rare one – would be incomplete without some account of the hopes he secretly cherishes and the naive reflections with which he sometimes keeps his spirits up.

You must face the fact that he does not expect the present school of theological thought to be everlasting. He thinks, perhaps wishfully thinks, that the whole thing may blow over. I have learned in other fields of study how transitory the 'assured results of modern scholarship' may be, how soon scholarship ceases to be modern. The confident treatment to which the New Testament is subjected is no longer applied to profane texts. There used to be English scholars who were prepared to cut up *Henry VI* between half a dozen authors and assign his share to each. We don't do that now. When I was a boy one would have been laughed at for supposing there had been a real Homer: the disintegrators seemed to have triumphed for ever. But Homer seems to be creeping back. Even the belief of the ancient Greeks that the Mycenaeans were their ancestors and spoke Greek has been surprisingly supported. We may without disgrace believe in a historical Arthur. Everywhere, except in theology, there has been a vigorous growth of scepticism about scepticism itself. We can't keep ourselves from murmuring *multa renascentur quae jam cecidere.*

Nor can a man of my age ever forget how suddenly and completely the idealist philosophy of his youth fell. McTaggart, Green, Bosanquet, Bradley seemed enthroned for ever; they went down as suddenly as the Bastille. And the interesting thing is that while I lived under that dynasty I felt various difficulties and objections which I never dared to express. They were so frightfully obvious that I felt sure they must be mere misunderstandings: the great men could not have made such very elementary mistakes as those which my objections implied. But very similar objections – though put, no doubt, far more cogently than I could have put them – were among the criticisms which finally prevailed. They would now be the stock answers to English Hegelianism. If anyone present tonight has felt the same shy and tentative doubts about the great Biblical critics, perhaps he need not feel quite certain that they are only his stupidity. They may have a future he little dreams of.

We derive a little comfort, too, from our mathematical colleagues. When a critic reconstructs the genesis of a text he usually has to use what may be called linked hypotheses. Thus Bultmann says that Peter's confession is 'an Easter-story projected backward into Jesus' life-time' (p. 26, op. cit.). The first hypothesis is that Peter made no such confession. Then, granting that, there is a second hypothesis as to how the false story of his having done so might have grown up. Now let us suppose – what I am far from granting – that the first hypothesis has a probability of 90 per cent. Let us assume that the second hypothesis also has a probability of 90 per cent. But the two together don't still have 90 per cent, for the second comes in only on the assumption of the first. You have not A plus B; you have a complex AB. And the mathematicians tell me that AB has only an 81 per cent probability. I'm not good enough at arithmetic to work it out, but you see that if, in a complex reconstruction, you go on thus superinducing hypothesis on hypothesis, you will in the end get a complex in which, though each hypothesis by itself has in a sense a high probability, the whole has almost none.

You must not, however, paint the picture too black. We are not fundamentalists. We think that different elements in this sort of theology have different degrees of strength. The nearer it sticks to mere textual criticism, of the old sort, Lachmann's sort, the more we are disposed to believe in it. And of course we agree that passages almost verbally identical cannot be independent. It is as we glide away from this into reconstructions of a subtler and more ambitious kind that our faith in the method wavers; and our faith in Christianity is proportionately corroborated. The sort of statement that arouses our deepest scepticism is the statement that something in a Gospel cannot be historical because it shows a theology or an ecclesiology too developed for so early a date. For this implies that we know, first of all, that there was any development in the matter, and secondly, how quickly it proceeded. It even implies an extraordinary homogeneity and continuity of development: implicitly denies that anyone could greatly have anticipated anyone else. This seems to involve knowing about a number of long dead people – for the early Christians were, after all, people – things of which I believe few of us could have given an accurate account if we had lived among them; all the forward and backward surge of discussion, preaching, and individual religious experience. I could not speak with similar confidence about the circle I have chiefly lived in myself. I could not describe the history even of my own thought as confidently as these men describe the history of the early Church's mind. And I am perfectly certain no one else could. Suppose a future scholar knew that I abandoned Christianity in my teens, and that, also in my teens, I went to an atheist tutor. Would not this seem far better evidence than most of what we have about the development of Christian theology in the first two centuries? Would he not conclude that my apostasy was due to the tutor? And then reject as 'backward projection' any story which represented me as an atheist before I went to that tutor? Yet he would be wrong. I am sorry to have become once more autobiographical. But reflection on the extreme improbability of his own life

– by historical standards – seems to me a profitable exercise for everyone. It encourages a due agnosticism.

For agnosticism is, in a sense, what I am preaching. I do not wish to reduce the sceptical element in your minds. I am only suggesting that it need not be reserved exclusively for the New Testament and the Creeds. Try doubting something else.

Such scepticism might, I think, begin at the very beginning with the thought which underlies the whole demythology of our time. It was put long ago by Tyrrell. As man progresses he revolts against 'earlier and inadequate expressions of the religious idea ... Taken literally, and not symbolically, they do not meet his need. And as long as he demands to picture to himself distinctly the term and satisfaction of that need he is doomed to doubt, for his picturings will necessarily be drawn from the world of his present experience.'[9]

In one way of course Tyrrell was saying nothing new. The Negative Theology of Pseudo-Dionysius had said as much, but it drew no such conclusions as Tyrrell. Perhaps this is because the older tradition found our conceptions inadequate to God whereas Tyrrell finds it inadequate to 'the religious idea'. He doesn't say whose idea. But I am afraid he means man's idea. We, being men, know what we think: and we find the doctrines of the Resurrection, the Ascension, and the Second Coming inadequate to our thoughts. But supposing these things were the expressions of God's thought?

It might still be true that 'taken literally and not symbolically' they are inadequate. From which the conclusion commonly drawn is that they must be taken symbolically, not literally; that is, wholly symbolically. All the details are equally symbolical and analogical.

But surely there is a flaw here. The argument runs like this. All the details are derived from our present experience; but the reality transcends our experience: therefore all the details are wholly and equally symbolical. But suppose a dog were trying to form a conception of human life. All the details in its picture would be derived from canine experience. Therefore all that the dog imagined could, at best, be only analogically true of human life. The conclusion is false. If the dog visualised our scientific researches in terms of ratting, this would be analogical; but if it thought that eating could be predicated of humans only in an analogical sense, the dog would be wrong. In fact if a dog could, *per impossibile*, be plunged for a day into human life, it would be hardly more surprised by hitherto

[9] George Tyrrell, 'The Apocalyptic Vision of Christ' in *Christianity at the Cross-Roads* (London, 1909), p. 125.

unimagined differences than by hitherto unsuspected similarities. A reverent dog would be shocked. A modernist dog, mistrusting the whole experience, would ask to be taken to the vet.

But the dog can't get into human life. Consequently, though it can be sure that its best ideas of human life are full of analogy and symbol, it could never point to any one detail and say, 'This is entirely symbolic.' You cannot know that everything in the representation of a thing is symbolical unless you have independent access to the thing and can compare it with the representation. Dr Tyrrell can tell that the story of the Ascension is inadequate to his religious idea, because he knows his own idea and can compare it with the story. But how if we are asking about a transcendent, objective reality to which the story is our sole access? 'We know not – oh we know not.' But then we must take our ignorance seriously.

Of course if 'taken literally and not symbolically' means 'taken in terms of mere physics', then this story is not even a religious story. Motion away from the earth – which is what Ascension physically means – would not in itself be an event of spiritual significance. Therefore, you argue, the spiritual reality can have nothing but an analogical connection with the story of an ascent. For the union of God with God and of man with God-man can have nothing to do with space. Who told you this? What you really mean is that we can't see how it could possibly have anything to do with it. That is a quite different proposition. When I know as I am known I shall be able to tell which parts of the story were purely symbolical and which, if any, were not; shall see how the transcendent reality either excludes and repels locality, or how unimaginably it assimilates and loads it with significance. Had we not better wait?

Such are the reactions of one bleating layman to Modern Theology. It is right you should hear them. You will not perhaps hear them very often again. Your parishioners will not often speak to you quite frankly. Once the layman was anxious to hide the fact that he believed so much less than the vicar: he now tends to hide the fact that he believes so much more. Missionary to the priests of one's own church is an embarrassing role; though I have a horrid feeling that if such mission work is not soon undertaken the future history of the Church of England is likely to be short.

[32]

THE LANGUAGE OF RELIGION

Lewis intended to read this paper at the Twelfth Symposium of the Colston Research Society, held at the University of Bristol in March 1960, but was unable to attend due to ill health. It was first published in Christian Reflections *(1998), although pages 4 and 5 of the text are missing.*

I have been asked to talk about religious language and the gist of what I have to say is that, in my opinion, there is no specifically religious language. I admit of course that some things said by religious people can't be treated exactly as we treat scientific statements. But I don't think that is because they are specimens of some special language. It would be truer to say that the scientific statements are in a special language. The language of religion, which we may presently have to distinguish from that of theology, seems to be, on the whole, either the same sort we use in ordinary conversation or the same sort we use in poetry, or somewhere between the two. In order to make this clearer, I am afraid I must turn away from the professed subject of my paper for some time and talk about language.

I begin with three sentences: (1) It was very cold. (2) There were 13 degrees of frost. (3) 'Ah, bitter chill it was! The owl, for all his feathers was a-cold; The hare limped trembling through the frozen grass, And silent was the flock in woolly fold: Numb'd were the Beadsman's fingers.'[1] I should describe the first as Ordinary language, the second as Scientific language, and the third as Poetic language. Of course there is no question here of different languages in the sense in which Latin and Chinese are different languages. Two and three are improved uses of the same language used in one. Scientific and Poetic language are two different artificial perfections of Ordinary: artificial, because they depend on skills;

---

[1] John Keats, *The Eve of St Agnes*, I, 1–5.

different, because they improve Ordinary in two different directions. Notice also that Ordinary could advance a little towards either so that you could pass by degrees into Scientific or Poetic. For 'very cold' you could substitute 'freezing hard' and, for 'freezing hard', 'freezing harder than last night'. That would be getting nearer to the Scientific. On the other hand you could say 'bitterly cold' and then you would be getting nearer the Poetic. In fact you would have anticipated one of the terms used in Keats's description.

The superiority of the Scientific description clearly consists in giving for the coldness of the night a precise quantitative estimate which can be tested by an instrument. The test ends all disputes. If the statement survives the test, then various inferences can be drawn from it with certainty: e.g., various effects on vegetable and animal life can be predicted. It is therefore of use in what Bacon calls 'operation'. We can take action on it. On the other hand it does not, of itself, give us any information about the quality of a cold night, does not tell us what we shall be feeling if we go out of doors. If, having lived all our lives in the tropics, we didn't know what a hard frost was like, the thermometer reading would not of itself inform us. Ordinary language would do that better – 'Your ears will ache' – 'You'll lose the feeling in your fingers'– 'You'll feel as if your ears were coming off.' If I could tell you (which unhappily I can't) the temperature of the coldest water I ever bathed in, it would convey the reality only to the few who had bathed in many temperatures and taken thermometer readings of them. When I tell you 'It was so cold that at first it felt like scalding hot water', I think you will get a better idea of it. And where a scientific statement could draw on no experience at all, like statements about optics made to a student born blind, then, though it might retain its proper virtues of precision, verifiability, and use in operation, it would in one sense convey nothing. Only in one sense, of course. The blind student could, presumably, draw inferences from it and use it to gain further knowledge.

I now turn to the Poetic. Its superiority to Ordinary language is, I am afraid, a much more troublesome affair. I feel fairly sure what it does not consist in: it does not consist either in discharging or arousing more emotion. It may often do one of these things or both, but I don't think that is its *differentia*. I don't think our bit of Keats differs from the Ordinary 'It was very cold' primarily or solely by getting off Keats's chest mere dislike of cold nights, nor by arousing mere dislike in me. There is, no doubt, some mere 'getting off the chest' in the exclamation 'Ah' and the catachresis 'bitter'. Personally, I don't feel the emotion to be either Keats's or mine. It is for me the imagined people in the story who are saying 'Ah' and 'bitter'; not with the result of making me share their discomfort, but of making me imagine how very cold it was. And the rest is all taken up with pictures of what might have been observed on such a night. The invitation is not to my emotions but to my senses. Keats seems to me to be simply conveying the quality of a cold night, and not imposing any emotions on me (except of course the emotion of pleasure at finding anything vividly conveyed to the imagination). He is in fact giving me all that concrete, qualitative information which the Scientific statement leaves out. But then, of course, he is not verifiable, nor precise, nor of much use for operation.

We must not, however, base our view on a single passage, which may have been unfairly chosen. Let us begin at quite another point. One of the most obvious differences between all the poetry I have ever read and all the straight prose (I say 'straight' to exclude prose which verges on the poetic) is this simple one, hardly ever stated: the poetry contains a great many more adjectives. This is perfectly obvious. From Homer, who never omits to tell us that the ships were black and the sea salty, or even wet, down to Eliot with his 'hollow valley' and 'multi-foliate rose', they all do it. Poets are always telling us that grass is green, or thunder loud, or lips red. It is not, except in bad poets, always telling us that things are shocking or delightful. It does not, in that direct way, attempt to discharge or excite emotion. On the contrary, it seems anxious to bombard us with masses of factual information which we might, on a prose view, regard as irrelevant or platitudinous.

[Here pages 4 and 5 of the manuscript are missing. Page 6 begins as follows:]

[In order to] discharge an emotion it is not necessary that we should make it clear to any audience. By 'expression' I mean that sort of utterance which will make clear to others how we are feeling. There are, of course, any number of intermediate stages between discharge and expression: but perfect expression in the presence of the perfect hearer would enable him to know exactly how you were feeling. To what extent this involves arousing the same emotion, or a replica of it in him – in other words, to what extent the perfect expression would be emotive – I don't know. But I think that to respond to expression is in principle different from having an emotion aroused in one, even though the arousing of some sort of phantom emotion may always be involved. There seems to me to be a difference between understanding another person's fear because he has expressed it well and being actually *infected* by his fear as so often happens. Or again, there seems to be a difference between under-standing the feelings of Shakespeare's Troilus before his assignation and being infected by similar feelings, as the writer of pornography intends to infect us.

But the really important point is the third[2] one. Even if Poetic language often expresses emotion and thereby (to some undefined extent) arouses emotion, it does not follow that the expression of emotion is always its sole, or even its chief function. For even in Ordinary language one of the best ways of describing something is to tell what reactions it provoked in us. If a man says, 'They kept their rooms terribly over-heated. Before I'd been in there five minutes, I was dripping', he is usually not concerned, as an end in itself, with giving us autobiographical fact that he perspired. He wants to make us realise how hot it was. And he takes the right way. Indeed in the last resort there is hardly any other way. To say that things were blue, or hard, or cool, or foul-smelling, or noisy, is to tell how they affected our senses. To say that someone is a bore, or a decent chap, or revolting, is to tell how he affected our emotions. In the same way, I think that Poetic language often expresses emotion not for its own sake but in order to inform us about the object which aroused the emotion. Certainly it seems to me to give us such information. Burns tells us that a woman is like a red, red rose,[3] and Wordsworth that another woman is like a violet by a mossy stone half hidden from the eye.[4] Now of course the one woman resembles a rose, and the other a half-hidden violet, not in size, weight, shape, colour, anatomy, or intelligence, but by arousing emotions in some way analogous to those which the flowers would arouse. But then we know quite well what sort of women (and how different from each other) they must have been to do so. The two state-ments do not in the least reduce to mere expressions of admiration. They tell us what kind of admiration and therefore what kind of woman. They are even, in their own proper way, verifiable or falsifiable: having seen the two women we might say 'I see what he meant in comparing her to a rose' and 'I see what he meant in comparing her to a violet', or might decide that the comparisons were bad. I am not of course denying that there are other love poems (some of Wyatt's, for example) where the poet is wholly concerned with his own emotions and we get no impression of the woman at all. I deny that this is the universal rule.

---

[2] Apparently referring to an enumeration of points Lewis made in the missing pages.
[3] Robert Burns, 'A red, red Rose', line 1.
[4] William Wordsworth, 'She dwelt among the untrodden ways', line 5.

Finally we have those instances where Poetic language expresses an experience which is not accessible to us in normal life at all, an experience which the poet himself may have imagined and not, in the ordinary sense, 'had'. An instance would be when Asia, in *Prometheus Unbound*, says 'My soul is an enchanted boat'.[5] If anyone thinks this is only a more musical and graceful way of saying 'Gee! this is fine', I disagree with him. An enchanted boat moves without oar or sail to its destined haven. Asia is at that moment undergoing a process of transfiguration, almost of apotheosis. Effortless and unimpeded movement to a goal desired but not yet seen is the point. If we were experiencing Asia's apotheosis we should feel like that. In fact we have never experienced apotheosis. Nor, probably, has Shelley. But to communicate the emotion which would accompany it is to make us know more fully than before what we meant by apotheosis.

This is the most remarkable of the powers of Poetic language: to convey to us the quality of experiences which we have not had, or perhaps can never have, to use factors within our experience so that they become pointers to something outside our experience – as two or more roads on a map show us where a town that is off the map must lie. Many of us have never had an experience like that which Wordsworth records near the end of *Prelude* XIII; but when he speaks of 'the visionary dreariness' I think we get an inkling of it. Other examples would be (for me) Marvell's 'green thought in a green shade',[6] and (for everyone) Pope's 'die of a rose in aromatic pain'.[7] Perhaps the most astonishing is in the *Paradiso* where Dante says that as he rose from one sphere of the Ptolemaic universe to the next, he knew that he had risen only by finding that he was moving forward more quickly.[8]

It must be remembered that I have been speaking simply of Poetic language not of poetry. Poetry of course has other characteristics besides its language. One of them is that it is very often fiction; it tells about people who never really lived and events that never really took place. Hence Plato's jibe that the poets are liars. But surely it would be a great confusion to attach the note of fiction to every specimen of Poetic *language*. You just can't tell whether Keats's description is of a winter night that really occurred or of one he imagined. The use of language in conveying the quality of a real place, or person, or thing is the same we should need to convey the quality of a feigned one.

---

[5] Percy Bysshe Shelley, *Prometheus Unbound*, II, v, 72.
[6] Andrew Marvell, 'The Garden', vi, 48.
[7] Alexander Pope, *An Essay on Man*, I, 200.
[8] I cannot find this in the *Paradiso*. It may be, however, a conflation of several passages. See *Paradiso* viii, 13; x, 35; and xiv, 85. — W.H.

My long, and perhaps tedious, digression on Poetic language is now almost at an end. My conclusion is that such language is by no means merely an expression, nor a stimulant, of emotion, but a real medium of information. Which information may, like any other, be true or false: true as Mr Young[9] on weirs, or false as the bit in *Beowulf* about the dragon sniffing along the path. It often does stimulate emotion, by expressing emotion, but usually in order to show us the object to which such emotion would be the response. A poet, Mr Robert Conquest, has put something like my view:

> *Observation of real events includes the observer, 'heart' and all;*
> *(The common measurable features are obtained by omitting this part.)*
>
> *But there is also a common aspect in the emotional*
> *Shared by other members of the species; this is conveyed by 'art'.*
>
> *The poem combines all these ...*[10]

Because events, as real events 'really' are and feigned events would 'really' be if they occurred, cannot be conveyed without bringing in the observer's heart and the common emotional reaction of the species, it has been falsely concluded that poetry represented the heart for its own sake, and nothing but the heart.

But I must not go too far. I think Poetic language does convey information, but it suffers from two disabilities in comparison with Scientific. (1) It is verifiable or falsifiable only to a limited degree and with a certain fringe of vagueness. Not all men, only men of some discrimination, would agree, on seeing Burns's mistress that the image of 'a red, red rose' was good, or (as might be) bad. In that sense, Scientific statements are, as people say now, far more easily 'cashed'. But the poet might of course reply that it always will be easier to cash a cheque for 30 shillings than one for 1000 pounds, that the Scientific statements are cheques, in one sense, for very small amounts, giving us, out of the teeming complexity of every concrete reality only 'the common measurable features'. (2) Such information as Poetic language has to give can be received only if you are ready

---

[9] Lewis is referring, I believe, to the Rev. Canon Andrew Young, whose poems, he felt, were something like a combination of Wordsworth and Marvell. An interesting reference to 'weirs' is found in Young's poem, 'The Slow Race'. For discussion on other possibilities see my letter, 'A C.S. Lewis Mystery', *Spectator* (28 October 1966), p. 546. — W.H.

[10] 'Excerpts from a Report to the Galactic Council', *The Listener*, Vol. LII (14 October 1954), p. 612.

THE LANGUAGE OF RELIGION

to meet it half way. It is no good holding a dialectical pistol to the poet's head and demanding how the deuce a river could have hair, or thought be green, or a woman a red rose. You may win, in the sense of putting him to a *non-plus*. But if he had anything to tell you, you will never get it by behaving in that way. You must begin by trusting him. Only by so doing will you find out whether he is trustworthy or not. *Credo ut intelligam* (it is time some theological expression came in) is here the only attitude.

Now, as I see it, the language in which we express our religious beliefs and other religious experiences, is not a special language, but something that ranges between the Ordinary and the Poetical. But even when it begins by being Ordinary, it can usually, under dialectical pressure, be found to become either Theological or Poetical. An example will best show what I mean by this trichotomy. I think the words 'I believe in God' are Ordinary language. If you press us by asking what we mean, we shall probably have to move in one of two directions. We might say, 'I believe in incorporeal entity, personal in the sense that it can be the subject and object of love, on which all other entities are unilaterally dependent.' That is what I call Theological language, though far from a first-class specimen of it. In it we are attempting, so far as is possible, to state religious matter in a form more like that we use for scientific matter. This is often necessary, for purposes of instruction, clarification, controversy and the like. But it is not the language religion naturally speaks. We are applying precise, and therefore abstract, terms to what for us is the supreme example of the concrete. If we do not always feel this fully, that, I think, is because nearly all who say or read such sentences (including unbelievers) really put into them much that they know from other sources – tradition, literature, etc. But for that, it would hardly be more information than 'There are 15 degrees of frost' would be to those who had never experienced frost.

And this is one of the great disadvantages under which the Christian apologist labours. Apologetics is controversy. You cannot conduct a controversy in those poetical expressions which alone convey the concrete: you must use terms as definable and univocal as possible, and these are always abstract. And this means that the thing we are really talking about can never appear in the discussion at all. We have to try to prove *that* God is in circumstances where we are denied every means of conveying *who* God is. It is faintly parallel to the state of a witness who has to try to convey something so concrete as the known character of a friend under cross-examination. Under other conditions he might possibly succeed in giving you a real impression of him; but not under hostile cross-examination. You remember Hamlet's speech to Horatio, 'Horatio thou art e'en as just a man', etc. But you could never have had it in a witness-box.

That, then, is one way in which we could go on from 'I believe in God' – the Theological: in a sense, alien to religion, crippling, omitting nearly all that really matters, yet, in spite of everything, sometimes successful.

On the other hand, you could go on, following the spontaneous tendency of religion, into poetical language. Asked what you meant by God, you might say 'God is love' or 'the Father of lights', or even 'underneath are the everlasting arms'. From what had gone before, you will understand that I do not regard these poetical expressions as merely expressions of emotion. They will of course express emotion in any who utters them, and arouse emotion in any who hears them with belief. But so would the sentence 'Fifty Russian divisions landed in the South of England this morning.' Momentous matter, if believed, will arouse emotion whatever the language. Further, these statements make use of emotion, as Burns makes use of our emotions about roses. All this is, in my view, consistent with their being essentially informative. But, of course, informative only to those who will meet them half way.

The necessity for such poetic expressions is closely connected with the grounds on which they are believed. They are usually two: authority, and religious experience.

Christians believe that Jesus Christ is the Son of God because He said so. The other evidence about Him has convinced them that He was neither a lunatic nor a quack. Now of course the statement cannot mean that He stands to God in the very same physical and temporal relation which exists between offspring and male parent in the animal world. It is then a poetical statement. And such expression must here be necessary because the reality He spoke of is outside our experience. And here once more the religious and the theological procedure diverge. The theologian will describe it as 'analogical', drawing our minds at once away from the subtle and sensitive exploitations of imagination and emotion with which poetry works to the clear-cut but clumsy analogies of the lecture-room. He will even explain in what respects the father-son relationship is *not* analogical to the reality, hoping by elimination to reach the respects in which it is. He may even supply other analogies of his own – the lamp and the light which flows from it, or the like. It is all unavoidable and necessary for certain purposes. But there is some death in it. The sentence 'Jesus Christ is the Son of God' cannot be all got into the form 'There is between Jesus and God an asymmetrical, social, harmonious relation involving homogeneity.' Religion takes it differently. A man who is both a good son and a good father, and who is continually urged to become a better son and a better father by meditation on the Divine Fatherhood and Sonship, and who thus comes in the end to make that Divine relation the norm to which his own human sonship and fatherhood are still merely analogical, is best receiving the revelation. It would be idle to tell such a man that the formula 'is the Son of God' tells us (what is almost zero) that an unknown X is in an unknown respect 'like' the relation of father and son. He has met it half way. Information has been given him: as far as I can see, in the only way possible.

Secondly, there is religious experience, ranging from the most ordinary experiences of the believer in worship, forgiveness, dereliction, and divine help, up to the high special experiences of the mystics. Through such experience Christians believe that they get a sort of verification (or perhaps sometimes falsification) of their tenets. Such experience cannot be conveyed to one another, much less to unbelievers, except by language which shares to some extent the nature of Poetic language. That is what leads some people to suppose that it can be nothing but emotion. For of course, if you accept the view that Poetic language is purely emotional, then things which can be expressed only in Poetic language will presumably be emotions. But if we don't equate Poetic language with emotional language, the question is still open.

Now it seems to me a mistake to think that our experience in general can be communicated by precise and literal language and that there is a special class of experiences (say, emotions) which cannot. The truth seems to me the opposite: there is a special region of experiences which can be communicated *without* Poetic language, namely, its 'common measurable features', but most experience cannot. To be incommunicable by Scientific language is, so far as I can judge, the normal state of experience. All our sensuous experience is in this condition, though this is somewhat veiled from us by the fact that much of it is very common and therefore everyone will understand our references to it at a hint. But if you have to describe to a doctor any unusual sensation, you will soon find yourself driven to use pointers of the same nature (essentially) as Asia's enchanted boat. An army doctor who suspected you of malingering would soon reduce you to halting and contradictory statements; but if by chance you had not been malingering he would have cut himself off from all knowledge of what might have turned out an interesting case.

But are there, as I have claimed, other experiences besides sensation (and, of course, emotion) which are in this predicament? I think there are. But, frankly, I am now getting into very deep water indeed. I am almost sure I shall fail to make myself clear, but the attempt must be made.

It seems to me that imagining is something other than having mental images. When I am imagining (say, Hamlet on the battlements or Herakles's journey to the Hyperboreans) there are images in my mind. They come and go rapidly and assist what I regard as the real imagining only if I take them all as provisional makeshifts, each to be dropped as soon as it has served its (instantaneous) turn. If any one of them becomes static and grows too clear and full, imagination proper is inhibited. A too lively visual imagination is the reader's, and writer's, bane; as toys, too elaborate and realistic, spoil children's play. They are, in the etymological sense, the *offal* (the off-fall) of imagination: the slag from the furnace. Again, thinking seems to me something other than the succession of linked concepts which we use when we successfully offer our 'thought' to another in argument. That appears to me to be always a sort of translation of a prior activity: and it was the prior activity which alone enabled us to find these concepts and links. The possibility of finding them may be a good test of the value of that previous activity; certainly the only test we have. It would be dangerous to indulge ourselves with the fancy of having valuable profundities within us which (unfortunately) we can't get out. But, perhaps, in others, where we are neutrals, we are sometimes not quite wrong in thinking that a sensible man, unversed in argument, has thought better than his mishandling of his own case suggests. If we lend him a helping hand and he replies 'Of course! That's it. That is what I really meant to say', he is not always a hypocrite. Finally, in all our joys and sorrows, religious, aesthetic, or natural, I seem to find things (almost indescribably) thus. They are *about* something. They are a by-product of the (logically) prior act of *attending to* or *looking towards* something.[11] We are not really concerned with the emotions: the emotions *are* our concern about something else. Suppose that a mother is anxious about her son who is on active service. It is no use going to her with the offer of some drug or hypnotism or spell that would obliterate her anxiety. What she wants is not the cessation of anxiety but the safety of her son. (I mean, on the whole. On one particular wakeful night, she might, no doubt, be glad of your magic.) Nor is it any use offering her a magic which would prevent her from feeling any grief if her son were killed: what she dreads is not grief but the death of her son. Similarly, it is no use offering me a drug which will give me over again the feelings I had on first hearing the overture to *The Magic Flute*. The feelings, by themselves – the flutter in the diaphragm – are of very mediocre interest to me. What gave them their value was the

[11] *Looking towards* is neither more nor less metaphorical than *attending to*. — C.S.L.

thing they were about. So in our Christian experiences. No doubt we experience sorrow when we repent and joy when we adore. But these were by-products of our attention to a particular Object.

If I have made myself at all clear (but I probably have not) you see what, for me, it adds up to. The very essence of our life as conscious beings, all day and every day, consists of something which cannot be communicated except by hints, similes, metaphors, and the use of those emotions (themselves not very important) which are pointers to it. I am not in the least talking about the Unconscious as psychologists understand it. At least, though it cannot be fully introspected, this region is, in many of us, very far from unconscious. I say 'in many of us'. But I sometimes wonder whether we may not be survivals. Evolution may not have ceased; and in evolution a species may lose old powers as well as acquire – possibly in order to acquire – new ones. There seem to be people about to whom imagination means only the presence of mental images (not to mention those like Professor Ryle who deny even that); to whom thought means only unuttered speech; and to whom emotions are final, as distinct from the things they are about. If this is so, and if they increase, then all real communications between them and the earlier type of man will finally be impossible.

Something like this may be happening. You remember Wells's *Country of the Blind*. Now its inhabitants, being men, must have descended from ancestors who could see. During centuries a gradual atrophy of sight must have spread through the whole race; but at no given moment, till it was complete, would it (probably) have been equally advanced in all individuals. During this intermediate period a very interesting linguistic situation would have arisen. They would have inherited from their unblind ancestors all the visual vocabulary – the names of the colours, words like 'see' and 'look' and 'dark' and 'light'. There would be some who still used them in the same sense as ourselves: archaic types who saw the green grass and perceived the light coming at dawn. There would be others who had faint vestiges of sight, and who used these words, with increasing vagueness, to describe sensations so evanescent as to be incapable of clear discrimination. (The moment at which they begin to think of them as sensations in their own eyeballs, not as externals, would mark an important step.) And there would be a third class who had achieved full blindness, to whom *see* was merely a synonym for *understand* and *dark* for *difficult*. And these would be the vanguard, and the future would be with them, and a very little cross-examination of the archaic type that still saw would convince them that its attempt to give some other meaning to the old visual words was merely a tissue of vague, emotive uses and category mistakes. This would be as clear to them as it is clear to many modern people that Job's words 'But now mine eye hath seen thee: wherefore I abhor myself and repent in dust and ashes' are, and can be, nothing but the expression of an emotion.[12]

As I say, this sometimes crosses my mind. But I am full of doubts about the whole subject, and everything I have said is merely tentative. Perhaps I should also point out that it is not apologetics. I have not tried to prove that the religious sayings are true, only that they are significant: if you meet them with a certain good will, a certain readiness to find meaning. For if they should happen to contain information about real things, you will not get it on any other terms. As for proof, I sometimes wonder whether the Ontological Argument did not itself arise as a partially unsuccessful translation of an experience without concept or words. I don't think we can initially argue from the *concept* of Perfect Being to its existence. But did they really, inside, argue from the experienced glory that it could not be generated subjectively?

[12] An interesting variation of this same theme is found in Lewis's poem, 'The Country of the Blind', *Poems*, ed. Walter Hooper (Collins, 1964), pp. 33f.

[33]

TRANSPOSITION

This sermon was first preached in Mansfield College, Oxford, and later appeared in They Asked for a Paper *(1962). An expanded version appeared in* Screwtape Proposes a Toast and Other Pieces *(1998).*

In the church to which I belong this day is set apart for commemorating the descent of the Holy Ghost upon the first Christians shortly after the Ascension. I want to consider one of the phenomena which accompanied, or followed, this descent; the phenomenon which our translation calls 'speaking with tongues' and which the learned call *glossolalia.* You will not suppose that I think this the most important aspect of Pentecost, but I have two reasons for selecting it. In the first place it would be ridiculous for me to speak about the nature of the Holy Ghost or the modes of His operation: that would be an attempt to teach when I have nearly all to learn. In the second place, *glossolalia* has often been a stumbling-block to me. It is, to be frank, an embarrassing phenomenon. St Paul himself seems to have been rather embarrassed by it in 1 Corinthians and labours to turn the desire and the attention of the Church to more obviously edifying gifts. But he goes no further. He throws in almost parenthetically the statement that he himself spoke with tongues more than anyone else, and he does not question the spiritual, or supernatural, source of the phenomenon.

The difficulty I feel is this. On the one hand, *glossolalia* has remained an intermittent 'variety of religious experience' down to the present day. Every now and then we hear that in some revivalist meeting one or more of those present has burst into a torrent of what appears to be gibberish. The thing does not seem to be edifying, and all non-Christian opinion would regard it as a kind of hysteria, an involuntary discharge of nervous excitement. A good deal even of Christian opinion would explain most instances of it in exactly the same way; and I must confess that it would be very hard to believe that in all instances of it the Holy Ghost is operating. We suspect, even if we cannot be sure, that it is usually an affair of the nerves. That is one horn of the dilemma. On the other hand, we cannot as Christians shelve the story of Pentecost or deny that there, at any rate, the speaking with tongues was miraculous. For the men spoke not gibberish but languages unknown to them though known to other people present. And the whole event of which this makes part is built into the very fabric of the birth-story of the Church. It is this very event which the risen Lord has told the Church to wait for – almost in the last words He uttered before His ascension. It looks, therefore, as if we shall have to say that the very same phenomenon which is sometimes not only natural but even pathological is at other times (or at least at one other time) the organ of the Holy Ghost. And this seems at first very surprising and very open to attack. The sceptic will certainly seize this opportunity to talk to us about Occam's razor, to accuse us of multiplying hypotheses. If most instances of *glossolalia* are covered by hysteria, is it not (he will ask) extremely probable that that explanation covers the remaining instances too?

It is to this difficulty that I would gladly bring a little ease if I can. And I will begin by pointing out that it belongs to a class of difficulties. The closest parallel to it within that class is raised by the erotic language and imagery we find in the mystics. In them we find a whole range of expressions – and therefore possibly of emotions – with which we are quite familiar in another context and which, in that other context, have a clear natural significance. But in the mystical writings it is claimed that these elements have a different cause. And once more the sceptic will ask why the cause which we are content to accept for ninety-nine instances of such language should not be held to cover the hundredth too. The hypothesis that mysticism is an erotic phenomenon will seem to him immensely more probable than any other.

Put in its most general terms our problem is that of the obvious continuity between things which are admittedly natural and things which, it is claimed, are spiritual; the reappearance in what professes to be our supernatural life of all the same old elements which make up our natural life and (it would seem) of no others. If we have really been visited by a revelation from beyond Nature, is it not very strange that an Apocalypse can furnish heaven with nothing more than selections from terrestrial experience (crowns, thrones, and music), that devotion can find no language but that of human lovers, and that the rite whereby Christians enact a mystical union should turn out to be only the old, familiar act of eating and drinking? And you may add that the very same problem also breaks out on a lower level, not only between spiritual and natural but also between higher and lower levels of the natural life. Hence cynics very plausibly challenge our civilised conception of the difference between love and lust by pointing out that when all is said and done they usually end in what is, physically, the same act. They similarly challenge the difference between justice and revenge on the ground that what finally happens to the criminal may be the same. And in all these cases, let us admit that the cynics and sceptics have a good *prima facie* case. The same acts do reappear in justice as well as in revenge: the consummation of humanised and conjugal love is physiologically the same as that of the merely biological lust; religious language and imagery, and probably religious emotion too, contains nothing that has not been borrowed from Nature.

Now it seems to me that the only way to refute the critic here is to show that the same *prima facie* case is equally plausible in some instance where we all know (not by faith or by logic, but empirically) that it is in fact false. Can we find an instance of higher and lower where the higher is within almost everyone's experience? I think we can. Consider the following quotation from *Pepys's Diary*:

> With my wife to the King's House to see *The Virgin Martyr*, and it is mighty pleasant … But that which did please me beyond anything in the whole world was the wind musick when the angel comes down, which is so sweet that it ravished me and, indeed, in a word, did wrap up my soul so that it made me really sick, just as I have formerly been when in love with my wife … and makes me resolve to practise wind musick and to make my wife do the like. (27 February 1688)

There are several points here that deserve attention. Firstly that the internal sensation accompanying intense aesthetic delight was indistinguishable from the sensation accompanying two other experiences, that of being in love and that of being, say, in a rough channel crossing. 2. That of these two other experiences one at least is the very reverse of pleasurable. No man enjoys nausea. 3. That Pepys was, nevertheless, anxious to have again the experience whose sensational accompaniment was identical with the very unpleasant accompaniments of sickness. That was why he decided to take up wind music.

Now it may be true that not many of us have fully shared Pepys's experience; but we have all experienced that sort of thing. For myself I find that if, during a moment of intense aesthetic rapture, one tries to turn round and catch by introspection what one is actually feeling, one can never lay one's hand on anything but a physical sensation. In my case it is a kind of kick or flutter in the diaphragm. Perhaps that is all Pepys meant by 'really sick'. But the important point is this: I find that this kick or flutter is exactly the same sensation which, in me, accompanies great and sudden anguish. Introspection can discover no difference at all between my neural response to very bad news and my neural response to the overture of *The Magic Flute*. If I were to judge simply by sensations I should come to the absurd conclusion that joy and anguish are the same thing, that what I most dread is the same with what I most desire. Introspection discovers nothing more or different in the one than in the other. And I expect that most of you, if you are in the habit of noticing such things, will report more or less the same.

Now let us take a step farther. These sensations – Pepys's sickness and my flutter in the diaphragm – do not merely accompany very different experiences as an irrelevant or neutral addition. We may be quite sure that Pepys hated that sensation when it came in real sickness: and we know from his own words that he liked it when it came with wind music, for he took measures to make as sure as possible of getting it again. And I likewise love this internal flutter in one context and call it a pleasure and hate it in another and call it misery. It is not a mere sign of joy and anguish: it becomes what it signifies. When the joy thus flows over into the nerves, that overflow is its consummation: when the anguish thus flows over, that physical symptom is the crowning horror. The very same thing which makes the sweetest drop of all in the sweet cup also makes the bitterest drop in the bitter.

And here, I suggest, we have found what we are looking for. I take our emotional life to be 'higher' than the life of our sensations – not, of course, morally higher, but richer, more varied, more subtle. And this is a higher level which nearly all of us know. And I believe that if anyone watches carefully the relation between his emotions and his sensations he will discover the following facts: 1. that the nerves do respond, and in a sense most adequately and exquisitely, to the emotions; 2. that their resources are far more limited, the possible variations of sense far fewer, than those of emotion; 3. and that the senses compensate for this by using the *same* sensation to express more than one emotion – even, as we have seen, to express opposite emotions.

Where we tend to go wrong is in assuming that if there is to be a correspondence between two systems it must be a one-for-one correspondence – that A in the one system must be represented by *a* in the other, and so on. But the correspondence between emotion and sensation turns out not to be of that sort. And there never could be correspondence of that sort where the one system was really richer than the other. If the richer system is to be represented in the poorer at all, this can only be by giving each element in the poorer system more than one meaning. The transposition of the richer into the poorer must, so to speak, be algebraical, not arithmetical. If you are to translate from a language which has a large vocabulary into a language that has a small vocabulary, then you must be allowed to use several words in more than one sense. If you are to write a language with twenty-two vowel sounds in an alphabet with only five vowel characters then you must be allowed to give each of those five characters more than one value. If you are making a piano version of a piece originally scored for an orchestra, then the same piano notes which represent flutes in one passage must also represent violins in another.

As the examples show we are all quite familiar with this kind of transposition or adaptation from a richer to a poorer medium. The most familiar example of all is the art of drawing. The problem here is to represent a three-dimensional world on a flat sheet of paper. The solution is perspective, and perspective means that we must give more than one value to a two-dimensional shape. Thus in a drawing of a cube we use an acute angle to represent what is a right angle in the real world. But elsewhere an acute angle on the paper may represent what was already an acute angle in the real world: for example, the point of a spear or the gable of a house. The very same shape which you must draw to give the illusion of a straight road receding from the spectator is also the shape you draw for a dunce's cap. As with the lines, so with the shading. Your brightest light in the picture is, in literal fact, only plain white paper: and this must do for the sun, or a lake in evening light, or snow, or human flesh.

I now make two comments on the instances of Transposition which are already before us:

1. It is clear that in each case what is happening in the lower medium can be understood only if we know the higher medium. The instance where this knowledge is most commonly lacking is the musical one. The piano version means one thing to the musician who knows the original orchestral score and another thing to the man who hears it simply as a piano piece. But the second man would be at an even greater disadvantage if he had never heard any instrument but a piano and even doubted the existence of other instruments. Even more, we understand pictures only because we know and inhabit the three-dimensional world. If we can imagine a creature who perceived only two dimensions and yet could somehow be aware of the lines as he crawled over them on the paper, we shall easily see how impossible it would be for him to understand. At first he might be prepared to accept on authority our assurance that there was a world in three dimensions. But when we pointed to the lines on the

paper and tried to explain, say, that 'This is a road', would he not reply that the shape which we were asking him to accept as a revelation of our mysterious other world was the very same shape which, on our own showing, elsewhere meant nothing but a triangle. And soon, I think, he would say, 'You keep on telling me of this other world and its unimaginable shapes which you call solid. But isn't it very suspicious that all the shapes which you offer me as images or reflections of the solid ones turn out on inspection to be simply the old two-dimensional shapes of my own world as I have always known it? Is it not obvious that your vaunted other world, so far from being the archetype, is a dream which borrows all its elements from this one?'

2. It is of some importance to notice that the word *symbolism* is not adequate in all cases to cover the relation between the higher medium and its transposition in the lower. It covers some cases perfectly, but not others. Thus the relation between speech and writing is one of symbolism. The written characters exist solely for the eye, the spoken words solely for the ear. There is complete discontinuity between them. They are not like one another, nor does the one cause the other to be. The one is simply a *sign* of the other and signifies it by a convention. But a picture is not related to the visible world in just that way. Pictures are part of the visible world themselves and represent it only by being part of it. Their visibility has the same source. The suns and lamps in pictures seem to shine only because real suns or lamps shine on them: that is, they seem to shine a great deal because they really shine a little in reflecting their archetypes. The sunlight in a picture is therefore not related to real sunlight simply as written words are to spoken. It is a sign, but also something more than a sign: and only a sign because it is also more than a sign, because in it the thing signified is really in a certain mode present. If I had to name the relation I should call it not symbolical but sacramental. But in the case we started from – that of emotion and sensation – we are even further beyond mere symbolism. For there, as we have seen, the very same sensation does not merely accompany, nor merely signify, diverse and opposite emotions, but becomes part of them. The emotion descends bodily, as it were, into the sensation and digests, transforms, transubstantiates it, so that the same thrill along the nerves *is* delight or *is* agony.

I am not going to maintain that what I call Transposition is the only possible mode whereby a poorer medium can respond to a richer: but I claim that it is very hard to imagine any other. It is therefore, at the very least, not improbable that Transposition occurs whenever the higher reproduces itself in the lower. Thus, to digress for a moment, it seems to me very likely that the real relation between mind and body is one of

Transposition. We are certain that, in this life at any rate, thought is intimately connected with the brain. The theory that thought therefore is merely a movement in the brain is, in my opinion, nonsense; for if so, that theory itself would be merely a movement, an event among atoms, which may have speed and direction but of which it would be meaningless to use the words 'true' or 'false'. We are driven then to some kind of correspondence. But if we assume a one-for-one correspondence this means that we have to attribute an almost unbelievable complexity and variety of events to the brain. But I submit that a one-for-one relation is probably quite unnecessary. All our examples suggest that the brain can respond – in a sense, adequately and exquisitely correspond – to the seemingly infinite variety of consciousness without providing one single physical modification for each single modification of consciousness.

But that is a digression. Let us now return to our original question, about Spirit and Nature, God and Man. Our problem was that in what claims to be our spiritual life all the elements of our natural life recur: and, what is worse, it looks at first glance as if no other elements were present. We now see that if the spiritual is richer than the natural (as no one who believes in its existence would deny) then this is exactly what we should expect. And the sceptic's conclusion that the so-called spiritual is really derived from the natural, that it is a mirage or projection or imaginary extension of the natural, is also exactly what we should expect; for, as we have seen, this is the mistake which an observer who knew only the lower medium would be bound to make in every case of Transposition. The brutal man never can by analysis find anything but lust in love; the Flatlander never can find anything but flat shapes in a picture; physiology never can find anything in thought except twitchings of the grey matter. It is no good browbeating the critic who approaches a Transposition from below. On the evidence available to him his conclusion is the only one possible.

Everything is different when you approach the Transposition from above, as we all do in the case of emotion and sensation or of the three-dimensional world and pictures, and as the spiritual man does in the case we are considering. Those who spoke with tongues, as St Paul did, can well understand how that holy phenomenon differed from the hysterical phenomenon – although be it remembered, they were in a sense exactly the same phenomenon, just as the very same sensation came to Pepys in love, in the enjoyment of music, and in sickness. Spiritual things are spiritually discerned. The spiritual man judges all things and is judged of none.

But who dares claim to be a spiritual man? In the full sense, none of us. And yet we are somehow aware that we approach from above, or from inside, at least some of those Transpositions which embody the Christian life in this world. With whatever sense of unworthiness, with whatever sense of audacity, we must affirm that we know a little of the higher system which is being transposed. In a way the claim we are making is not a very startling one. We are only claiming to know that our apparent devotion, whatever else it may have been, was not simply erotic, or that our apparent desire for Heaven, whatever else it may have been, was not simply a desire for longevity or jewellery or social splendours. Perhaps we have never really attained at all to what St Paul would describe as spiritual life. But at the very least we know, in some dim and confused way, that we were trying to use natural acts and images and language with a new value, have at least desired a repentance which was not merely prudential and a love which was not self-centred. At the worst, we know enough of the spiritual to know that we have fallen short of it: as if the picture knew enough of the three-dimensional world to be aware that it was flat.

It is not only for humility's sake (that, of course) that we must emphasise the dimness of our knowledge. I suspect that, save by God's direct miracle, spiritual experience can never abide introspection. If even our emotions will not do so (since the attempt to find out what we are now *feeling* yields nothing more than a physical sensation), much less will the operations of the Holy Ghost. The attempt to discover by introspective analysis our own spiritual condition is to me a horrible thing which reveals, at best, not the secrets of God's spirit and ours, but their transpositions in intellect, emotion and imagination, and which at worst may be the quickest road to presumption or despair.

I believe that this doctrine of Transposition provides for most of us a background very much needed for the theological virtue of Hope. We can hope only for what we can desire. And the trouble is that any adult and philosophically respectable notion we can form of Heaven is forced to deny of that state most of the things our nature desires. There is no doubt a blessedly ingenuous faith, a child's or a savage's faith which finds no difficulty. It accepts without awkward questionings the harps and golden streets and the family reunions pictured by hymn-writers. Such a faith is deceived, yet, in the deepest sense, not deceived; for while it errs in mistaking symbol for fact, yet it apprehends Heaven as joy and plenitude and love. But it is impossible for most of us. And we must not try, by artifice, to make ourselves more naive than we are. A man does not 'become as a little child' by aping childhood. Hence our notion of Heaven involves perpetual negations; no food, no drink, no sex, no movement, no mirth, no events, no time, no art.

Against all these, to be sure, we set one positive: the vision and enjoyment of God. And since this is an infinite good we hold (rightly) that it outweighs them all. That is, the reality of the Beatific Vision would, or will, outweigh, would infinitely outweigh, the reality of the negations. But can our present notion of it outweigh our present notion of them? That is quite a different question. And for most of us at most times the answer is No. How it may be for great saints and mystics I cannot tell. But for others the conception of that Vision is a difficult, precarious and fugitive extrapolation from a very few and ambiguous moments in our earthly experience: while our idea of the negated natural goods is vivid and persistent, loaded with the memories of a lifetime, built into our nerves and muscles and therefore into our imaginations.

Thus the negatives have, so to speak, an unfair advantage in every competition with the positive. What is worse, their presence – and most when we most resolutely try to suppress or ignore them – vitiates even such a faint and ghostlike notion of the positive as we might have had. The exclusion of the lower goods begins to seem the essential characteristic of the higher good. We feel, if we do not say, that the vision of God will come not to fulfil but to destroy our nature; this bleak fantasy often underlies our very use of such words as 'holy' or 'pure' or 'spiritual'.

We must not allow this to happen if we can possibly prevent it. We must believe – and therefore in some degree imagine – that every negation will be only the reverse side of a fulfilling. And we must mean by that the fulfilling, precisely, of our humanity; not our transformation into angels nor our absorption into Deity. For though we shall be 'as the angels' and made 'like unto' our Master, I think this means 'like with the likeness proper to men': as different instruments that play the same air but each in its own fashion. How far the life of the risen man will be sensory, we do not know. But I surmise that it will differ from the sensory life we know here, not as emptiness differs from water or water from wine but as a flower differs from a bulb or a cathedral from an architect's drawing. And it is here that Transposition helps me.

Let us construct a fable. Let us picture a woman thrown into a dungeon. There she bears and rears a son. He grows up seeing nothing but the dungeon walls, the straw on the floor, and a little patch of the sky seen through the grating, which is too high up to show anything except sky. This unfortunate woman was an artist, and when they imprisoned her she managed to bring with her a drawing pad and a box of pencils. As she never loses the hope of deliverance she is constantly teaching her son about that outer world which he has never seen. She does it very largely by drawing him pictures. With her pencil she attempts to show him what fields, rivers, mountains, cities and waves on a beach are like. He is a dutiful boy and he does his best to believe her when she tells him that that outer world is far more interesting and glorious than anything in the dungeon. At times he succeeds. On the whole he gets on tolerably well until, one day, he says something that gives his mother pause. For a minute or two they are at cross-purposes. Finally it dawns on her that he has, all these years, lived under a misconception. 'But,' she gasps, 'you didn't think that the real world was full of lines drawn in lead pencil?' 'What?' says the boy. 'No pencil-marks there?' And instantly his whole notion of the outer world becomes a blank. For the lines, by which alone he was imagining it, have now been denied of it. He has no idea of that which will exclude and dispense with the lines, that of which the lines were merely a transposition – the waving tree-tops, the light dancing on the weir, the coloured three-dimensional realities which are not enclosed in lines but define their own shapes at every moment with a delicacy and multiplicity which no drawing could ever achieve. The child will get the idea that the real world is somehow less visible than his mother's pictures. In reality it lacks lines because it is incomparably more visible.

So with us. 'We know not what we shall be'; but we may be sure we shall be more, not less, than we were on earth. Our natural experiences (sensory, emotional, imaginative) are only like the drawing, like pencilled lines on flat paper. If they vanish in the risen life, they will vanish only as pencil lines vanish from the real landscape; not as a candle flame that is put out but as a candle flame which becomes invisible because someone has pulled up the blind, thrown open the shutters, and let in the blaze of the risen sun.

You can put it whichever way you please. You can say that by Transposition our humanity, senses and all, can be made the vehicle of beatitude. Or you can say that the heavenly bounties by Transposition are embodied during this life in our temporal experience. But the second way is the better. It is the present life which is the diminution, the symbol, the etiolated, the (as it were) 'vegetarian' substitute. If flesh and blood cannot inherit the Kingdom, that is not because they are too solid, too gross, too distinct, too 'illustrious with being'. They are too flimsy, too transitory, too phantasmal.

With this my case, as the lawyers say, is complete. But I have just four points to add:

1. I hope it is quite clear that the conception of Transposition, as I call it, is distinct from another conception often used for the same purpose – I mean the conception of development. The Developmentalist explains the continuity between things that claim to be spiritual and things that are certainly natural by saying that the one slowly turned into the other. I believe this view explains some facts, but I think it has been much

overworked. At any rate it is not the theory I am putting forward. I am not saying that the natural act of eating after millions of years somehow blossoms into the Christian sacrament. I am saying that the Spiritual Reality, which existed before there were any creatures who ate, gives this natural act a new meaning, and more than a new meaning: makes it in a certain context to be a different thing. In a word, I think that real landscapes enter into pictures, not that pictures will one day sprout into real trees and grass.

2. I have found it impossible, in thinking of what I call Transposition, not to ask myself whether it may help us to conceive the Incarnation. Of course if Transposition were merely a mode of symbolism it could give us no help at all in this matter: on the contrary, it would lead us wholly astray, back into a new kind of Docetism (or would it be only the old kind?) and away from the utterly historical and concrete reality which is the centre of all our hope, faith and love. But then, as I have pointed out, Transposition is not always symbolism. In varying degrees the lower reality can actually be drawn into the higher and become part of it. The sensation which accompanies joy becomes itself joy: we can hardly choose but say 'incarnates joy'. If this is so, then I venture to suggest, though with great doubt and in the most provisional way, that the concept of Transposition may have some contribution to make to the theology – or at least to the philosophy – of the Incarnation. For we are told in one of the creeds that the Incarnation worked 'not by conversion of the Godhead into flesh, but by taking of the Manhood into God'. And it seems to me that there is a real analogy between this and what I have called Transposition: that humanity, still remaining itself, is not merely counted as, but veritably drawn into, Deity, seems to me like what happens when a sensation (not in itself a pleasure) is drawn into the joy it accompanies. But I walk *in mirabilibus supra me* and submit all to the verdict of real theologians.

3. I have tried to stress throughout the inevitableness of the error made about every transposition by one who approaches it from the lower medium only. The strength of such a critic lies in the words 'merely' or 'nothing but'. He sees all the facts but not the meaning. Quite truly, therefore, he claims to have seen all the facts. There *is* nothing else there; except the meaning. He is therefore, as regards the matter in hand, in the position of an animal. You will have noticed that most dogs cannot understand *pointing*. You point to a bit of food on the floor: the dog, instead of looking at the floor, sniffs at your finger. A finger is a finger to him, and that is all. His world is all fact and no meaning. And in a period when factual realism is dominant we shall find people deliberately

inducing upon themselves this dog-like mind. A man who has experienced love from within will deliberately go about to inspect it analytically from outside and regard the results of this analysis as truer than his experience. The extreme limit of this self-blinding is seen in those who, like the rest of us, have consciousness, yet go about to study the human organism as if they did not know it was conscious. As long as this deliberate refusal to understand things from above, even where such understanding is possible, continues, it is idle to talk of any final victory over materialism. The critique of every experience from below, the voluntary ignoring of meaning and concentration on fact, will always have the same plausibility. There will always be evidence, and every month fresh evidence, to show that religion is only psychological, justice only self-protection, politics only economics, love only lust, and thought itself only cerebral biochemistry.

4. Finally, I suggest that what has been said of Transposition throws a new light on the doctrine of the resurrection of the body. For in a sense Transposition can do anything. However great the difference between Spirit and Nature, between aesthetic joy and that flutter in the diaphragm, between reality and picture, yet the Transposition can be in its own way adequate. I said before that in your drawing you had only plain white paper for sun and cloud, snow, water, and human flesh. In one sense, how miserably inadequate! Yet in another, how perfect. If the shadows are properly done, that patch of white paper will, in some curious way, be very like blazing sunshine; we shall almost feel cold while we look at the paper snow and almost warm our hands at the paper fire. May we not, by a reasonable analogy, suppose likewise that there is no experience of the spirit so transcendent and supernatural, no vision of Deity Himself so close and so far beyond all images and emotions, that to it there cannot be an appropriate correspondence on the sensory level? Not by a new sense but by the incredible flooding of those very sensations we now have with a meaning, a transvaluation, of which we have here no faintest guess?

PART 3

THE CHRISTIAN
IN THE WORLD

[34]
WHY I AM NOT A PACIFIST

Read to a pacifist society in Oxford in 1940, this was published in an expanded edition of The Weight of Glory and Other Addresses *(US, 1980), then in* Timeless at Heart *(1987) and in* Compelling Reason *(1988).*

The question is whether to serve in the wars at the command of the civil society to which we belong is a wicked action, or an action morally indifferent or an action morally obligatory. In asking how to decide this question, we are raising a much more general question: how do we decide what is good or evil? The usual answer is that we decide by conscience. But probably no one thinks now of conscience as a separate faculty, like one of the senses. Indeed, it cannot be so thought of. For an autonomous faculty like a sense cannot be argued with; you cannot argue a man into seeing green if he sees blue. But the conscience can be altered by argument; and if you did not think so, you would not have asked me to come and argue with you about the morality of obeying the civil law when it tells us to serve in the wars. Conscience, then, means the whole man engaged in a particular subject matter.

But even in this sense conscience still has two meanings. It can mean (a) the pressure a man feels upon his will to do what he thinks is right; (b) his judgement as to what the content of right and wrong are. In sense (a) conscience is always to be followed. It is the sovereign of the universe, which 'if it had power as it has right, would absolutely rule the world'. It is not to be argued with, but obeyed, and even to question it is to incur guilt. But in sense (b) it is a very different matter. People may be mistaken about wrong and right; most people in some degree are mistaken. By what means are mistakes in this field to be corrected?

The most useful analogy here is that of Reason – by which I do not mean some separate faculty but, once more, the whole man judging, only judging this time not about good and evil, but about truth and falsehood. Now any concrete train of reasoning involves three elements.

Firstly, there is the reception of facts to reason about. These facts are received either from our own senses, or from the report of other minds; that is, either experience or authority supplies us with our material. But each man's experience is so limited that the second source is the more usual; of every hundred facts upon which to reason, ninety-nine depend on authority.

Secondly, there is the direct, simple act of the mind perceiving self-evident truth, as when we see that if A and B both equal C, then they equal each other. This act I call intuition.

Thirdly, there is an art or skill of arranging the facts so as to yield a series of such intuitions which linked together produce a proof of the truth or falsehood of the proposition we are considering. Thus in a geometrical proof each step is seen by intuition, and to fail to see it is to be not a bad geometrician but an idiot. The skill comes in arranging the material into a series of intuitable 'steps'. Failure to do this does not mean idiocy, but only lack of ingenuity or invention. Failure to follow it need not mean idiocy, but either inattention or defect of memory which forbids us to hold all the intuitions together.

Now all correction of errors in reasoning is really correction of the first or the third element. The second, the intuitional element, cannot be corrected if it is wrong, nor supplied if it is lacking. You can give the man new facts. You can invent a simpler proof, that is, a simple concatenation of intuitable truths. But when you come to an absolute inability to see any one of the self-evident steps out of which the proof is built, then you can do nothing. No doubt this absolute inability is much rarer than we suppose. Every teacher knows that people are constantly protesting that they 'can't see' some self-evident inference, but the supposed inability is usually a refusal to see, resulting either from some passion which *wants* not to see the truth in question or else from sloth which does not want to think at all. But when the inability is real, argument is at an end. You cannot produce rational intuition by argument, because argument depends upon rational intuition. Proof rests upon the unprovable which has to be just 'seen'. Hence faulty intuition is incorrigible. It does not follow that it cannot be trained by practice in attention and in the morti-fication of disturbing passions, or corrupted by the opposite habits. But it is not amenable to correction by argument.

Before leaving the subject of Reason, I must point out that authority not only combines with experience to produce the raw material, the 'facts', but also has to be frequently used instead of reasoning itself as a method of getting conclusions. For example, few of us have followed the reasoning on which even 10 per cent of the truths we believe are based.

WHY I AM NOT A PACIFIST

We accept them on authority from the experts and are wise to do so, for though we are thereby sometimes deceived, yet we should have to live like savages if we did not.

Now all three elements are found also in conscience. The facts, as before, come from experience and authority. I do not mean 'moral facts' but those facts about actions without holding which we could not raise moral questions at all – for we should not even be discussing Pacifism if we did not know what war and killing meant, nor Chastity, if we had not yet learned what schoolmasters used to call 'the facts of life'. Secondly, there are the pure intuitions of utterly simple good and evil as such. Third, there is the process of argument by which you arrange the intuitions so as to convince a man that a particular act is wrong or right. And finally, there is authority as a substitute for argument, telling a man of some wrong or right which he would not otherwise have discovered, and rightly accepted if the man has good reason to believe the authority wiser and better than himself. The main difference between Reason and Conscience is an alarming one. It is thus: that while the unarguable intuitions on which all depend are liable to be corrupted by passion when we are considering truth and falsehood, they are much more liable, they are almost certain to be corrupted when we are considering good and evil. For then we are concerned with some action to be here and now done or left undone by ourselves. And we should not be considering that action at all unless we had some wish either to do or not to do it, so that in this sphere we are bribed from the very beginning. Hence the value of authority in checking, or even superseding, our own activity is much greater in this sphere than in that of Reason. Hence, too, human beings must be trained in obedience to the moral intuitions almost before they have them, and years before they are rational enough to discuss them, or they will be corrupted before the time for discussion arrives.

These basic moral intuitions are the only element in Conscience which cannot be argued about; if there can be a difference of opinion which does not reveal one of the parties as a moral idiot, then it is not an intuition. They are the ultimate preferences of the will for love rather than hatred, and happiness rather than misery. There are people so corrupted as to have lost even these, just as there are people who can't see the simplest proof, but in the main these can be said to be the voice of humanity as such. And they are unarguable. But here the trouble begins. People are constantly claiming this unarguable and unanswerable status for moral judgements which are not really intuitions at all but remote consequences or particular applications of them, eminently open to discussion since the consequences may be illogically drawn or the application falsely made.

Thus you may meet a 'temperance' fanatic who claims to have an unanswerable intuition that all strong drink is forbidden. Really he can have nothing of the sort. The real intuition is that health and harmony are good. Then there is a generalisation from facts to the effect that drunkenness produces disease and quarrelling, and perhaps also, if the fanatic is Christian, the voice of Authority saying that the body is the temple of the Holy Ghost. Then there is a conclusion that what can always be abused had better never be used at all – a conclusion eminently suited for discussion. Finally, there is the process whereby early associations, arrogance, and the like turn the remote conclusion into something which the man thinks unarguable because he does not wish to argue about it.

This, then, is our first canon for moral decision. Conscience in the (a) sense, the thing that moves us to do right, has absolute authority, but conscience in the (b) sense, our judgement as to what is right, is a mixture of inarguable intuitions and highly arguable processes of reasoning or of submission to authority; and nothing is to be treated as an intuition unless it is such that no good man has ever dreamed of doubting. The man who 'just feels' that total abstinence from drink or marriage is obligatory is to be treated like the man who 'just feels sure' that *Henry VIII* is not by Shakespeare, or that vaccination does no good. For a mere unargued conviction is in place only when we are dealing with the axiomatic; and these views are not axiomatic.

I therefore begin by ruling out one Pacifist position which probably no one present holds, but which conceivably might be held – that of the man who claims to know on the ground of immediate intuition that all killing of human beings is in all circumstances an absolute evil. With the man who reaches the same result by reasoning or authority, I can argue. Of the man who claims not to reach it but to start there, we can only say that he can have no such intuition as he claims. He is mistaking an opinion, or, more likely, a passion, for an intuition. Of course, it would be rude to say this to him. *To* him we can only say that if he is not a moral idiot, then unfortunately the rest of the human race, including its best and wisest, are, and that argument across such a chasm is impossible.

Having ruled out this extreme case, I return to enquire how we are to decide on a question of morals. We have seen that every moral judgement involves facts, intuition and reasoning, and, if we are wise enough to be humble, it will involve some regard for authority as well. Its strength depends on the strength of these four factors. Thus if I find that the facts on which I am working are clear and little disputed, that the basic intuition is unmistakably an intuition, that the reasoning which connects this intuition with the particular judgement is strong, and that I am in agreement or (at worst) not in disagreement with authority, then I can trust my moral judgement with reasonable confidence. And if, in addition, I find little reason to suppose that any passion has secretly swayed my mind, this confidence is confirmed. If, on the other hand, I find the facts doubtful, the supposed intuition by no means obvious to all good men, the reasoning weak, and authority against me, then I ought to conclude that I am probably wrong. And if the conclusion which I have reached turns out also to flatter some strong passion of my own, then my suspicion should deepen into moral certainty. By 'moral certainty' I mean that degree of certainty proper to moral decisions; for mathematical certainty is not here to be looked for. I now apply these tests to the judgement, 'It is immoral to obey when the civil society of which I am a member commands me to serve in the wars!'

First as to the facts. The main relevant fact admitted by all parties is that war is very disagreeable. The main contention urged as fact by pacifists would be that wars always do more harm than good. How is one to find out whether this is true? It belongs to a class of historical generalisations which involve a comparison between the actual consequences of some actual event and a consequence which might have followed if that event had not occurred. 'Wars do no good' involves the proposition that if the Greeks had yielded to Xerxes and the Romans to Hannibal, the course of history ever since would have been perhaps better, but certainly no worse than it actually has been; that a Mediterranean world in which Carthaginian power succeeded Persian would have been at least as good and happy and as fruitful for all posterity as the actual Mediterranean world in which Roman power succeeded Greek. My point is not that such an opinion seems to me overwhelmingly improbable. My point is that both opinions are merely speculative; there is no conceivable way of convincing a man of either. Indeed it is doubtful whether the whole conception of 'what would have happened' – that is, of unrealised possibilities – is more than an imaginative technique for giving a vivid rhetorical account of what did happen.

That wars do no good is then so far from being a fact that it hardly ranks as a historical opinion. Nor is the matter mended by saying 'modern wars'; how are we to decide whether the total effect would have been better or worse if Europe had submitted to Germany in 1914? It is, of course, true that wars never do half the good which the leaders of the belligerents say they are going to do. Nothing ever does half the good – perhaps nothing ever does half the evil – which is expected of it. And that may be a sound argument for not pitching one's propaganda too high. But it is no argument against war. If a Germanised Europe in 1914 would have been an evil, then the war which prevented that evil was, so far, justified. To call it useless because it did not also cure slums and unemployment is like coming up to a man who has just succeeded in defending himself from a man-eating tiger and saying, 'It's no good, old chap. This hasn't really cured your rheumatism!'

On the test of the fact, then, I find the Pacifist position weak. It seems to me that history is full of useful wars as well as of useless wars. If all that can be brought against the frequent appearance of utility is mere speculation about what could have happened, I am not converted.

I turn next to the intuition. There is no question of discussion once we have found it; there is only the danger of mistaking for an intuition something which is really a conclusion and therefore needs argument. We want something which no good man has ever disputed; we are in search of platitude. The relevant intuition seems to be that love is good and hatred bad, or that helping is good and harming bad.

We have next to consider whether reasoning leads us from this intuition to the Pacifist conclusion or not. And the first thing I notice is that intuition can lead to no action until it is limited in some way or other. You cannot do *simply* good to *simply* Man; you must do this or that good to this or that man. And if you do *this* good, you can't at the same time do *that*; and if you do it to *these* men, you can't also do it to *those*. Hence from the outset the law of beneficence involves not doing some good to some men at some times. Hence those rules which so far as I know have never been doubted, as that we should help one we have promised to help rather than another, or a benefactor rather than one who has no special claims on us, or a compatriot more than a stranger, or a kinsman rather than a mere compatriot. And this in fact most often means helping A at the expense of B, who drowns while you pull A on board. And sooner or later, it involves helping A by actually doing some degree of violence to B. But when B is up to mischief against A, you must either do nothing (which disobeys the intuition) or you must help one against the other. And certainly no one's conscience tells him to help B, the guilty. It remains, therefore, to help A. So far, I suppose, we all agree. If the argument is not to end in an anti-Pacifist conclusion, one or other of two stopping places must be selected. You must either say that violence to B is lawful only if it stops short of killing, or else that killing of individuals is indeed lawful but the mass killing of a war is not. As regards the first, I admit the general proposition that the lesser violence done to B is always preferable to the greater, provided that it is equally efficient in restraining him and equally good for everyone concerned, including B, whose claim is inferior to all the other claims involved but not nonexistent. But I do not therefore conclude that to kill B is always wrong. In some instances – for instance in a small, isolated community – death may be the only efficient method of restraint. In any community its effect on the population, not simply as a deterrent through fear, but also as an expression of the moral importance of certain crimes, may be valuable. And as for B himself, I think a bad man is at least as likely to make a good end in the execution shed some weeks after the crime as in the prison hospital twenty years later. I am not producing arguments to show that capital punishment is certainly right; I am only maintaining that it is not certainly wrong; it is a matter on which good men may legitimately differ.

As regards the second, the position seems to be much clearer. It is arguable that a criminal can always be satisfactorily dealt with without the death penalty. It is certain that a whole nation cannot be prevented from taking what it wants except by war. It is almost equally certain that the absorption of certain societies by certain other societies is a greater evil. The doctrine that war is always a great evil seems to imply a materialist ethic, a belief that death and pain are the greatest evils. But I do not think they are. I think the suppression of a higher religion by a lower, or even a higher secular culture by a lower, a much greater evil. Nor am I greatly moved by the fact that many of the individuals we strike down in war are innocent. That seems, in a way, to make war not worse but better. All men die, and most men miserably. That two soldiers on opposite sides, each believing his own country to be in the right, each at the moment when his selfishness is most in abeyance and his will to sacrifice in the ascendant, should kill each other in plain battle seems to me by no means one of the most terrible things in this very terrible world. Of course, one of them (at least) must be mistaken. And of course war is a very great evil. But that is not the question. The question is whether war is the greatest evil in the world, so that any state of affairs which might result from submission is certainly preferable. And I do not see any really cogent arguments for that view.

Another attempt to get a Pacifist conclusion from the intuition is of a more political and calculating kind. If not the greatest evil, yet war is a great evil. Therefore, we should all like to remove it if we can. But every war leads to another war. The removal of war must therefore be attempted. We must increase by propaganda the number of Pacifists in each nation until it becomes great enough to deter that nation from going to war. This seems to me wild work. Only liberal societies tolerate Pacifists. In the liberal society, the number of Pacifists will either be large enough to cripple the state as a belligerent, or not. If not, you have done nothing. If it is large enough, then you have handed over the state which does tolerate Pacifists to its totalitarian neighbour who does not. Pacifism of this kind is taking the straight road to a world in which there will be no Pacifists.

It may be asked whether, faint as the hope is of abolishing war by Pacifism, there is any other hope. But the question belongs to a mode of thought which I find quite alien to me. It consists in assuming that the great permanent miseries in human life must be curable if only we can find the right cure; and it then proceeds by elimination and concludes that whatever is left, however unlikely to prove a cure, must nevertheless do so. Hence the fanaticism of Marxists, Freudians, Eugenists, Spiritualists, Douglasites, Federal Unionists, Vegetarians, and all the rest. But I have received no assurance that anything we can do will eradicate suffering. I think the best results are obtained by people who work quietly away at their objectives, such as the abolition of the slave trade, or prison reform, or factory acts, or tuberculosis, not by those who think they can achieve universal justice, or health, or peace. I think the art of life consists in tackling each immediate evil as well as we can. To avert or postpone one particular war by wise policy, or to render one particular campaign shorter by strength and skill or less terrible by mercy to the conquered and the civilians, is more useful than all the proposals for universal peace that have ever been made; just as the dentist who can stop one toothache has deserved better of humanity than all the men who think they have some scheme for producing a perfectly healthy race.

I do not therefore find any very clear and cogent reason for inferring from the general principle of beneficence the conclusion that I must disobey if I am called on by lawful authority to be a soldier. I turn next to consider Authority. Authority is either special or general, and again either human or divine.

The special human authority which rests on me in this matter is that of the society to which I belong. That society by its declaration of war has decided the issue against Pacifism in this particular instance, and by its institutions and practice for centuries has decided against Pacifism in general. If I am Pacifist, I have Arthur and Aelfred, Elizabeth and Cromwell, Walpole and Burke, against me. I have my university, my school, and my parents against me. I have the literature of my country against me, and cannot even open my *Beowulf*, my Shakespeare, my Johnson or my Wordsworth without being reproved. Now, of course, this authority of England is not final. But there is a difference between conclusive authority and authority of no weight at all. Men may differ as to the weight they would give the almost unanimous authority of England. I am not here concerned with assessing it but merely with noting that whatever weight it has is against Pacifism. And, of course, my duty to take that authority into account is increased by the fact that I am indebted to that society for my birth and my upbringing, for the education which has allowed me to become a Pacifist, and the tolerant laws which allow me to remain one.

So much for special human authority. The sentence of general human authority is equally clear. From the dawn of history down to the sinking of the *Terris Bay*, the world echoes with the praise of righteous war. To be a Pacifist, I must part company with Homer and Virgil, with Plato and Aristotle, with Zarathustra and the *Bhagavad-Gita*, with Cicero and Montaigne, with Iceland and with Egypt. From this point of view, I am almost tempted to reply to the Pacifist as Johnson replied to Goldsmith, 'Nay Sir, if you will not take the universal opinion of mankind, I have no more to say.'

I am aware that, though Hooker thought 'the general and perpetual voice of men is as the sentence of God Himself', yet many who hear will give it little or no weight. This disregard of human authority may have two roots. It may spring from the belief that human history is a simple, unilinear movement from worse to better – what is called a belief in Progress – so that any given generation is always in all respects wiser than all previous generations. To those who believe thus, our ancestors are superseded and there seems nothing improbable in the claim that the whole world was wrong until the day before yesterday and now has suddenly become right. With such people I confess I cannot argue, for I do not share their basic assumption. Believers in progress rightly note that in the world of machines the new model supersedes the old; from this they falsely infer a similar kind of supercession in such things as virtue and wisdom.

But human authority may be discounted on a quite different ground. It may be held, at least by a Christian Pacifist, that the human race is fallen and corrupt, so that even the consent of great and wise human teachers and great nations widely separated in time and place affords no clue whatsoever to the good. If this contention is being made, we must then turn to our next head, that of Divine Authority.

I shall consider Divine Authority only in terms of Christianity. Of the other civilised religions I believe that only one – Buddhism – is genuinely Pacifist; and anyway I am not well enough informed about them to discuss them with profit. And when we turn to Christianity, we find Pacifism based almost exclusively on certain of the sayings of Our Lord Himself. If those sayings do not establish the Pacifist position, it is vain to try to base it on the general *securus judicat* of Christendom as a whole. For when I seek guidance there, I find Authority on the whole against me. Looking at the statement which is my immediate authority as an Anglican, the Thirty-Nine Articles, I find it laid down in black and white that 'it is lawful for Christian men, at the commandment of the Magistrate, to wear weapons and serve in the wars'. Dissenters may not accept this; then I can refer them to the history of the Presbyterians, which is by no means Pacifist. Papists may not accept this; then I can refer them to the ruling of Thomas Aquinas that 'even as princes lawfully defend their land by the sword against disturbance from within, so it belongs to them to defend it by the sword from enemies without'. Or if you demand patristic authority, I give you St Augustine, 'If Christian discipleship wholly reprobated war, then to those who sought the counsel of salvation in the Gospel this answer would have been given first, that they should throw away their arms and withdraw themselves altogether from being soldiers. But what was really said to them was, "Do violence to no man and be content with your pay". When he bade them to be content with their due soldiers' pay, he forbade them not to be paid as soldiers.' But of checking individual voices, there would be no end. All bodies that claim to be Churches – that is, who claim apostolic succession and accept the Creeds – have constantly blessed what they regarded as righteous arms. Doctors, bishops and popes – including, I think, the present Pope [Pius XII] – have again and again discountenanced the Pacifist position. Nor, I think, do we find a word about Pacifism in the apostolic writings, which are older than the Gospels and represent, if anything does, that original Christendom whereof the Gospels themselves are a product.

The whole Christian case for Pacifism rests, therefore, on certain Dominical utterances, such as 'Resist not evil: but whosoever shall smite thee on thy right cheek, turn to him the other also.' I am now to deal with the Christian who says this is to be taken without qualification. I need not point out – for it has doubtless been pointed out to you before – that such a Christian is obliged to take all the other hard sayings of Our Lord in the same way. For the man who has done so, who has on every occasion given to all who ask and has finally given all he has to the poor, no one will fail to feel respect. With such a man I must suppose myself to be arguing; for who would deem worth answering that inconsistent person who takes Our Lord's words *à la rigueur* when they dispense him from a possible obligation, and takes them with latitude when they demand that he should become a pauper?

There are three ways of taking the command to turn the other cheek. One is the Pacifist interpretation; it means what it says and imposes a duty of non-resistance on all men in all circumstances. Another is the minimising interpretation; it does not mean what it says but is merely an orientally hyperbolical way of saying that you should put up with a lot and be placable. Both you and I agree in rejecting this view. The conflict is therefore between the Pacifist interpretation and a third one which I am now going to propound. I think the text means exactly what it says, but with an understood reservation in favour of those obviously exceptional cases which every hearer would naturally assume to be exceptions without being told. Or to put the same thing in more logical language, I think the duty of non-resistance is here stated as regards injuries *simpliciter*, but without prejudice to anything we may have to allow later about injuries *secundum quid*. That is, in so far as the only relevant factors in the case are an injury to me by my neighbour and a desire on my part to retaliate, then I hold that Christianity commands the absolute mortification of that desire. No quarter whatever is given to the voice within us which says, 'He's done it to me, so I'll do the same to him'. But the moment you introduce other factors, of course, the problem is altered. Does anyone suppose that Our Lord's hearers understood Him to mean that if a homicidal maniac, attempting to murder a third party, tried to knock me out of the way, I must stand aside and let him get his victim? I at any rate think it impossible they could have so understood Him. I think it equally impossible that they supposed Him to mean that the best way of bringing up a child was to let it hit its parents whenever it was in a temper, or, when it had grabbed at the jam, to give it the honey also. I think the meaning of the words was perfectly clear – 'In so far as you are simply an angry man who has been hurt, mortify your anger and do not hit back' – even, one would have assumed that in so far as you are a magistrate struck by a private person, a parent struck by a child, a teacher by a scholar, a sane man by a lunatic, or a soldier by the public enemy, your duties may be very different, different because they may be then other motives than egoistic retaliation for hitting back. Indeed, as the audience were private people in a disarmed nation, it seems unlikely that they would have ever supposed Our Lord to be referring to war. War was not what they would have been thinking of. The frictions of daily life among villagers were more likely to be in their minds.

That is my chief reason for preferring this interpretation to yours. Any saying is to be taken in the sense it would naturally have borne in the time and place of utterance. But I also think that, so taken, it harmonises better with St John Baptist's words to the soldiers, and with the fact that one of the few persons whom Our Lord praised without reservation was a Roman centurion. It also allows me to suppose that the New Testament is consistent with itself. St Paul approves of the magistrate's use of the sword (Romans 13:4) and so does St Peter (1 Peter 2:14). If Our Lord's words are taken in that unqualified sense which the Pacifist demands, we shall then be forced to the conclusion that Christ's true meaning, concealed from those who lived in the same time and spoke the same language, and whom He Himself chose to be His messengers to the world, as well as from all their successors, has at last been discovered in our own time. I know there are people who will not find this sort of thing difficult to believe, just as there are people ready to maintain that the true meaning of Plato or Shakespeare, oddly concealed from their contemporaries and immediate successors, has preserved its virginity for the daring embraces of one or two modern professors. But I cannot apply to divine matters a method of exegesis which I have already rejected with contempt in my profane studies. Any theory which bases itself on a supposed 'historical Jesus', to be dug out of the Gospels and then set up in opposition to Christian teaching, is suspect. There have been too many historical Jesuses – a liberal Jesus, a pneumatic Jesus, a Barthian Jesus, a Marxist Jesus. They are the cheap crop of each publisher's list like the new Napoleons and new Queen Victorias. It is not to such phantoms that I look for my faith and my salvation.

Christian authority, then, fails me in my search for Pacifism. It remains to inquire whether, if I still remain a Pacifist, I ought to suspect the secret influence of any passion. I hope you will not here misunderstand me. I do not intend to join in any of the jibes to which those of your persuasion are exposed in the popular press. Let me say at the outset that I think it unlikely there is anyone present less courageous than myself. But let me also say that there is no man alive so virtuous that he need feel himself insulted at being asked to consider the possibility of a warping passion when the choice is one between so much happiness and so much misery. For let us make no mistake. All that we fear from all the kinds of adversity, severally, is collected together in the life of a soldier on active service. Like sickness, it threatens pain and death. Like poverty, it threatens ill lodging, cold, heat, thirst and hunger. Like slavery, it threatens toil, humiliation, injustice and arbitrary rule. Like exile, it separates you from all you love. Like the galleys, it imprisons you at close quarters with uncongenial companions. It threatens *every* temporal evil – every evil except dishonour and final perdition, and those who bear it like it no better than you would like it. On the other side, though it may not be your fault, it is certainly a fact that Pacifism threatens you with almost nothing. Some public opprobrium, yes, from people whose opinion you discount and whose society you do not frequent, soon recompensed by the warm mutual approval which exists, inevitably, in any minority group. For the rest it offers you a continuance of the life you know and love, among the people and in the surroundings you know and love. It offers you time to lay the foundations of a career; for whether you will or no, you can hardly help getting the jobs for which the discharged soldiers will one day look in vain. You do not even have to fear, as Pacifists may have had to fear in the last war, that public opinion will punish you when the peace comes. For we have learned now that though the world is slow to forgive, it is quick to forget.

This, then, is why I am not a Pacifist. If I tried to become one, I should find a very doubtful factual basis, an obscure train of reasoning, a weight of authority both human and Divine against me, and strong grounds for suspecting that my wishes had directed my decision. As I have said, moral decisions do not admit of mathematical certainty. It may be, after all, that Pacifism is right. But it seems to me very long odds, longer odds than I would care to take with the voice of almost all humanity against me.

DANGERS OF
NATIONAL REPENTANCE

Published in The Guardian *(15 March 1940), this essay was reproduced in* Undeceptions *(1971) and* Christian Reunion *(1990).*

The idea of national repentance seems at first sight to provide such an edifying contrast to that national self-righteousness of which England is so often accused and with which she entered (or is said to have entered) the last war, that a Christian naturally turns to it with hope. Young Christians especially – last year undergraduates and first year curates – are turning to it in large numbers. They are ready to believe that England bears part of the guilt for the present war, and ready to admit their own share in the guilt of England. What that share is, I do not find it easy to determine. Most of these young men were children, and none of them had a vote or the experience which would enable them to use a vote wisely, when England made many of those decisions to which the present disorders could plausibly be traced. Are they, perhaps, repenting what they have in no sense done?

If they are, it might be supposed that their error is very harmless: men fail so often to repent their real sins that the occasional repentance of an imaginary sin might appear almost desirable. But what actually happens (I have watched it happening) to the youthful national penitent is a little more complicated than that. England is not a natural agent, but a civil society. When we speak of England's actions we mean the actions of the British Government. The young man who is called upon to repent of England's foreign policy is really being called upon to repent the acts of his neighbour; for a Foreign Secretary or a Cabinet Minister is certainly a neighbour. And repentance presupposes condemnation. The first and fatal charm of national repentance is, therefore, the encouragement it gives us to turn from the bitter task of repenting our own sins to the congenial one of bewailing – but, first, of denouncing – the conduct of others. If it were clear to the young penitent that this is what he is doing, no doubt he would remember the law of charity. Unfortunately the very

terms in which national repentance is recommended to him conceal its
true nature. By a dangerous figure of speech, he calls the Government not
'they' but 'we'. And since, as penitents, we are not encouraged to be charitable to our own sins, nor to give ourselves the benefit of any doubt, a
Government which is called 'we' is *ipso facto* placed beyond the sphere of
charity or even of justice. You can say anything you please about it. You
can indulge in the popular vice of detraction without restraint, and yet
feel all the time that you are practising contrition. A group of such young
penitents will say, 'Let us repent our national sins'; what they mean is,
'Let us attribute to our neighbour (even our Christian neighbour) in the
Cabinet, whenever we disagree with him, every abominable motive that
Satan can suggest to our fancy.'

Such an escape from personal repentance into that tempting region

> *Where passions have the privilege to work*
> *And never hear the sound of their own names,*[1]

would be welcome to the moral cowardice of anyone. But it is doubly
attractive to the young intellectual. When a man over forty tries to repent
the sins of England and to love her enemies, he is attempting something
costly; for he was brought up to certain patriotic sentiments which
cannot be mortified without a struggle. But an educated man who is now
in his twenties usually has no such sentiment to mortify. In art, in literature, in politics, he has been, ever since he can remember, one of an angry
and restless minority; he has drunk-in almost with his mother's milk a
distrust of English statesmen and a contempt for the manners, pleasures
and enthusiasms of his less-educated fellow countrymen. All Christians
know that they must forgive their enemies. But 'my enemy' primarily
means the man whom I am really tempted to hate and traduce. If you
listen to young Christian intellectuals talking, you will soon find out who
their real enemy is. He seems to have two names – Colonel Blimp and
'the businessman'. I suspect that the latter usually means the speaker's
father, but that is speculation. What is certain is that in asking such
people to forgive the Germans and Russians and to open their eyes to the
sins of England, you are asking them, not to mortify, but to indulge, their
ruling passion. I do not mean that what you are asking them is not right
and necessary in itself; we must forgive all our enemies or be damned. But
it is emphatically not the exhortation which your audience needs. The

[1] Wordsworth, *The Prelude*, XI, 230.

communal sins which they should be told to repent are those of their own age and class – its contempt for the uneducated, its readiness to suspect evil, is self-righteous provocations of public obloquy, its breaches of the Fifth Commandment.[2] Of these sins I have heard nothing among them. Till I do, I must think their candour towards the national enemy a rather inexpensive virtue. If a man cannot forgive the Colonel Blimp next door whom he has seen, how shall he forgive the Dictators whom he hath not seen?

Is it not, then, the duty of the Church to preach national repentance? I think it is. But the office – like many others – can be profitably discharged only by those who discharge it with reluctance. We know that a man may have to 'hate' his mother for the Lord's sake.[3] The sight of a Christian rebuking his mother, though tragic, may be edifying; but only if we are quite sure that he has been a good son and that, in his rebuke, spiritual zeal is triumphing, not without agony, over strong natural affection. The moment there is reason to suspect that he *enjoys* rebuking her – that he believes himself to be rising above the natural level while he is still, in reality, grovelling below it in the unnatural – the spectacle becomes merely disgusting. The hard sayings of our Lord are wholesome to those only who find them hard. There is a terrible chapter in M. Mauriac's *Vie de Jésus*. When the Lord spoke of brother and child against parent, the other disciples were horrified. No so Judas. He took to it as a duck takes to water: *'Pourquoi cette stupeur?, se demande Judas ... Il aime dans le Christ cette vue simple, ce regard de Dieu sur l'horreur humaine.'*[4] For there are two states of mind which face the Dominical paradoxes without flinching. God guard us from one of them.

[2] Honour thy father and thy mother; that thy days may be long in the land which the Lord thy God giveth thee' (Exodus 22:12).
[3] Luke 14:26: 'If any man come to me, and hate not his father, and mother, and wife, and children, and brethren, and sisters, yea, and his own life also, he cannot be my disciple.'
[4] François Mauriac, *Vie de Jésus* (Paris, 1936), ch. 9. ' "Why this stupefaction?" asked Judas ... He loved in Christ his simple view of things, his divine glance at human depravity.'

36

TWO WAYS WITH THE SELF

This essay was first published in The Guardian *(3 May 1940) and was reproduced in* Undeceptions *(1971) and* Christian Reunion *(1990).*

Self-renunciation is thought to be, and indeed is, very near the core of Christian ethics. When Aristotle writes in praise of a certain kind of self-love, we may feel, despite the careful distinctions which he draws between the legitimate and the illegitimate *Philautia,*[1] that here we strike something essentially sub-Christian. It is more difficult, however, to decide what we think of St François de Sales's chapter, *De la douceur envers nous-mêmes,*[2] where we are forbidden to indulge resentment even against ourselves and advised to reprove even our own faults *avec des remonstrances douces et tranquilles,*[3] feeling more compassion than passion. In the same spirit, Lady Julian of Norwich would have us 'loving and peaceable', not only to our 'even-Christians', but to 'ourself'.[4] Even the New Testament bids me love my neighbour 'as myself',[5] which would be a horrible command if the self were simply to be hated. Yet Our Lord also says that a true disciple must 'hate his own life'.[6]

We must not explain this apparent contradiction by saying that self-love is right up to a certain point and wrong beyond that point. The question is not one of degree. There are two kinds of self-hatred which look rather alike in their earlier stages, but of which one is wrong from the beginning and the other right to the end. When Shelley speaks of self-contempt as the source of cruelty, or when a later poet says that he has no stomach for the man 'who loathes his neighbour as himself', they are

---

[1] *Nicomachean Ethics*, Book 9, ch. 8.
[2] Part III, ch. 9, 'Of Meekness towards Ourselves' in the *Introduction to the Devout Life* (Lyons, 1609).
[3] With mild and calm remonstrances.
[4] *Sixteen Revelations of Divine Love*, ch. 44.
[5] Matthew 19:19; 22:39; Mark 12:31, 33; Romans 13:9; Galatians 5:14; James 2:8.
[6] Luke 14:26; John 12:25.

referring to a very real and very unChristian hatred of the self which may make diabolical a man whom common selfishness would have left (at least, for a while) merely animal. The hard-boiled economist or psychologist of our own day, recognising the 'ideological taint' or Freudian motive in his own make-up, does not necessarily learn Christian humility. He may end in what is called a 'low view' of all souls, including his own, which expresses itself in cynicism or cruelty, or both. Even Christians, if they accept in certain forms the doctrine of total depravity, are not always free from the danger. The logical conclusion of the process is the worship of suffering – for others as well as for the self – which we see, if I read it aright, in Mr David Lindsay's *Voyage to Arcturus,* or that extraordinary vacancy which Shakespeare depicts at the end of *Richard 111.* Richard in his agony tries to turn to self-love. But he has been 'seeing through' all emotions so long that he 'sees through' even this. It becomes a mere tautology: 'Richard loves Richard; that is, I am I'.[7]

Now, the self can be regarded in two ways. On the one hand, it is God's creature, an occasion of love and rejoicing; now, indeed, hateful in condition, but to be pitied and healed. On the other hand, it is that one self of all others which is called *I* and *me,* and which on that ground puts forward an irrational claim to preference. This claim is to be not only hated, but simply killed; 'never', as George MacDonald says, 'to be allowed a moment's respite from eternal death'. The Christian must wage endless war against the clamour of the *ego* as *ego:* but he loves and approves selves as such, though not their sins. The very self-love which he has to reject is to him a specimen of how he ought to feel to all selves; and he may hope that when he has truly learned (which will hardly be in this life) to love his neighbour as himself, he may then be able to love himself as his neighbour: that is, with charity instead of partiality. The other kind of self-hatred, on the contrary, hates selves as such. It begins by accepting the special value of the particular self called *me,* then, wounded in its pride to find that such a darling object should be so disappointing, it seeks revenge, first upon that self, then on all. Deeply egoistic, but now with an inverted egoism, it uses the revealing argument, 'I don't spare myself' – with the implication 'then *a fortiori* I need not spare others' – and becomes like the centurion in Tacitus, *immitior quia toleraverat.*[8]

The wrong asceticism torments the self: the right kind kills the selfness. We must die daily: but it is better to love the self than to love nothing, and to pity the self than to pity no one.

[7] *Richard III*, v, iii, 184.
[8] 'More relentless because he had endured (it himself).' *Annals,* Book I, section 10, line 14.

37

MEDITATION ON THE
THIRD COMMANDMENT

First published in The Guardian *(10 January 1941) this essay was
reproduced in* Undeceptions *(1971) and* Christian Reunion *(1990).*

From many letters to *The Guardian,* and from much that is printed elsewhere, we learn of the growing desire for a Christian 'party', a Christian
'front', or a Christian 'platform' in politics. Nothing is so earnestly to be
wished as a real assault by Christianity on the politics of the world:
nothing, at first sight, so fitted to deliver this assault as a Christian Party.
But it is odd that certain difficulties in this programme should be already
neglected while the printer's ink is hardly dry on M. Maritain's
Scholastiscism and Politics.[1]

The Christian Party must either confine itself to stating what ends are
desirable and what means are lawful, or else it must go further and select
from among the lawful means those which it deems possible and efficacious and give to these its practical support. If it chooses the first alternative, it will not be a political party. Nearly all parties agree in professing
ends which we admit to be desirable – security, a living wage, and the best
adjustment between the claims of order and freedom. What distinguishes
one party from another is the championship of means. We do not dispute
whether the citizens are to be made happy, but whether an egalitarian or a
hierarchical State, whether capitalism or socialism, whether despotism or
democracy is most likely to make them so.

What, then, will the Christian Party actually do? Philarchus, a devout
Christian, is convinced that temporal welfare can flow only from a
Christian life, and that a Christian life can be promoted in the community only by an authoritarian State which has swept away the last vestiges
of the hated 'Liberal' infection. He thinks Fascism not so much an evil as
a good thing perverted, regards democracy as a monster whose victory

---

[1] J. Maritain, *Scholasticism and Politics*, M.J. Adler (London, 1950).

would be a defeat for Christianity, and is tempted to accept even Fascist assistance, hoping that he and his friends will prove the leaven in a lump of British Fascists.

Stativus is equally devout and equally Christian. Deeply conscious of the Fall and therefore convinced that no human creature can be trusted with more than the minimum power over his fellows, and anxious to preserve the claims of God from any infringement by those of Caesar, he still sees in democracy the only hope of Christian freedom. He is tempted to accept aid from champions of the *status quo* whose commercial or imperial motives bear hardly even a veneer of theism.

Finally, we have Spartacus, also a Christian and also sincere, full of the prophetic and dominical denunciations of riches, and certain that the 'historical Jesus', long betrayed by the Apostles, the Fathers, and the churches, demands of us a Left revolution. And he also is tempted to accept help from unbelievers who profess themselves quite openly to be the enemies of God.

The three types represented by these three Christians presumably come together to form a Christian Party. Either a deadlock ensues (and there the history of the Christian Party ends) or else one of the three succeeds in floating a party and driving the other two, with their followers, out of its ranks. The new party – being probably a minority of the Christians who are themselves a minority of the citizens – will be too small to be effective. In practice, it will have to attach itself to the unChristian party nearest to it in beliefs about means – to the Fascists if Philarchus has won, to the Conservatives if Stativus, to the Communists if Spartacus. It remains to ask how the resulting situation will differ from that in which Christians find themselves today.

It is not reasonable to suppose that such a Christian Party will acquire new powers of leavening the infidel organisation to which it is attached. Why should it? Whatever it calls itself, it will represent, not Christendom, but a part of Christendom. The principle which divides it from its brethren and unites it to its political allies will not be theological. It will have no authority to speak for Christianity; it will have no more power than the political skill its members give it to control the behaviour of its unbelieving allies. But there will be a real, and most disastrous, novelty. It will be not simply a *part* of Christendom, but *a part claiming to be the whole*. By the mere act of calling itself the Christian Party it implicitly accuses all Christians who do not join it of apostasy and betrayal. It will be exposed, in an aggravated degree, to that temptation which the Devil spares none of us at any time – the temptation of claiming for our favourite opinions that kind and degree of certainty and authority which really belongs only to our Faith. The danger of mistaking our merely natural, though perhaps legitimate, enthusiasms for holy zeal, is always great. Can any more fatal expedient be devised for increasing it than that of dubbing a small band of Fascists, Communists, or Democrats 'the Christian Party'? The demon inherent in every party is at all times ready enough to disguise himself as the Holy Ghost; the formation of a Christian Party means handing over to him the most efficient make-up we can find. And when once the disguise has succeeded, his commands will presently be taken to abrogate all moral laws and to justify whatever the unbelieving allies of the 'Christian' Party wish to do. If ever Christian men can be brought to think treachery and murder the lawful means of establishing the *régime* they desire, and faked trials, religious persecution and organised hooliganism the lawful means of maintaining it, it will, surely, be by just such a process as this. The history of the late medieval pseudo-Crusaders, of the Covenanters,[2] of the Orangemen,[3] should be remembered. On those who add 'Thus saith the Lord' to their merely human utterances descends the doom of a conscience which seems clearer and clearer the more it is loaded with sin.

All this comes from pretending that God has spoken when He has not spoken. He will not settle the two brothers' inheritance: 'Who made Me a judge or a divider over you?' (Luke 12:14). By the natural light He has shown us what means are lawful: to find out which one is efficacious He has given us brains. The rest He has left to us.

M. Maritain has hinted at the only way in which Christianity (as opposed to schismatics blasphemously claiming to represent it) can influence politics. Nonconformity has influenced modern English history not because there was a Nonconformist Party but because there was a Nonconformist conscience which all parties had to take into account. An interdenominational Christian Voters' Society might draw up a list of assurances about ends and means which every member was expected to exact from any political party as the price of his support. Such a society might claim to represent Christendom far more truly than any 'Christian Front'; and for that reason I should be prepared, in principle, for membership and obedience to be obligatory on Christians. 'So all it comes down to is pestering MPs with letters?' Yes: just that. I think such pestering combines the dove and the serpent. I think it means a world

[2] The bodies of Presbyterians in Scotland who in the sixteenth and seventeenth centuries bound themselves by religious and political oaths to maintain the cause of their religion.

[3] Members of the Orange Association (founded in 1795) who defended the cause of Protestantism in Ireland.

where parties have to take care not to alienate Christians, instead of a world where Christians have to be 'loyal' to infidel parties. Finally, I think a minority can influence politics only by 'pestering' or by becoming a 'party' in the new continental sense (that is, a secret society of murderers and blackmailers) which is impossible to Christians. But I had forgotten. There is a third way – by becoming a majority. He who converts his neighbour has performed the most practical Christian-political act of all.

[38]
ON ETHICS

Probably written a few years before The Abolition of Man *(1943), this essay was published for the first time in* Christian Reflections *(1998).*

It is often asserted in modern England that the world must return to Christian ethics in order to preserve civilisation, or even in order to save the human species from destruction. It is sometimes asserted in reply that Christian ethics have been the greatest obstacle to human progress and that we must take care never to return to a bondage from which we have at last so fortunately escaped. I will not weary you with a repetition of the common arguments by which either view could be supported. My task is a different one. Though I am myself a Christian, and even a dogmatic Christian untinged with Modernist reservations and committed to supernaturalism in its full rigour, I find myself quite unable to take my place beside the upholders of the first view. The whole debate between those who demand and those who deprecate a return to Christian ethics, seems to me to involve presuppositions which I cannot allow. The question between the contending parties has been wrongly put.

I must begin by distinguishing the senses in which we may speak of ethical systems and of the differences between them. We may, on the one hand, mean by an ethical system a body of ethical injunctions. In this sense, when we speak of Stoical Ethics we mean the system which strongly commends suicide (under certain conditions) and enjoins Apathy in the technical sense, the extinction of the emotions: when we speak of Aristotelian ethics we mean the system which finds in Virtuous Pride or Magnanimity the virtue that presupposes and includes all other virtues; when we speak of Christian ethics we mean the system that commands humility, forgiveness, and (in certain circumstances) martyrdom. The differences, from this point of view, are differences of content. But we also sometimes speak of Ethical Systems when we mean systematic analyses and explanations of our moral experience. Thus the expression 'Kantian Ethics' signifies not primarily a body of commands – Kant did not differ remarkably from other men on the content of ethics – but the doctrine of the Categorical Imperative. From this point of view Stoical Ethics is the system which defines moral behaviour by conformity to Nature, or the whole, or Providence – terms almost interchangeable in Stoical thought: Aristotelian ethics is the system of eudaemonism: Christian ethics, the system which, whether by exalting Faith above Works, by asserting that love fulfils the Law, or by demanding Regeneration, makes duty a self-transcending concept and endeavours to escape from the region of mere morality.

It would of course be naive to suppose that there is no profound connection between an ethical system in the one sense and an ethical system in the other. The philosopher's or theologian's theory of ethics arises out of the practical ethics he already holds and attempts to obey; and again, the theory, once formed, reacts on his judgement of what ought to be done. That is a truth in no danger of being neglected by an age so steeped in historicism[1] as ours. We are, if anything, too deeply imbued with the sense of period, too eager to trace a common spirit in the ethical practice and ethical theory, in the economics, institutions, art, dress and language of a society. It must, however, also be insisted that Ethical Systems in the one sense do not differ in a direct ratio to the difference of Ethical Systems in another. The number of actions about whose ethical quality a Stoic, an Aristotelian, a Thomist, a Kantian, and a Utilitarian would agree is, after all, very large. The very act of studying diverse ethical theories, as theories, exaggerates the practical differences between them. While we are studying them from that point of view we naturally and, for that purpose, rightly seize on the marginal case where the theoretical difference goes with a contradiction between the injunctions, because it is the *experimentum crucis*. But the exaggeration useful in one inquiry must not be carried over into other inquiries.

When modern writers urge us to return, or not to return, to Christian Ethics, I presume they mean Christian Ethics in our first sense; a body of injunctions, not a theory as to the origin, sanctions, or ultimate significance, of those injunctions. If they do not mean that, then they should not talk about a return to Christian Ethics but simply about a return to Christianity. I will at any rate assume that in this debate Christian Ethics means a body of injunctions.

And now my difficulties begin. A debate about the desirability of adopting Christian Ethics seems to proceed upon two presuppositions.

[1] See Lewis's essay on 'Historicism', p. 621.

(1) That Christian Ethics is one among several alternative bodies of injunctions, so clearly distinct from one another that the whole future of our species in this planet depends on our choice between them. (2) That we to whom the disputants address their pleadings, are for the moment standing outside all these systems in a sort of ethical vacuum, ready to enter whichever of them is most convincingly recommended to us. And it does not appear to me that either presupposition corresponds at all closely or sensitively to the reality.

Consider with me for a moment the first presupposition. Did Christian Ethics really enter the world as a novelty, a new, peculiar set of commands, to which a man could be in the strict sense *converted*? I say converted to the practical ethics: he could of course be converted to the Christian faith, he could accept, not only as a novelty, but as a transcendent novelty, a mystery hidden from all eternity, the deity and resurrection of Jesus, the Atonement, the forgiveness of sins. But these novelties themselves set a rigid limit to the novelty we can assume in the ethical injunctions. The convert accepted forgiveness of sins. But of sins against what Law? Some new law promulgated by the Christians? But that is nonsensical. It would be the mockery of a tyrant to forgive a man for doing what had never been forbidden until the very moment at which the forgiveness was announced. The idea (at least in its grossest and most popular form) that Christianity brought a new ethical code into the world is a grave error. If it had done so, then we should have to conclude that all who first preached it wholly misunderstood their own message: for all of them, its Founder, His precursor, His apostles, came demanding repentance and offering forgiveness, a demand and an offer both meaningless except on the assumption of a moral law already known and already broken.

It is far from my intention to deny that we find in Christian ethics a deepening, an internalisation, a few changes of emphasis, in the moral code. But only serious ignorance of Jewish and Pagan culture would lead anyone to the conclusion that it is a radically new thing. Essentially, Christianity is not the promulgation of a moral discovery. It is addressed only to penitents, only to those who admit their disobedience to the known moral law. It offers forgiveness for having broken, and supernatural help towards keeping, that law, and by so doing reaffirms it. A Christian who understands his own religion laughs when unbelievers expect to trouble

---

[2] Readers will have already recognized themes in this paper which recall the main argument of Lewis's *Abolition of Man* – a book which is, in my opinion, an all but indispensable introduction to the entire *corpus* of Lewisiana. Though I am unable to establish a date for this paper, my guess is that it anticipates the *Abolition* by a year or so. On the similarities in various ethical systems, see his 'Illustrations of the *Tao*' (= The Way, or the Natural Law) which forms the Appendix to *The Abolition of Man.* — W.H.

him by the assertion that Jesus uttered no command which had not been anticipated by the Rabbis – few, indeed, which cannot be paralleled in classical, ancient Egyptian, Ninevite, Babylonian, or Chinese texts.[2] We have long recognised that truth with rejoicing. Our faith is not pinned on a crank.

The second presupposition – that of an ethical vacuum in which we stand deciding what code we will adopt – is not quite so easily dealt with, but I believe it to be, in the long run, equally misleading. Of course, historically or chronologically, a man need not be supposed to stand outside all ethical codes at the moment when you exhort him to adopt Christian ethics. A man who is attending one lecturer or one physician may be advised to exchange him for another. But he cannot come to a decision without first reaching a moment of indecision. There must be a point at which he feels himself attached to neither and weighs their rival merits. Adherence to either is inconsistent with choice. In the same way, the demand that we should reassume, or refrain from reassuming, the Christian code of ethics, invites us to enter a state in which we shall be unattached.

I am not, of course, denying that some men at some times can be in an ethical vacuum, adhering to no Ethical System. But most of those who are in that state are by no means engaged in deciding what system they shall adopt, for such men do not often propose to adopt any. They are more often concerned with getting out of gaols or asylums. Our question is not about them. Our question is whether the sort of men who urge us to return (or not to return) to Christian Ethics, or the sort of men who listen to such appeals, can enter the ethical vacuum which seems to be involved in the very conception of choosing an ethical code. And the best way of answering this question is (as sometimes happens) by asking another first. Supposing we can enter the vacuum and view all Ethical Systems from the outside, what sort of motives can we then expect to find for entering any one of them?

One thing is immediately clear. We can have no *ethical* motives for adopting any of these systems. It cannot, while we are in the vacuum, be our duty to emerge from it. An act of duty is an act of obedience to the moral law. But by definition we are standing outside all codes of moral law. A man with no ethical allegiance can have no ethical motive for adopting one. If he had, it would prove that he was not really in the vacuum at all. How then does it come about that men who talk as if we could stand outside all moralities and choose among them as a woman chooses a hat, nevertheless exhort us (and often in passionate tones) to make some one particular choice? They have a ready answer.

Almost invariably they recommend some code of ethics on the ground that it, and it alone, will preserve civilisation, or the human race. What they seldom tell us is whether the preservation of the human race is itself a duty or whether they expect us to aim at it on some other ground.

Now if it is a duty, then clearly those who exhort us to it are not themselves really in a moral vacuum, and do not seriously believe that we are in a moral vacuum. At the very least they accept, and count on our accepting, one moral injunction. Their moral code is, admittedly, singularly poor in content. Its solitary command, compared with the richly articulated codes of Aristotle, Confucius, or Aquinas, suggests that it is a mere residuum; as the arts of certain savages suggest that they are the last vestige of a vanished civilisation. But there is a profound difference between having a fanatical and narrow morality and having no morality at all. If they were really in a moral vacuum, whence could they have derived the idea of even a single duty?

In order to evade the difficulty, it may be suggested that the preservation of our species is not a moral imperative but an end prescribed by Instinct. To this I reply, firstly, that it is very doubtful whether there is such an instinct; and secondly, that if there were, it would not do the work which those who invoke instinct in this context demand of it.

Have we in fact such an instinct? We must here be careful about the meaning of the word. In English the word *instinct* is often loosely used for what ought rather to be called appetite: thus we speak of the sexual instinct. *Instinct* in this sense means an impulse which appears in consciousness as desire, and whose fulfilment is marked by pleasure. That we have no instinct (in this sense) to preserve our species, seems to me self-evident. Desire is directed to the concrete – this woman, this plate of soup, this glass of beer: but the preservation of the species is a high abstraction which does not even enter the mind of unreflective people, and affects even cultured minds most at those times when they are least instinctive. But instinct is also, and more properly, used to mean Behaviour as if from knowledge. Thus certain insects carry out complicated actions which have in fact the result that their eggs are hatched and their larvae nourished: and since (rightly or wrongly) we refuse to attribute conscious design and foreknowledge to the agent we say that it has acted 'by instinct'. What that means on the subjective side, how the matter appears, if it appears at all, to the insect, I suppose we do not know. To say, in this sense, that we have an instinct to preserve the human race, would be to say that we find ourselves compelled, we know not how, to perform acts which in fact (though that was not our purpose) tend to its preservation. This seems very unlikely.

What are these acts? And if they exist, what is the purpose of urging us to preserve the race by adopting (or avoiding) Christian Ethics? Had not the job better be left to instinct?

Yet again, *Instinct* may be used to denote these strong impulses which are, like the appetites, hard to deny though they are not, like the appetites, directed to concrete physical pleasure. And this, I think, is what people really mean when they speak of an instinct to preserve the human race. They mean that we have a natural, unreflective, spontaneous impulse to do this, as we have to preserve our own offspring. And here we are thrown back on the debatable evidence of introspection. I do not find that I have this impulse, and I do not see evidence that other men have it. Do not misunderstand me. I would not be thought a monster. I acknowledge the preservation of man as an end to which my own preservation and happiness are subordinate; what I deny is that that end has been prescribed to me by a powerful, spontaneous impulse. The truth seems to me to be that we have such an impulse to preserve our children and grandchildren, an impulse which progressively weakens as we carry our minds further and further into the abyss of future generations, and which, if left to its own spontaneous strength, soon dies out altogether. Let me ask anyone in this audience who is a father whether he has a spontaneous impulse to sacrifice his own son for the sake of the human species in general. I am not asking whether he would so sacrifice his son. I am asking whether, if he did so, he would be obeying a spontaneous impulse. Will not every father among you reply that if this sacrifice were demanded of him and if he made it, he would do so not in obedience to a natural impulse but in hard-won defiance of it? Such an act, no less than the immolation of oneself, would be a triumph over nature.

But let us leave that difficulty on one side. Let us suppose, for purposes of argument, that there really is an 'instinct' (in whatever sense) to preserve civilisation, or the human race. Our instincts are obviously in conflict. The satisfaction of one demands the denial of another. And obviously the instinct, if there is one, to preserve humanity, is the one of all others whose satisfaction is likely to entail the greatest frustration of my remaining instincts. My hunger and thirst, my sexual desires, my family affections, are all going to be interfered with. And remember, we are still supposed to be in the vacuum, outside all ethical systems. On what conceivable ground, in an ethical void, on the assumption that the preservation of the species is not a moral but a merely instinctive end, can I be asked to gratify my instinct for the preservation of the species by adopting a moral code? Why should this instinct be preferred to all my others? It is certainly not my strongest. Even if it were, why should I not fight against it as a dipsomaniac is exhorted to fight against his tyrannous desire? Why do my advisers assume from the very outset, without argument, that this instinct should be given a dictatorship in my soul? Let us not be cheated with words. It is no use to say that this is the deepest, or highest, or most fundamental, or noblest of my instincts. Such words either mean that it is my strongest instinct (which is false and would be no reason for obeying it even if it were true) or else conceal a surreptitious reintroduction of the ethical.

And in fact the ethical has been reintroduced. Or, more accurately, it has never really been banished. The moral vacuum was from the outset a mere figment. Those who expect us to adopt a moral code as a means to the preservation of the species have themselves already a moral code and tacitly assume that we have one too. Their starting point is a purely moral maxim *That humanity ought to be preserved*. The introduction of instinct is futile. If you do not arrange our instincts in a hierarchy of comparative dignity, it is idle to tell us to obey instinct, for the instincts are at war. If you do, then you are arranging them in obedience to a moral principle, passing an ethical judgement upon them. If instinct is your only standard, no instinct is to be preferred to another: for each of them will claim to be gratified at the expense of all the rest. Those who urge us to choose a moral code are already moralists. We may throw away the preposterous picture of a wholly unethical man confronted with a series of alternative codes and making his free choice between them. Nothing of the kind occurs. When a man is wholly unethical he does not choose between ethical codes. And those who say they are choosing between ethical codes are already assuming a code.

What, then, shall we say of the maxim which turns out to be present from the beginning – *That humanity ought to be preserved*? Where do we get it from? Or, to be more concrete, where do I get it from? Certainly, I can point to no moment in time at which I first embraced it. It is, so far as I can make out, a late and abstract generalisation from all the moral teaching I have ever had. If I now wanted to find authority for it, I should have no need to appeal to my own religion. I could point to the confession of the righteous soul in the Egyptian *Book of the Dead* – 'I have not slain men.' I could find in the Babylonian Hymn that he who meditates oppression will find his house overturned. I would find, nearer home in the Elder Edda, that 'Man is man's delight.' I would find in Confucius that the people should first be multiplied, then enriched, and then instructed. If I wanted the spirit of all these precepts generalised I could find in Locke that 'by the fundamental law of Nature Man is to be preserved as much as possible'.

Thus from my point of view there is no particular mystery about this maxim. It is what I have been taught, explicitly and implicitly, by my nurse, my parents, my religion, by sages or poets from every culture of which I have any knowledge. To reach this maxim I have no need to choose one ethical code among many and excogitate impossible motives for adopting it. The difficulty would be to find codes that contradict it. And when I had found them they would turn out to be, not radically different things, but codes in which the same principle is for some reason restricted or truncated: in which the preservation and perfection of Man shrinks to that of the tribe, the class, or the family, or the nation. They could all be reached by mere subtraction from what seems to be the general code: they differ from it not as ox from man but as dwarf from man.

Thus far as concerns myself. But where do those others get it from, those others who claimed to be standing outside all ethical codes? Surely there is no doubt about the answer. They found it where I found it. They hold it by inheritance and training from the general (if not strictly universal) human tradition. They would never have reached their solitary injunction if they had really begun in an ethical vacuum. They have trusted the general human tradition at least to the extent of taking over from it one maxim.

But of course in that tradition the maxim did not stand alone. I found beside it many other injunctions: special duties to parents and elders, special duties to my wife and child, duties of good faith and veracity, duties to the weak, the poor and the desolate (these latter not confined, as some think, to the Judaic-Christian texts). And for me, again, there is no difficulty. I accept all these commands, all on the same authority. But there is surely a great difficulty for those who retain one and desire to drop the rest? And now we come to the heart of our subject.

There are many people in the modern world who offer us, as they say, new moralities. But as we have just seen there can be no moral motive for entering a new morality unless the motive is borrowed from the traditional morality, which is neither Christian nor Pagan, neither Eastern nor Western, neither ancient nor modern, but general. The question then arises as to the reasonableness of taking one maxim and rejecting the rest. If the remaining maxims have no authority, what is the authority of the one you have selected to retain? If it has authority, why have the others no authority? Thus a scientific Humanist may urge us to get rid of what he might call our inherited *Taboo* morality and realise that the total exploitation of nature for the comfort and security of posterity is the sole end. His system clashes with mine, say, at the point where he demands the compulsory euthanasia of the aged or the unfit. But the duty of caring for posterity, on which he bases his whole system, has no other source than that some tradition which bids me honour my parents and do no murder (a prohibition I find in the *Voluspa* as well as in the Decalogue). If, as he would have me believe, I have been misled by the tradition when it taught me my duty to my parents, how do I know it has not misled me equally in prescribing a duty to posterity? Again, we may have a fanatical Nationalist who tells me to throw away my anti-quated scruples about universal justice and benevolence and adopt a system in which nothing but the wealth and power of my own country matters. But the difficulty is the same. I learned of a special duty to my own country in the same place where I also learned of a general duty to men as such. If the tradition was wrong about the one duty, on what ground does the Nationalist ask me to believe that it was right about the other? The Communist is in the same position. I may well agree with him that exploitation is an evil and that those who do the work should reap the reward. But I only believe this because I accept certain traditional notions of justice. When he goes on to attack justice as part of my *bourgeois* ideology, he takes away the very ground on which I can reasonably be asked to accept his new communistic code.

Let us very clearly understand that, in a certain sense, it is no more possible to invent a new ethics than to place a new sun in the sky. Some precept from traditional morality always has to be assumed. We never start from a *tabula rasa*: if we did, we should end, ethically speaking, with a *tabula rasa*. New moralities can only be contractions or expansions of something already given. And all the specifically modern attempts at new moralities are contractions. They proceed by retaining some traditional precepts and rejecting others: but the only real authority behind those which they retain is the very same authority which they flout in rejecting others. Of course this inconsistency is concealed; usually, as we have seen, by a refusal to recognise the precepts that are retained as moral precepts at all.

But many other causes contribute to the concealment. As in the life of the individual so in that of a community, particular circumstances set a temporary excess of value on some one end. When we are in love, the beloved, when we are ill, health, when we are poor, money, when we are frightened, safety, seems the only thing worth having. Hence he who speaks to a class, a nation, or a culture, in the grip of some passion, will not find it difficult to insinuate into their minds the fatal idea of some one finite good which is worth achieving at all costs, and building an eccentric ethical system on that foundation. It is, of course, no genuinely new system. Whatever the chosen goal may be, the idea that I should seek it for my class or culture or nation at the expense of my own personal satisfaction has no authority save that which it derives from traditional morality. But in the emotion of the moment this is overlooked.

Added to this, may we not recognise in modern thought a very serious exaggeration of the ethical differences between different cultures? The conception which dominates our thought is enshrined in the word *ideologies*, in so far as that word suggests that the whole moral and philosophical outlook of a people can be explained without remainder in terms of their method of production, their economic organisation, and their geographical position. On that view, of course, differences, and differences to any extent, are to be expected between ideologies as between languages and costumes. But is this what we actually find? Much anthropology seems at first to encourage us to answer Yes. But if I may venture on an opinion in a field where I am by no means an expert, I would suggest that the appearance is somewhat illusory. It seems to me to result from a concentration on those very elements in each culture which are most variable (sexual practice and religious ritual) and also from a concentration on the savage. I have even found a tendency in some thinkers to treat the savage as the normal or archetypal man. But surely he is the exceptional man. It may indeed be true that we were all savages once, as it is certainly true that we were all babies once. But we do not treat as normal man the imbecile who remains in adult life what we all were (intellectually) in the cradle. The savage has had as many generations of ancestors as the civilised man: he is the man who, in the same number of centuries, either has not learned or has forgotten, what the rest of the human race know. I do not see why we should attach much significance to the diversity and eccentricity (themselves often exaggerated) of savage codes. And if we turn to civilised man, I claim that we shall find far fewer differences of ethical injunction than is now popularly believed. In triumphant monotony the same indispensable platitudes will meet us in culture after culture. The idea that any of the new moralities now offered us would be simply one more addition to a variety already almost infinite, is not in accordance with the facts. We are not really justified in speaking of different moralities as we speak of different languages or different religions.

You will not suspect me of trying to reintroduce in its full Stoical or medieval rigour the doctrine of Natural Law. Still less am I claiming as the source of this substantial ethical agreement anything like Intuition or Innate Ideas. Nor, Theist though I am, do I here put forward any surreptitious argument for Theism. My aim is more timid. It is even negative. I deny that we have any choice to make between clearly differentiated ethical systems. I deny that we have any power to make a new ethical system. I assert that wherever and whenever ethical discussion begins we find already before us an ethical code whose validity has to be assumed before we can even criticise it. For no ethical attack on any of the traditional precepts can be made except on the ground of some other traditional precept. You can attack the concept of justice because it interferes with the feeding of the masses, but you have taken the duty of feeding the masses from the world-wide code. You may exalt patriotism at the expense of mercy; but it was the old code that told you to love your country. You may vivisect your grandfather in order to deliver your grandchildren from cancer: but, take away traditional morality, and why should you bother about your grandchildren?

Out of these negatives, there springs a positive. Men say 'How are we to act, what are we to teach our children, now that we are no longer Christians?' You see, gentlemen, how I would answer that question. You are deceived in thinking that the morality of your father was based on Christianity. On the contrary, Christianity presupposed it. That morality stands exactly where it did; its basis has not been withdrawn for, in a sense, it never had a basis. The ultimate ethical injunctions have always been premises, never conclusions. Kant was perfectly right on that point at least: the imperative is categorical. Unless the ethical is assumed from the outset, no argument will bring you to it.

In thus recalling men to traditional morality I am not of course maintaining that it will provide an answer to every particular moral problem with which we may be confronted. M. Sartre seems to me to be the victim of a curious misunderstanding when he rejects the conception of general moral rules on the ground that such rules may fail to apply clearly to all concrete problems of conduct. Who could ever have supposed that by accepting a moral code we should be delivered from all questions of casuistry? Obviously it is moral codes that create questions of casuistry, just as the rules of chess create chess problems. The man without a moral code, like the animal, is free from moral problems. The man who has not learned to count is free from mathematical problems. A man asleep is free from all problems. Within the framework of general human ethics problems will, of course, arise and will sometimes be solved wrongly. This possibility of error is simply the symptom that we are awake, not asleep, that we are men, not beasts or gods. If I were pressing on you a panacea, if I were recommending traditional ethics as a means to some end, I might be tempted to promise you the infallibility which I actually deny. But that, you see, is not my position. I send you back to your nurse and your father, to all the poets and sages and law givers, because, in a sense, I hold that you are already there whether you recognise it or not: that there is really no ethical alternative: that those who urge us to adopt new moralities are only offering us the mutilated or expurgated text of a book which we already possess in the original manuscript. They all wish us to depend on them instead of on that original, and then to deprive us of our full humanity. Their activity is in the long run always directed against our freedom.

[39]
THREE KINDS OF MEN

First published in The Sunday Times *(21 March 1943), this essay was published in* Present Concerns *(1986) and then in* Compelling Reason *(1998).*

There are three kinds of people in the world. The first class is of those who live simply for their own sake and pleasure, regarding Man and Nature as so much raw material to be cut up into whatever shape may serve them. In the second class are those who acknowledge some other claim upon them – the will of God, the categorical imperative, or the good of society – and honestly try to pursue their own interests no further than this claim will allow. They try to surrender to the higher claim as much as it demands, like men paying a tax, but hope, like other taxpayers, that what is left over will be enough for them to live on. Their life is divided, like a soldier's or a schoolboy's life, into time 'on parade' and 'off parade', 'in school' and 'out of school'. But the third class is of those who can say like St Paul that for them 'to live is Christ' (Philippians 1:21). These people have got rid of the tiresome business of adjusting the rival claims of Self and God by the simple expedient of rejecting the claims of Self altogether. The old egoistic will has been turned round, reconditioned, and made into a new thing. The will of Christ no longer limits theirs; it is theirs. All their time, in belonging to Him, belongs also to them, for they are His.

And because there are three classes, any merely twofold division of the world into good and bad is disastrous. It overlooks the fact that the members of the second class (to which most of us belong) are always and necessarily unhappy. The tax which moral conscience levies on our desires does not in fact leave us enough to live on. As long as we are in this class we must either feel guilt because we have not paid the tax or penury because we have. The Christian doctrine that there is no 'salvation' by works done according to the moral law is a fact of daily experience. Back or on we must go. But there is no going on simply by our own efforts. If the new Self, the new Will, does not come at His own good pleasure to be born in us, we cannot produce Him synthetically.

The price of Christ is something, in a way, much easier than moral effort – it is to want Him. It is true that the wanting itself would be beyond our power but for one fact. The world is so built that, to help us desert our own satisfactions, they desert us. War and trouble and finally old age take from us one by one all those things that the natural Self hoped for at its setting out. Begging is our only wisdom, and want in the end makes it easier for us to be beggars. Even on those terms the Mercy will receive us.

[40]

ANSWERS TO QUESTIONS
ON CHRISTIANITY

First published as a pamphlet by the Electrical and Musical Industries Christian Fellowship (Hayes, Middlesex, 1944), and subsequently in Undeceptions *(1971) and* Timeless at Heart *(1991).*

Lewis: I have been asked to open with a few words on Christianity and Modern Industry. Now Modern Industry is a subject of which I know nothing at all. But for that very reason it may illustrate what Christianity, in my opinion, does and does not do. Christianity does *not* replace the technical. When it tells you to feed the hungry it doesn't give you lessons in cookery. If you want to learn *that*, you must go to a cook rather than a Christian. If you are not a professional economist and have no experience of industry, simply being a Christian won't give you the answer to industrial problems. My own idea is that modern industry is a radically hopeless system. You can improve wages, hours, conditions, etc., but all that doesn't cure the deepest trouble: i.e. that numbers of people are kept all their lives doing dull repetition work which gives no full play to their faculties. How that is to be overcome, I do not know. If a single country abandoned the system it would merely fall a prey to the other countries which hadn't abandoned it. I don't know the solution: that is not the kind of thing Christianity teaches a person like me. Let's now carry on with the questions:

Question 1
Christians are taught to love their neighbours. How, therefore, can they justify their attitude of supporting the war?

Lewis: You are told to love your neighbour as yourself. How do you love yourself? When I look into my own mind, I find that I do not love myself by thinking myself a dear old chap or having affectionate feelings. I do not think that I love myself because I am particularly good, but just because I am myself and quite apart from my character. I might detest something which I have done. Nevertheless, I do not cease to love myself. In other words, that definite distinction that Christians make between hating sin and loving the sinner is one that you have been making in your own case since you were born. You dislike what you have done, but you don't cease to love yourself. You may even think that you ought to be hanged. You may even think that you ought to go to the police and own up and be hanged. Love is not affectionate feeling, but a steady wish for the loved person's ultimate good as far as it can be obtained. It seems to me, therefore, that when the worst comes to the worst, if you cannot restrain a man by any method except by trying to kill him, then a Christian must do that. That is my answer. But I may be wrong. It is very difficult to answer, of course.

Question 2

Supposing a factory worker asked you: 'How can I find God?' How would you reply?

Lewis: I don't see how the problem would be different for a factory worker than for anyone else. The primary thing about any man is that he is a human being, sharing all the ordinary human temptations and assets. What is the special problem about the factory worker? But perhaps it is worth saying this:

Christianity really does two things about conditions here and now in this world:

1. It tries to make them as good as possible, i.e. to reform them; but also
2. It fortifies you against them in so far as they remain bad.

If what was in the questioner's mind was this problem of repetition work, then the factory worker's difficulty is the same as any other man confronted with any sorrow or difficulty. People will find God if they consciously seek from Him the right attitude towards all unpleasant things … if that is the point of the question?

Question 3

Will you please say how you would define a practising Christian. Are there any other varieties?

Lewis: Certainly there are a great many other varieties. It depends, of course, on what you mean by 'practising Christian'. If you mean one who has practised Christianity in every respect at every moment of his life, then there is only One on record – Christ Himself. In that sense there are no practising Christians, but only Christians who, in varying degrees, try to practise it and fail in varying degrees and then start again. A perfect practice of Christianity would, of course, consist in a perfect imitation of the life of Christ – I mean, in so far as it was applicable in one's own particular circumstances. Not in an idiotic sense – it doesn't mean that every Christian should grow a beard, or be a bachelor, or become a travelling preacher. It means that every single act and feeling, every experience, whether pleasant or unpleasant, must be referred to God. It means looking at everything as something that comes from Him, and always looking to Him and asking His will first, and saying: 'How would He wish me to deal with this?'

A kind of picture or pattern (in a very remote way) of the relation between the perfect Christian and his God, would be the relation of the good dog to its master. This is only a very imperfect picture, though, because the dog hasn't reason like its master: whereas we do share in God's reason, even if in an imperfect and uninterrupted way ('interrupted' because we don't think rationally for very long at a time – it's too tiring – and we haven't information to understand things fully, and our intelligence itself has certain limitations). In that way we are more like God than the dog is like us, though, of course, there are other ways in which the dog is more like us than we are like God. It is only an illustration.

Question 4

What justification on ethical grounds and on the grounds of social expediency exists for the Church's attitude towards Venereal Disease and prophylaxis and publicity in connection with it?

Lewis: I need further advice on that question, and then perhaps I can answer it. Can the questioner say which Church he has in mind?

Voice: The Church concerned is the Church of England, and its attitude, though not written, is implicit in that it has more or less banned all publicity in connection with prophylactic methods of combating Venereal Disease. The view of some is that moral punishment should not be avoided.

Lewis: I haven't myself met any clergyman of the Church of England who held that view: and I don't hold it myself. There are obvious objections to it. After all, it isn't only Venereal Disease that can be regarded as a punishment for bad conduct. Indigestion in old age may be the result of overeating in earlier life: but no one objects to advertisements for Beecham's Pills. I, at any rate, strongly dissent from the view that you've mentioned.

Question 5

Many people feel resentful or unhappy because they think they are the target of unjust fate. These feelings are stimulated by bereavement, illness, deranged domestic or working conditions, or the observation of suffering in others. What is the Christian view of this problem?

Lewis: The Christian view is that men are created to be in a certain relationship to God (if we are in that relation to Him, the right relation to one another will follow inevitably). Christ said it was difficult for 'the rich' to enter the Kingdom of Heaven (Matthew 19:23; Mark 10:23; Luke 18:24), referring, no doubt, to 'riches' in the ordinary sense. But I think it really covers riches in every sense – good fortune, health, popularity, and all the things one wants to have. All these things tend – just as money tends – to make you feel independent of God, because if you have them you are happy already and contented in this life. You don't want to turn away to anything more, and so you try to rest in a shadowy happiness as if it could last for ever. But God wants to give you a real and eternal happiness. Consequently He may have to take all these 'riches' away from you: if He doesn't, you will go on relying on them. It sounds cruel, doesn't it? But I am beginning to find out that what people call the cruel doctrines are really the kindest ones in the long run. I used to think it was a 'cruel' doctrine to say that troubles and sorrows were 'punishments'. But I find in practice that when you are in trouble, the moment you regard it as a 'punishment', it becomes easier to bear. If you think of this world as a place intended simply for our happiness, you find it quite intolerable: think of it as a place of training and correction and it's not so bad.

Imagine a set of people all living in the same building. Half of them think it is a hotel, the other half think it is a prison. Those who think it a hotel might regard it as quite intolerable, and those who thought it was a prison might decide that it was really surprisingly comfortable. So that what seems the ugly doctrine is one that comforts and strengthens you in the end. The people who try to hold an optimistic view of this world would become pessimists: the people who hold a pretty stern view of it become optimistic.

Question 6

Materialists and some astronomers suggest that the solar planetary system and life as we know it was brought about by an accidental stellar collision. What is the Christian view of this theory?

Lewis: If the solar system was brought about by an accidental collision, then the appearance of organic life on this planet was also an accident, and the whole evolution of Man was an accident too. If so, then all our present thoughts are mere accidents – the accidental by-product of the movement of atoms. And this holds for the thoughts of the materialists and astronomers as well as for anyone else's. But if *their* thoughts – i.e. of materialism and astronomy – are merely accidental by-products, why should we believe them to be true? I see no reason for believing that one accident should be able to give me a correct account of all the other accidents. It's like expecting that the accidental shape taken by the splash when you upset a milk jug should give you a correct account of how the jug was made and why it was upset.

Question 7

Is it true that Christianity (especially the Protestant forms) tends to produce a gloomy, joyless condition of society which is like a pain in the neck to most people?

Lewis: As to the distinction between Protestant and other forms of Christianity, it is very difficult to answer. I find by reading about the sixteenth century, that people like Sir Thomas More, for whom I have a great respect, always regarded Martin Luther's doctrines not as gloomy thinking, but as wishful thinking. I doubt whether we can make a distinction between Protestant and other forms in this respect. Whether Protestantism is gloomy and whether Christianity at all produces gloominess, I find it very difficult to answer, as I have never lived in a completely non-Christian society nor a completely Christian one, and I wasn't there in the sixteenth century, and only have my knowledge from reading books. I think there is about the same amount of fun and gloom in all periods. The poems, novels, letters, etc., of every period all seem to show that. But again, I don't really know the answer, of course. I wasn't there.

Question 8

Is it true that Christians must be prepared to live a life of personal discomfort and self-sacrifice in order to qualify for 'Pie in the Sky'?

Lewis: All people, whether Christians or not, must be prepared to live a life of discomfort. It is impossible to accept Christianity for the sake of finding comfort: but the Christian tries to lay himself open to the will of God, to do what God wants him to do. You don't know in advance whether God is going to set you to do something difficult or painful, or something that you will quite like; and some people of heroic mould are disappointed when the job doled out to them turns out to be something quite nice. But you must be prepared for the unpleasant things and the discomforts. I don't mean fasting, and things like that. They are a different matter. When you are training soldiers in manoeuvres, you practise with blank ammunition because you would like them to have practice before meeting the real enemy. So we must practise in abstaining from pleasures which are not in themselves wicked. If you don't abstain from pleasure, you won't be good when the time comes along. It is purely a matter of practice.

Voice: Are not practices like fasting and self-denial borrowed from earlier or more primitive religions?

Lewis: I can't say for certain which bits came into Christianity from earlier religions. An enormous amount did. I should find it hard to believe Christianity if that were not so. I couldn't believe that nine hundred and ninety-nine religions were completely false and the remaining one true. In reality, Christianity is primarily the fulfilment of the Jewish religion, but also the fulfilment of what was vaguely hinted in all the religions at their best. What was vaguely seen in them all comes into focus in Christianity – just as God Himself comes into focus by becoming a Man. I take it that the speaker's remarks on earlier religions are based on evidence about modern savages. I don't think it is good evidence. Modern savages usually represent some decay in culture – you find them doing things which look as if they had a fairly civilised basis once, which they have forgotten. To assume that primitive man was exactly like the modern savage is unsound.

Voice: Could you say any more on how one discovers whether a task is laid on one by God, or whether it comes in some other way? If we cannot distinguish between the pleasant and the unpleasant things, it is a complicated matter.

Lewis: We are guided by the ordinary rules of moral behaviour, which I think are more or less common to the human race and quite reasonable and demanded by the circumstances. I don't mean anything like sitting down and waiting for a supernatural vision.

Voice: We don't qualify for heaven by practice, but salvation is obtained at the Cross. We do nothing to obtain it, but follow Christ. We may have pain or tribulation, but nothing we do qualifies us for heaven, but Christ.

Lewis: The controversy about faith and works is one that has gone on for a very long time, and it is a highly technical matter. I personally rely on the paradoxical text: 'Work out your own salvation ... for it is God that worketh in you' (Philippians 2:12–13). It looks as if in one sense we do nothing, and in another case we do a damned lot. 'Work out your own salvation with fear and trembling,' but you must have it in you before you can work it out. But I have no wish to go further into it, as it would interest no one but the Christians present, would it?

Question 9

Would the application of Christian standards bring to an end or greatly reduce scientific and material progress? In other words, is it wrong for a Christian to be ambitious and strive for personal success?

Lewis: It is easier to think of a simplified example. How would the application of Christianity affect anyone on a desert island? Would he be less likely to build a comfortable hut? The answer is 'No'. There might come a particular moment, of course, when Christianity would tell him to bother less about the hut, i.e. if he were in danger of coming to think that the hut was the most important thing in the universe. But there is no evidence that Christianity would prevent him from building it.

Ambition! We must be careful what we mean by it. If it means the desire to get ahead of other people – which is what I think it does mean – then it is bad. If it means simply wanting to do a thing well, then it is good. It isn't wrong for an actor to want to act his part as well as it can possibly be acted, but the wish to have his name in bigger type than the other actors is a bad one

Voice: It's all right to be a General, but if it is one's ambition to be a General, then you shouldn't become one.

Lewis: The mere event of becoming a General isn't either right or wrong in itself. What matters morally is your attitude towards it. The man may be thinking about winning a war; he may be wanting to be a General because he honestly thinks that he has a good plan and is glad of a chance to carry it out. That's all right. But if he is thinking: 'What can I get out of the job?' or 'How can I get on the front page of the *Illustrated News*?' then it is all wrong. And what we call 'ambition' usually means the wish to be more conspicuous or more successful than someone else. It is this competitive element in it that is bad. It is perfectly reasonable to want to dance well or to look nice. But when the dominant wish is to dance better or look nicer than the others – when you begin to feel that if the others danced as well as you or looked as nice as you, that would take all the fun out of it – then you are going wrong.

Voice: I am wondering how far we can ascribe to the work of the Devil those very legitimate desires that we indulge in. Some people have a very sensitive conception of the presence of the Devil. Others haven't. Is the Devil as real as we think he is? That doesn't trouble some people, since they have no desire to be good, but others are continually harassed by the Old Man himself.

Lewis: No reference to the Devil or devils is included in any Christian Creeds, and it is quite possible to be a Christian without believing in them. I do believe such beings exist, but that is my own affair. Supposing there to be such beings, the degree to which humans were conscious of their presence would presumably vary very much. I mean, the more a man was in the Devil's power, the less he would be aware of it, on the principle that a man is still fairly sober as long as he knows he's drunk. It is the people who are fully awake and trying hard to be good who would be most aware of the Devil. It is when you start arming against Hitler that you first realise your country is full of Nazi agents. Of course, they don't want you to know they are there. In the same way, the Devil doesn't want you to believe in the Devil. If devils exist, their first aim is to give you an anaesthetic – to put you off your guard. Only if that fails, do you become aware of them.

Voice: Does Christianity retard scientific advancement? Or does it approve of those who help spiritually others who are on the road to perdition, by scientifically removing the environmental causes of the trouble?

Lewis: Yes. In the abstract it is certainly so. At a particular moment, if most human beings are concentrating only on material improvements in the environment, it may be the duty of Christians to point out (and pretty loudly) that this isn't the only thing that matters. But as a general rule it is in favour of all knowledge and all that will help the human race in any way.

Question 10

The Bible was written thousands of years ago for people in a lower state of mental development than today. Many portions seem preposterous in the light of modern knowledge. In view of this, should not the Bible be rewritten with the object of discarding the fabulous and reinterpreting the remainder?

Lewis: First of all as to the people in a lower state of mental development. I am not so sure what lurks behind that. If it means that people ten thousand years ago did not know a good many things that we know now, of course, I agree. But if it means that there has been any advance in *intelligence* in that time, I believe there is no evidence for any such thing. The Bible can be divided into two parts – the Old and the New Testaments. The Old Testament contains fabulous elements. The New Testament consists mostly of teaching, not of narrative at all: but where it *is* narrative, it is, in my opinion, historical. As to the fabulous element in the Old Testament, I very much doubt if you would be wise to chuck it out. What you get is something *coming gradually into focus.* First you get, scattered through the heathen religions all over the world – but still quite vague and mythical – the idea of a god who is killed and broken and then comes to life again. No one knows where he is supposed to have lived and died; he's not historical. Then you get the Old Testament. Religious ideas get a bit more focused. Everything is now connected with a particular nation. And it comes still more into focus as it goes on. Jonah and the Whale (the Book of Jonah), Noah and his Ark (Genesis 6–8) are fabulous; but the court history of King David (2 Samuel 2 – 1 Kings 2) is probably as reliable as the court history of Louis XIV. Then, in the New Testament the *thing really happens*. The dying god really appears – as a historical Person, living in a definite place and time. If we *could* sort out all the fabulous elements in the earlier stages and separate them from the historical ones, I think we might lose an essential part of the whole process. That is my own idea.

Question 11

Which of the religions of the world gives to its followers the greatest happiness?

Lewis: Which of the religions of the world gives to its followers the greatest happiness? While it lasts, the religion of worshipping oneself is the best.

I have an elderly acquaintance of about eighty, who has lived a life of unbroken selfishness and self-admiration from the earliest years, and is, more or less, I regret to say, one of the happiest men I know. From the moral point of view it is very difficult! I am not approaching the question from that angle. As you perhaps know, I haven't always been a Christian. I didn't go to religion to make me happy. I always knew a bottle of port would do that. If you want a religion to make you feel really comfortable, I certainly don't recommend Christianity. I am certain there must be a patent American article on the market which will suit you far better, but I can't give any advice on it.

Question 12

Are there any unmistakable outward signs in a person surrendered to God? Would he be cantankerous? Would he smoke?

Lewis: I think of the advertisements for 'White Smiles' Tooth Paste, saying that it is the best on the market. If they are true, it would follow that:

1. Anyone who starts using it will have better teeth.
2. Anyone using it has better teeth than he would have if he weren't using it.

But you can't test it in the case of one who has naturally bad teeth and uses it, and compare him with a healthy Negro who has never used toothpaste at all.

Take the case of a sour old maid, who is a Christian, but cantankerous. On the other hand, take some pleasant and popular fellow, but who has never been to church. Who knows how much more cantankerous the old maid might be if she were *not* a Christian, and how much more likeable the nice fellow might be if he *were* a Christian? You can't judge Christianity simply by comparing the *product* in those two people; you would need to know what kind of raw material Christ was working on in both cases.

As an illustration, let us take a case of industrialism. Let us take two factories:

Factory A with poor and inadequate plant, and
Factory B with first-class modern plant.

You can't judge by the outside. You must consider the plant and methods by which they are run, and considering the plant at Factory A, it may be a wonder it does anything at all; and considering the new machinery at Factory B, it may be a wonder it doesn't do better.

Question 13
What is your opinion about raffles within the plant – no matter how good the cause – which, not infrequently, is given less prominence than the alluring list of prizes?

Lewis: Gambling ought never to be an important part of a man's life. If it is a way in which large sums of money are transferred from person to person without doing any good (e.g. producing employment, good will, etc.) then it is a bad thing. If it is carried out on a small scale, I am not sure that it is bad. I don't know much about it, because it is about the only vice to which I have no temptation at all, and I think it is a risk to talk about things which are not in my own make-up, because I don't understand them. If anyone comes to me asking me to play bridge for money, I just say: 'How much do you hope to win? Take it and go away.'

Question 14
Many people are quite unable to understand the theological differences which have caused divisions in the Christian Church. Do you consider that these differences are fundamental, and is the time now ripe for reunion?

Lewis: The time is always ripe for reunion. Divisions between Christians are a sin and a scandal, and Christians ought at all times to be making contributions towards reunion, if it is only by their prayers. I am only a layman and a recent Christian, and I do not know much about these things, but in all the things which I have written and thought I have always stuck to traditional, dogmatic positions. The result is that letters of agreement reach me from what are ordinarily regarded as the most different kinds of Christians; for instance, I get letters from Jesuits, monks, nuns, and also from Quakers and Welsh Dissenters, and so on. So it seems to me that the 'extreme' elements in every Church are nearest one another, and the liberal and 'broad-minded' people in each Body could never be united at all. The world of dogmatic Christianity is a place in which thousands of people of quite different types keep on saying the same thing, and the world of 'broad-mindedness' and watered-down 'religion' is a world where a small number of people (all of the same type) say totally different things and change their minds every few minutes. We shall never get reunion from them.

Question 15

In the past the Church used various kinds of compulsion in attempts to force a particular brand of Christianity on the community. Given sufficient power, is there not a danger of this sort of thing happening again?

Lewis: Yes. I hear nasty rumours coming from Spain. Persecution is a temptation to which all men are exposed. I had a postcard signed 'M.D.' saying that anyone who expressed and published his belief in the Virgin Birth should be stripped and flogged. That shows you how easily persecution of Christians by the non-Christians might come back. Of course, they wouldn't call it persecution: they'd call it 'Compulsory re-education of the ideologically unfit', or something like that. But, of course, I have to admit that Christians themselves have been persecutors in the past. It was worse of them, because *they* ought to have known better: they weren't worse in any other way. I detest every kind of religious compulsion: only the other day I was writing an angry letter to *The Spectator* about Church Parades in the Home Guard!

Question 16

Is attendance at a place of worship or membership with a Christian community necessary to a Christian way of life?

Lewis: That's a question which I cannot answer. My own experience is that when I first became a Christian, about fourteen years ago, I thought that I could do it on my own, by retiring to my rooms and reading theology, and I wouldn't go to the churches and gospel halls; and then later I found that it was the only way of flying your flag; and, of course, I found that this meant being a target. It is extraordinary how inconvenient to your family it becomes for you to get up early to go to church. It doesn't matter so much if you get up early for anything else, but if you get up early to go to church it's very selfish of you and you upset the house. If there is anything in the teaching of the New Testament which is in the nature of a command, it is that you are obliged to take the Sacrament,[1] and you can't do it without going to church. I disliked very much their hymns, which I considered to be fifth-rate poems set to sixth-rate music. But as I went on I saw the great merit of it. I came up against different people of quite different outlooks and different education, and then gradually my conceit just began peeling off. I realised that the hymns (which were just sixth-rate music) were, nevertheless, being sung with devotion and benefit by an old saint in elastic-sided boots in the opposite pew, and then you realise that you aren't fit to clean those boots. It gets you out of your solitary conceit. It is not for me to lay down laws, as I am only a layman, and I don't know much.

Question 17

If it is true that one has only to want God enough in order to find Him, how can I make myself want Him enough to enable myself to find Him?

Lewis: If you don't want God, why are you so anxious to want to want Him? I think that in reality the want is a real one, and I should say that this person has in fact found God, although it may not be fully recognised yet. We are not always aware of things at the time they happen. At any rate, what is more important is that God has found this person, and that is the main thing.

---

[1] John 6:53–54: 'Except ye eat the flesh of the Son of man, and drink his blood, ye have no life in you. Whoso eateth my flesh, and drinketh my blood, hath eternal life; and I will raise him up at the last day.'

[41]

THE LAWS OF NATURE

First published in The Coventry Evening Telegraph *(4 April 1945) and reproduced in* Undeceptions *(1971), this also appeared in* God in the Dock *(1998).*

'Poor woman,' said my friend. 'One hardly knows what to say when they talk like that. She thinks her son survived Arnhem because she prayed for him. It would be heartless to explain to her that he really survived because he was standing a little to the left or a little to the right of some bullet. That bullet was following a course laid down by the laws of nature. It couldn't have hit him. He just happened to be standing off its line ... and so all day long as regards every bullet and every splinter of shell. His survival was simply due to the laws of nature.'

At that moment my first pupil came in and the conversation was cut short, but later in the day I had to walk across the park to a committee meeting and this gave me time to think the matter over. It was quite clear that once a bullet had been fired from point A in direction B, the wind being C, and so forth, it would pursue a certain path. But might our young friend have been standing somewhere else? And might the German have fired at a different moment or in a different direction? If men have free will it would appear that they might. On that view we get a rather more complicated picture of the battle of Arnhem. The total course of events would be a kind of amalgam derived from two sources – on the one hand, from acts of human will (which might presumably have been otherwise), and, on the other, from the laws of physical nature. And this would seem to provide all that is necessary for the mother's belief that her prayers had some place among the causes of her son's preservation. God might continually influence the wills of all the combatants so as to allot death, wounds, and survival in the way He thought best, while leaving the behaviour of the projectile to follow its normal course.

But I was still not quite clear about the physical side of this picture. I had been thinking (vaguely enough) that the bullet's flight was *caused* by the laws of nature. But is this really so? Granted that the bullet is set in motion, and granted the wind and the earth's gravitation and all the other relevant factors, then it is a 'law' of nature that the bullet must take the course it did. But then the pressing of the trigger, the side wind, and even the earth, are not exactly *laws*. They are facts or events. They are not laws but things that obey laws. Obviously, to consider the pressing of the trigger would only lead us back to the free will side of the picture. We must, therefore, choose a simpler example.

The laws of physics, I understand, decree that when one billiard ball (A) sets another billiard ball (B) in motion, the momentum lost by A exactly equals the momentum gained by B. This is a *law*. That is, this is the pattern to which the movement of the two billiard balls must conform. Provided, of course, that something sets ball A in motion. And here comes the snag. The *law* won't set it in motion. It is usually a man with a cue who does that. But a man with a cue would send us back to free will, so let us assume that it was lying on a table in a liner and that what set it in motion was a lurch of the ship. In that case it was not the law which produced the movement; it was a wave. And that wave, though it certainly moved *according* to the laws of physics, was not moved by them. It was shoved by other waves, and by winds, and so forth. And however far you traced the story back you would never find the *laws* of nature causing anything.

The dazzlingly obvious conclusion now arose in my mind: *in the whole history of the universe the laws of nature have never produced a single event.* They are the pattern to which every event must conform, provided only that it can be induced to happen. But how do you get it to do that? How do you get a move on? The laws of nature can give you no help there. All events obey them, just as all operations with money obey the laws of arithmetic. Add six pennies to six and the result will certainly be a shilling. But arithmetic by itself won't put one farthing into your pocket. Up till now I had had a vague idea that the laws of nature could make things happen. I now saw that this was exactly like thinking that you could increase your income by doing sums about it. The *laws* are the pattern to which events conform: the source of events must be sought elsewhere.

This may be put in the form that the laws of nature explain everything except the source of events. But this is rather a formidable exception. The laws, in one sense, cover the whole of reality except – well, except that continuous cataract of real events which makes up the actual universe. They explain everything except what we should ordinarily call 'everything'. The only thing they omit is – the whole universe. I do not mean that a knowledge of these laws is useless. Provided we can take over the actual universe as a going concern, such knowledge is useful and indeed indispensable for manipulating it; just as, if only you have some money, arithmetic is indispensable for managing it. But the events themselves, the money itself – that is quite another affair.

Where, then, do actual events come from? In one sense the answer is easy. Each event comes from a previous event. But what happens if you trace this process backwards? To ask this is not exactly the same as to ask where *things* come from – how there came to be space and time and matter at all. Our present problem is not about things but about events; not, for example, about particles of matter but about this particle colliding with that. The mind can perhaps acquiesce in the idea that the 'properties' of the universal drama somehow 'just happen to be there': but whence comes the play, the story?

Either the stream of events had a beginning or it had not. If it had, then we are faced with something like creation. If it had not (a supposition, by the way, which some physicists find difficult), then we are faced with an everlasting impulse which, by its very nature, is opaque to scientific thought. Science, when it becomes perfect, will have explained the connection between each link in the chain and the link before it. But the actual existence of the chain will remain wholly unaccountable. We learn more and more about the pattern. We learn nothing about that which 'feeds' real events into the pattern. If it is not God, we must at the very least call it Destiny – the immaterial, ultimate, one-way pressure which keeps the universe on the move.

The smallest event, then, if we face the fact that it occurs (instead of concentrating on the pattern into which, if it can be persuaded to occur, it must fit) leads us back to a mystery which lies outside natural science. It is certainly a possible supposition that behind this mystery some mighty Will and Life is at work. If so, any contrast between His acts and the laws of Nature is out of the question. It is His act alone that gives the laws any events to apply to. The laws are an empty frame; it is He who fills that frame – not now and then on specially 'providential' occasions, but at every moment. And He, from His vantage point above Time, can, if He pleases, take all prayers into account in ordaining that vast complex event which is the history of the universe. For what we call 'future' prayers have always been present to Him.

In *Hamlet* a branch breaks and Ophelia is drowned. Did she die because the branch broke or because Shakespeare wanted her to die at that point in the play? Either – both – whichever you please. The alternative suggested by the question is not a real alternative at all – once you have grasped that Shakespeare is making the whole play.

[42]

MEMBERSHIP

This was read to the Society of St Alban and St Sergius, Oxford, and published in Sobornost, *No. 31 (June 1945). It was later reprinted in* Transposition and Other Addresses *(1949) and* Fern-seed and Elephants *(1998).*

No Christian and, indeed, no historian could accept the epigram which defines religion as 'what a man does with his solitude'. It was one of the Wesleys, I think, who said that the New Testament knows nothing of solitary religion. We are forbidden to neglect the assembling of ourselves together. Christianity is already institutional in the earliest of its documents. The Church is the Bride of Christ. We are members of one another.

In our own age the idea that religion belongs to our private life – that it is, in fact, an occupation for the individual's hour of leisure – is at once paradoxical, dangerous, and natural. It is paradoxical because this exaltation of the individual in the religious field springs up in an age when collectivism is ruthlessly defeating the individual in every other field. I see this even in a university. When I first went to Oxford the typical undergraduate society consisted of a dozen men, who knew one another intimately, hearing a paper by one of their own number in a small sitting-room and hammering out their problem till one or two in the morning. Before the war the typical undergraduate society had come to be a mixed audience of one or two hundred students assembled in a public hall to hear a lecture from some visiting celebrity. Even on those rare occasions when a modern undergraduate is not attending some such society he is seldom engaged in those solitary walks, or walks with a single companion, which built the minds of the previous generations. He lives in a crowd; caucus has replaced friendship. And this tendency not only exists both within and without the university, but is often approved. There is a crowd of busybodies, self-appointed masters of ceremonies, whose life is devoted to destroying solitude wherever solitude still exists.

They call it 'taking the young people out of themselves', or 'waking them up', or 'overcoming their apathy'. If an Augustine, a Vaughan, a Traherne or a Wordsworth should be born in the modern world, the leaders of a youth organization would soon cure him. If a really good home, such as the home of Alcinous and Arete in the *Odyssey* or the Rostovs in *War and Peace* or any of Charlotte M. Yonge's families, existed today, it would be denounced as bourgeois and every engine of destruction would be levelled against it. And even where the planners fail and someone is left physically by himself, the wireless has seen to it that he will be – in a sense not intended by Scipio – never less alone than when alone. We live, in fact, in a world starved for solitude, silence, and privacy: and therefore starved for meditation and true friendship.

That religion should be relegated to solitude in such an age is, then, paradoxical. But it is also dangerous for two reasons. In the first place, when the modern world says to us aloud, 'You may be religious when you are alone,' it adds under its breath, 'and I will see to it that you never are alone.' To make Christianity a private affair while banishing all privacy is to relegate it to the rainbow's end or the Greek calends. That is one of the enemy's stratagems. In the second place, there is the danger that real Christians who know that Christianity is not a solitary affair may react against that error by simply transporting into our spiritual life that same collectivism which has already conquered our secular life. That is the enemy's other stratagem. Like a good chess player he is always trying to manoeuvre you into a position where you can save your castle only by losing your bishop. In order to avoid the trap we must insist that though the private conception of Christianity is an error it is a profoundly natural one, and is clumsily attempting to guard a great truth. Behind it is the obvious feeling that our modern collectivism is an outrage upon human nature and that from this, as from all other evils, God will be our shield and buckler.

This feeling is just. As personal and private life is lower than participation in the Body of Christ, so the collective life is lower than the personal and private life and has no value save in its service. The secular community, since it exists for our natural good and not for our supernatural, has no higher end than to facilitate and safeguard the family, and friendship, and solitude. To be happy at home, said Johnson, is the end of all human endeavour. As long as we are thinking only of natural values we must say that the sun looks down on nothing half so good as a household laughing together over a meal, or two friends talking over a pint of beer, or a man alone reading a book that interests him; and that all economics, politics, laws, armies, and institutions, save in so far as they prolong and multiply such scenes, are a mere ploughing the sand and sowing the ocean, a meaningless vanity and vexation of spirit. Collective activities are, of course, necessary; but this is the end to which they are necessary. Great sacrifices of this private happiness by those who have it may be necessary in order that it may be more widely distributed. All may have to be a little hungry in order that none may starve. But do not let us mistake necessary evils for good. The mistake is easily made. Fruit has to be tinned if it is to be transported, and has to lose thereby some of its good qualities. But one meets people who have learned actually to prefer the tinned fruit to the fresh. A sick society must think much about politics, as a sick man must think much about his digestion: to ignore the subject may be fatal cowardice for the one as for the other. But if either comes to regard it as the natural food of the mind – if either forgets that we think of such things only in order to be able to think of something else – then what was undertaken for the sake of health has become itself a new and deadly disease.

There is, in fact, a fatal tendency in all human activities for the means to encroach upon the very ends which they were intended to serve. Thus money comes to hinder the exchange of commodities, and rules of art to hamper genius, and examinations to prevent young men from becoming learned. It does not, unfortunately, always follow that the encroaching means can be dispensed with. I think it probable that the collectivism of our life is necessary and will increase; and I think that our only safeguard against its deathly properties is in a Christian life; for we were promised that we could handle serpents and drink deadly things and yet live. That is the truth behind the erroneous definition of religion with which we started. Where it went wrong was in opposing to the collective mass mere solitude. The Christian is called, not to individualism but to membership in the mystical body. A consideration of the differences between the secular collective and the mystical body is therefore the first step to understanding how Christianity without being individualistic can yet counteract collectivism.

At the outset we are hampered by a difficulty of language. The very word *membership* is of Christian origin, but it has been taken over by the world and emptied of all meaning. In any book on logic you may see the expression 'members of a class'. It must be most emphatically stated that the items or particulars included in a homogeneous class are almost the reverse of what St Paul meant by *members*. By *members* (μέλη) he meant what we should call *organs*, things essentially different from, and complementary to, one another: things differing not only in structure and function but also in dignity. Thus, in a club, the committee as a whole, and the servants as a whole, may both properly be regarded as 'members'; what we should call the members of the club are merely units. A row of identically dressed and identically trained soldiers set side by side, or a number of citizens listed as voters in a constituency, are not members of anything in the Pauline sense. I am afraid that when we describe a man as 'a member of the Church' we usually mean nothing Pauline: we mean only that he is a unit – that he is one more specimen of some kind of things as X and Y and Z. How true membership in a body differs from inclusion in a collective may be seen in the structure of a family. The grandfather, the parents, the grown-up son, the child, the dog, and the cat are true members (in the organic sense) precisely because they are not members or units of a homogeneous class. They are not interchangeable. Each person is almost a species in himself. The mother is not simply a different person from the daughter, she is a different kind of person. The grown-up brother is not simply one unit in the class children, he is a separate estate of the realm. The father and grandfather are almost as different as the cat and the dog. If you subtract any one member you have not simply reduced the family in number, you have inflicted an injury on its structure. Its unity is a unity of unlikes, almost of incommensurables.

A dim perception of the richness inherent in this kind of unity is one reason why we enjoy a book like *The Wind in the Willows*; a trio such as Rat, Mole, and Badger symbolises the extreme differentiation of persons in harmonious union which we know intuitively to be our true refuge both from solitude and from the collective. The affection between such oddly matched couples as Dick Swiveller and the Marchioness, or Mr Pickwick and Sam Weller, pleases in the same way. That is why the modern notion that children should call their parents by their Christian names is so perverse. For this is an effort to ignore the difference in kind which makes for real organic unity. They are trying to inoculate the child with the preposterous view that one's mother is simply a fellow-citizen like anyone else, to make it ignorant of what all men know and insensible to what all men feel. They are trying to drag the featureless repetitions of the collective into the fuller and more concrete world of the family.

A convict has a number instead of a name. That is the collective idea carried to its extreme. But a man in his own house may also lose his name, because he is called simply 'Father'. That is membership in a body. The loss of the name in both cases reminds us that there are two opposite ways of departing from isolation.

The society into which the Christian is called at baptism is not a collective but a Body. It is in fact that Body of which the family is an image on the natural level. If anyone came to it with the misconception that

335

membership of the Church was membership in a debased modern sense – a massing together of persons as if they were pennies or counters – he would be corrected at the threshold by the discovery that the head of this Body is so unlike the inferior members that they share no predicate with him save by analogy. We are summoned from the outset to combine as creatures with our creator, as mortals with immortal, as redeemed sinners with sinless Redeemer. His presence, the interaction between him and us, must always be the overwhelmingly dominant factor in the life we are to lead within the Body; and any conception of Christian fellowship which does not mean primarily fellowship with him is out of court. After that it seems almost trivial to trace further down the diversity of operations to the unity of the Spirit. But it is very plainly there. There are priests divided from the laity, catechumens divided from those who are in full fellowship. There is authority of husbands over wives and parents over children. There is, in forms too subtle for official embodiment, a continual interchange of complementary ministrations. We are all constantly teaching and learning, forgiving and being forgiven, representing Christ to man when we intercede, and man to Christ when others intercede for us. The sacrifice of selfish privacy which is daily demanded of us is daily repaid a hundredfold in the true growth of personality which the life of the Body encourages. Those who are members of one another become as diverse as the hand and the ear. That is why the worldlings are so monotonously alike compared with the almost fantastic variety of the saints. Obedience is the road to freedom, humility the road to pleasure, unity the road to personality.

And now I must say something that may appear to you a paradox. You have often heard that, though in the world we hold different stations, yet we are all equal in the sight of God. There are of course senses in which this is true. God is no accepter of persons: his love for us is not measured by our social rank or our intellectual talents. But I believe there is a sense in which this maxim is the reverse of the truth. I am going to venture to say that artificial equality is necessary in the life of the State, but that in the Church we strip off this disguise, we recover our real inequalities, and are thereby refreshed and quickened.

I believe in political equality. But there are two opposite reasons for being a democrat. You may think all men so good that they deserve a share in the government of the commonwealth, and so wise that the commonwealth needs their advice. That is, in my opinion, the false, romantic doctrine of democracy. On the other hand, you may believe fallen men to be so wicked that not one of them can be trusted with any irresponsible power over his fellows.

That I believe to be the true ground of democracy. I do not believe that God created an egalitarian world. I believe the authority of parent over child, husband over wife, learned over simple, to have been as much a part of the original plan as the authority of man over beast. I believe that if we had not fallen Filmer would be right, and patriarchal monarchy would be the sole lawful government. But since we have learned sin, we have found, as Lord Acton says, that 'all power corrupts, and absolute power corrupts absolutely.' The only remedy has been to take away the powers and substitute a legal fiction of equality. The authority of father and husband has been rightly abolished on the legal plane, not because this authority is in itself bad (on the contrary, it is, I hold, divine in origin) but because fathers and husbands are bad. Theocracy has been rightly abolished not because it is bad that learned priests should govern ignorant laymen, but because priests are wicked men like the rest of us. Even the authority of man over beast has had to be interfered with because it is constantly abused.

Equality is for me in the same position as clothes. It is a result of the Fall and the remedy for it. Any attempt to retrace the steps by which we have arrived at egalitarianism and to reintroduce the old authorities on the political level is for me as foolish as it would be to take off our clothes. The Nazi and the nudist make the same mistake. But it is the naked body, still there beneath the clothes of each one of us, which really lives. It is the hierarchical world, still alive and (very properly) hidden behind a façade of equal citizenship, which is our real concern.

Do not misunderstand me. I am not in the least belittling the value of this egalitarian fiction which is our only defence against one another's cruelty. I should view with the strongest disapproval any proposal to abolish manhood suffrage, or the Married Women's Property Act. But the function of equality is purely protective. It is medicine, not food. By treating human persons (in judicious defiance of the observed facts) as if they were all the same kind of thing, we avoid innumerable evils. But it is not on this that we were made to live. It is idle to say that men are of equal value. If value is taken in a worldly sense – if we mean that all men are equally useful or beautiful or good or entertaining – then it is nonsense. If it means that all are of equal value as immortal souls then I think it conceals a dangerous error. The infinite value of each human soul is not a Christian doctrine. God did not die for man because of some value he perceived in him. The value of each human soul considered simply in itself, out of relation to God, is zero. As St Paul writes, to have died for valuable men would have been not divine but merely heroic; but God died for sinners. He loved us not because we were lovable, but because he is Love. It may be that he loves all equally – he certainly loved all to the death – and I am not certain what the expression means. If there is equality it is in his love, not in us.

Equality is a quantitative term and therefore love often knows nothing of it. Authority exercised with humility and obedience accepted with delight are the very lines along which our spirits live. Even in the life of the affections, much more in the Body of Christ, we step outside that world which says 'I am as good as you'. It is like turning from a march to a dance. It is like taking off our clothes. We become, as Chesterton said, taller when we bow; we become lowlier when we instruct. It delights me that there should be moments in the services of my own Church when the priest stands and I kneel. As democracy becomes more complete in the outer world and opportunities for reverence are successively removed, the refreshment, the cleansing, and invigorating returns to inequality, which the Church offers us, become more and more necessary.

In this way then, the Christian life defends the single personality from the collective, not by isolating him but by giving him the status of an organ in the mystical Body. As the book of Revelation says, he is made 'a pillar in the temple of God'; and it adds, 'he shall go no more out.' That introduces a new side of our subject. That structural position in the Church which the humblest Christian occupies is eternal and even cosmic. The Church will outlive the universe; in it the individual person will outlive the universe. Everything that is joined to the immortal head will share his immortality. We hear little of this from the Christian pulpit today. What has come of our silence may be judged from the fact that recently addressing the Forces on this subject, I found that one of my audience regarded this doctrine as 'theosophical'. If we do not believe it let us be honest and relegate the Christian faith to museums. If we do, let us give up the pretence that it makes no difference. For this is the real answer to every excessive claim made by the collective. It is mortal; we shall live for ever. There will come a time when every culture, every institution, every nation, the human race, all biological life, is extinct, and every one of us is still alive. Immortality is promised to us, not to these generalities. It was not for societies or states that Christ died, but for men. In that sense Christianity must seem to secular collectivists to involve an almost frantic assertion of individuality. But then it is not the individual as such who will share Christ's victory over death. We shall share the victory by being in the Victor. A rejection, or in Scripture's strong language, a crucifixion of the natural self is the passport to everlasting life. Nothing that has not died will be resurrected. That is just how Christianity cuts across the antithesis between individualism and collectivism. There lies the maddening ambiguity of our faith as it must appear to outsiders. It sets its face relentlessly against our natural individualism; on the other hand, it gives back to those who abandon individualism an eternal possession of their own personal being, even of their bodies. As mere biological entities, each with its separate will to live and to expand, we are apparently of no account; we are cross-fodder. But as organs in the Body of Christ, as stones and pillars in the temple, we are assured of our eternal self-identity and shall live to remember the galaxies as an old tale.

This may be put in another way. Personality is eternal and inviolable. But then, personality is not a datum from which we start. The individualism in which we all begin is only a parody or shadow of it. True personality lies ahead – how far ahead, for most of us, I dare not say. And the key to it does not lie in ourselves. It will not be attained by development from within outwards. It will come to us when we occupy those places in the structure of the eternal cosmos for which we were designed or invented. As a colour first reveals its true quality when placed by an excellent artist in its pre-elected spot between certain others, as a spice reveals its true flavour when inserted just where and when a good cook wishes among the other ingredients, as the dog becomes really doggy only when he has taken his place in the household of man, so we shall then first be true persons when we have suffered ourselves to be fitted into our places. We are marble waiting to be shaped, metal waiting to be run into a mould. No doubt there are already, even in the unregenerate self, faint hints of what mould each is designed for, or what sort of pillar he will be. But it is, I think, a gross exaggeration to picture the saving of a soul as being, normally, at all like the development from seed to flower. The very words repentance, regeneration, the New Man, suggest something very different. Some tendencies in each natural man may have to be simply rejected. Our Lord speaks of eyes being plucked out and hands lopped off – a frankly Procrustean method of adaptation.

The reason we recoil from this is that we have in our day started by getting the whole picture upside down. Starting with the doctrine that every individuality is 'of infinite value' we then picture God as a kind of employment committee whose business it is to find suitable careers for souls, square holes for square pegs. In fact, however, the value of the individual does not lie in him. He is capable of receiving value. He receives it by union with Christ. There is no question of finding for him a place in the living temple which will do justice to his inherent value and give scope to his natural idiosyncrasy. The place was there first. The man was created for it. He will not be himself till he is there. We shall be true and everlasting and really divine persons only in heaven, just as we are, even now, coloured bodies only in the light.

To say this is to repeat what everyone here admits already – that we are saved by grace, that in our flesh dwells no good thing, that we are, through and through, creatures not creators, derived beings, living not of ourselves but from Christ. If I seem to have complicated a simple matter, you will, I hope, forgive me. I have been anxious to bring out two points. I have wanted to try to expel that quite unchristian worship of the human individual simply as such which is so rampant in modern thought side by side with our collectivism; for one error begets the opposite error and, far from neutralising, they aggravate each other. I mean the pestilent notion (one sees it in literary criticism) that each of us starts with a treasure called 'personality' locked up inside him, and that to expand and express this, to guard it from interference, to be 'original', is the main end of life. This is Pelagian, or worse, and it defeats even itself. No man who values originality will ever be original. But try to tell the truth as you see it, try to do any bit of work as well as it can be done for the work's sake, and what men call originality will come unsought. Even on that level, the submission of the individual to the function is already beginning to bring true personality to birth. And secondly, I have wanted to show that Christianity is not, in the long run, concerned either with individuals or communities. Neither the individual nor the community as popular thought understands them can inherit eternal life: neither the natural self, nor the collective mass, but a new creature.

[43]
THE SERMON AND THE LUNCH

Published in The Church of England Newspaper *(21 September 1945) and reproduced in* Undeceptions *(1971), as well as in* First and Second Things *(1985).*

'And so,' said the preacher, 'the home must be the foundation of our national life. It is there, all said and done, that character is formed. It is there that we appear as we really are. It is there we can fling aside the weary disguises of the outer world and be ourselves. It is there that we retreat from the noise and stress and temptation and dissipation of daily life to seek the sources of fresh strength and renewed purity ...' And as he spoke I noticed that all confidence in him had departed from every member of that congregation who was under thirty. They had been listening well up to this point. Now the shufflings and coughings began. Pews creaked; muscles relaxed. The sermon, for all practical purposes, was over; the five minutes for which the preacher continued talking were a total waste of time – at least for most of us.

Whether I wasted them or not is for you to judge. I certainly did not hear any more of the sermon. I was thinking; and the starting-point of my thought was the question, 'How can he? How can *he* of all people?' For I knew the preacher's own home pretty well. In fact, I had been lunching there that very day, making a fifth to the Vicar and the Vicar's wife and the son (RAF) and the daughter (ATS), who happened both to be on leave. I could have avoided it, but the girl had whispered to me, 'For God's sake stay to lunch if they ask you. It's always a little less frightful when there's a visitor.'

Lunch at the vicarage nearly always follows the same pattern. It starts with a desperate attempt on the part of the young people to keep up a bright patter of trivial conversation: trivial not because they are trivially minded (you can have real conversation with them if you get them alone), but because it would never occur to either of them to say at home anything they were really thinking, unless it is forced out of them by anger. They are talking only to try to keep their parents quiet. They fail. The Vicar, ruthlessly interrupting, cuts in on a quite different subject. He is telling us how to re-educate Germany. He has never been there and seems to know nothing either of German history or the German language. 'But Father,' begins the son, and gets no further. His mother is now talking, though nobody knows exactly when she began. She is in the middle of a complicated story about how badly some neighbour has treated her. Though it goes on a long time, we never learn either how it began or how it ended: it is all middle. 'Mother, that's not quite fair,' says the daughter at last. 'Mrs Walker never said –' but her father's voice booms in again. He is telling his son about the organisation of the RAF. So it goes on until either the Vicar or his wife say something so preposterous that the boy or the girl contradicts and insists on making the contradiction heard. The real minds of the young people have at last been called into action. They talk fiercely, quickly, contemptuously. They have facts and logic on their side. There is an answering flare up from the parents. The father storms; the mother is (oh blessed domestic queen's move!) 'hurt' – plays pathos for all she is worth. The daughter becomes ironical. The father and son, elaborately ignoring each other, start talking to me. The lunch party is in ruins.

The memory of that lunch worries me during the last few minutes of the sermon. I am not worried by the fact that the Vicar's practice differs from his precept. That is, no doubt, regrettable, but it is nothing to the purpose. As Dr Johnson said, precept may be very sincere (and, let us add, very profitable) where practice is very imperfect,[1] and no one but a fool would discount a doctor's warnings about alcoholic poisoning because the doctor himself drank too much. What worries me is the fact that the Vicar is not telling us at all that home life is difficult and has, like every form of life, its own proper temptations and corruptions. He keeps on talking as if 'home' were a panacea, a magical charm which of itself was bound to produce happiness and virtue. The trouble is not that he is insincere but that he is a fool. He is not talking from his own experience of family life at all: he is automatically reproducing a sentimental tradition – and it happens to be a false tradition. That is why the congregation have stopped listening to him.

If Christian teachers wish to recall Christian people to domesticity – and I, for one, believe that people must be recalled to it – the first necessity is to stop telling lies about home life and to substitute realistic

[1] James Boswell, *Life of Johnson*, ed. George Birkbeck Hill (Oxford, 1934), Vol. IV, p. 397 (2 December 1784).

teaching. Perhaps the fundamental principles would be something like this.

1. Since the Fall no organisation or way of life whatever has a natural tendency to go right. In the Middle Ages some people thought that if only they entered a religious order they would find themselves automatically becoming holy and happy: the whole native literature of the period echoes with the exposure of that fatal error. In the nineteenth century some people thought that monogamous family life would automatically make them holy and happy; the savage anti-domestic literature of modern times – the Samuel Butlers, the Gosses, the Shaws – delivered the answer. In both cases the 'debunkers' may have been wrong about principles and may have forgotten the maxim *abusus non tollit usum:*[2] but in both cases they were pretty right about matters of fact. Both family life and monastic life were often detestable, and it should be noticed that the serious defenders of both are well aware of the dangers and free of the sentimental illusion. The author of the *Imitation of Christ* knows (no one better) how easily monastic life goes wrong. Charlotte M. Yonge makes it abundantly clear that domesticity is no passport to heaven on earth but an arduous vocation – a sea full of hidden rocks and perilous ice shores only to be navigated by one who uses a celestial chart. That is the first point on which we must be absolutely clear. The family, like the nation, can be offered to God, can be converted and redeemed, and will then become the channel of particular blessings and graces. But, like everything else that is human, it needs redemption. Unredeemed, it will produce only particular temptations, corruptions, and miseries. Charity begins at home: so does uncharity.

2. By the conversion or sanctification of family life we must be careful to mean something more than the preservation of 'love' in the sense of natural affection. Love (in that sense) is not enough. Affection, as distinct from charity, is not a cause of lasting happiness. Left to its natural bent affection becomes in the end greedy, naggingly solicitous, jealously exacting, timorous. It suffers agony when its object is absent – but is not repaid by any long enjoyment when the object is present. Even at the Vicar's lunch table affection was partly the cause of the quarrel. That son would have borne patiently and humorously from any other old man the silliness which enraged him in his father. It is because he still (in some fashion) 'cares' that he is impatient. The Vicar's wife would not be quite that endless whimper of self-pity which she now is if she did not (in a sense) 'love' the family: the continued disappointment of her continued

---

[2] The abuse does not abolish the use.

and ruthless demand for sympathy, for affection, for appreciation has helped to make her what she is. I do not think this aspect of affection is nearly enough noticed by most popular moralists. The greed to be loved is a fearful thing. Some of those who say (and almost with pride) that they live only for love come, at last, to live in incessant resentment.

3. We must realise the yawning pitfall in that very characteristic of home life which is so often glibly paraded as its principal attraction. 'It is there that we appear as we really are: it is there that we can fling aside the disguises and be ourselves.' These words, in the Vicar's mouth, were only too true and he showed at the lunch table what they meant. Outside his own house he behaves with ordinary courtesy. He would not have interrupted any other young man as he interrupted his son. He would not, in any other society, have talked confident nonsense about subjects of which he was totally ignorant: or, if he had, he would have accepted correction with good temper. In fact, he values home as the place where he can 'be himself' in the sense of trampling on all the restraints which civilised humanity has found indispensable for tolerable social intercourse. And this, I think, is very common. What chiefly distinguishes domestic from public conversation is surely very often simply its selfishness, slovenliness, incivility – even brutality. And it will often happen that those who praise home life most loudly are the worst offenders in this respect: they praise it – they are always glad to get home, hate the outer world, can't stand visitors, can't be bothered meeting people, etc. – because the freedoms in which they indulge themselves at home have ended by making them unfit for civilised society. If they practised elsewhere the only behaviour they now find 'natural' they would simply be knocked down.

4. How, then, *are* people to behave at home. If a man can't be comfortable and unguarded, can't take his ease and 'be himself' in his own house, where can he? That is, I confess, the trouble. The answer is an alarming one. There is *nowhere* this side of heaven where one can safely lay the reins on the horse's neck. It will never be lawful simply to 'be ourselves' until 'ourselves' have become sons of God. It is all there in the hymn – 'Christian, seek not yet repose.' This does not mean, of course, that there is no difference between home life and general society. It does mean that home life has its own rule of courtesy – a code more intimate, more subtle, more sensitive, and therefore, in some ways more difficult, than that of the outer world.

5. Finally, must we not teach that if the home is to be a means of grace it must be a place of *rules?* There cannot be a common life without a *regula*. The alternative to rule is not freedom but the unconstitutional (and often unconscious) tyranny of the most selfish member.

In a word, must we not either cease to preach domesticity or else begin to preach it seriously? Must we not abandon sentimental eulogies and begin to give practical advice on the high, hard, lovely, and adventurous art of really creating the Christian family?

[44]

SCRAPS

Published in St James' Magazine *(St James's Church, Birkdale, Southport, December 1945), and reproduced in* Undeceptions *(1971) and* Christian Reunion *(1990).*

1

'Yes', my friend said. 'I don't see why there shouldn't be books in Heaven. But you will find that your library in Heaven contains only some of the books you had on earth.' 'Which?', I asked. 'The ones you gave away or lent.' 'I hope the lent ones won't still have all the borrowers' dirty thumb-marks', said I. 'Oh yes they will', said he. 'But just as the wounds of the martyrs will have turned into beauties, so you will find that the thumb-marks have turned into beautiful illuminated capitals or exquisite marginal woodcuts.'

2

'The angels', he said. 'have no senses; their experience is purely intellec-tual and spiritual. That is why we know something about God which they don't. There are particular aspects of His love and joy which can be communicated to a created being only by sensuous experience. Something of God which the Seraphim can never quite understand flows into us from the blue of the sky, the taste of honey, the delicious embrace of water whether cold or hot, and even from sleep itself.'

3

'You are always dragging me down', said I to my Body. 'Dragging *you* down' replied my Body. 'Well I like that! Who taught me to like tobacco and alcohol? You, of course, with your idiotic adolescent idea of being "grown-up". My palate loathed both at first: but you would have your way. Who put an end to all those angry and revengeful thoughts last night? Me, of course, by insisting on going to sleep. Who does his best to keep you from talking too much and eating too much by giving you dry throats and headaches and indigestion? Eh?' 'And what about sex?', said I. 'Yes, what about it?' retorted the Body. 'If you and your wretched imagination would leave me alone I'd give you no trouble. That's Soul all over; you give me orders and then blame me for carrying them out.'

4

'Praying for particular things', said I, 'always seems to me like advising God how to run the world. Wouldn't it be wiser to assume that He knows best?' 'On the same principle,' said he 'I suppose you never ask a man next to you to pass the salt, because God knows best whether you ought to have salt or not. And I suppose you never take an umbrella, because God knows best whether you ought to be wet or dry.' 'That's quite different', I protested. 'I don't see why', said he. 'The odd thing is that He should let us influence the course of events at all. But since He lets us do it in one way, I don't see why He shouldn't let us do it in the other.'

[45]
AFTER PRIGGERY — WHAT?

Published in The Spectator, *Volume CLXXV (7 December 1945), and reprinted in* Present Concerns *(1991).*

No doubt priggery is a horrid thing, and the more moral the horrider. To avoid a man's society because he is poor or ugly or stupid may be bad; but to avoid it because he is wicked – with the all but inevitable implication that you are less wicked (at least in some respect) – is dangerous and disgusting. We could all go on to develop this theme at any length and without the slightest effort. Smug – complacent – Pharasaical – Victorian – parable of the Pharisee and the Publican ... it writes itself. Upon my word, I have some difficulty in bridling the pen.

But the real question is what are we to put in the place of priggery. Private vices, we were taught long ago, are public benefits. Which means that when you remove a vice you must put a virtue in its place – a virtue which will produce the same public benefits. It will not do simply to cut out priggery and leave it at that.

These reflections arose out of the sort of conversation one often has. Suppose a man tells me that he has recently been lunching with a gentleman who we will call Cleon. My informant is an honest man and a man of good will. Cleon is a wicked journalist, a man who disseminates for money falsehoods calculated to produce envy, hatred, suspicion and confusion. At least that is what I believe Cleon to be; I have caught him lying myself. But it does not matter for purposes of the present argument whether my judgement of Cleon is correct or no. The point is that my honest friend fully agreed with it. The very reason why he mentioned the lunch party was that he wanted to tell me some more than usually foetid instance of Cleon's mendacity.

That, then, is the position we are in after the expulsion of priggery. My friend believes Cleon to be as false as hell; but he meets him on perfectly friendly terms over a lunch table. In a priggish or self-righteous society Cleon would occupy the same social status as a prostitute. His social contacts would extend only to clients, fellow-professionals, moral welfare-workers, and the police. Indeed, in a society which was rational as well as priggish (if such a combination could occur) his status would be a good deal lower than hers. The intellectual virginity which he has sold is a dearer treasure than her physical virginity. He gives his patrons a baser pleasure than she. He infects them with more dangerous diseases. Yet not one of us hesitates to eat with him, drink with him, joke with him, shake his hand, and, what is much worse, very few of us refrain from reading what he writes.

It will hardly be maintained that this complaisance springs from a sudden increase of our charity. We are not associating with Cleon as a friar or a clergyman from a mission or a member of the Salvation Army might associate with the prostitute. It is not our Christian love for the villain that has conquered our hatred of the villainy. We do not even pretend to love the villain; I have never in my life heard anyone speak well of him. As for the villainy, if we do not love it, we take it as a thing of course with a tolerant laugh or a shrug. We have lost the invaluable faculty of being shocked – a faculty which has hitherto almost distinguished the Man or Woman from the beast or the child. In a word, we have not risen above priggery; we have sunk below it.

The result is that things are a good deal too easy for Cleon. Even when the rewards of dishonesty are strictly alternative to those of honesty some men will choose them. But Cleon finds he can have both. He can enjoy all the sense of secret power and all the sweets of a perpetually gratified inferiority complex while at the same time having the *entrée* to honest society. From such conditions what can we expect but an increasing number of Cleons? And that must be our ruin. If we remain a democracy they render impossible the formation of any healthy public opinion. If – *absit omen* – the totalitarian threat is realised, they will be the cruellest and dirtiest tools of government.

I submit, therefore, that the rest of us must really return to the old and 'priggish' habit of sending such people to Coventry.[1] And I am not quite convinced that we need to be prigs in doing so. The charge brought against us – Cleon himself will do it very well, possibly next week – will be that in cold-shouldering a man for his vices we are claiming to be better than he. This sounds very dreadful but I wonder whether it may not be a turnip ghost?

If I meet a friend in the street who is drunk and pilot him home, I do, by the mere act of piloting him, imply that I am sober. If you press it this

---

[1] i.e., to refuse to associate with them.

implies the claim that I am, for that one moment and in that one respect, 'better' than he. Mince it as you will, the mere brute fact is that I can walk straight and he can't. I am not saying in the least that I am in general a better man. Or again, in a lawsuit, I say I am in the right and the other man is in the wrong. I claim that particular superiority over him. It is really quite off the point to remind me that he has qualities of courage, good-temper, unselfishness and the like. It may well be so. I never denied it. But the question was about the title to a field or the damage done by a cow.

Now it seems to me that we can (and should) blackball Cleon at every club and avoid his society and boycott his paper without in the least claiming any general superiority to him. We know perfectly well that he may be in the last resort a better man that we. We do not know by what stages he became the thing he is, nor how hard he may have struggled to be something better. Perhaps a bad heredity ... unpopularity at school ... complexes ... a disgraceful record from the last war but one still nagging him on wakeful nights ... a disastrous marriage. Who knows? Perhaps strong and sincere political convictions first bred intense desire that his side should prevail, and this first taught him to lie for what seemed a good cause and then, little by little, lying became his profession. God knows, we are not saying that we, placed as Cleon, would have done better. But for the moment, however it came about – and let us sing *non nobis* loud enough to lift the roof – we are not professional liars and he is. We may have a hundred vices from which he is free. But on one particular matter we are, if you insist, 'better' than he.

And that one thing which he does and we do not do is poisoning the whole nation. To prevent the poisoning is an urgent necessity. It cannot be prevented by the law: partly because we do not wish the law to have too much power over freedom of speech, and partly, perhaps, for another reason. The only safe way of silencing Cleon is by discrediting him. What cannot be done – and indeed ought not to be done – by law, can be done by public opinion. A 'sanitary cordon' can be drawn round Cleon. If no one but Cleon's like read his paper, much less meet him on terms of social intercourse, his trade will soon be reduced to harmless proportions.

To abstain from reading – and *a fortiori* from buying – a paper which you have once caught telling lies seems a very moderate form of asceticism. Yet how few practise it! Again and again I find people with Cleon's dirty sheets in their hands. They admit that he is a rogue but 'one must keep up with the times, must know what is being said'. That is one of the ways Cleon puts it across us. It is a fallacy. If we must find out what bad men are writing, and must therefore buy their papers, and therefore enable their papers to exist, who does not see that this supposed necessity of observing the evil is just what maintains the evil? It may in general be dangerous to ignore an evil; but not if the evil is one that perishes by being ignored.

But, you say, even if we ignore it others will not. Cleon's readers are not all the half-heartedly honest people whom I describe. Some of them are real rascals like Cleon himself. They are not interested in truth. That, no doubt, is so. But I am not convinced that the number of thoroughgoing rascals is large enough to keep Cleon afloat. In the present 'tolerant' age he has the support and countenance not only of the rascals but of thousands of honest people as well. Is it not at least worth our while to try the experiment of leaving him and the rascals alone? We might try it for five years. Let him for five years be sent to Coventry. I doubt if you will find him still rampant at the end. And why not begin today by counter-manding your order for his paper?

[46]
MAN OR RABBIT?

Originally published as a pamphlet by the Student Christian Movement in Schools (probably in 1946), this essay was reproduced in Undeceptions *(1971) and* God in the Dock *(1998).*

'Can't you lead a good life without believing in Christianity?' This is the question on which I have been asked to write, and straightaway, before I begin trying to answer it, I have a comment to make. The question sounds as if it were asked by a person who said to himself, 'I don't care whether Christianity is in fact true or not. I'm not interested in finding out whether the real universe is more like what the Christians say than what the Materialists say. All I'm interested in is leading a good life. I'm going to choose beliefs not because I think them true but because I find them helpful.' Now frankly, I find it hard to sympathise with this state of mind. One of the things that distinguishes man from the other animals is that he wants to know things, wants to find out what reality is like, simply for the sake of knowing. When that desire is completely quenched in anyone, I think he has become something less than human. As a matter of fact, I don't believe any of you have really lost that desire. More probably, foolish preachers, by always telling you how much Christianity will help you and how good it is for society, have actually led you to forget that Christianity is not a patent medicine. Christianity claims to give an account of *facts* – to tell you what the real universe is like. Its account of the universe may be true, or it may not, and once the question is really before you, then your natural inquisitiveness must make you want to know the answer. If Christianity is untrue, then no honest man will want to believe it, however helpful it might be: if it is true, every honest man will want to believe it, even if it gives him no help at all.

As soon as we have realised this, we realise something else. If Christianity should happen to be true, then it is quite impossible that those who know this truth and those who don't should be equally well equipped for leading a good life. Knowledge of the facts must make a

difference to one's actions. Suppose you found a man on the point of starvation and wanted to do the right thing. If you had no knowledge of
medical science, you would probably give him a large solid meal; and as a
result your man would die. That is what comes of working in the dark. In
the same way a Christian and a non-Christian may both wish to do good
to their fellow men. The one believes that men are going to live for ever,
that they were created by God and so built that they can find their true
and lasting happiness only by being united to God, that they have gone
badly off the rails, and that obedient faith in Christ is the only way back.
The other believes that men are an accidental result of the blind workings
of matter, that they started as mere animals and have more or less steadily
improved, that they are going to live for about seventy years, that their
happiness is fully attainable by good social services and political organisations, and that everything else (e.g. vivisection, birth-control, the judicial
system, education) is to be judged to be 'good' or 'bad' simply in so far as
it helps or hinders that kind of 'happiness'.

Now there are quite a lot of things which these two men could agree in
doing for their fellow citizens. Both would approve of efficient sewers and
hospitals and a healthy diet. But sooner or later the difference of their
beliefs would produce differences in their practical proposals. Both, for
example, might be very keen about education: but the kinds of education
they wanted people to have would obviously be very different. Again,
where the Materialist would simply ask about a proposed action 'Will it
increase the happiness of the majority?', the Christian might have to say,
'Even if it does increase the happiness of the majority, we can't do it. It is
unjust.' And all the time, one great difference would run through their
whole policy. To the Materialist things like nations, classes, civilisations
must be more important than individuals, because the individuals live
only seventy odd years each and the group may last for centuries. But to
the Christian, individuals are more important, for they live eternally; and
races, civilisations and the like, are in comparison the creatures of a day.

The Christian and the Materialist hold different beliefs about the
universe. They can't both be right. The one who is wrong will act in a
way which simply doesn't fit the real universe. Consequently, with the
best will in the world, he will be helping his fellow creatures to their
destruction.

With the best will in the world ... then it won't be his fault? Surely God
(if there is a God) will not punish a man for honest mistakes? But was *that*
all you were thinking about? Are we ready to run the risk of working in
the dark all our lives and doing infinite harm, provided only someone will
assure us that our own skins will be safe, that no one will punish us or

blame us? I will not believe that the reader is quite on that level. But even if he were, there is something to be said to him.

The question before each of us is not 'Can *someone* lead a good life without Christianity?' The question is, 'Can *I*?' We all know there have been good men who were not Christians; men like Socrates and Confucius who had never heard of it, or men like J. S. Mill who quite honestly couldn't believe it. Supposing Christianity to be true, these men were in a state of honest ignorance or honest error. If their intentions were as good as I suppose them to have been (for of course I can't read their secret hearts) I hope and believe that the skill and mercy of God will remedy the evils which their ignorance, left to itself, would naturally produce both for them and for those whom they influenced. But the man who asks me, 'Can't I lead a good life without believing in Christianity?' is clearly not in the same position. If he hadn't heard of Christianity he would not be asking this question. If, having heard of it, and having seriously considered it, he had decided that it was untrue, then once more he would not be asking the question. The man who asks this question has heard of Christianity and is by no means certain that it may not be true. He is really asking, 'Need I bother about it? Mayn't I just evade the issue, just let sleeping dogs lie, and get on with being "good"? Aren't good intentions enough to keep me safe and blameless without knocking at that dreadful door and making sure whether there is, or isn't, someone inside?'

To such a man it might be enough to reply that he is really asking to be allowed to get on with being 'good' before he has done his best to discover what *good* means. But that is not the whole story. We need not enquire whether God will punish him for his cowardice and laziness; they will punish themselves. The man is shirking. He is deliberately trying not to know whether Christianity is true or false, because he foresees endless trouble if it should turn out to be true. He is like the man who deliberately 'forgets' to look at the notice board because, if he did, he might find his name down for some unpleasant duty. He is like the man who won't look at his bank account because he's afraid of what he might find there. He is like the man who won't go to the doctor when he first feels a mysterious pain, because he is afraid of what the doctor may tell him.

The man who remains an unbeliever for such reasons is not in a state of honest error. He is in a state of dishonest error, and that dishonesty will spread through all his thoughts and actions: a certain shiftiness, a vague worry in the background, a blunting of his whole mental edge, will result. He has lost his intellectual virginity. Honest rejection of Christ, however mistaken, will be forgiven and healed – 'Whosoever shall speak a word against the Son of Man, it shall be forgiven him' (Luke 12:10). But to *evade* the Son of Man, to look the other way, to pretend you haven't noticed, to become suddenly absorbed in something on the other side of the street, to leave the receiver off the telephone because it might be He who was ringing up, to leave unopened certain letters in a strange hand-writing because they might be from Him – this is a different matter. You may not be certain yet whether you ought to be a Christian; but you do know you ought to be a man, not an ostrich, hiding its head in the sands.

But still – for intellectual honour has sunk very low in our age – I hear someone whimpering on with his question, 'Will it help me? Will it make me happy? Do you really think I'd be better if I became a Christian?' Well, if you must have it, my answer is 'Yes'. But I don't like giving an answer at all at this stage. Here is a door, behind which, according to some people, the secret of the universe is waiting for you. Either that's true, or it isn't. And if it isn't, then what the door really conceals is simply the greatest fraud, the most colossal 'sell' on record. Isn't it obviously the job of every man (that is a man and not a rabbit) to try to find out which, and then to devote his full energies either to serving this tremendous secret or to exposing and destroying this gigantic humbug? Faced with such an issue, can you really remain wholly absorbed in your blessed 'moral development'?

All right, Christianity will do you good – a great deal more good than you ever wanted or expected. And the first bit of good it will do you is to hammer into your head (you won't enjoy *that*!) the fact that what you have hitherto called 'good' – all that about 'leading a decent life' and 'being kind' – isn't quite the magnificent and all-important affair you supposed. It will teach you that in fact you can't be 'good' (not for twenty-four hours) on your own moral efforts. And then it will teach you that even if you were, you still wouldn't have achieved the purpose for which you were created. Mere *morality* is not the end of life. You were made for something quite different from that. J.S. Mill and Confucius (Socrates was much nearer the reality) simply didn't know what life is about. The people who keep on asking if they can't lead a decent life without Christ, don't know what life is about; if they did they would know that 'a decent life' is mere machinery compared with the thing we men are really made for. Morality is indispensable: but the Divine Life, which gives itself to us and which calls us to be gods, intends for us something in which morality will be swallowed up. We are to be re-made. All the rabbit in us is to disappear – the worried, conscientious, ethical rabbit as well as the cowardly and sensual rabbit. We shall bleed and squeal as the handfuls of fur come out; and then, surprisingly, we shall find underneath it all a thing we have never yet imagined: a real man, an ageless god, a son of God, strong, radiant, wise, beautiful, and drenched in joy.

'When that which is perfect is come, then that which is in part shall be done away' (1 Corinthians 13:10). The idea of reaching 'a good life' without Christ is based on a double error. Firstly, we cannot do it; and secondly, in setting up 'a good life' as our final goal, we have missed the very point of our existence. Morality is a mountain which we cannot climb by our own efforts; and if we could we should only perish in the ice and unbreathable air of the summit, lacking those wings with which the rest of the journey has to be accomplished. For it is *from* there that the real ascent begins. The ropes and axes are 'done away' and the rest is a matter of flying.

[47]
'THE TROUBLE WITH "X" ...'

First published in The Bristol Diocesan Gazette, *Volume XXVII (August 1948), it was reproduced in* Undeceptions *(1971) and in* God in the Dock *(1998).*

I suppose I may assume that seven out of ten of those who read these lines are in some kind of difficulty about some other human being. Either at work or at home, either the people who employ you or those whom you employ, either those who share your house or those whose house you share, either your in-laws or parents or children, your wife or your husband, are making life harder for you than it need be even in these days. It is to be hoped that we do not often mention these difficulties (especially the domestic ones) to outsiders. But sometimes we do. An outside friend asks us why we are looking so glum; and the truth comes out.

On such occasions the outside friend usually says, 'But why don't you tell them? Why don't you go to your wife (or husband, or father, or daughter, or boss, or landlady, or lodger) and have it all out? People are usually reasonable. All you've got to do is to make them see things in the right light. Explain it to them in a reasonable, quiet, friendly way.' And we, whatever we say outwardly, think sadly to ourselves, 'He doesn't know "X".' We do. We know how utterly hopeless it is to make 'X' see reason. Either we've tried it over and over again – tried it till we are sick of trying it – or else we've never tried it because we saw from the beginning how useless it would be. We know that if we attempt to 'have it all out with "X"' there will either be a 'scene', or else 'X' will stare at us in blank amazement and say 'I don't know what on earth you're talking about'; or else (which is perhaps worst of all) 'X' will quite agree with us and promise to turn over a new leaf and put everything on a new footing – and then, twenty-four hours later, will be exactly the same as 'X' has always been.

You know, in fact, that any attempt to talk things over with 'X' will shipwreck on the old, fatal flaw in 'X's' character. And you see, looking back, how all the plans you have ever made always have shipwrecked on that fatal flaw – on 'X's' incurable jealousy, or laziness, or touchiness, or muddle-headedness, or bossiness, or ill temper, or changeableness. Up to a certain age you have perhaps had the illusion that some external stroke of good fortune – an improvement in health, a rise of salary, the end of the war – would solve your difficulty. But you know better now. The war is over, and you realise that even if the other things happened, 'X' would still be 'X', and you would still be up against the same old problem. Even if you became a millionaire, your husband would still be a bully, or your wife would still nag or your son would still drink, or you'd still have to have your mother-in-law to live with you.

It is a great step forward to realise that this is so; to face the fact that even if all external things went right, real happiness would still depend on the character of the people you have to live with – and that you can't alter their characters. And now comes the point. When you have seen this you have, for the first time, had a glimpse of what it must be like for God. For, of course, this is (in one way) just what God Himself is up against. He has provided a rich, beautiful world for people to live in. He has given them intelligence to show them how it can be used, and conscience to show them how it ought to be used. He has contrived that the things they need for their biological life (food, drink, rest, sleep, exercise) should be positively delightful to them. And, having done all this, He then sees all His plans spoiled – just as our little plans are spoiled – by the crookedness of the people themselves. All the things He has given them to be happy with they turn into occasions for quarrelling and jealousy, and excess and hoarding, and tomfoolery.

You may say it is very different for God because He could, if He pleased, alter people's characters, and we can't. But this difference doesn't go quite as deep as we may at first think. God has made it a rule for Himself that He won't alter people's character by force. He can and will alter them – but only if the people will let Him. In that way He has really and truly limited His power. Sometimes we wonder why He has done so, or even wish that He hadn't. But apparently He thinks it worth doing. He would rather have a world of free beings, with all its risks, than a world of people who did right like machines because they couldn't do anything else. The more we succeed in imagining what a world of perfect automatic beings would be like, the more, I think, we shall see His wisdom.

I said that when we see how all our plans shipwreck on the characters of the people we have to deal with, we are 'in one way' seeing what it must be like for God. But only in one way. There are two respects in which God's view must be very different from ours. In the first place, He sees (like you) how all the people in your home or your job are in various degrees awkward or difficult; but when He looks into that home or factory or office He sees one more person of the same kind – the one you never do see. I mean, of course, yourself. That is the next great step in wisdom – to realise that you also are just that sort of person. You also have a fatal flaw in your character. All the hopes and plans of others have again and again shipwrecked on your character just as your hopes and plans have shipwrecked on theirs.

It is no good passing this over with some vague, general admission such as 'Of course, I know I have my faults.' It is important to realise that there is some really fatal flaw in you: something which gives the others just that same feeling of *despair* which their flaws give you. And it is almost certainly something you don't know about – like what the advertisements call 'halitosis', which everyone notices except the person who has it. But why, you ask, don't the others tell me? Believe me, they have tried to tell you over and over again, and you just couldn't 'take it'. Perhaps a good deal of what you call their 'nagging' or 'bad temper' or 'queerness' are just their attempts to make you see the truth. And even the faults you do know you don't know fully. You say, 'I admit I lost my temper last night'; but the others know that you're always doing it, that you are a bad-tempered person. You say, 'I admit I drank too much last Saturday'; but everyone else knows that you are a habitual drunkard.

That is one way in which God's view must differ from mine. He sees all the characters: I see all except my own. But the second difference is this. He loves the people in spite of their faults. He goes on loving. He does not let go. Don't say, 'It's all very well for Him; He hasn't got to live with them.' He has. He is inside them as well as outside them. He is *with* them far more intimately and closely and incessantly than we can ever be. Every vile thought within their minds (and ours), every moment of spite, envy, arrogance, greed and self-conceit comes right up against His patient and longing love, and grieves His spirit more than it grieves ours.

The more we can imitate God in both these respects, the more progress we shall make. We must love 'X' more; and we must learn to see ourselves as a person of exactly the same kind. Some people say it is morbid to be always thinking of one's own faults. That would be all very well if most of us could stop thinking of our own without soon beginning to think about those of other people. For unfortunately we *enjoy* thinking about other people's faults: and in the proper sense of the word 'morbid', that is the most morbid pleasure in the world.

We don't like rationing which is imposed upon us, but I suggest one form of rationing which we ought to impose on ourselves. Abstain from all thinking about other people's faults, unless your duties as a teacher or parent make it necessary to think about them. Whenever the thoughts come unnecessarily into one's mind, why not simply shove them away? And think of one's own faults instead? For there, with God's help, one *can* do something. Of all the awkward people in your house or job there is only one whom you can improve very much. That is the practical end at which to begin. And really, we'd better. The job has to be tackled some day: and every day we put it off will make it harder to begin.

What, after all, is the alternative? You see clearly enough that nothing, not even God with all His power, can make 'X' really happy as long as 'X' remains envious, self-centred, and spiteful. Be sure there is something inside you which, unless it is altered, will put it out of God's power to prevent your being eternally miserable. While that something remains there can be no Heaven for you, just as there can be no sweet smells for a man with a cold in the nose, and no music for a man who is deaf. It's not a question of God 'sending' us to Hell. In each of us there is something growing up which will of itself *be Hell* unless it is nipped in the bud. The matter is serious: let us put ourselves in His hands at once – this very day, this hour.

[48]

ON LIVING IN
AN ATOMIC AGE

Published in the last issue of an annual magazine called Informed
Reading, *Volume VI (1948), this essay was reproduced in* Present
Concerns *(1981) and* Compelling Reason *(1998).*

In one way we think a great deal too much of the atomic bomb. 'How are
we to live in an atomic age?' I am tempted to reply: 'Why, as you would
have lived in the sixteenth century when the plague visited London
almost every year, or as you would have lived in a Viking age when raiders
from Scandinavia might land and cut your throat any night; or indeed, as
you are already living in an age of cancer, an age of syphilis, an age of
paralysis, an age of air raids, an age of railway accidents, an age of motor
accidents.'

In other words, do not let us begin by exaggerating the novelty of our
situation. Believe me, dear sir or madam, you and all whom you love were
already sentenced to death before the atomic bomb was invented: and
quite a high percentage of us were going to die in unpleasant ways. We
had, indeed, one very great advantage over our ancestors – anaesthetics;
but we have that still. It is perfectly ridiculous to go about whimpering and
drawing long faces because the scientists have added one more chance of
painful and premature death to a world which already bristled with such
chances and in which death itself was not a chance at all, but a certainty.

This is the first point to be made: and the first action to be taken is to
pull ourselves together. If we are all going to be destroyed by an atomic
bomb, let that bomb when it comes find us doing sensible and human
things – praying, working, teaching, reading, listening to music, bathing
the children, playing tennis, chatting to our friends over a pint and a
game of darts – not huddled together like frightened sheep and thinking
about bombs. They may break our bodies (a microbe can do that) but they
need not dominate our minds.

'But,' you reply, 'it is not death – not even painful and premature death
– that we are bothering about. Of course the chance of *that* is not new.

What is new is that the atomic bomb may finally and totally destroy civilisation itself. The lights may be put out for ever.'

This brings us much nearer to the real point; but let me try to make clear exactly what I think that point is. What were your views about the ultimate future of civilization *before* the atomic bomb appeared on the scene? What did you think all this effort of humanity was to come to in the end? The real answer is known to almost everyone who has even a smattering of science; yet, oddly enough, it is hardly ever mentioned. And the real answer (almost beyond doubt) is that, with or without atomic bombs, the whole story is going to end in NOTHING. The astronomers hold out no hope that this planet is going to be permanently inhabitable. The physicists hold out no hope that organic life is going to be a permanent possibility in any part of the material universe. Not only this earth, but the whole show, all the suns of space, are to run down. Nature is a sinking ship. Bergson talks about the *élan vital*, and Mr Shaw talks about the 'Life-force' as if they could surge on for ever and ever. But that comes of concentrating on biology and ignoring the other sciences. There is really no such hope. Nature does not, in the long run, favour life. If Nature is all that exists – in other words, if there is no God and no life of some quite different sort somewhere outside Nature – then all stories will end in the same way: in a universe from which all life is banished without possibility of return. It will have been an accidental flicker, and there will be no one even to remember it. No doubt atomic bombs may cut its duration on this present planet shorter than it might have been; but the whole thing, even if it lasted for billions of years, must be so infinitesimally short in relation to the oceans of dead time which precede and follow it that I cannot feel excited about its curtailment.

What the wars and the weather (are we in for another of those periodic ice ages?) and the atomic bomb have really done is to remind us forcibly of the sort of world we are living in and which, during the prosperous period before 1914, we were beginning to forget. And this reminder is, so far as it goes, a good thing. We have been waked from a pretty dream, and now we can begin to talk about realities.

We see at once (when we have been waked) that the important question is not whether an atomic bomb is going to obliterate 'civilisation'. The important question is whether 'Nature' – the thing studied by the sciences – is the only thing in existence. Because if you answer *yes* to the second question, then the first question only amounts to asking whether the inevitable frustration of all human activities may be hurried on by our own action instead of coming at its natural time. That is, of course, a question that concerns us very much. Even on a ship which will certainly sink sooner or later, the news that the boiler might blow up *now* would not be heard with indifference by anyone. But those who knew that the ship was sinking in any case would not, I think, be quite so desperately excited as those who had forgotten this fact, and were vaguely imagining that it might arrive somewhere.

It is, then, on the second question that we really need to make up our minds. And let us begin by supposing that Nature is all that exists. Let us suppose that nothing ever has existed or ever will exist except this meaningless play of atoms in space and time: that by a series of hundredth chances it has (regrettably) produced things like ourselves – conscious beings who now know that their own consciousness is an accidental result of the whole meaningless process and is therefore itself meaningless, though to us (alas!) it *feels* significant.

In this situation there are, I think, three things one might do:

1. You might commit suicide. Nature which has (blindly, accidentally) given me for my torment this consciousness which demands meaning and value in a universe that offers neither, has luckily also given me the means of getting rid of it. I return the unwelcome gift. I will be fooled no longer.

2. You might decide simply to have as good a time as possible. The universe is a universe of nonsense, but since you are here, grab what you can. Unfortunately, however, there is, on these terms, so very little left to grab – only the coarsest sensual pleasures. You can't, except in the lowest animal sense, be in love with a girl if you know (and keep on remembering) that all the beauties both of her person and of her character are a momentary and accidental pattern produced by the collision of atoms, and that your own response to them is only a sort of psychic phosphorescence arising from the behaviour of your genes. You can't go on getting any very serious pleasure from music if you know and remember that its air of significance is a pure illusion, that you like it only because your nervous system is irrationally conditioned to like it. You may still, in the lowest sense, have a 'good time'; but just in so far as it becomes very good, just in so far as it ever threatens to push you on from cold sensuality into real warmth and enthusiasm and joy, so far you will be forced to feel the hopeless disharmony between your own emotions and the universe in which you really live.

3. You may defy the universe. You may say, 'Let it be irrational, I am not. Let it be merciless, I will have mercy. By whatever curious chance it has produced me, now that I am here I will live according to human values. I know the universe will win in the end, but what is that to me? I will go down fighting. Amid all this wastefulness I will persevere; amid all this competition, I will make sacrifices. Be damned to the universe!'

I suppose that most of us, in fact, while we remain materialists, adopt a more or less uneasy alternation between the second and the third attitude. And although the third is incomparably the better (it is, for instance, much more likely to 'preserve civilisation'), both really shipwreck on the same rock. That rock – the disharmony between our own hearts and Nature – is obvious in the second. The third seems to avoid the rock by accepting disharmony from the outset and defying it. But it will not really work. In it, you hold up our own human standards against the idiocy of the universe. That is, we talk as if our own standards were something *outside* the universe which can be contrasted with it; as if we could judge the universe by some standard borrowed *from another source.* But if (as we were supposing) Nature – the space-time-matter system – is the only thing in existence, then of course there can be no other source for our standards. They must, like everything else, be the unintended and meaningless outcome of blind forces. Far from being a light from beyond Nature whereby Nature can be judged, they are only the way in which anthropoids of our species feel when the atoms under our own skulls get into certain states – those states being produced by causes quite irrational, unhuman, and non-moral. Thus the very ground on which we defy Nature crumbles under our feet. The standard we are applying is tainted at the source. If our standards are derived from this meaningless universe they must be as meaningless as it.

For most modern people, I think, thoughts of this kind have to be gone through before the opposite view can get a fair hearing. All Naturalism leads us to this in the end – to a quite final and hopeless discord between what our minds claim to be and what they really must be if Naturalism is true. They claim to be spirit; that is, to be reason, perceiving universal intellectual principles and universal moral laws and possessing free will. But if Naturalism is true they must in reality be merely arrangements of atoms in skulls, coming about by irrational causation. We never think a thought because it is true, only because blind Nature forces us to think it. We never do an act because it is right, only because blind Nature forces us to do it. It is when one has faced this preposterous conclusion that one is at last ready to listen to the voice that whispers: 'But suppose we really are spirits? Suppose we are not the offspring of Nature ...?'

For, really, the naturalistic conclusion is unbelievable. For one thing, it is only through trusting our own minds that we have come to know Nature herself. If Nature when fully known seems to teach us (that is, if the sciences teach us) that our own minds are chance arrangements of atoms, then there must have been some mistake; for if that were so, then the sciences themselves would be chance arrangements of atoms and we should have no reason for believing in them. There is only one way to avoid this deadlock. We must go back to a much earlier view. We must simply accept it that we are spirits, free and rational beings, at present inhabiting an irrational universe, and must draw the conclusion that we are *not derived from it*. We are strangers here. We come from somewhere else. Nature is not the only thing that exists. There is 'another world', and that is where we come from. And that explains why we do not feel at home here. A fish feels at home in the water. If we 'belonged here' we should feel at home here. All that we say about 'Nature red in tooth and claw', about death and time and mutability, all our half-amused, half-bashful attitude to our own bodies, is quite inexplicable on the theory that we are simply natural creatures. If this world is the only world, how did we come to find its laws either so dreadful or so comic? If there is no straight line elsewhere, how did we discover that Nature's line is crooked?

But what, then, is Nature, and how do we come to be imprisoned in a system so alien to us? Oddly enough, the question becomes much less sinister the moment one realises that Nature is not all. Mistaken for our mother, she is terrifying and even abominable. But if she is only our sister – if she and we have a common Creator – if she is our sparring partner – then the situation is quite tolerable. Perhaps we are not here as prisoners but as colonists: only consider what we have done already to the dog, the horse, or the daffodil. She is indeed a rough playfellow. There are elements of evil in her. To explain that would carry us far back: I should have to speak of Powers and Principalities and all that would seem to a modern reader most mythological. This is not the place, nor do these questions come first. It is enough to say here that Nature, like us but in her different way, is much alienated from her Creator, though in her, as in us, gleams of the old beauty remain. But they are there not to be worshipped but to be enjoyed. She has nothing to teach us. It is our business to live by our own law not by hers: to follow, in private or in public life, the law of love and temperance even when they seem to be suicidal, and not the law of competition and grab, even when they seem to be necessary to our survival. For it is part of our spiritual law never to put survival first: not even the survival of our species. We must resolutely train ourselves to feel that the survival of Man on this Earth, much more of our own nation or culture or class, is not worth having unless it can be had by honourable and merciful means.

The sacrifice is not so great as it seems. Nothing is more likely to destroy a species or a nation than a determination to survive at all costs. Those who care for something else more than civilisation are the only people by whom civilisation is at all likely to be preserved. Those who want Heaven most have served Earth best. Those who love Man less than God do most for Man.

[49]
LILIES THAT FESTER

Published in Twentieth Century, *Volume CLVII (April 1955), this essay was reproduced in* The World's Last Night *(US 1960),* They Asked for a Paper *(Geoffrey Bles, 1962) and* Christian Reunion *(1990).*

In the 'Cambridge number' of the *Twentieth Century* (1955) Mr John Allen asked why so many people 'go to such lengths to prove to us that really they are not intellectuals at all and certainly not cultured'. I believe I know the answer. Two parallels may help to ease it into the reader's mind.

We all know those who shudder at the word *refinement* as a term of social approval. Sometimes they express their dislike of this usage by facetiously spelling it *refanement,* with the implication that it is likely to be commonest in the mouths of those whose speech has a certain varnished vulgarity. And I suppose we can all understand the shudder, whether we approve it or not. He who shudders feels that the quality of mind and behaviour which we call *refined* is nowhere less likely to occur than among those who aim at, and talk much about, *refinement.* Those who have this quality are not obeying any idea of *refinement* when they abstain from swaggering, spitting, snatching, triumphing, calling names, boasting or contradicting. These modes of behaviour do not occur to them as possibles: if they did, that training and sensibility which constitute refinement would reject them as disagreeables, without reference to any ideal of conduct, just as we reject a bad egg without reference to its possible effect on our stomachs. *Refinement,* in fact, is a name given to certain behaviour from without. From within, it does not appear as *refinement;* indeed, it does not appear, does not become an object of consciousness, at all. Where it is most named it is most absent.

I produce my next parallel with many different kinds of reluctance. But I think it too illuminating to be omitted. The word *religion* is extremely rare in the New Testament or the writings of mystics. The reason is simple. Those attitudes and practices to which we give the collective name of *religion* are themselves concerned with religion hardly at all. To be religious is to have one's attention fixed on God and on one's neighbour in relation to God. Therefore, almost by definition, a religious man, or a man when he is being religious, is not thinking about *religion;* he hasn't the time. *Religion* is what we (or he himself at a later moment) call his activity from outside.

Of course those who disdain the words *refinement* and *religion* may be doing so from bad motives; they may wish to impress us with the idea that they are well-bred or holy. Such people are regarding chatter about *refinement* or *religion* simply as symptomatic of vulgarity or worldliness, and eschew the symptom to clear themselves from the suspicion of the disease. But there are others who sincerely and (I believe) rightly think that such talk is not merely a symptom of, but a cause active in producing, that disease. The talk is inimical to the thing talked of, likely to spoil it where it exists and to prevent its birth where it is unborn.

Now *culture* seems to belong to the same class of dangerous and embarrassing words. Whatever else it may mean, it certainly covers deep and genuine enjoyment of literature and the other arts. (By using the word *enjoyment* I do not mean to beg the vexed question about the role of pleasure in our experience of the arts. I mean *frui,* not *delectari;* as we speak of a man 'enjoying' good health or an estate.) Now if I am certain of anything in the world, I am certain that while a man is, in this sense, enjoying *Don Giovanni* or the *Oresteia* he is not caring one farthing about *culture.* Culture? the irrelevance of it! For just as to be fat or clever means to be fatter or cleverer than most, so to be called *cultured* must mean to be more so than most, and thus the very word carries the mind at once to comparisons, and groupings, and life in society. And what has all that to do with the horns that blow as the statue enters, or Clytæmnestra crying, 'Now you have named me aright'? In *Howard's End* Mr E.M. Forster excellently describes a girl listening to a symphony. She is not thinking about *culture:* nor about 'Music'; nor even about 'this music'. She sees the whole world through the music. *Culture,* like religion, is a name given from outside to activities which are not themselves interested in *culture* at all, and would be ruined the moment they were.

I do not mean that we are never to talk of things from the outside. But when the things are of high value and very easily destroyed, we must talk with great care, and perhaps the less we talk the better. To be constantly engaged with the idea of *culture,* and (above all) of *culture* as something enviable, or meritorious, or something that confers prestige, seems to me to endanger those very 'enjoyments' for whose sake we chiefly value it.

If we encourage others, or ourselves, to hear, see, or read great art, on the ground that it is a *cultured* thing to do, we call into play precisely those elements in us which must be in abeyance before we can enjoy art at all. We are calling up the desire for self-improvement, the desire for distinction, the desire to revolt (from one group) and to agree (with another), and a dozen busy passions which, whether good or bad in themselves, are, in relation to the arts, simply a blinding and paralysing distraction.

At this point some may protest that by *culture* they do not mean the 'enjoyments' themselves, but the whole habit of mind which such experiences, reacting upon one another, and reflected on, build up as a permanent possession. And some will wish to include the sensitive and enriching social life which, they think, will arise among groups of people who share this habit of mind. But this reinterpretation leaves me with the same difficulty. I can well imagine a lifetime of such enjoyments leading a man to such a habit of mind, but on one condition; namely, that he went to the arts for no such purpose. Those who read poetry to improve their minds will never improve their minds by reading poetry. For the true enjoyments must be spontaneous and compulsive and look to no remoter end. The Muses will submit to no marriage of convenience. The desirable habit of mind, if it is to come at all, must come as a by-product, unsought. The idea of making it one's aim suggests that shattering confidence which Goethe made to Eckermann: 'In all my youthful amours the object I had in view was my own ennoblement.' To this, I presume, most of us would reply that, even if we believe a love-affair can ennoble a young man, we feel sure that a love-affair undertaken for that purpose would fail of its object. Because of course it wouldn't be a love-affair at all.

So much for the individual. But the claims made for the 'cultured' group raise an embarrassing question. What, exactly, is the evidence that *culture* produces among those who share it a sensitive and enriching social life? If by 'sensitive' we mean 'sensitive to real or imagined affronts', a case could be made out. Horace noted long ago that 'bards are a touchy lot'. The lives and writings of the Renaissance Humanists and the correspondence in the most esteemed literary periodicals of our own century will show that critics and scholars are the same. But *sensitive* in that meaning cannot be combined with *enriching*. Competitive and resentful egoisms can only impoverish social life. The sensitivity that enriches must be of the sort that guards a man from wounding others, not of the sort that makes him ready to feel wounded himself. Between this sensitivity and *culture,* my own experience does not suggest any causal connection. I have often found it among the uncultured. Among the cultured I have sometimes found it and sometimes not.

Let us be honest. I claim to be one of the cultured myself and have no wish to foul my own nest. Even if that claim is disallowed, I have at least lived among them and would not denigrate my friends. But we are speaking here among ourselves – behind closed doors. Frankness is best. The real traitor to our order is not the man who speaks, within that order, of its faults, but the man who flatters our corporate self-complacency. I gladly admit that we number among us men and women whose modesty, courtesy, fair-mindedness, patience in disputation and readiness to see an antagonist's point of view, are wholly admirable. I am fortunate to have known them. But we must also admit that we show as high a percentage as any group whatever of bullies, paranoiacs and poltroons, of backbiters, exhibitionists, mopes, milksops and world-without-end bores. The loutishness that turns every argument into a quarrel is really no rarer among us than among the sub-literate; the restless inferiority complex ('stern to inflict' but not 'stubborn to endure') which bleeds at a touch but scratches like a wildcat is almost as common among us as among schoolgirls.

If you doubt this, try an experiment. Take any one of those who vaunt most highly the adjusting, cleansing, liberating and civilising effects of *culture* and ask him about other poets, other critics, other scholars, not in the mass but one by one and name by name. Nine times out of ten he will deny of each what he claimed for all. He will certainly produce very few cases in which, on his own showing, *culture* has had its boasted results. Sometimes we suspect that he can think of only one. The conclusion most naturally to be drawn from his remarks is that the praise our order can most securely claim is that which Dr Johnson gave to the Irish. 'They are an honest people; they never speak well of one another.'

It is then (at best) extremely doubtful whether *culture* produces any of those qualities which will enable people to associate with one another graciously, loyally, understandingly, and with permanent delight. When Ovid said that it 'softened our manners', he was flattering a barbarian king. But even if *culture* did all these things, we could not embrace it for their sake. This would be to use consciously and self-consciously, as means to extraneous ends, things which must lose all their power of conducing to those ends by the very fact of being so used. For many modern exponents of *culture* seem to me to be 'impudent' in the etymological sense; they lack *pudor,* they have no shyness where men ought to be shy. They handle the most precious and fragile things with the roughness of an auctioneer, and talk of our most intensely solitary and fugitive experiences as if they were selling us a Hoover. It is all really very well summed up in Mr Allen's phrase in the *Twentieth Century,* 'the faith in culture'. A 'faith in culture' is as bad as a faith in religion; both expressions imply a turning away from those very things which culture and religion are about. 'Culture' as a collective name for certain very valuable activities is a permissible word; but *culture* hypostatised, set up on its own, made into a faith, a cause, a banner, a 'platform', is unendurable. For none of the activities in question cares a straw for that faith or cause. It is like a return to early Semitic religion where names themselves were regarded as powers.

Now a step further. Mr Allen complained that, not content with creeping out of earshot when we can hear the voices of certain *culture*-mongers no longer, we then wantonly consort, or pretend that we consort, with the lowest of the low brows, and affect to share their pleasures. There are at this point a good many allusions which go over my head. I don't know what AFN is, I am not fond of cellars, and modern whisky suits neither my purse, my palate, nor my digestion. But I think I know the sort of thing he has in mind, and I think I can account for it. As before, I will begin with a parallel. Suppose you had spent an evening among very young and very transparent snobs who were feigning a discriminating enjoyment of a great port, though anyone who knew could see very well that, if they had ever drunk port in their lives before, it came from a grocer's. And then suppose that on your journey home you went into a grubby little teashop and there heard an old body in a feather boa say to another old body, with a smack of her lips, 'That was a nice cup o'tea dearie, that was. Did me good.' Would you not, at that moment, feel that this was like fresh mountain air? For here, at last, would be something real. Here would be a mind really concerned about that in which it expressed concern. Here would be pleasure, here would be undebauched experience, spontaneous and compulsive, from the fountain head. A live dog is better than a dead lion. In the same way, after a certain kind of sherry party, where there have been cataracts of *culture* but never one word or one glance that suggested a real enjoyment of any art, any person, or any natural object, my heart warms to the schoolboy on the bus who is reading *Fantasy and Science Fiction,* rapt and oblivious of all the world beside. For here also I should feel that I had met something real and live and unfabricated; genuine literary experience, spontaneous and compulsive, disinterested. I should have hopes of that boy. Those who have greatly cared for any book whatever may possibly come to care, some day, for good books. The organs of appreciation exist in them. They are not impotent. And even if this particular boy is never going to like anything severer than science fiction, even so.

The child whose love is here, at least doth reap
One precious gain, that he forgets himself.

I should still prefer the live dog to the dead lion; perhaps, even, the wild dog to the over-tame poodle or Peke.

I should not have spent so many words on answering Mr Allen's question (neither of us matters sufficiently to justify it) unless I thought that the discussion led to something of more consequence. This I will now try to develop. Mr Forster feels anxious because he dreads Theocracy. Now if he expects to see a Theocracy set up in modern England, I myself believe his expectation to be wholly chimerical. But I wish to make it very clear that, if I thought the thing in the least probable, I should feel about it exactly as he does. I fully embrace the maxim (which he borrows from a Christian) that 'all power corrupts'. I would go further. The loftier the pretensions of the power, the more meddlesome, inhuman and oppressive it will be. Theocracy is the worst of all possible governments. All political power is at best a necessary evil: but it is least evil when its sanctions are most modest and commonplace, when it claims no more than to be useful or convenient and sets itself strictly limited objectives. Anything transcendental or spiritual, or even anything very strongly ethical, in its pretensions is dangerous, and encourages it to meddle with our private lives. Let the shoemaker stick to his last. Thus the Renaissance doctrine of Divine Right is for me a corruption of monarchy; Rousseau's General Will, of democracy; racial mysticisms, of nationality. And Theocracy, I admit and even insist, is the worst corruption of all. But then I don't think we are in any danger of it. What I think we are really in danger of is something that would be only one degree less intolerable, and intolerable in almost the same way. I would call it Charientocracy; not the rule of the saints but the rule of the χαρίεντες, the *venustiores*, the Hotel de Rambouillet, the Wits, the Polite, the 'Souls', the 'Apostles', the Sensitive, the *Cultured*, the Integrated, or whatever the latest password may be. I will explain how I think it could come about.

The old social classes have broken up. Two results follow. On the one hand, since most men, as Aristotle observed, do not like to be merely equal with all other men, we find all sorts of people building themselves into groups within which they can feel superior to the mass; little unofficial, self-appointed aristocracies. The *Cultured* increasingly form such a group. Notice their tendency to use the social term *vulgar* of those who disagree with them. Notice that Mr Allen spoke of rebels against, or deserters from, this group, as denying not that they are 'intellectual' but that they are 'intellectuals', not hiding a quality but deprecating inclusion in a class. On the other hand, inevitably, there is coming into existence a new, real, ruling class: what has been called the Managerial Class. The coalescence of these two groups, the unofficial, self-appointed aristocracy of the *Cultured* and the actual Managerial rulers, will bring us to Charientocracy.

But the two groups are already coalescing because eduction is increasingly the means of access to the Managerial Class. And of course eduction, in some sense, is a very proper means of access, we do not want our rulers to be dunces. But education is coming to have a new significance. It aspires to do, and can do, far more to the pupil than education (except, perhaps, that of the Jesuits) has ever done before.

For one thing, the pupil is now far more defenceless in the hands of his teachers. He comes increasingly from businessmen's flats or workmen's cottages in which there are few books or none. He has hardly ever been alone. The educational machine seizes him very early and organises his whole life, to the exclusion of all unsuperintended solitude or leisure. The hours unsponsored, uninspected, perhaps even forbidden, reading, the ramblings, and the 'long, long thoughts' in which those of luckier generations first discovered literature and nature and themselves are a thing of the past. If a Traherne or a Wordsworth were born today he would be 'cured' before he was twelve. In short, the modern pupil is the ideal patient for those masters who, not content with teaching a subject, would create a character; helpless Plasticine. Or if by chance (for nature will be nature) he should have any powers of resistance, they know how to deal with him. I am coming to that point in a moment.

Secondly, the nature of the teaching has changed. In a sense it had changed for the better: that is, it demands far more of the master and, in recompense, makes his work more interesting. It has become far more intimate and penetrating; more inward. Not content with making sure that the pupil has read and remembered the text, it aspires to teach him appreciation. It seems harsh to quarrel with what at first sounds so reasonable an aim. Yet there is a danger in it. Everyone now laughs at the old test paper with its context questions and the like, and people ask, 'What good can that sort of thing do a boy?' But surely to demand that the test paper should do the boy good is like demanding that a thermometer should heat a room. It was the reading of the text which was supposed to do the boy good; you set the paper to find out if he had read it. And just because the paper did not force the boy to produce, or to feign, appreciation, it left him free to develop in private, spontaneously, as an out-of-school activity which would never earn any marks, such appreciation as he could. That was a private affair between himself and

Virgil or himself and Shakespeare. Nine times out of ten, probably, nothing happened at all. But wherever appreciation did occur (and quite certainly it sometimes did) it was genuine; suited to the boy's age and character; no exotic, but the healthy growth of its native soil and weather. But when we substitute exercises in 'practical criticism' for the old, dry papers, a new situation arises. The boy will not get good marks (which means, in the long run, that he will not get into the Managerial Class) unless he produces the kind of responses, and the kind of analytic method, which commend themselves to his teacher. This means at best that he is trained to the precocious anticipation of responses, and of a method, inappropriate to his years. At worst it means that he is trained in the (not very difficult) art of simulating the orthodox responses. For nearly all boys are good mimics. Depend upon it, before you have been teaching for a term, everyone in the form knows pretty well 'the sort of stuff that goes down with Prickly Pop-eye'. In the old days also they knew what 'went down', but the only thing that 'went down' was correct answers to factual questions, and there were only two ways of producing those: working or cheating.

The thing would not be so bad if the responses which the pupils had to make were even those of the individual master. But we have already passed that stage. Somewhere (I have not yet tracked it down) there must be a kind of *culture*-mongers' central bureau which keeps a sharp look out for deviationists. At least there is certainly someone who sends little leaflets to schoolmasters, printing half a dozen poems on each and telling the master not only which the pupils must be made to prefer, but exactly on what grounds. (The impertinence of it! We know what Mulcaster or Boyer would have done with those leaflets.)

Thus to say that, under the nascent régime, education alone will get you into the ruling class, may not mean simply that the failure to acquire certain knowledge and to reach a certain level of intellectual competence will exclude you. That would be reasonable enough. But it may come to mean, perhaps means already, something more. It means that you cannot get in without becoming, or without making your masters believe that you have become, a very specific kind of person, one who makes the right responses to the right authors. In fact, you can get in only by becoming, in the modern sense of the word, *cultured*. This situation must be distinguished from one that has often occurred before. Nearly all ruling classes, sooner or later, in some degree or other, have taken up *culture* and patronised the arts. But when that happens the *culture* is the result of their position; one of the luxuries or privileges of their order. The situation we are now facing will be almost the opposite. Entry into the ruling class will be the reward of *culture*. Thus we reach Charientocracy.

Not only is the thing likely to happen; it is already planned and avowed. Mr J.W. Saunders has set it all out in an excellent article entitled 'Poetry in the Managerial Age' *(Essays in Criticism,* iv, 3, July 1954). He there faces the fact that modern poets are read almost exclusively by one another. He looks about for a remedy. Naturally he does not suggest that the poets should do anything about it. For it is taken as basic by all the *culture* of our age that whenever artists and audience lose touch, the fault must be wholly on the side of the audience. (I have never come across the great work in which this important doctrine is proved.) The remedy which occurs to Mr Saunders is that we should provide our poets with a conscript audience; a privilege last enjoyed, I believe, by Nero. And he tells us how this can be done. We get our 'co-ordinators' through eduction; success in examinations is the road into the ruling class. All that we need do, therefore, is to make not just poetry, but 'the intellectual discipline, which the critical reading of poetry can foster', the backbone of our educational system. In order words, practical criticism or something of the sort, exercised, no doubt, chiefly on modern poets, is to be the indispensable subject, failure in which excludes you from the Managerial Class. And so our poets get their conscript readers. Every boy or girl who is born is presented with the choice. 'Read the poets whom we, the *cultured,* approve, and say the sort of things we say about them, or be a prole.' And this (picking up on a previous point) shows how Charientocracy can deal with the minority of pupils who have tastes of their own and are not pure Plasticine. They get low marks. You kick them off the educational ladder at a low rung and they disappear into the proletariat.

Another advantage is that, besides providing poets with a conscript audience for the moment, you can make sure that the regnant literary dynasty will reign almost for ever. For the deviationists whom you have kicked off the ladder will of course include all those troublesome types who, in earlier ages, were apt to start new schools and movements. If there had been a sound Charientocracy in their day, the young Chaucer, the young Donne, the young Wordsworth and Coleridge, could have been dealt with. And thus literary history, as we have known it in the past, may come to an end. Literary man, so long a wild animal, will have become a tame one.

Having explained why I think a Charientocracy probable, I must conclude by explaining why I think it undesirable.

Culture is a bad qualification for a ruling class because it does not qualify men to rule. The things we really need in our rulers – mercy, financial integrity, practical intelligence, hard work, and the like – are no more likely to be found in cultured persons than in anyone else.

Culture is a bad qualification in the same way as sanctity. Both are hard to diagnose and easy to feign. Of course not every charientocrat will be a cultural hypocrite nor every theocrat a Tartuffe. But both systems encourage hypocrisy and make the disinterested pursuit of the quality they profess to value more difficult.

But hypocrisy is not the only evil they encourage. There are, as in piety, so in *culture,* states which, if less culpable, are no less disastrous. In the one we have the 'Goody-goody'; the docile youth who has neither revolted against nor risen above the routine pietisms and respectabilities of his home. His conformity has won the approval of his parents, his influential neighbours, and his own conscience. He does not know that he has missed anything and is content. In the other, we have the adaptable youth to whom poetry has always been something 'Set' for 'evaluation'. Success in this exercise has given him pleasure and let him into the ruling class. He does not know what he has missed, does not know that poetry ever had any other purpose, and is content.

Both types are much to be pitied: but both can sometimes be very nasty. Both may exhibit spiritual pride, but each in its proper form; since the one has succeeded by acquiescence and repression, but the other by repeated victory in competitive performances. To the pride of the one, sly, simpering and demure, we might apply Mr Allen's word 'smug' (especially if we let in a little of its older sense). My epithet for the other would, I think, be 'swaggering'. It tends in my experience to be raw, truculent, eager to give pain, insatiable in its demands for submission, resentful and suspicious of disagreement. Where the goody-goody slinks and sidles and purrs (and sometimes scratches) like a cat, his opposite number in the ranks of the *cultured* gobbles like an enraged turkey. And perhaps both types are less curable than the hypocrite proper. A hypocrite might (conceivably) repent and mend; or he might be unmasked and rendered innocuous. But who could bring to repentance, and who can unmask, those who were attempting no deception? who don't know that they are not the real thing because they don't know that there ever was a real thing?

Lastly I reach the point where my objections to Theocracy and to Charientocracy are almost identical 'Lilies that fester smell far worse than weeds.' The higher the pretensions of our rulers are, the more meddlesome and impertinent their rule is likely to be, and the more the thing in whose name they rule will be defiled. The highest things have the most precarious foothold in our nature. By making sanctity or culture a *moyen de parvenir* you help to drive them out of the world. Let our masters leave these two, at least, alone; leave us some region where the spontaneous, the unmarketable, the utterly private, can still exist.

As far as I am concerned, Mr Allen fell short of the mark when he spoke of a 'retreat from the faith in culture'. I don't want retreat; I want attack or, if you prefer the word, rebellion. I write in the hope of rousing others to rebel. So far as I can see, the question has nothing to do with the difference between Christians and those who (unfortunately, since the word has long borne a useful, and wholly different, meaning) have been called 'humanists'. I hope that red herring will not be brought in. I would gladly believe that many atheists and agnostics care for the things I care for. It is for them I have written. To them I say: the 'faith in culture' is going to strangle all those things unless we can strangle it first. And there is no time to spare.

[50]

GOOD WORK AND
GOOD WORKS

This first appeared in The Catholic Art Quarterly, *then in* Good Work, *XXIII (Christmas 1959), and later in* The World's Last Night and Other Essays *(US, 1960). It also appeared in* Screwtape Proposes a Toast *(1998).*

'Good works' in the plural is an expression much more familiar to modern Christendom than 'good work'. Good works are chiefly alms-giving or 'helping' in the parish. They are quite separate from one's 'work'. And good works need not be good work, as anyone can see by inspecting some of the objects made to be sold at bazaars for charitable purposes. This is not according to our example. When our Lord provided a poor wedding party with an extra glass of wine all round, he was doing good works. But also good work; it was a wine really worth drinking. Nor is the neglect of goodness in our 'work', our job, according to precept. The apostle says everyone must not only work but work to produce what is 'good'.

The idea of Good Work is not quite extinct among us, though it is not, I fear, especially characteristic of religious people. I have found it among cabinet-makers, cobblers, and sailors. It is no use at all trying to impress sailors with a new liner because she is the biggest or costliest ship afloat. They look for what they call her 'lines': they predict how she will behave in a heavy sea. Artists also talk of Good Work; but decreasingly. They begin to prefer words like 'significant', 'important', 'contemporary', or 'daring'. These are not, to my mind, good symptoms.

But the great mass of men in all fully industrialised societies are the victims of a situation which almost excludes the idea of Good Work from the outset. 'Built-in obsolescence' becomes an economic necessity. Unless an article is so made that it will go to pieces in a year or two and thus have to be replaced, you will not get a sufficient turnover. A hundred years ago, when a man got married, he had built for him (if he were rich enough) a carriage in which he expected to drive for the rest of his life. He now buys a car which he expects to sell again in two years. Work nowadays must *not* be good.

For the wearer, zip fasteners have this advantage over buttons: that, while they last, they will save him an infinitesimal amount of time and trouble. For the producer, they have a much more solid merit; they don't remain in working order long. Bad work is the *desideratum*.

We must avoid taking a glibly moral view of this situation. It is not solely the result of original or actual sin. It has stolen upon us, unforeseen and unintended. The degraded commercialism of our minds is quite as much its result as its cause. Nor can it, in my opinion, be cured by purely moral efforts.

Originally things are made for use, or delight, or (more often) for both. The savage hunter makes himself a weapon of flint or bone; makes it as well as he can, for if it is blunt or brittle he will kill no meat. His woman makes a clay pot to fetch water in; again as well as she can, for she will have to use it. But they do not for long (if at all) abstain from decorating these things; they want to have (like Dogberry) 'everything handsome about them'. And while they work, we may be sure they sing or whistle or at least hum. They may tell stories too.

Into this situation, unobtrusive as Eden's snake and at first as innocent as that snake once was, there must sooner or later come a change. Each family no longer makes all it needs. There is a specialist, a potter making pots for the whole village, a smith making weapons for all; a bard (poet and musician in one) singing and story-telling for all. It is significant that in Homer the smith of the gods is lame, and the poet among men is blind. That may be how the thing began. The defectives, who are no use as hunters or warriors, may be set aside to provide both necessaries and recreation for those who are.

The importance of this change is that we now have people making things (pots, swords, lays) not for their own use and delight but for the use and delight of others. And of course they must, in some way or other, be rewarded for doing it. The change is necessary unless society and arts are to remain in a state not of paradisal, but of feeble, blundering, and impoverishing simplicity. It is kept healthy by two facts. First, these specialists will do their work as well as they can. They are right up against the people who are going to use it. You'll have all the women in the village after you if you make bad pots. You'll be shouted down if you sing a dull lay. If you make bad swords, then at best the warriors will come back and thrash you; at worst, they won't come back at all, for the enemy will have killed them, and your village will be burned and you yourself enslaved or knocked on the head. And secondly, because the specialists are doing as well as they can something that is indisputably worth doing, they will delight in their work. We must not idealise. It will not all be delight. The smith may be overworked. The bard may be frustrated when the village insists on hearing his last lay over again (or a new one exactly like it) while he is longing to get a hearing for some wonderful innovation. But, by and large, the specialists have a life fit for a man; usefulness, a reasonable amount of honour, and the joy of exercising skill.

I lack space and, of course, knowledge, to trace the whole process from this state of affairs to that in which we are living today. But I think we can now disengage the essence of the change. Granted the departure from the primitive condition in which everyone makes things for himself, and granted, therefore, a condition in which many work for others (who will pay them), there are still two sorts of job. Of one sort, a man can truly say, 'I am doing work which is worth doing. It would still be worth doing if nobody paid for it. But as I have no private means, and need to be fed and housed and clothed, I must be paid while I do it.' The other kind of job is that in which people do work whose sole purpose is the earning of money: work which need not be, ought not to be, or would not be, done by anyone in the whole world unless it were paid.

We may thank God there are still plenty of jobs in the first category. The agricultural labourer, the policeman, the doctor, the artist, the teacher, the priest, and many others, are doing what is worth doing in itself; what quite a number of people would do, and do, without pay; what every family would attempt to do for itself, in some amateurish fashion, if it lived in primitive isolation. Of course jobs of this kind need not be agreeable. Ministering to a leper settlement is one of them.

The opposite extreme may be represented by two examples. I do not necessarily equate them morally, but they are alike by our present classification. One is the work of the professional prostitute. The peculiar horror of her work – if you say we should not call it work, think again – the thing that makes it so much more horrible than ordinary fornication, is that it is an extreme example of an activity which has no possible end in view except money. You cannot go further in that direction than sexual intercourse, not only without marriage, not only without love, but even without lust. My other example is this. I often see a hoarding which bears a notice to the effect that thousands look at this space and your firm ought to hire it for an advertisement of its wares. Consider by how many stages this is separated from 'making that which is good'. A carpenter has made this hoarding; that, in itself, has no use. Printers and paper-makers have worked to produce the notice – worthless until someone hires the space – worthless to him until he pastes on it another notice, still worthless to him unless it persuades someone else to buy his goods; which themselves may be ugly, useless, and pernicious luxuries that no mortal would have bought unless the advertisement, by its sexy or snobbish incantations, had conjured up in him a factitious desire for them. At every stage of the process, work is being done whose sole value lies in the money it brings.

Such would seem to be the inevitable result of a society which depends predominantly on buying and selling. In a rational world, things would be made because they were wanted; in the actual world, wants have to be created in order that people may receive money for making the things. That is why the distrust or contempt of trade which we find in earlier societies should not be too hastily set down as mere snobbery. The more important trade is, the more people are condemned to – and, worse still, learn to prefer – what we have called the second kind of job. Work worth doing apart from its pay, enjoyable work, and good work become the privilege of a fortunate minority. The competitive search for customers dominates international situations.

Within my lifetime in England money was (very properly) collected to buy shirts for some men who were out of work. The work they were out of was the manufacture of shirts.

That such a state of affairs cannot be permanent is easily foreseen. But unfortunately it is most likely to perish by its own internal contradictions in a manner which will cause immense suffering. It can be ended painlessly only if we find some way of ending it voluntarily; and needless to say I have no plan for doing that, and none of our masters – the Big Men behind government and industry – would take any notice if I had. The only hopeful sign at the moment is the 'space-race' between America and Russia. Since we have got ourselves into a state where the main problem is not to provide people with what they need or like, but to keep people making things (it hardly matters what), great powers could not easily be better employed than in fabricating costly objects which they then fling overboard. It keeps money circulating and factories working, and it won't do space much harm – or not for a long time. But the relief is partial and temporary. The main practical task for most of us is not to give the Big Men advice about how to end our fatal economy – we have none to give and they wouldn't listen – but to consider how we can live within it as little hurt and degraded as possible.

It is something even to recognise that it is fatal and insane. Just as the Christian has a great advantage over other men, not by being less fallen than they nor less doomed to live in a fallen world, but by knowing that he *is* a fallen man in a fallen world; so we shall do better if we remember at every moment what Good Work was and how impossible it has now become for the majority. We may have to earn our living by taking part in the production of objects which are rotten in quality and which, even if they were good in quality, would not be worth producing – the demand or 'market' for them having been simply engineered by advertisement. Beside the waters of Babylon – or the assembly belt – we shall still say inwardly, 'If I forget thee, O Jerusalem, may my right hand forget its cunning.' (It will.)

And of course we shall keep our eyes skinned for any chance of escape. If we have any 'choice of a career' (but has one man in a thousand any such thing?) we shall be after the sane jobs like greyhounds and stick there like limpets. We shall try, if we get the chance, to earn our living by doing well what would be worth doing even if we had not our living to earn. A considerable mortification of our avarice may be necessary. It is usually the insane jobs that lead to big money; they are often also the least laborious.

But beyond all this there is something subtler. We must take great care to preserve our habits of mind from infection by those which the situation has bred. Such an infection has, in my opinion, deeply corrupted our artists.

Until quite recently – until the latter part of the last century – it was taken for granted that the business of the artist was to delight and instruct his public. There were, of course, different publics; the street-songs and the oratorios were not addressed to the same audience (though I think a good many people liked both). And an artist might lead his public on to appreciate finer things than they had wanted at first; but he could do this only by being, from the first, if not merely entertaining, yet entertaining, and if not completely intelligible, yet very largely intelligible. All this has changed. In the highest aesthetic circles one now hears nothing about the artist's duty to us. It is all about our duty to him. He owes us nothing; we owe him 'recognition', even though he has never paid the slightest attention to our tastes, interests, or habits. If we don't give it to him, our name is mud. In this shop, the customer is always wrong.

But this change is surely part of our changed attitude to all work. As 'giving employment' becomes more important than making things men need or like, there is a tendency to regard every trade as something that exists chiefly for the sake of those who practise it. The smith does not work in order that the warriors may fight; the warriors exist and fight in order that the smith may be kept busy. The bard does not exist in order to delight the tribe: the tribe exists in order to appreciate the bard.

In industry highly creditable motives, as well as insanity, lie behind this change of attitude. A real advance in charity stopped us talking about 'surplus population' and started us talking instead about 'unemploy-ment'. The danger is that this should lead us to forget that employment is not an end in itself. We want people to be employed only as a means to their being fed – believing (whether rightly, who knows?) that it is better to feed them for making things badly than for doing nothing.

But though we have a duty to feed the hungry, I doubt whether we have a duty to 'appreciate' the ambitious. This attitude to art is fatal to good work. Many modern novels, poems, and pictures, which we are brow-beaten into 'appreciating', are not good work because they are not *work* at all. They are mere puddles of spilled sensibility or reflection. When an artist is in the strict sense working, he of course takes into account the existing taste, interests, and capacity of his audience. These, no less than the language, the marble, or the paint, are part of his raw material; to be used, tamed, sublimated, not ignored nor defied. Haughty indifference to them is not genius nor integrity; it is laziness and incompetence. You have not learned your job. Hence, real honest-to-God work, so far as the arts are concerned, now appears chiefly in low-brow art; in the film, the detective story, the children's story. These are often sound structures; seasoned wood, accurately dovetailed, the stresses all calculated; skill and labour successfully used to do what is intended. Do not misunderstand. The high-brow productions may, of course, reveal a finer sensibility and profounder thought. But a puddle is not a work, whatever rich wines or oils or medicines have gone into it.

'Great works' (of art) and 'good works' (of charity) had better also be Good Work. Let choirs sing well or not at all. Otherwise we merely confirm the majority in their conviction that the world of Business, which does with such efficiency so much that never really needed doing is the real, the adult, and the practical world; and that all this 'culture' and all this 'religion' (horrid words both) are essentially marginal, amateurish, and rather effeminate activities.

A SLIP OF THE TONGUE

An enlarged version of 'Thoughts of a Cambridge Don', this was published in The Lion, *the magazine of St Mark's, Dundela, Belfast (January 1963). It was also preached as a sermon in Magdalene College Chapel, Cambridge, in 1956. First published in* They Asked for a Paper *(1962), it was reprinted in* Screwtape Proposes a Toast *(1998).*

When a layman has to preach a sermon I think he is most likely to be useful, or even interesting, if he starts exactly from where he is himself; not so much presuming to instruct as comparing notes.

Not long ago when I was using the collect for the fourth Sunday after Trinity in my private prayers I found that I had made a slip of the tongue. I had meant to pray that I might so pass through things temporal that I finally lost not the things eternal; I found I had prayed so to pass through things eternal that I finally lost not the things temporal. Of course I don't think that a slip of the tongue is a sin. I am not sure that I am even a strict enough Freudian to believe that all such slips, without exception, are deeply significant. But I think some of them are significant, and I thought this was one of that sort. I thought that what I had inadvertently said very nearly expressed something I had really wished.

Very nearly; not, of course, precisely. I had never been quite stupid enough to think that the eternal could, strictly, be 'passed through'. What I had wanted to pass through without prejudice to my things temporal was those hours or moments in which I attended to the eternal, in which I exposed myself to it.

I mean this sort of thing. I say my prayers, I read a book of devotion, I prepare for, or receive, the Sacrament. But while I do these things there is, so to speak, a voice inside me that urges caution. It tells me to be careful; to keep my head; not to go too far; not to burn my boats. I come into the presence of God with a great fear lest anything should happen to me within that presence which will prove too intolerably inconvenient when I have come out again into my 'ordinary' life. I don't want to be carried away into any resolution which I shall afterwards regret. For I know I shall be feeling quite different after breakfast; I don't want anything to happen to me at the altar which will run up too big a bill to pay then. It would be very disagreeable, for instance, to take the duty of charity (while I am at the altar) so seriously that, after breakfast, I had to tear up the really stunning reply I had written to an impudent correspondent yesterday and meant to post today. It would be very tiresome to commit myself to a programme of temperance which would cut off my after-breakfast cigarette (or, at best, make it cruelly alternative to a cigarette later in the morning). Even repentance of past acts will have to be paid for. By repenting one acknowledges them as sins – therefore not to be repeated. Better leave that issue undecided.

The root principle of all these precautions is the same: to guard the things temporal. And I find some evidence that this temptation is not peculiar to me. A good author (whose name I have forgotten) asks somewhere, 'Have we never risen from our knees in haste for fear God's will should become too unmistakable if we prayed longer?' The following story was told as true. An Irishwoman who had just been at confession met on the steps of the chapel the other woman who was her greatest enemy in the village. The other woman let fly a torrent of abuse. 'Isn't it a shame for ye,' replied Biddy, 'to be talking to me like that, ye coward, and me in a state of Grace the way I can't answer ye? But you wait. I won't be in a state of Grace long.' There is an excellent tragi-comic example in Trollope's *Last Chronicle*. The Archdeacon was angry with his eldest son. He at once made a number of legal arrangements to the son's disadvantage. They could all easily have been made a few days later, but Trollope explains why the Archdeacon would not wait. To reach the next day, he had to pass through his evening prayers, and he knew that he might not be able to carry his hostile plans safely through the clause, 'Forgive us our trespasses as we forgive.' So he got in first, he decided to present God with a *fait accompli*. This is an extreme case of the precautions I am talking about; the man will not venture within reach of the eternal until he has made the things temporal safe in advance.

This is my endlessly recurrent temptation: to go down to that Sea (I think St John of the Cross called God a sea) and there neither dive nor swim nor float, but only dabble and splash, careful not to get out of my depth and holding on to the lifeline which connects me with my things temporal.

It is different from the temptations that met us at the beginning of the Christian life. Then we fought (at least I fought) against admitting the claims of the eternal at all. And when we had fought, and been beaten, and surrendered, we supposed that all would be fairly plain sailing. This temptation comes later. It is addressed to those who have already admitted the claim in principle and are even making some sort of effort to meet it. Our temptation is to look eagerly for the minimum that will be accepted. We are in fact very like honest but reluctant taxpayers. We approve of an income tax in principle. We make our returns truthfully. But we dread a rise in the tax. We are very careful to pay no more than is necessary. And we hope – we very ardently hope – that after we have paid it there will still be enough left to live on.

And notice that those cautions which the tempter whispers in our ears are all plausible. Indeed, I don't think he often tries to deceive us (after early youth) with a direct lie. The plausibility is this. It is really possible to be carried away by religious emotion – *enthusiasm* as our ancestors called it – into resolutions and attitudes which we shall, not sinfully but rationally, not when we are more worldly but when we are wiser, have cause to regret. We can become scrupulous or fanatical; we can, in what seems zeal but is really presumption, embrace tasks never intended for us. That is the truth in the temptation. The lie consists in the suggestion that our best protection is a prudent regard for the safety of our pocket, our habitual indulgences, and our ambitions. But that is quite false. Our real protection is to be sought elsewhere; in common Christian usage, in moral theology, in steady rational thinking, in the advice of good friends and good books, and (if need be) in a skilled spiritual director. Swimming lessons are better than a lifeline to the shore.

For of course that lifeline is really a death-line. There is no parallel to paying taxes and living on the remainder. For it is not so much of our time and so much of our attention that God demands; it is not even all our time and all our attention: it is our selves. For each of us the Baptist's words are true: 'He must increase and I decrease.' He will be infinitely merciful to our repeated failures; I know no promise that He will accept a deliberate compromise. For He has, in the last resort, nothing to give us but Himself; and He can give that only in so far as our self-affirming will retires and makes room for Him in our souls. Let us make up our minds to it; there will be nothing 'of our own' left over to live on; no 'ordinary' life. I do not mean that each of us will necessarily be called to be a martyr or even an ascetic. That's as may be. For some (nobody knows which) the Christian life will include much leisure, many occupations we naturally like. But these will be received from God's hands. In a perfect Christian they would be as much part of his 'religion', his 'service', as his hardest duties, and his feasts would be as Christian as his fasts. What cannot be admitted – what must exist only as an undefeated but daily resisted enemy – is the idea of something that is 'our own', some area in which we are to be 'out of school', on which God has no claim.

For he claims all, because He is love and must bless. He cannot bless us unless He has us. When we try to keep within us an area that is our own, we try to keep an area of death. Therefore, in love, He claims all. There's no bargaining with Him.

This is, I take it, the meaning of all those sayings that alarm me most. Thomas More said, 'If ye make indentures with God how much ye will serve Him, ye shall find ye have signed both of them yourself.' Law, in his terrible, cool voice, said, 'Many will be rejected at the last day, not because they have taken no time or pains about their salvation, but because they have not taken time and pains enough'; and later, in his richer, Behmenite period, 'If you have not chosen the Kingdom of God, it will make in the end no difference what you have chosen instead.' Those are hard words to take. Will it really make no difference whether it was women or patriotism, cocaine or art, whisky or a seat in the Cabinet, money or science? Well, surely no difference that matters. We shall have missed the end for which we are formed and rejected the only thing that satisfies. Does it matter to a man dying in a desert, by which choice of route he missed the only well?

It is a remarkable fact that on this subject Heaven and Hell speak with one voice. The tempter tells me, 'Take care. Think how much this good resolve, the acceptance of this Grace, is going to cost.' But Our Lord equally tells us to count the cost. Even in human affairs great importance is attached to the agreement of those whose testimony hardly ever agrees. Here, more. Between them it would seem to be pretty clear that paddling is of little consequence. What matters, what Heaven desires and Hell fears, is precisely that further step; out of our depth, out of our own control.

And yet, I am not in despair. At this point I become what some would call very Evangelical; at any rate very un-Pelagian. I do not think any efforts of my own will can end once and for all this craving for limited liabilities, this fatal reservation, only God can. I have good faith and hope He will. Of course I don't mean that I can therefore, as they say, 'sit back'. What God does for us, He does in us. The process of doing it will appear to me (and not falsely) to be the daily or hourly repeated exercises of my own will in renouncing this attitude; especially each morning, for it grows all over me like a new shell each night. Failures will be forgiven; it is acquiescence that is fatal, the permitted, regularised presence of an area in ourselves which we still claim for our own. We may never, this side of death, drive the invader out of our territory; but we must be in the Resistance, not in the Vichy government. And this, so far as I can yet see, must be begun again every day. Our morning prayer should be that in the *Imitation: Da hodie perfecte incipere* – grant me to make an unflawed beginning today, for I have done nothing yet.

[52]

WE HAVE NO
'RIGHT TO HAPPINESS'

The last thing Lewis wrote before his death in November 1963, this appeared shortly afterwards in The Saturday Evening Post, CCXXXVI *(21–28 December 1963), then in* Undeceptions *(1971) and* God in the Dock *(1998).*

'After all,' said Clare, 'they had a right to happiness.'

We were discussing something that once happened in our own neighbourhood. Mr A. had deserted Mrs A. and got his divorce in order to marry Mrs B., who had likewise got her divorce in order to marry Mr A. And there was certainly no doubt that Mr A. and Mrs B. were very much in love with one another. If they continued to be in love, and if nothing went wrong with their health or their income, they might reasonably expect to be very happy.

It was equally clear that they were not happy with their old partners. Mrs B. had adored her husband at the outset. But then he got smashed up in the war. It was thought he had lost his virility, and it was known that he had lost his job. Life with him was no longer what Mrs B. had bargained for. Poor Mrs A., too. She had lost her looks – and all her liveliness. It might be true, as some said, that she consumed herself by bearing his children and nursing him through the long illness that overshadowed their earlier married life.

You mustn't, by the way, imagine that A. was the sort of man who nonchalantly threw a wife away like the peel of an orange he'd sucked dry. Her suicide was a terrible shock to him. We all knew this, for he told us so himself. 'But what could I do?' he said. 'A man has a right to happiness. I had to take my one chance when it came.'

I went away thinking about the concept of a 'right to happiness'.

At first this sounds to me as odd as the right to good luck. For I believe – whatever one school of moralists may say – that we depend for a very great deal of our happiness or misery on circumstances outside all human control. A right to happiness doesn't, for me, make much more sense than a right to be six feet tall, or to have a millionaire for your father, or to get good weather whenever you want to have a picnic.

I can understand a right as a freedom guaranteed me by the laws of the society I live in. Thus, I have a right to travel along the public roads because society gives me that freedom; that's what we mean by calling the roads 'public'. I can also understand a right as a claim guaranteed me by the laws, and correlative to an obligation on someone else's part. If I have a right to receive £100 from you, this is another way of saying that you have a duty to pay me £100. If the laws allow Mr A. to desert his wife and seduce his neighbour's wife, then, by definition, Mr A. has a legal right to do so, and we need bring in no talk about 'happiness'.

But of course that was not what Clare meant. She meant that he had not only a legal but a moral right to act as he did. In other words, Clare is – or would be if she thought it out – a classical moralist after the style of Thomas Aquinas, Grotius, Hooker and Locke. She believes that behind the laws of the state there is a Natural Law.

I agree with her. I hold this conception to be basic to all civilisation. Without it, the actual laws of the state become an absolute, as in Hegel. They cannot be criticised because there is no norm against which they should be judged.

The ancestry of Clare's maxim, 'They have a right to happiness', is august. In words that are cherished by all civilised men, but especially by Americans, it has been laid down that one of the rights of man is a right to 'the pursuit of happiness'. And now we get to the real point.

What did the writers of that august declaration mean?

It is quite certain what they did not mean. They did not mean that man was entitled to pursue happiness by any and every means – including, say, murder, rape, robbery, treason and fraud. No society could be built on such a basis.

They meant 'to pursue happiness by all lawful means'; that is, by all means which the Law of Nature eternally sanctions and which the laws of the nation shall sanction.

Admittedly this seems at first to reduce their maxim to the tautology that men (in pursuit of happiness) have a right to do whatever they have a right to do. But tautologies, seen against their proper historical context, are not always barren tautologies. The declaration is primarily a denial of the political principles which long governed Europe: a challenge flung down to the Austrian and Russian empires, to England before the Reform Bills, to Bourbon France. It demands that whatever means of pursuing happiness are lawful for any should be lawful for all; that 'man', not men of some particular caste, class, status or religion, should be free to use them. In a century when this is being unsaid by nation after nation and party after party, let us not call it a barren tautology.

But the question as to what means are 'lawful' – what methods of pursuing happiness are either morally permissible by the Law of Nature or should be declared legally permissible by the legislature of a particular nation – remains exactly where it did. And on that question I disagree with Clare. I don't think it is obvious that people have the unlimited 'right to happiness' which she suggests.

For one thing, I believe that Clare, when she says 'happiness', means simply and solely 'sexual happiness'. Partly because women like Clare never use the word 'happiness' in any other sense. But also because I never heard Clare talk about the 'right' to any other kind. She was rather leftist in her politics, and would have been scandalised if anyone had defended the actions of a ruthless man-eating tycoon on the ground that his happiness consisted in making money and he was pursuing his happiness. She was also a rabid teetotaller; I never heard her excuse an alcoholic because he was happy when he was drunk.

A good many of Clare's friends, and especially her female friends, often felt – I've heard them say so – that their own happiness would be perceptibly increased by boxing her ears. I very much doubt if this would have brought her theory of a right to happiness into play.

Clare, in fact, is doing what the whole western world seems to me to have been doing for the last forty-odd years. When I was a youngster, all the progressive people were saying, 'Why all this prudery? Let us treat sex just as we treat all our other impulses.' I was simple-minded enough to believe they meant what they said. I have since discovered that they meant exactly the opposite. They meant that sex was to be treated as no other impulse in our nature has ever been treated by civilised people. All the others, we admit, have to be bridled. Absolute obedience to your instinct for self-preservation is what we call cowardice; to your acquisitive impulse, avarice. Even sleep must be resisted if you're a sentry. But every unkindness and breach of faith seems to be condoned provided that the object aimed at is 'four bare legs in a bed'.

It is like having a morality in which stealing fruit is considered wrong – unless you steal nectarines.

And if you protest against this view you are usually met with chatter about the legitimacy and beauty and sanctity of 'sex' and accused of harbouring some Puritan prejudice against it as something disreputable or shameful. I deny the charge. Foam-born Venus ... golden Aphrodite ... Our Lady of Cyprus ... I never breathed a word against you. If I object to boys who steal my nectarines, must I be supposed to disapprove of nectarines in general? Or even of boys in general? It might, you know, be stealing that I disapproved of.

The real situation is skilfully concealed by saying that the question of Mr A.'s 'right' to desert his wife is one of 'sexual morality'. Robbing an orchard is not an offence against some special morality called 'fruit morality'. It is an offence against honesty. Mr A.'s action is an offence against good faith (to solemn promises), against gratitude (towards one to whom he was deeply indebted) and against common humanity.

Our sexual impulses are thus being put in a position of preposterous privilege. The sexual motive is taken to condone all sorts of behaviour which, if it had any other end in view, would be condemned as merciless, treacherous and unjust.

Now though I see no good reason for giving sex this privilege, I think I see a strong cause. It is this.

It is part of the nature of a strong erotic passion – as distinct from a transient fit of appetite – that it makes more towering promises than any other emotion. No doubt all our desires make promises, but not so impressively. To be in love involves the almost irresistible conviction that one will go on being in love until one dies, and that possession of the beloved will confer, not merely frequent ecstasies, but settled, fruitful, deep-rooted, lifelong happiness. Hence *all* seems to be at stake. If we miss this chance we shall have lived in vain. At the very thought of such doom we sink into fathomless depths of self-pity.

Unfortunately these promises are found often to be quite untrue. Every experienced adult knows this to be so as regards all erotic passions (except the one he himself is feeling at the moment). We discount the world-without-end pretensions of our friends' amours easily enough. We know that such things sometimes last – and sometimes don't. And when they do last, this is not because they promised at the outset to do so. When two people achieve lasting happiness, this is not solely because they are great lovers but because they are also – I must put it crudely – good people; controlled, loyal, fair-minded, mutually adaptable people.

If we establish a 'right to (sexual) happiness' which supersedes all the ordinary rules of behaviour, we do so not because of what our passion shows itself to be in experience but because of what it professes to be while we are in the grip of it. Hence, while the bad behaviour is real and works miseries and degradations, the happiness which was the object of the behaviour turns out again and again to be illusory. Everyone (except Mr A. and Mrs B.) knows that Mr A. in a year or so may have the same reason for deserting his new wife as for deserting his old. He will feel again that all is at stake. He will see himself again as the great lover, and his pity for himself will exclude all pity for the woman.

Two further points remain.

One is this. A society in which conjugal infidelity is tolerated must always be in the long run a society adverse to women. Women, whatever a few male songs and satires may say to the contrary, are more naturally monogamous than men: it is a biological necessity. Where promiscuity prevails, they will therefore always be more often the victims than the culprits. Also, domestic happiness is more necessary to them than to us. And the quality by which they most easily hold a man, their beauty, decreases every year after they have come to maturity, but this does not happen to those qualities of personality – women don't really care twopence about our *looks* – by which we hold women. Thus in the ruthless war of promiscuity women are at a double disadvantage. They play for higher stakes and are also more likely to lose. I have no sympathy with moralists who frown at the increasing crudity of female provocativeness. These signs of desperate competition fill me with pity.

Secondly, though the 'right to happiness' is chiefly claimed for the sexual impulse, it seems to me impossible that the matter should stay there. The fatal principle, once allowed in that department, must sooner or later seep through our whole lives. We thus advance towards a state of society in which not only each man but every impulse in each man claims *carte blanche*. And then, though our technological skill may help us survive a little longer, our civilization will have died at heart, and will – one dare not even add 'unfortunately' – be swept away.

PART 4

THE CHURCH

[53]

CHRISTIAN REUNION

An Anglican Speaks to Roman Catholics

Written at the invitation of Roman Catholic friends, this essay was discovered – on the back of a few sheets of broadcasts made in 1944 – after Lewis's death in 1963, and was published for the first time in Christian Reunion *(1990).*

I have been asked to write on Christian reunion: but I am afraid that what I have to say will amount to little more than a rough analysis of the actual disunity and a suggestion as to how most of us ought to behave while our tragic and sinful divisions continue.

I will begin by saying that, whether for good or ill, the nature of the disunity has changed with the centuries: it has become more strictly, or clearly, theological. I have been well placed for noticing this because I grew up in a very archaic society – that of Northern Ireland – amidst conditions which had even then long since passed away in England. I have thus had a glimpse of the *old* disunity – the kind that descended from the sixteenth century. In it the strictly theological differences were hopelessly entangled with differences of nationality, class, politics, and the less essential differences of ritual. (I do not suggest that all differences of ritual are unessential.) They were also very embittered. A Protestant mother whose son turned from Atheism to Rome, or a Roman mother whose son turned from Atheism to Protestantism, would both have felt (I think) simple grief.

That state of affairs has passed away. On the question of ritual, indeed, it has almost turned upside down. In southern England the Romans are now *not ritualistic enough* to please the High Anglicans, and Congregationalists may (I am told) be as 'high' as either. Whatever the barrier now is, it is no longer a barrier of candles: whatever the fog, it is not a fog of incense.

And on the purely theological level I think I may say that the barrier is no longer that between a doctrine of Faith and a doctrine of Works. I am not myself convinced that any good Roman ever did hold the doctrine of

Works in that form of which Protestants accused him, or that any good Protestant ever did hold the doctrine of Faith in that form of which Romans accused him. At any rate I feel certain that no man of good will today hopes to see God either by *Pecca fortiter* or by founding an abbey. It would still be difficult (especially in Germany) to get an agreed formula: but I think that difficulty now springs rather from the mysteriousness of the subject itself than from two clearly held and mutually exclusive doctrines.

The difficulty that remains, and which becomes sharper as it becomes narrower, is our disagreement about the seat and nature of doctrinal Authority. The real reason, I take it, why you cannot be in communion with us is not your disagreement with this or that particular Protestant doctrine, so much as the absence of any real 'Doctrine', in your sense of the word, at all. It is, you feel, like asking a man to say he agrees not with a speaker but with a debating society. And the real reason why I cannot be in communion with you is not my disagreement with this or that Roman doctrine, but that to accept your Church means, not to accept a given body of doctrine, but to accept in advance any doctrine your Church hereafter produces. It is like being asked to agree not only to what a man has said but to what he's going to say.

To you the real vice of Protestantism is the formless drift which seems unable to retain the Catholic truths, which loses them one by one and ends in a 'modernism' which cannot be classified as Christian by any tolerable stretch of the word. To us the terrible thing about Rome is the recklessness (as we hold) with which she has added to the *depositum fidei* – the tropical fertility, the proliferation, of *credenda*. You see in Protestantism the Faith dying out in a desert: we see in Rome the Faith smothered in a jungle.

I know no way of bridging this gulf. Nor do I think it the business of the private layman to offer much advice on bridge-building to his betters. My only function as a Christian writer is to preach 'mere Christianity' not *ad clerum* but *ad populum*. Any success that has been given me has, I believe, been due to my strict observance of those limits. By attempting to do otherwise I should only add one more recruit (and a very ill-qualified recruit) to the ranks of the controversialists. After that I should be no more use to anyone.

I have, however, a strong premonition as to the way in which reunion will *not* come. It will not come at the edges. 'Liberal' Romans and 'high' Anglicans will not be the ones who will meet first. For the odd thing is that the nearer you get to the heart of each communion, the less you notice its difference from the other.

It is important at this point that I should not be misunderstood. What I am trying to say might be interpreted to mean that doctrines 'don't matter', and that the essence of the spiritual life lay either in the affections or in some 'mystical' experience to which the intelligence is simply irrelevant. I do not believe it is so. That the spiritual life transcends both intelligence and morality, we are probably all agreed. But I suppose it transcends them as poetry transcends grammar, and does not merely exclude them as algebra excludes grammar. I should distrust a mysticism to which they ever became simply irrelevant. That is not the way in which the divisions grow less important at the centre. To the very last, when two people differ in doctrine, logic proclaims that though both might be in error, it is impossible for both to be right. And error always to some extent disables.

When therefore we find a certain heavenly unity existing between really devout persons of differing creeds – a mutual understanding and even a power of mutual edification which each may lack towards a lukewarm member of his own denomination – we must ascribe this to the work of Christ who, in the erroneous one, sterilises his errors and inhibits the evil consequences they would naturally have ('If ye drink any deadly thing it shall not hurt you' [Mark 16:18]) and opens the eyes of the other party to all the truths mingled in his friend's errors, which are, of course, likely to be truths he particularly needs.

[54]
PRIESTESSES IN THE CHURCH?

Originally published as 'Notes on the Way' in Time and Tide, *Volume XXIX (14 August 1948), and reproduced in* Undeceptions *(1971), this also appeared in* God in the Dock *(1998).*

'I should like Balls infinitely better,' said Caroline Bingley, 'if they were carried on in a different manner ... It would surely be much more rational if conversation instead of dancing made the order of the day.' 'Much more rational, I dare say,' replied her brother, 'but it would not be near so much like a Ball.'[1] We are told that the lady was silenced: yet it could be maintained that Jane Austen has not allowed Bingley to put forward the full strength of his position. He ought to have replied with a *distinguo*. In one sense conversation is more rational for conversation may exercise the reason alone, dancing does not. But there is nothing irrational in exercising other powers than our reason. On certain occasions and for certain purposes the real irrationality is with those who will not do so. The man who would try to break a horse or write a poem or beget a child by pure syllogising would be an irrational man; though at the same time syllogising is in itself a more rational activity than the activities demanded by these achievements. It is rational not to reason, or not to limit oneself to reason, in the wrong place; and the more rational a man is the better he knows this.

These remarks are not intended as a contribution to the criticism of *Pride and Prejudice.* They came into my head when I heard that the Church of England was being advised to declare women capable of Priests' Orders. I am, indeed, informed that such a proposal is very unlikely to be seriously considered by the authorities. To take such a revolutionary step at the present moment, to cut ourselves off from the Christian past and to widen the divisions between ourselves and other

[1] *Pride and Prejudice*, ch. 11.

Churches by establishing an order of priestesses in our midst, would be an almost wanton degree of imprudence. And the Church of England herself would be torn in shreds by the operation. My concern with the proposal is of a more theoretical kind. The question involves something even deeper than a revolution in order.

I have every respect for those who wish women to be priestesses. I think they are sincere and pious and sensible people. Indeed, in a way they are too sensible. That is where my dissent from them resembles Bingley's dissent from his sister. I am tempted to say that the proposed arrangement would make us much more rational 'but not near so much like a Church'.

For at first sight all the rationality (in Caroline Bingley's sense) is on the side of the innovators. We are short of priests. We have discovered in one profession after another that women can do very well all sorts of things which were once supposed to be in the power of men alone. No one among those who dislike the proposal is maintaining that women are less capable than men of piety, zeal, learning and whatever else seems necessary for the pastoral office. What, then, except prejudice begotten by tradition, forbids us to draw on the huge reserves which could pour into the priesthood if women were here, as in so many other professions, put on the same footing as men? And against this flood of common sense, the opposers (many of them women) can produce at first nothing but an inarticulate distaste, a sense of discomfort which they themselves find it hard to analyse.

That this reaction does not spring from any contempt for women is, I think, plain from history. The Middle Ages carried their reverence for one Woman to a point at which the charge could plausibly be made that the Blessed Virgin became in their eyes almost 'a fourth Person of the Trinity'. But never, so far as I know, in all those ages was anything remotely resembling a sacerdotal office attributed to her. All salvation depends on the decision which she made in the words *Ecce ancilla*;[2] she is united in nine months' inconceivable intimacy with the eternal Word; she stands at the foot of the cross (John 19:25). But she is absent both from the Last Supper (Matthew 26:26; Mark 14:22; Luke 22:19) and from the descent of the Spirit at Pentecost (Acts 2:1f). Such is the record of Scripture. Nor can you daff it aside by saying that local and temporary conditions condemned women to silence and private life. There were female preachers. One man had four daughters who all 'prophesied', i.e.,

---

[2] After being told by the angel Gabriel that she has found favour with God and that she should bear the Christ Child, the Virgin exclaims, 'Behold the handmaid of the Lord' (Luke 1:38). The *Magnificat* follows in verses 46–55.

preached (Acts 21:9). There were prophetesses even in Old Testament times. Prophetesses, not priestesses.

At this point the common sensible reformer is apt to ask why, if women can preach, they cannot do all the rest of a priest's work. This question deepens the discomfort of my side. We begin to feel that what really divides us from our opponents is a difference between the meaning which they and we give to the word 'priest'. The more they speak (and speak truly) about the competence of women in administration, their tact and sympathy as advisers, their natural talent for 'visiting', the more we feel that the central thing is being forgotten. To us a priest is primarily a representative, a double representative, who represents us to God and God to us. Our very eyes teach us this in church. Sometimes the priest turns his back on us and faces the East – he speaks to God for us: sometimes he faces us and speaks to us for God. We have no objection to a woman doing the first: the whole difficulty is about the second. But why? Why should a woman not in this sense represent God? Certainly not because she is necessarily, or even probably, less holy or less charitable or stupider than a man. In that sense she may be as 'God-like' as a man; and a given woman much more so than a given man. The sense in which she cannot represent God will perhaps be plainer if we look at the thing the other way round.

Suppose the reformer stops saying that a good woman may be like God and begins saying that God is like a good woman. Suppose he says that we might just as well pray to 'Our Mother which art in Heaven' as to 'Our Father'. Suppose he suggests that the Incarnation might just as well have taken a female as a male form, and the Second Person of the Trinity be as well called the Daughter as the Son. Suppose, finally, that the mystical marriage were reversed, that the Church were the Bridegroom and Christ the Bride. All this, as it seems to me, is involved in the claim that a woman can represent God as a priest does.

Now it is surely the case that if all these supposals were ever carried into effect we should be embarked on a different religion. Goddesses have, of course, been worshipped: many religions have had priestesses. But they are religions quite different in character from Christianity. Common sense, disregarding the discomfort, or even the horror, which the idea of turning all our theological language into the feminine gender arouses in most Christians, will ask 'Why not? Since God is in fact not a biological being and has no sex, what can it matter whether we say *He* or *She*, *Father* or *Mother*, *Son* or *Daughter*?'

But Christians think that God Himself has taught us how to speak of Him. To say that it does not matter is to say either that all the masculine imagery is not inspired, is merely human in origin, or else that, though inspired, it is quite arbitrary and unessential. And this is surely intolerable: or, if tolerable, it is an argument not in favour of Christian priestesses but against Christianity. It is also surely based on a shallow view of imagery. Without drawing upon religion, we know from our poetical experience that image and apprehension cleave closer together than common sense is here prepared to admit; that a child who had been taught to pray to a Mother in Heaven would have a religious life radically different from that of a Christian child. And as image and apprehension are in an organic unity, so, for a Christian, are human body and human soul.

The innovators are really implying that sex is something superficial, irrelevant to the spiritual life. To say that men and women are equally eligible for a certain profession is to say that for the purposes of that profession their sex is irrelevant. We are, within that context, treating both as neuters. As the State grows more like a hive or an ant-hill it needs an increasing number of workers who can be treated as neuters. This may be inevitable for our secular life. But in our Christian life we must return to reality. There we are not homogeneous units, but different and complementary organs of a mystical body. Lady Nunburnholme has claimed that the equality of men and women is a Christian principle.[3] I do not remember the text in Scripture nor the Fathers, nor Hooker, nor the Prayer Book which asserts it; but that is not here my point. The point is that unless 'equal' means 'interchangeable', equality makes nothing for the priesthood of women. And the kind of equality which implies that the equals are interchangeable (like counters or identical machines) is, among humans, a legal fiction. It may be a useful legal fiction, but in church we turn our back on fictions. One of the ends for which sex was created was to symbolise to us the hidden things of God. One of the functions of human marriage is to express the nature of the union between Christ and the Church. We have no authority to take the living and seminal figures which God has painted on the canvas of our nature and shift them about as if they were mere geometrical figures.

This is what common sense will call 'mystical'. Exactly. The Church claims to be the bearer of a revelation. If that claim is false then we want not to make priestesses but to abolish priests. If it is true, then we would expect to find in the Church an element which unbelievers will call irrational and which believers will call suprarational. There ought to be

---

[3] Lady Nunburnholme, 'A petition to the Lambeth Conference', *Time and Tide*, vol. XXIX, No. 28 (10 July 1948), p. 720.

something in it opaque to our reason though not contrary to it – as the facts of sex and sense on the natural level are opaque. And that is the real issue. The Church of England can remain a church only if she retains this opaque element. If we abandon that, if we retain only what can be justified by standards of prudence and convenience at the bar of enlightened common sense, then we exchange revelation for that old wraith Natural Religion.

It is painful, being a man, to have to assert the privilege, or the burden, which Christianity lays upon my own sex. I am crushingly aware how inadequate most of us are, in our actual and historical individualities to fill the place prepared for us. But it is an old saying in the army that you salute the uniform, not the wearer. Only one wearing the masculine uniform can (provisionally, and till the *Parousia*)[4] represent the Lord to the Church: for we are all, corporately and individually, feminine to Him. We men may often make very bad priests. That is because we are insufficiently masculine. It is no cure to call in those who are not masculine at all. A given man may make a very bad husband; you cannot mend matters by trying to reverse the roles. He may make a bad male partner in a dance. The cure for that is that men should more diligently attend dancing classes; not that the ballroom should henceforward ignore distinctions of sex and treat all dancers as neuter. That would, of course, be eminently sensible, civilised, and enlightened, but, once more, 'not near so much like a ball'.

And this parallel between the Church and the ball is not so fanciful as some would think. The Church ought to be more like a ball than it is like a factory or a political party. Or, to speak more strictly, they are at the circumference and the Church at the centre and the ball comes in between. The factory and the political party are artificial creations – 'a breath can make them as a breath has made'. In them we are not dealing with human beings in their concrete entirety – only with 'hands' or voters. I am not of course using 'artificial' in any derogatory sense. Such artifices are necessary: but because they are our artifices we are free to shuffle, scrap and experiment as we please. But the ball exists to stylise something which is natural and which concerns human beings in their entirety – namely, courtship. We cannot shuffle or tamper so much. With the Church, we are farther in: for there we are dealing with male and female not merely as facts of nature but as the live and awful shadows of realities utterly beyond our control and largely beyond our direct knowledge. Or rather, we are not dealing with them but (as we shall soon learn if we meddle) they are dealing with us.

---

[4] The future return of Christ in glory.

[55]
ON CHURCH MUSIC

Published in English Church Music, *Volume XIX (April 1949) and written at the invitation of the Editor, Leonard Blake. It was reprinted in* Christian Reflections *(1998).*

I am a layman and one who can boast no musical education. I cannot even speak from the experience of a life-long church-goer. It follows that Church Music is a subject on which I cannot, even in the lowest degree, appear as a teacher. My place is in the witness box. If it concerns the court to know how the whole matter appears to such as I (not only *laicus* but *laicissimus*) I am prepared to give my evidence.

I assume from the outset that nothing should be done or sung or said in church which does not aim directly or indirectly either at glorifying God or edifying the people or both. A good service may of course have a cultural value as well, but that is not what it exists for; just as, in an unfamiliar landscape, a church may help me to find the points of the compass, but was not built for that purpose.

These two ends, of edifying and glorifying, seem to me to be related as follows. Whenever we edify, we glorify, but when we glorify we do not always edify. The edification of the people is an act of charity and obedience and therefore in itself a glorification of God. But it is possible for a man to glorify God in modes that do not edify his neighbour. This fact confronted the Church at an early stage in her career, in the phenomenon called 'speaking with tongues'. In 1 Corinthians 14, St Paul points out that the man who is inspired to speak in an unknown tongue may do very well, as far as he himself is concerned, but will not profit the congregation unless his utterance can be translated. Thus glorifying and edifying may come to be opposed.

Now at first sight to speak with unknown tongues and to sing anthems which are beyond the musical capacity of the people would seem to be very much the same kind of thing. It looks as if we ought to extend to the one the embargo which St Paul places on the other. And this would lead to the forbidding conclusion that no Church Music is legitimate except that which suits the existing taste of the people.

In reality, however, the parallel is not perhaps so close as it seems. In the first place, the mode after which a speech in an unknown tongue could glorify God was not, I suppose, the same as the mode after which learned music is held to do so. It is (to say the least) doubtful whether the speeches in 'tongues' claimed to glorify God by their aesthetic quality. I suppose that they glorified God firstly by being miraculous and involuntary, and secondly by the ecstatic state of mind in which the speaker was. The idea behind Church Music is very different. It glorifies God by being excellent in its own kind; almost as the birds and flowers and the heavens themselves glorify Him. In the composition and highly-trained execution of sacred music we offer our natural gifts at their highest to God, as we do also in ecclesiastical architecture, in vestments, in glass and gold and silver, in well-kept parish accounts, or the careful organisation of a Social. And in the second place, the incapacity of the people to 'understand' a foreign language and their incapacity to 'understand' good music are not really the same. The first applies absolutely and equally (except for a lucky accident) to all the members of the congregation. The second is not equally present or equally incurable perhaps in any two individuals. And finally, the alternative to speech in an unknown tongue was speech in a known tongue. But in most discussions about Church Music the alternative to learned music is popular music – giving the people 'what they like' and allowing them to sing (or shout) their 'old favourites'.

It is here that the distinction between our problem and St Paul's seems to me to be the sharpest. That words in a known tongue might edify was obvious. Is it equally obvious that the people are edified by being allowed to shout their favourite hymns? I am well aware that the people like it. They equally like shouting *Auld Lang Syne* in the streets on New Year's Eve or shouting the latest music-hall song in a tap-room. To make a communal familiar noise is certainly a pleasure to human beings. And I would not be thought to despise this pleasure. It is good for the lungs, it promotes good fellowship, it is humble and unaffected, it is in every way a wholesome, innocent thing – as wholesome and innocent as a pint of beer, a game of darts, or a dip in the sea. But is it, any more than these, a means of edification? No doubt it can be done – all these things can be done – eating can be done – to the glory of God. We have an Apostle's word for it. The perfected Christian can turn all his humblest, most secular, most economic, actions in that direction. But if this is accepted as an argument for popular hymns it will also be an argument for a good many other things. What we want to know is whether untrained communal singing is in itself any more edifying than other popular plea-sures. And of this I, for one, am still wholly unconvinced. I have often heard this noise; I have sometimes contributed to it. I do not yet seem to have found any evidence that the physical and emotional exhilaration which it produces is necessarily, or often, of any religious relevance. What I, like many other laymen, chiefly desire in church are fewer, better, and shorter hymns; especially fewer.

The case for abolishing all Church Music whatever thus seems to me far stronger than the case for abolishing the difficult work of the trained choir and retaining the lusty roar of the congregation. Whatever doubts I feel about the spiritual value of the first I feel at least equally about the spiritual value of the second.

The first and most solid conclusion which (for me) emerges is that both musical parties, the High Brows and the Low, assume far too easily the spiritual value of the music they want. Neither the greatest excellence of a trained performance from the choir, nor the heartiest and most enthusiastic bellowing from the pews, must be taken to signify that any specifically religious activity is going on. It may be so, or it may not. Yet the main sense of Christendom, reformed and unreformed, would be against us if we tried to banish music from the Church. It remains to suggest, very tentatively, the ways in which it can really be pleasing to God or help to save the souls of men.

There are two musical situations on which I think we can be confident that a blessing rests. One is where a priest or an organist, himself a man of trained and delicate taste, humbly and charitably sacrifices his own (aesthetically right) desires and gives the people humbler and coarser fare than he would wish, in a belief (even, as it may be, the erroneous belief) that he can thus bring them to God. The other is where the stupid and unmusical layman humbly and patiently, and above all silently, listens to music which he cannot, or cannot fully, appreciate, in the belief that it somehow glorifies God, and that if it does not edify him this must be his own defect. Neither such a High Brow nor such a Low Brow can be far out of the way. To both, Church Music will have been a means of grace; not the music they have liked, but the music they have disliked. They have both offered, sacrificed, their taste in the fullest sense. But where the opposite situation arises, where the musician is filled with the pride of skill or the virus of emulation and looks with contempt on the unappreciative congregation, or where the unmusical, complacently entrenched in their own ignorance and conservatism, look with the restless and resentful hostility of an inferiority complex on all who would try to improve their taste – there, we may be sure, all that both offer is unblessed and the spirit that moves them is not the Holy Ghost.

These highly general reflections will not, I fear, be of much practical use to any priest or organist in devising a working compromise for a particular church. The most they can hope to do is to suggest that the problem is never a merely musical one. Where both the choir and the congregation are spiritually on the right road no insurmountable difficulties will occur. Discrepancies of taste and capacity will, indeed, provide matter for mutual charity and humility.

For us, the musically illiterate mass, the right way is not hard to discern; and as long as we stick to it, the fact that we are capable only of a confused rhythmical noise will not do very much harm, if, when we make it, we really intend the glory of God. For if that is our intention it follows of necessity that we shall be as ready to glorify Him by silence (when required) as by shouts. We shall also be aware that the power of shouting stands very low in the hierarchy of natural gifts, and that it would be better to learn to sing if we could. If anyone tries to teach us we will try to learn. If we cannot learn, and if this is desired, we will shut up. And we will also try to listen intelligently. A congregation in this state will not complain if a good deal of the music they hear in church is above their heads. It is not the mere ignorance of the unmusical that really resists improvements. It is jealousy, arrogance, suspicion, and the wholly detestable species of conservatism which those vices engender. How far it may be politic (part of the wisdom of the serpent) to make concessions to the 'old guard' in a congregation, I would not like to determine. But I do not think it can be the business of the Church greatly to co-operate with the modern State in appeasing inferiority complexes and encouraging the natural man's instinctive hatred of excellence. Democracy is all very well as a political device. It must not intrude into the spiritual, or even the aesthetic, world.

The right way for the musicians is perhaps harder, and I, at any rate, can speak of it with much less confidence. But it seems to me that we must define rather carefully the way, or ways, in which music can glorify God. There is, as I hinted above, a sense in which all natural agents, even inanimate ones, glorify God continually by revealing the powers He has given them. And in that sense we, as natural agents, do the same. On that level our wicked actions, in so far as they exhibit our skill and strength, may be said to glorify God, as well as our good actions. An excellently performed piece of music, as a natural operation which reveals in a very high degree the peculiar powers given to man, will thus always glorify God whatever the intention of the performers may be. But that is a kind of glorifying which we share with 'the dragons and great deeps', with the 'frosts and snows'. What is looked for in us, as men, is another kind of glorifying, which depends on intention. How easy or how hard it may be for a whole choir to preserve that intention through all the discussions and decisions, all the corrections and disappointments, all the temptations to pride, rivalry and ambition, which precede the performance of a great work, I (naturally) do not know. But it is on the intention that all depends. When it succeeds, I think the performers are the most enviable of men; privileged while mortals to honour God like angels and, for a few golden moments, to see spirit and flesh, delight and labour, skill and worship, the natural and the supernatural, all fused into that unity they would have had before the Fall. But I must insist that no degree of excellence in the music, simply as music, can assure us that this paradisal state has been achieved. The excellence proves 'keenness'; but men can be 'keen' for natural, or even wicked, motives. The absence of keenness would prove that they lacked the right spirit; its presence does not prove that they have it. We must beware of the naive idea that our music can 'please' God as it would please a cultivated human hearer. That is like thinking, under the old Law, that He really needed the blood of bulls and goats. To which an answer came, 'Mine are the cattle upon a thousand hills', and 'if I am hungry, I will not tell *thee*'. If God (in that sense) wanted music, He would not tell *us*. For all our offerings, whether of music or martyrdom, are like the intrinsically worthless present of a child, which a father values indeed, but values only for the intention.[1]

---

[1] Before this article was written, Lewis was invited by the Rev. Erik Routley to become a member of the panel of the Hymn Society of Great Britain and Ireland, to whom new hymns are submitted in order that their merit might be assessed. As could be expected, Lewis refused. However, his answers to the request were published (with Mr Routley's letters) as 'Correspondence with an Anglican who Dislikes Hymns', *The Presbyter*, VI, No. 2 (1948), pp. 15–20. (The two letters from Lewis, dated 16 July 1946 and 21 September 1946, are printed over the initials 'A.B.') (See p. 771.)

[PART 5]

LETTERS

These letters on theological subjects were originally published in various journals, and then in Undeceptions *(1971) and* Timeless at Heart *(1987). Though only Lewis's own letters are reprinted here, they are placed in their proper contexts by citing the sources of the letters from the various correspondents whom Lewis was answering, or who were answering him. Thus the sub-divisions (a), (b), (c), and so forth.*

[56]

THE CONDITIONS FOR A JUST WAR

(a) E.L. Mascall, 'The Christian and the Next War', *Theology*, Vol. XXXVIII (January 1939), pp. 53–8.
(b) C.S. Lewis, 'The Conditions for a Just War', ibid. (May 1939), pp. 373–4.

Sir,

In your January number Mr Mascall mentions six conditions for a just war which have been laid down by 'theologians'. I have one question to ask, and a number of problems to raise, about these rules. The question is merely historical. Who are these theologians, and what kind or degree of authority can they claim over members of the Church of England? The problems are more difficult. Condition 4 lays down that 'it must be morally certain that the losses, to the belligerents, the world, and religion, will not outweigh the advantages of winning'; and 6, that 'there must be a considerable probability of winning'. It is plain that equally sincere people can differ to any extent and argue for ever as to whether a proposed war fulfils these conditions or not. The practical question, therefore, which faces us is one of authority. Who has the duty of deciding when the conditions are fulfilled, and the right of enforcing his decision? Modern discussions tend to assume without argument that the answer is 'The private conscience of the individual', and that any other answer is immoral and totalitarian. Now it is certain, in some sense, that 'no duty of obedience can justify a sin', as Mr Mascall says. Granted that capital punishment is compatible with Christianity, a Christian may lawfully be a hangman; but he must not hang a man whom he knows to be innocent. But will anyone interpret this to mean that the hangman has the *same* duty of investigating

411

the prisoner's guilt which the judge has? If so, no executive can work and no Christian state is possible; which is absurd. I conclude that the hangman has done his duty if he has done his share of the general duty, resting upon all citizens alike, to ensure, so far as in him lies, that we have an honest judicial system; if, in spite of this, and unknowingly, he hangs an innocent man, then a sin has been committed, but not by him. This analogy suggests to me that it must be absurd to give to the private citizen the *same* right and duty of deciding the justice of a given war which rests on governments; and I submit that the rules for determining what wars are just were originally rules for the guidance of princes, not subjects. This does not mean that private persons must obey governments commanding them to do what they know is sin; but perhaps it does mean (I write it with some reluctance) that the ultimate decision as to what the situation at a given moment is in the highly complex field of international affairs is one which must be delegated. No doubt we must make every effort which the constitution allows to ensure a good government and to influence public opinion; but in the long run, the nation, as a nation, must act, and it can act only through its government. (It must be remembered that there are risks in both directions: if war is ever lawful, then peace is sometimes sinful.) What is the alternative? That individuals ignorant of history and strategy should decide for themselves whether condition 6 ('a considerable probability of winning') is, or is not, fulfilled? – or that every citizen, neglecting his own vocation and not weighing his capacity, is to become an expert on all the relevant, and often technical, problems?

Decisions by the private conscience of each Christian in the light of Mr Mascall's six rules would divide Christians from each other and result in no clear Christian witness to the pagan world around us. But a clear Christian witness might be attained in a different way. If all Christians consented to bear arms at the command of the magistrate, and if all, after that, refused to obey anti-Christian orders, should we not get a clear issue? A man is much more certain that he ought not to murder prisoners or bomb civilians than he ever can be about the justice of a war. It is perhaps here that 'conscientious objection' ought to begin. I feel certain that one Christian airman shot for refusing to bomb enemy civilians would be a more effective martyr (in the etymological sense of the word) than a hundred Christians in jail for refusing to join the army.

Christendom has made two efforts to deal with the evil of war – chivalry and pacifism. Neither succeeded. But I doubt whether chivalry has such an unbroken record of failure as pacifism.

The question is a very dark one. I should welcome about equally refutation, or development, of what I have said.

[57]

THE CONFLICT IN ANGLICAN THEOLOGY

(a) Oliver C. Quick, 'The Conflict in Anglican Theology', *Theology*, Vol. LXI
   (October 1940), pp. 234–7.
(b) C.S. Lewis, ibid. (November 1940), p. 304.

Sir,

In an admirable letter contributed to your October number Canon Quick remarks, ' "Moderns" of every kind have one characteristic in common: they hate Liberalism.' Would it not be equally true to say, more shortly, ' "Moderns" of every kind have one characteristic in common: they *hate*?' The matter deserves, perhaps, more attention than it has received.

[58]

MIRACLES

(a) Peter May, 'Miracles', *The Guardian* (9 October 1942), p. 323.
(b) C.S. Lewis, ibid. (16 October 1942), p. 331.

Sir,

In answer to Mr May's question, I reply that whether the birth of St John Baptist were a miracle or no, it was not the same miracle as the birth of our Lord.[1] What was abnormal about St Elizabeth's pregnancy was that she was an elderly (married) woman, hitherto sterile. That Zacharias was the father of St John is implied in the text ('shall bear *thee* a son', Luke 1:13).

Of the natural conversion of water into wine, what I said was: 'God creates the vine and teaches it to draw up water by its roots and, *with the aid of the sun*, to turn that water into a juice *which will ferment* and take on certain qualities.'[2] For completeness I should, no doubt, have added 'with the aid of the soil', and perhaps other things; but this would not, from my point of view, have materially altered what I was saying. My answer to Mr May's question – where the other raw materials came from – would be the same, whether the list of raw materials be reduced to the mere vegetable and

---

[1] Mr May was criticising Lewis's essay on 'Miracles' in *God in the Dock*.
[2] *God in the Dock*, p. 7.

sunlight I mentioned, or extended to bring in all that the skilled botanist might add. I think they came from the same source at Cana whence they come in nature. I agree with Mr May, of course, that on the hypothesis of the story being fiction, we can attach to it, as our ancestors did to the miracles in Ovid, any number of edifying *moralitates*. What I was doing was to combat that particular argument for its falsity which rests on the idea that, if it occurred, such an event would be arbitrary and meaningless.

[59]

MR C.S. LEWIS ON CHRISTIANITY

(a) W.R. Childe, 'Mr C.S. Lewis on Christianity', *The Listener*, Vol. XXXI (2 March 1944), p. 245.
(b) C.S. Lewis, ibid. (9 March 1944), p. 273.

I agree with Mr W.R. Childe that it is no use to say 'Lord, Lord', if we do not do what Christ tells us: that, indeed, is one of the reasons why I think an aesthetic religion of 'flowers and music' insufficient.[1] My reason for thinking that a mere statement of even the highest ethical principles is not enough is precisely that to know these things is not necessarily to do them, and if Christianity brought no healing to the impotent will, Christ's teaching would not help us. I cannot blame Mr Childe for misunderstanding me, because I am naturally no judge of my own lucidity; but I take it very hard that a total stranger whom I have never knowingly injured or offended, on the first discovery of a difference in theological opinion between us, should publicly accuse me of being a potential torturer, murderer and tyrant – for that is what Mr Childe's reference to faggots means if it means anything. How little I approve of compulsion in religion may be gauged from a recent letter of mine to the *Spectator* protesting against the intolerable tyranny of compulsory church parades for the Home Guard. If Mr Childe can find any passage in my works which favours religious or anti-religious compulsion I will give five pounds to any (not militantly anti-Christian) charity he cares to name. If he cannot, I ask him, for justice and charity's sake, to withdraw his charge.

(c) W.R. Childe, ibid. (16 March 1944), p. 301.

[1] Mr Childe had taken exception to a passage in Lewis's BBC broadcast 'The Map and the Ocean' in which he said, in speaking of a 'vague religion', that 'you will not get eternal life by just feeling the presence of God in flowers or music.' *The Listener*, Vol. XXXI (24 February 1944), p. 216. The broadcast was later to become a chapter in Lewis's *Mere Christianity* (London, 1952), Bk. IV, ch. i.

[60]

A VILLAGE EXPERIENCE

C.S. Lewis, 'A Village Experience', *The Guardian* (31 August 1945), p. 335.

Sir,

I think your readers should, and will, be interested in the following extract from a letter I have just received; the writer is an invalid lady in a village:

'This used to be a God-fearing village with a God-fearing parson who visited and ran the Scouts ("Lovely troop he 'ad. *And* you should have 'eard our choir of a Sunday", says my bricklayer host). The young were polished up and sent to Sunday school, their parents filled the church to the brim. *Now* they have an octogenarian. No harm in that! My late uncle – at that age – was going as strong as most two-year-olds. But this one – I noted for myself, seeing him pass – has been dead for years ... He does not visit the sick, even if asked. He does nothing. And – listen – he stuck up a notice in the church: *No children admitted without their parents or an adult.* The village ... went instantly Pagan. I must get away from it. Never before but in the vile pagan West Indies have I been without so much as an *extorted* Holy Sacrament. (*Can* one forbid the church to a Crissom Child? – legally, I mean? Pass me a Bishop.)'

[61]

CORRESPONDENCE WITH AN ANGLICAN
WHO DISLIKES HYMNS[1]

(a) Summary of a letter from Erik Routley to Lewis (dated 13 July 1946), p. 15.

'... The Hymn Society of Great Britain and Ireland is opening a file of new hymns to which modern hymn-writers are to be asked to contribute. I have been asked to write to you and ask if you will be a member of the panel to whom new hymns may be submitted in order that their merit may be assessed ...'

---

[1] The 'correspondence' consists of two letters from Erik Routley to Lewis and two letters from Lewis, all of which were published together in *The Presbyter*, Vol. VI, No. 2 (1948), pp. 15–20. Lewis's letters were published over the initials. — 'A.B.'

(b) C.S. Lewis to Erik Routley (dated 16 July 1946), p. 15.

Dear Mr Routley,

The truth is that I'm not in sufficient sympathy with the project to help you. I know that many of the congregation like singing hymns: but am not yet convinced that their enjoyment is of a spiritual kind. It may be: I don't know. To the minority, of whom I am one, the hymns are mostly the dead wood of the service. Recently in a party of six people I found that all without exception would like *fewer* hymns. Naturally, one holding this view can't help you.

(c) Erik Routley to Lewis (dated 18 September 1946), pp. 15–20.

(d) C.S. Lewis to Erik Routley (dated 21 September 1946), p. 20.

I can't quite remember my own last letter; but I was wrong if I said or implied that (*a*) variables, (*b*) active participation by the people, or (*c*) hymns were bad in principle. I would agree that anything the congregation *can do* may properly and profitably be offered to God in public worship. If one had a congregation (say, in Africa) who had a high tradition in sacred dancing and could do it really well I would be perfectly in favour of making a dance part of the service. But I wouldn't transfer the practice to a Willesden congregation whose best dance was a ballroom shuffle. In modern England, however, we can't sing – as the Welsh and Germans can. Also (a great pity, but a fact) the art of poetry has developed for two centuries in a private and subjective direction. That is why I find hymns 'dead wood'. But I spoke only for myself and a few others. If an improved hymnody – or even the present hymnody – does edify other people, of course it is an elementary duty of charity and humility for me to submit. I have never spoken in public *against* the use of hymns: on the contrary I have often told 'highbrow' converts that a humble acquiescence in anything that may edify their uneducated brethren (however frightful it seems to the educated 'natural man') is the first lesson they must learn. The door is *low* and one must stoop to enter.

[62]

THE CHURCH'S LITURGY, INVOCATION,
AND INVOCATION OF SAINTS

(a) E.L. Mascall, 'Quadringentesimo Anno', *Church Times*, Vol CXXXII (6 May 1949), p. 282.
(b) C.S. Lewis, 'The Church's Liturgy', ibid. (20 May 1949), p. 319.

Sir,

If it is not harking back too far, I would like to make two layman's comments on the liturgical articles in your issue of 6th May. Firstly, I would underline the necessity for uniformity, if in nothing else, yet in the time taken by the rite. We laymen may not be busier than the clergy but we usually have much less choice in our hours of business. The celebrant who lengthens the service by ten minutes may, for us, throw the whole day into hurry and confusion. It is difficult to keep this out of our minds: it may even be difficult to avoid some feeling of resentment. Such temptations may be good for us but it is not the celebrant's business to supply them: God's permission and Satan's diligence will see to that part of our education without his assistance.

Secondly, I would ask the clergy to believe that we are more interested in orthodoxy and less interested in liturgiology as such than they can easily imagine. Dr Mascall rightly says that variations are permissible when they do not alter doctrine. But after that he goes on almost casually to mention 'devotions to the Mother of God and to the hosts of heaven' as a possible liturgical variant. That the introduction of such devotions into any parish not accustomed to them would divide the congregation into two camps, Dr Mascall well knows. But if he thinks that the issue between those camps would be a liturgical issue, I submit that he is mistaken. It would be a doctrinal issue. Not one layman would be asking whether these devotions marred or mended the beauty of the rite; everyone would be asking whether they were lawful or damnable. It is no part of my object to discuss that question here, but merely to point out that it is the question.

What we laymen fear is that the deepest doctrinal issues should be tacitly and implicitly settled by what seem to be, or are avowed to be, merely changes in liturgy. A man who is wondering whether the fare set before him is food or poison is not reassured by being told that this course is now restored to its traditional place in the *menu* or that the tureen is of the Sarum pattern. We laymen are ignorant and timid. Our lives are ever in our hands, the avenger of blood is on our heels, and of each of us his soul may this night be required. Can you blame us if the reduction of grave doctrinal issues to merely liturgical issues fills us with something like terror?

(c) W.D.F. Hughes, ibid. (24 June 1949), p. 409.

(d) C.S. Lewis, ibid. (1 July 1949). p. 427.

Sir,

I agree with Dean Hughes that the connection of belief and liturgy is close, but doubt if it is 'inextricable'. I submit that the relation is healthy when liturgy expresses the belief of the Church, morbid when liturgy creates in the people by suggestion beliefs which the Church has not publicly professed, taught, and defended. If the mind of the Church is, for example, that our fathers erred in abandoning the Romish invocations of saints and angels, by all means let our corporate recantation, together with its grounds in scripture, reason and tradition be published, our solemn acts of penitence be performed, the laity re-instructed, and the proper changes in liturgy be introduced.

What horrifies me is the proposal that individual priests should be encouraged to behave as if all this had been done when it has not been done. One correspondent compared such changes to the equally stealthy and (as he holds) irresistible changes in a language. But that is just the parallel that terrifies me, for even the shallowest philologist knows that the unconscious linguistic process is continually degrading good words and blunting useful distinctions. *Absit omen!* Whether an 'enrichment' of liturgy which involves a change of doctrine is allowable, surely depends on whether our doctrine is changing from error to truth or from truth to error. Is the individual priest the judge of that?

(e) Edward Every, 'Doctrine and Liturgy', ibid. (8 July 1949), pp. 445–6.

(f) C.S. Lewis 'Invocation', ibid. (15 July 1949), pp. 463–4.

Sir,

Mr Every (quite legitimately) gives the word *invocation* a wider sense than I. The question then becomes how far we can infer propriety of *devotion* from propriety of *invocation*? I accept the authority of the *Benedicite*[1] for the propriety of *invoking* (in Mr Every's sense) saints. But

---

[1] Found in the Prayer Book service of Morning Prayer, the original source of which is *The Song of the Three Holy Children* (vv. 35–66) in the Old Testament Apocrypha.

if I thence infer the propriety of *devotions* to saints, will not an argument force me to approve devotions to stars, frosts and whales?

I am also quite ready to admit that I overlooked a distinction. Our fathers might disallow a particular medieval doctrine and yet not disallow some other doctrine which we laymen easily confuse with it. But if the issue is so much finer than I thought, this merely redoubles my anxiety that it should be openly and authoritatively decided.

If I feared lest the suggestions of liturgy might beguile us laymen on a simple issue, I am not likely to be comforted by finding the issue a subtle one. If there is one kind of devotion to created beings which is pleasing and another which is displeasing to God, when is the Church, as a Church, going to instruct us in the distinction?

Meanwhile, what better opportunity for the stealthy insinuation of the wrong kind than the unauthorised and sporadic practice of devotions to creatures before uninstructed congregations would our ghostly foe desire? Most of us laymen, I think, have no *parti pris* in the matter. We desire to believe as the Church believes.

(g) Edward Every 'Invocation of Saints', ibid. (22 July 1949), pp. 481–2.

(h) C.S. Lewis, ibid. (5 August 1949), p. 513.

Sir,

I hope Mr Every has not misunderstood me. There is, I believe, a *prima facie* case for regarding devotions to saints in the Church of England as a controversial question (see Jewel, *Apologia Ecclesiae Anglicanae*, Pt. II, ch. xxviii, *Homilies*, Bk. II, *Peril of Idolatry*, Pt. III; Laud, *Conference with Fisher*, Sect. XXIII; Taylor, *Dissuasive from Popery*, Pt. I, ch. ii, sect. 8. I merely claim that the controversy exists. I share Mr Every's wish that it should cease. But there are two ways in which a controversy can cease: by being settled, or by gradual and imperceptible change of custom. I do not want any controversy to cease in the second way.

I implore priests to remember what Aristotle tells us about unconscious revolution (πολλάκις λανθάνει μεγάλη γινομένη μεταβάσις τῶν νομίμων, *Politics* 1303 a 22).[2] When such unconscious revolution produces a result we like, we are all tempted to welcome it; thus I am tempted to welcome it when it leads to prayers for the dead. But then I see that the very same process can be used, and is used, to introduce modernist dilutions of the faith which, I am sure, Mr Every and I equally

[2] The occurrence of an important transition in customs often passes unnoticed.

abominate. I conclude that a road so dangerous should never be trodden, whether the destination to which it seems to point is in itself good or bad. To write 'No Thoroughfare' over that road is my only purpose.

[63]
THE HOLY NAME

(a) Leslie E.T. Bradbury, 'The Holy Name', *Church Times*, Vol. CXXXIV (3 August 1951), p. 525.
(b) C.S. Lewis, ibid. (10 August 1951), p. 541.

Sir,

Having read Mr Bradbury's letter on the Holy Name, I have a few comments to make. I do not think we are entitled to assume that all who use this Name without reverential prefixes are making a 'careless' use of it; otherwise, we should have to say that the Evangelists were often careless. I do not think we are entitled to assume that the use of the word *Blessed* when we speak of the Virgin Mary is 'necessary'; otherwise, we should have to condemn both the Nicene and the Apostles' Creed for omitting it. Should we not rather recognise that the presence or absence of such prefixes constitute a difference, not in faith or morals, but simply in style? I know that as their absence is 'irritating' to some, so their frequent recurrence is irritating to others. Is not each party innocent in its temperamental preference but grossly culpable if it allows anything so subjective, contingent, and (with a little effort) conquerable as a temperamental preference to become a cause of division among brethren? If we cannot lay down our tastes, along with other carnal baggage, at the church door, surely we should at least bring them in to be humbled and, if necessary, modified, not to be indulged?

[64]
MERE CHRISTIANS

(a) R. D. Daunton-Fear, 'Evangelical Churchmanship', *Church Times*, Vol. CXXXV (1 February 1952), p. 77.
(b) C.S. Lewis, 'Mere Christians', ibid. (8 February 1952), p. 95.

Sir,

I welcome the letter from the Rural Dean of Gravesend, though I am sorry that anyone should have rendered it necessary by describing the Bishop of Birmingham as an Evangelical. To a layman, it seems obvious that what unites the Evangelical and the Anglo-Catholic against the 'Liberal' or 'Modernist' is something very clear and momentous, namely, the fact that both are thoroughgoing supernaturalists, who believe in the Creation, the Fall, the Incarnation, the Resurrection, the Second Coming, and the Four Last Things. This unites them not only with one another, but with the Christian religion as understood *ubique et ab omnibus*.[1]

The point of view from which this agreement seems less important than their divisions, or than the gulf which separates both from any non-miraculous version of Christianity, is to me unintelligible. Perhaps the trouble is that as supernaturalists, whether 'Low' or 'High' Church, thus taken together, they lack a name. May I suggest 'Deep Church'; or, if that fails in humility, Baxter's 'mere Christians'?

[65]

CANONISATION

(a) Eric Pitt, 'Canonisation', *Church Times*, Vol. CXXXV (17 October 1952), p. 743.
(b) C.S. Lewis, ibid. (24 October 1952), p. 763.

Sir,

I am, like Mr Eric Pitt, a layman, and would like to be instructed on several points before the proposal to set up a 'system' of Anglican canonisation is even discussed. According to the *Catholic Encyclopaedia*, 'saints' are dead people whose virtues have made them 'worthy' of God's 'special' love. Canonisation makes *dulia* 'universal and obligatory'; and, whatever else it asserts, it certainly asserts that the person concerned 'is in heaven'.

Unless, then, the word 'canonisation' is being used in a sense distinct from the Roman (and, if so, some other word would be much more convenient), the proposal to set up a 'system' of canonisation means that someone (say, the Archbishops) shall be appointed

(a) To tell us that certain named people are (i) 'in heaven', and (ii) are 'worthy' of God's 'special' love.

---

[1] 'everywhere and by all'. See St Vincent of Lérins, *Commonitorium*, ii.

(b) To lay upon us (under pain of excommunication?) the duty of *dulia* towards those they have named.

Now it is very clear that no one ought to tell us what he does not know to be true. Is it, then, held that God has promised (and, if so, when and where?) to the Church universal a knowledge of the state of certain departed souls? If so, is it clear that this knowledge will discern varying degrees or kinds of salvation such as are, I suppose, implicit in the word 'special'? And if it does, will the promulgation of such knowledge help to save souls now *in via*? For it might well lead to a consideration of 'rival claims', such as we read of in the *Imitation of Christ* (Bk. III, ch. 58), where we are warned, 'Ask not which is greater in the Kingdom of Heaven ... the search into such things brings no profit, but rather offends the saints themselves.'

Finally there is the practical issue: by which I do not mean the *Catholic Encyclopaedia*'s neat little account of 'the ordinary actual expenses of canonisation' (though that too can be read with profit), but the danger of schism. Thousands of members of the Church of England doubt whether *dulia* is lawful. Does anyone maintain that it is necessary to salvation? If not, whence comes our obligation to run such frightful risks?

[66]

PITTENGER-LEWIS AND VERSION VERNACULAR

(a) W. Norman Pittenger, 'Pittenger-Lewis', *The Christian Century*, Vol. LXXV (24 December 1958), pp. 1485–6.
(b) C.S. Lewis, 'Version Vernacular', ibid. (31 December 1958), p. 515.

Sir,

Thank you for publishing my 'Rejoinder to Dr Pittenger' (26th November). Now would you, please, complete your kindness by publishing the statement that '*populam*' is either my typist's or your printer's error for '*populum*'?

An article on 'translation such as Dr Pittenger suggests in his letter in the 24th December issue certainly needs doing, but I could not usefully do it for Americans. The vernacular into which they would have to translate is not quite the same as that into which I have translated. Small differences, in addressing proletarians, may be all-important.

In both countries an essential part of the ordination exam ought to be a passage from some recognised theological work set for translation into vulgar English – just like doing Latin prose. Failure on this paper should mean failure on the whole exam. It is absolutely disgraceful that we expect missionaries to the Bantus to learn Bantu but never ask whether our missionaries to the Americans or English can speak American or English. Any fool can write *learned* language. The vernacular is the real test. If you can't turn your faith into it, then either you don't understand it or you don't believe it.

[67]

CAPITAL PUNISHMENT AND DEATH PENALTY

(a) C.S. Lewis, 'Capital Punishment', *Church Times*, Vol. CXLIV (1 December 1961), p. 7.

Sir,

I do not know whether capital punishment should or should not be abolished, for neither the natural light, nor scripture, nor ecclesiastical authority seems to tell me. But I am concerned about the grounds on which its abolition is being sought.

To say that by hanging a man we presumptuously judge him to be irredeemable is, I submit, simply untrue. My Prayer Book includes an exhortation to those under sentence of death which throughout implies the exact opposite. The real question is whether a murderer is more likely to repent and make a good end three weeks hence in the execution shed, or, say, thirty years later in the prison infirmary. No mortal can know. But those who have most right to an opinion are those who know most by experience about the effects of prolonged prison life. I wish some prison chaplains, governors and warders would contribute to the discussion.

The suggestion of compensation of the relatives of the murdered man is in itself reasonable, but it ought not to be even remotely connected with the case for or against capital punishment. If it is, we shall be giving countenance to the archaic, and surely erroneous, view that murder is primarily an offence not against society but against individuals.

Hanging is not a more irrevocable act than any other. You can't bring an innocent man to life: but neither can you give him back the years which wrongful imprisonment has eaten.

Other correspondents have pointed out that a theory of punishment which is purely exemplary or purely reformatory, or both, is shockingly immoral. Only the concept of desert connects punishment with morality at all. If deterrence is all that matters, the execution of an innocent man, provided the public think him guilty, would be fully justified. If reformation alone is in question, then there is nothing against painful and compulsory reform for all our defects, and a Government which believes Christianity to be a neurosis will have a perfectly good right to hand us all over to their straighteners for 'cure' tomorrow.

(b) Claude Davis, ibid (8 December 1961), p. 14.

(c) C.S. Lewis, 'Death Penalty', ibid. (15 December 1961), p. 12.

Sir,

Mr Davis rightly reproves me for using the word *society* as I did. This hypostatised abstraction has already done harm enough. But I only meant 'all of us'. The absurdity of the view which treats murder as an offence against a single family is best illustrated in the case in the private speeches of Demosthenes (I can't turn it up at the moment, but your more scholarly readers no doubt can).[1]

A man, *A*, set free a female slave, *B*, his old nurse. *B* married. Her husband died without issue. Someone then murdered *B*. But under Athenian law no one could prosecute because there was no injured party. *A* could not act because *B*, when murdered, was no longer his property. There was no widower, and there were no orphans.

I am on neither side in the present controversy. But I still think the abolitionists conduct their case very ill. They seem incapable of stating it without imputing vile motives to their opponents. If unbelievers often look at your correspondence column, I am afraid they may carry away a bad impression of our logic, manners and charity.

[1] *The Orations of Demosthenes*, 'The Oration against Euergus and Mnesibulus', sections 1155–62.

ACKNOWLEDGEMENTS

The Publishers and Editor gratefully acknowledge permission to reproduce the essays, short stories and letters in this book, which are copyright © C.S. Lewis Pte Ltd. All material is published by HarperCollins *Publishers*, London.

INDEX OF ESSAYS

The C.S. Lewis Signature Classics

SURPRISED BY JOY

'He is admirably equipped to write spiritual autobiography for the plain man, for his outstanding gift is clarity.'   *Sunday Times*

C.S. Lewis was for many years an atheist, and in *Surprised by Joy* he vividly describes the spiritual quest which eventually convinced him of the truth and reality of the Christian faith. This autobiography of his early life focuses on the spiritual crisis which was to determine the shape of his entire life and career.

'You can take it at two levels, a straight autobiography, or as a kind of spiritual thriller, a detective's probing of clue and motive that led up to his return to the Christianity he had lost in child-hood.'   *Sunday Times*

The C.S. Lewis Signature Classics

THE FOUR LOVES

'He has never written better. Nearly every page scintillates with observations which are illuminating, provocative and original.'

Church Times

Millions of words have been written on the true nature of love, but few are as succinct as in this book. This seminal inspirational work divides 'love' into four categories: Affection, Friendship, Eros and Charity. The first three come naturally, but without Charity, C.S. Lewis shows how all love can become distorted, bitter and even dangerous.

'I read C.S. Lewis for comfort and pleasure many years ago, and a glance into the books revives my old admiration.'

JOHN UPDIKE